The team members leaned forward expectantly

"I want each man down for this, hard-charging and no questions asked. I have a thousand pounds and a plane ticket to anywhere for any man who wants out, and thank you for your time."

The men just stared.

Bolan's War Everlasting had pitted him against drug lords, mafias and terrorists with vast financial backing. During his war, he had confiscated fortunes. The money in his war chest was slated for situations such as this.

"I'll have one hundred thousand pounds deposited into an account set up in the Cayman Islands for each man who's in. In the event of your death or incarceration, the money will go to your family. Each of you has to write a short statement as to how you want that to work."

Stunned silence reigned.

Bolan scooped up a can of beer and pulled the tab. "So who's in?"

2

Don Pendleton's Mack Bolan®

THE KILLING RULE

A GOLD EAGLE BOOK FROM

WORLDWIDE®

TORONTO • NEW YORK • LONDON
AMSTERDAM • PARIS • SYDNEY • HAMBURG
STOCKHOLM • ATHENS • TOKYO • MILAN
MADRID • WARSAW • BUDAPEST • AUCKLAND

First edition January 2008

ISBN-13: 978-0-373-61521-6
ISBN-10:   0-373-61521-3

Special thanks and acknowledgment to
Chuck Rogers for his contribution to this work.

THE KILLING RULE

Old soldiers never die;
They only fade away!

—British Army song
[c.1915]

I have taken my War Everlasting to every continent on Earth and seen selfless sacrifice from some of the greatest fighting men and women the modern world has known. There is no greater sacrifice than a soldier willing to lay down his or her life for the greater good.

—Mack Bolan

CHAPTER ONE

Mack Bolan, aka the Executioner, cat footed through the London fog. He'd already picked up a tail, which was all right with him. Bolan was spoiling for a fight this evening, anyway. In fact, it was the number-one item on his agenda. He turned up the collar of his peacoat and pulled his watch cap low over his forehead against the chill, and moved toward his target.

London was one of the most cosmopolitan cities on Earth. Nearly every immigrant group on the planet, including their organized crime and terrorist syndicates, had an enclave in the city. Since ancient times, the Irish had been one of the first and foremost.

The Irish Republican Army was on Bolan's plate this night.

Pub Claddagh was his destination.

It was a well-known IRA meet-and-greet watering hole. Not surprisingly, Pub Claddagh was well used to visits by the English bobbies, inspectors from Scotland Yard and undercover agents from MI-5. It had also received visits from two CIA field agents in the past three months, both of whom had wound up floating dead in the Thames River with severe contusions, multiple broken bones and a .223-caliber bullet through the backs of their heads. Ballistics had shown that the bullets had come from AR-18 assault rifles, one of the IRA's weapons of choice—one they were so pleased with they had come to nickname the AR-18 "Widowmaker." Both CIA men had left widows behind.

Now Pub Claddagh was about to have its first visit from the Executioner.

But first Bolan was going to have to get to the door. The two men tailing him were making no more attempts at stealth. Their boots thudded on the cobblestones as they briskly caught up with him. An Irish brogue broke through the thick fog blanketing the street. "Hey! Yank!"

Bolan turned to his opponents. They were large men and heavily built. One wore his hair cropped short, the other had shaved his head. Their lumpish faces, poorly set broken noses, scarred brows and cauliflower ears only added to the "goon" effect. They looked like archetypal British soccer hooligans, only they spoke with Irish accents that could be cut with a knife. The skinhead leaned forward, jutting a jaw you could break a croquet mallet on.

"And where d'you think you're going?"

Bolan spit casually on the pavement between them. "What's it to you, Paddy?"

"Paddy!" The skinhead grinned happily. "D'you hear that, Liam?"

"Oh, I do, Shane." Liam smiled like a shark. "A bold boy, this one."

Both men were dressed in Team Ireland football jerseys voluminous enough to hide some significant weapons. Bolan suspected this was to be a beating, albeit a brutal one, rather than an assassination or a kidnapping.

"If you two are looking to beg a fiver, bugger off. If you're looking to get buggered, you've got each other."

Shane laughed delightedly. The American was being very obliging.

Liam's eyes narrowed slightly. He was a predator, but he sensed something was wrong. The American wasn't belligerent or filled with drunken defiance. He was showing no fear whatsoever, and his burning blue eyes were disturbing even in the dim light. Liam folded his arms across his thick chest and tsked sadly, still confident in his and his partner's control of the situation. That was his first and last mistake.

Bolan took the opportunity to kick Shane in the shin.

During the early years of the Cold War, the OSS and other intelligence agencies had issued shoes with steel toecaps for crippling opponents in sudden struggles. Such modifications couldn't make it through today's airport X-ray or metal detector screenings, but Bolan had the modern equivalent made out of polycarbonate Lexan that had the tensile strength of industrial-grade cast zinc. They weren't quite as strong as steel, but then again neither was Shane's tibia. The bone cracked with an audible click noise.

Shane let out an amazingly high-pitched scream for a man of his size.

Liam had made the unforgivable mistake of crossing his arms and posturing when he should have been attacking. He unfolded his arms with alacrity, but he was already behind the curve.

Bolan's hand blurred into motion, and he slapped Liam. But rather than slapping the man across the face, the soldier slapped into it. He cupped his palm as he hit Liam to create an air pocket, and the blow sounded like a gunshot. The cupped air concentrated the blow and drove the force into Liam's Gasserian ganglion, where the trigeminal nerves carrying information from the eyes, ears and face met. Tears geysered out of Liam's eyes and blood burst from his nose from the force of the blow. The trauma beneath the surface was far more severe. The Gasserian ganglion had a direct route to the brain, and by crushing the nerve bundle Bolan's blow had reproduced the symptoms of facial neuralgia, which many medical resources described as the most terrible pain a human being was capable of experiencing.

Liam dropped to his knees, clawing at his face, his screams slurred by his malfunctioning jaw. Within heartbeats he collapsed and went fetal in blissful unconsciousness. Shane was still hopping around on one foot, screaming and clutching his fractured left shin, so Bolan stepped in and fractured his right.

Shane toppled, howling, to the cobbles.

Bolan took their wallets and removed their ID cards before moving on up the street. Above a green-painted oaken door thick enough for a medieval castle hung a classic tin pub sign. On it was painted a golden claddagh symbol, a heart topped by a crown and held by two hands. The heart symbolized love, the hands friendship and the crown loyalty. Bolan pushed open the heavy door and the smells of cigarette smoke and shepherd's pie washed over him. Warmth radiated from a glowing fireplace. The interior was classic pub. The wood was ancient dark varnished oak, crushed red-velvet upholstery covered the walls and the furniture and gleaming brass was everywhere. There were about thirty patrons in the pub; most sat at tables or in booths. A few sat at the bar watching the football scores on the television.

Bolan pulled off his watch cap and walked up to the bar. The bartender was an immense man in formal bartender attire. His red hair was cut close to his skull and was the same shade as his short beard and mustache. He looked like a jolly Irish Santa. He had a lazy eye, and one eye looked at Bolan while the other one appeared to be taking note of the scorers on the television above the bar. He smiled at Bolan benignly. "What'll it be, mate?"

Bolan ran his gaze across the taps. "Half and half."

The bartender nodded wisely and filled a pint glass half full of Harp lager. He filled the rest of the glass with Guinness stout poured down the side of the glass over a spoon to create two distinct layers of light and dark beer. He topped it with a flourish that left a four-leaf clover shape in the foamy head. Bolan sipped his beer and acknowledged its perfect execution with a grin. He reached into his coat and produced pictures of the two dead CIA agents. "You seen either of these two in the past couple of months?"

The bartender squinted at the photos and shrugged. "Can't say's I have, but then I can't say's I haven't." He gave Bolan a merry smile. "Y'see we are London's most famous Irish pub. We get a lot of American tourists and businessmen coming in."

Bolan hadn't said the two dead agents were Americans, but he was willing to chalk that up to an assumption on the bartender's part. Bolan took out Liam's and Shane's ID cards and placed them on the bar. "You know these two?"

The bartender had an excellent poker face, but his face froze for the barest instant and he knew it. He lost his veneer of friendliness. "And where'd you get those, then?"

"From Liam and Shane," Bolan said.

"Are they under arrest?"

"No." Bolan smiled. "But I left their crippled asses lying in the street a couple of minutes ago."

The bartender's thick fingers clenched into fists. He took a long breath and unclenched them. "You know, I think you'd best be leaving."

Bolan feigned surprise. "But I haven't finished my beer yet."

The bartender's lazy eye suddenly swung into line and the big man glared at Bolan in binocular anger. He slowly leaned forward, worked his jaws a moment and spit into Bolan's half and half. "Take your time, then."

Bolan scooped up his pictures and pushed away from the bar. He went from table to table, showing the pictures and asking the same questions while he felt the bartender's eyes burning holes in his back. A glance back showed him the bartender talking rapidly into a cell phone. Bolan went on with his interviews. Most of the Claddagh's patrons genuinely didn't recognize the pictures. A few clearly recognized Liam and Shane. When Bolan responded that no, he was not with the police, he was informed of several unique places he could "bugger off" to.

The big American concluded his interviews, leaving a card with a phone number and the address of the hotel he was staying at with whomever would accept one. Bolan pulled on his cap and stepped out into the London night.

Liam and Shane were gone. Rooted in the same spot where the fight had occurred stood two men of equally goonlike dimensions. They wore long coats with hooded black sweatshirts underneath. The hoods were pulled low over the men's brows to throw their faces into shadow. A similar pair of men stood directly across the street from Bolan. One of them held a cell phone to his ear. Standing there like stones with the fog creeping around them, they looked like the IRA's own Four Horsemen of the Apocalypse.

Bolan's hand went to the grips of the Beretta 93-R machine pistol beneath his coat.

The IRA was different from a lot of terrorist organizations. They had what some might describe as a vaguely achievable goal of driving the British out of Northern Ireland and uniting their country. Driving the Protestants into the sea was part of it, but driving out the British had to come first. IRA members also tended not to be suicidal. Martyrdom usually wasn't on the agenda, and they wanted to get away with their bombings and killings. However, like any such organization, they had their hardcore "soldiers." Men who were ready to die beneath the bullets of British soldiers or do a life sentence in an English supermax prison standing on their heads and not talking.

Bolan faced four of them now.

One of the men across the street took a single step forward. He twisted his wrist and a length of wood slid down out of his sleeve. The weapon was a shillelagh, the ancient Irish war club. Only this wasn't one of the walking sticks sold to tourists in the airports. The tapering blackthorn terminated in a root-ball the size of a human fist.

The weapon was not a total anachronism.

During a riot when British soldiers were wielding batons, firing tear gas and shooting rubber bullets and the rioters responded with bricks and stones, an IRA man could produce his shillelagh and crush the skull of a traitor or political target. One more fatal head trauma would go unnoticed in the melee.

Bolan didn't currently want to shoot any of these men. He wanted the men controlling *them*. The Executioner took out his cell phone and punched a preset number. A cheerful Englishwoman asked him if he required a cab and he provided the address of the pub and then waited. He stared at the Irish, and they stared at him.

A London black cab turned the corner and proceeded up the street. The clubman threw his weapon, and it clattered across the cobblestones to rest at Bolan's feet. The four men melted away into the fog. Bolan scooped up the shillelagh, surprised at its weight and heft. He tucked it under his coat and climbed into his cab. The club was a challenge. The IRA had dropped a punk card for Bolan and dared him to pick it up.

The Executioner had picked it up, and he'd left ample calling cards in the bar.

CHAPTER TWO

Bolan lay on the bed of his hotel room and examined his new club. The three-foot length of blackthorn was three inches in diameter and varnished against the elements. The Irish craftsman had added a brass cap on the tapered end to prevent splitting. The most interesting aspect of it was the business end. The ugly lump of the root-ball had been partially drilled out, and molten lead had been poured in to "load" the stick. It was a club that would not just crack a human skull but go through it.

He sat up as the satellite link peeped at him from its aluminum case. Bolan flipped open the attached laptop and clicked a key. Aaron "The Bear" Kurtzman's craggy, bearded face appeared on the eleven-inch monitor in real time all the way from Stony Man Farm in Virginia. Bolan held up his shillelagh for the camera. "Look what I got."

Kurtzman's brow furrowed. "Nice battle bludgeon you got there. Who gave it to you?"

"A nice Irish lad." Bolan tossed the cudgel onto the bed. "Speaking of likely lads, what did you get on the two IDs I faxed you?"

United Kingdom criminal justice forms began to scroll on the screen beneath Kurtzman's image. Liam and Shane had rap sheets. "We have Shane O'Maonlai and Liam Mac-Gowan, both born in Ulster, Northern Ireland. Shane did two years for assault at Magilligan prison where apparently he was recruited by Liam. Both men have had multiple cases of assault lodged against them, though in almost all cases the charges have been dropped."

Bolan nodded. "They're low-level muscle."

"Yeah," the computer expert agreed. "Their MO seems to be cracking heads and keeping people in line for the IRA in London, but by their rap sheets they've also dabbled in leg-breaking and loan-sharking for the London Mob to earn pocket money." His eyes flicked to the bed. "The shillelagh strikes me as a bit odd. Liam and Shane do their work with their hands."

"I didn't get it from them. Like you said, they're leg-breakers. When I left them on the ground and started poking my nose around the pub, the bartender called in some heavy hitters."

Kurtzman frowned. "You took it off one of them?"

"No, they gave it to me."

"As a gift?"

"No, it's a challenge."

Kurtzman sighed. It was one of Bolan's usual tactics. When all else failed, he stuck his head out and waited to see who took a swing at it. "I don't suppose you got any fingerprints off it?"

"They were wearing gloves, and it's as clean as whistle."

The computer wizard regarded Bolan dryly. "I gather you left a road map to your exact location."

"Pretty much," Bolan admitted. "You get anything on the bartender at the Claddagh?"

"Ronald Caron, former Irish wrestling champion, former military policeman in the Irish Defence Forces, suspected of gun trafficking, suspected of harboring fugitives, suspected of assault, twice arrested on conspiracy charges but released for lack of evidence and a 'person of interest' in nearly every alleged IRA action in London for the past two decades."

Bolan nodded. The bartender might be a hundred pounds over his fighting weight, but underneath the jolly exterior he had given off the vibe of a very dangerous man.

Kurtzman pulled up MacGowan's file again. "It's of note that Liam MacGowan and Caron both served at the same time in the Irish Defence Forces. Though MacGowan was light infantry rather than an MP."

That didn't come as a surprise, either. The Irish Defence Forces were small by nature, generally equipped with obsolescent equipment due to budget constraints, and chronically short of manpower. English recruiting officers for the U.K.'s armed forces were only a ferry ride across the Irish Sea and offered better pay, better benefits, better terms of service and were always happy to enlist Irishmen. The only reason to join the Irish Army was that you were Irish and wanted to.

The Irish government denied it, but there had always been cells of the IRA within the Irish Defence Forces, who used the Irish military as an IRA recruiting and training ground, as well as using the military structure for networking. He had no doubt that Caron had probably recruited MacGowan. When it came to petty intrigues, strong-arming and IRA errand-running on the streets of London, Caron was MacGowan's and O'Maonlai's control officer.

Still, killing CIA agents seemed somewhat above their pay grade. There was something bigger happening, and bigger fish were involved. Bolan was sure of it.

His phone rang. "Just a sec, Bear." Bolan picked up the phone. "Yeah?"

A basso profundo, distorted voice that had obviously been put through a voice scrambler spoke over the line. "You're dead here."

Bolan pushed a button on his electronic warfare suite. The trace started, but he doubted his caller would stay on the line. Bolan had his suspicions about the caller. "That you, fatso?"

"Get out of England or you'll wind up like the other two." The line clicked dead.

"Well, that was pretty cut and dried," Kurtzman commented. "So you think they have the hotel surrounded?"

"I'm sure they've got an eye on it." Bolan checked his watch. It was 2:15 a.m. He doubted they would have an assassination attempt or a snatch set up this quickly. The call was more designed to egg him on rather than to warn him off.

Bolan decided to be egged. "Well, I'm going out for a ride." He scooped up the shillelagh and took a few choice items out of a suitcase.

"You're not going back to the pub."

"Oh, yeah. I'll check back in a little later." Bolan clicked off the satellite link, tested the security measures in the room, then took the elevator down to the garage. His Renault rental vehicle was nondescript, but had enough power to suit his needs. Bolan key-carded the gate and tore out into the night. There was little traffic in the late hour other than cabs, so he quickly arrived at Pub Claddagh. The light over the sign was off and the windows shuttered closed. The ancient, thick oak door would probably withstand minutes of abuse from a police handheld door ram.

Bolan exited his vehicle and pulled a short length of flexible charge out of his coat pocket. He peeled off the adhesive backing, inserted a detonator pin and pressed the charge against the door lock. He stepped back and pushed a preset cell phone number. Yellow fire cracked like a halo around the lock, and Bolan put his foot against the door and shoved.

The lights were on. The fire in the fireplace still crackled. Caron blinked in surprise from behind the bar. MacGowan and O'Maonlai looked up from their beers in horror. Two men sat with the thugs. Bolan didn't know them, but he recognized their long, dark coats and the hoods they'd pushed back onto their shoulders.

The Executioner closed the distance in three strides. Both of O'Maonlai's lower legs were in casts, and a pair of crutches leaned against the table. The left side of MacGowan's face was swollen as if a rugby ball had grown under the skin. The bruising had turned an ugly black and his left eye was swollen shut. He was drinking his pint of stout through a straw. He winced and sputtered beer as Bolan advanced. He couldn't work his jaw to speak.

O'Maonlai shouted and pointed hysterically. "It's him! He's the man who—"

Bolan rammed his heel into the man's chest and toppled him and his chair backward. MacGowan started to rise and Bolan lunged, thrusting his forefinger like a fencer into his opponent's distorted left cheek. Liam let out a high, thin scream and fell backward over his chair.

Bolan grasped his new shillelagh. The two men Bolan didn't know had recovered from their initial surprise. The closer man slapped a hand down on the table to push himself up and his other reached under his jacket. Bolan swung the club like a hammer and brought it down on the man's hand. The man jerked and cringed with shock. The Executioner then swung the shillelagh in a tennis forehand and swatted the hand clawing beneath the coat. The man slid out of his chair, screaming and tucking his crushed hands against his sides.

The other man was up, his coat thrown back, and his silenced PB pistol had just cleared leather, but the combination of the long sound suppressor and a shoulder holster made for a slow draw. Bolan lunged again, ramming the brutal head of the shillelagh into his opponent's solar plexus. The blood drained from the man's face as his sternum cracked beneath the lead-loaded club. Bolan brought the weapon down across the gunman's wrist. The ulna cracked and the pistol fell to the floor.

The assassin joined it a second later.

Ronald Caron leisurely came around the bar with his own shillelagh. He tapped the huge knob into a hand the size of a bunch of bananas and smiled at the weapon Bolan held. "Oh, boyo, you should have brought a gun."

Bolan smiled back. "I did."

Caron continued to advance, apparently without a care in the world. "You should've used it, then. When you had the chance."

Bolan took a step back and put the table between them. He didn't want to shoot Caron, but Cro-Magnon club fighting was the Irishman's game, not his. Caron stepped over MacGowan's mewling form and continued to advance. He tsked at the weapon in Bolan's hand. "You know, I never much cared for the leaded ones. It ruins the balance." He dropped his club to his side and began making small, lazy figure eights. "Of course some say it adds power. But as for me?"

Caron moved with speed belying a man of his age and bulk. He swung the shillelagh up and around, not like a man with a club but a man cracking a whip. The club crashed down and smashed the pub table between them in two. Caron recovered instantly and tapped the knob into his palm again, smiling at the carnage he'd wrought. "I say it's the man behind the shillelagh that matters." He stepped forward, wood crunching beneath his feet and his smile going ugly. "What d'you have behind yours, boyo?"

Crossing clubs with the big man was suicide.

Bolan flung his shillelagh. He threw it down like a game of mumblety-peg being played with sledgehammers. Caron should have had polycarbonate Lexan inserts in his shoes. The giant Irishman grimaced and tottered with his first two toes broken. "Oh, you'll—"

Bolan was already airborne. He sailed across the broken table and delivered a flying side kick into Caron's chest. It was like kicking a beer keg. Caron grunted and budged half a step back. Bolan pistoned his right fist into exactly the same spot over Caron's heart, and for the first time the man's face registered genuine pain. His left hand shot out and covered Bolan's face like a catcher's mitt, his fingers vising down in an iron claw. It wasn't quite the facial neuralgia he'd induced in MacGowan, but it felt like cold chisels were attempting to crash through his facial bones.

Bolan thrust his thumbs into Caron's carotids, but the bull-like neck resisted the blow.

The giant Irishman yanked the soldier into his embrace by the face and rammed it with his hip. A second later he'd spun Bolan and stood behind him, the huge shillelagh pressed against one side of his throat, a brawny arm squeezed against the other. The huge hand had slid from Bolan's face to the back of his head and shoved his face forward into the strangle. It was the figure-four choke out, aided and abetted by three feet of Irish firewood.

Caron whispered in Bolan's ear like a lover. "Yer going to go to sleep now, boyo, and when you wake? It'll be me standing over you. Not with my pride and joy, now—" Caron cinched the strangle deeper with a practiced shrug of his shoulders "—but with a knife from the kitchen. We'll have a long talk you and I, before I send you to the Old Place, at the bottom of the Thames."

Bolan couldn't break the hold. His trachea compressed and sparkly things danced in his vision. He regretted not having drawn his pistol. The Beretta was in a small-of-the-back holster and wedged against Caron's massive middle. He was swiftly running out of air and options. Caron knew what Bolan was thinking from long practice, and he buried his face into Bolan's back to prevent any eye gouging.

The Executioner lifted his knee to his chest and stomped down with all of his might on the Irishman's two broken digits, breaking a third in the bargain. Caron groaned, and Bolan raised his foot and stomped his heel down again. The Irishman couldn't help himself. He instinctively lifted his mangled foot from the floor to protect it. Tottering on one leg, he lost all his leverage. Bolan grabbed the club pressed against his neck, dropped to one knee and heaved.

The three-hundred-pounder flew over Bolan's shoulder in a textbook judo "flying-mare" throw.

O'Maonlai screamed as the giant beached like a whale across his broken legs. Bolan gasped air into his lungs. Caron was already struggling to rise. The soldier strode forward and kicked the Irishman in the side of the neck. The blow had far more power than a karate chop, and the bartender went limp. The shooter with the broken sternum lay gasping weakly and staring up into the lights. His gun hand lay like a broken bird protectively between his legs. MacGowan was reaching through the rubble for Bolan's fallen shillelagh. His open eye widened in terror as Bolan loomed over him. The soldier gave him another finger poke in the swollen hinge of his jaw. The thug passed out without even screaming.

The remaining shooter had risen to his knees and elbows

and was making an admirable attempt to wrap his broken hands around his silenced pistol. He looked up just in time to receive Bolan's foot in his teeth. He fell onto his back and took the soldier's second kick between the legs. He curled fetal, spitting teeth and vomiting up stout.

Bolan relieved both shooters of their pistols. He shot out the overhead lights, blew out the mirror behind the bar and with a twinge of conscience expended the remaining bullets on the vintage ports and the decades-aged single malts on the top shelf. It was a shame to shoot up a historic pub like this, but it had become a nest of serpents, and it was a calculated affront. He wanted the IRA enraged. He wanted the hotheads among them to search him out for payback.

Bolan tossed the spent pistols onto pile of humanity on the floor. He tucked his shillelagh back up his sleeve and scooped up Caron's, as well.

Now he had two.

CHAPTER THREE

"Well, Bear—" Bolan held up wood in each hand for the satellite camera "—now I have two."

Kurtzman grinned. "That's very nice, Striker, but did you really have to go back and beat up everyone a second time?"

Bolan considered. "No, but I felt like it."

Kurtzman's faced showed what he thought of that, and Bolan knew he was right. It had been close. Two CIA field agents were dead, and so far all Bolan had to show for it were two pub brawls and a couple of bludgeons. He just had to hope he'd stirred things up enough that someone higher up the food chain would reveal himself. "Have Shane, Caron or any of the boys showed up in any hospitals?"

Kurtzman shook his head.

It was a long shot. The IRA would have some doctors in London to take care of these kinds of things on the quiet. Bolan considered all they had, which wasn't much. The Pentagon had gotten hold of some pretty wild chatter about the IRA getting its hands on weapons of mass destruction. Britain's MI-5 had put the vague rumors on their very low order of probability list and continued with much more promising lines of investigation of terrorism in the U.K. However, the CIA had a sleeper asset in place with the IRA. That asset had gone active, quietly investigating the rumor, and he had swiftly wound up dead. So had his replacement. Despite their losses, MI-5 seemed to consider the matter a nonissue. At least they did not appear to be assigning any of their own assets to it.

Of course MI-5 probably wasn't pleased that the U.S. had gone ahead and staged an operation on U.K. soil without telling them. Intelligence agencies, even those of staunch allies, were extremely territorial. There would be directors in MI-5 who on some level were secretly pleased and felt the "Yanks" had gotten a deserved comeuppance for playing cowboy games on British soil. Still, two dead CIA agents should have merited some attention. Hard-won instincts told Bolan that there was something wrong with the situation. He couldn't say why, but to him it felt like the whole matter was being swept under the rug.

"Bear, who would have the power to hush this up?"

"A whole lot of people, but you also have to factor that the CIA blundered and got a bloody nose. It's causing quite a little stink between our intelligence communities. There's every reason to suspect that MI-5 is running its own operation on the matter right now and feels no compunction at all to inform the U.S. about it much less involve us." Kurtzman pointed a condemning finger. "For that matter, once the Brits find out that you're running your own gambit over there, which they will, considering how you're leaving a trail of broken Irishmen everywhere you go, things are going to get downright frosty across the pond."

Bolan knew that all too well. "Well, I guess I'm just going to have to pay MI-5 a visit."

Kurtzman just stared. "Really."

"Like you said, they're going to find out about me sooner or later. I might as well give them a courtesy call."

"They're going to read you the riot act and have you shipped home, and that's best-case scenario."

"Probably, but there's something going on here. Something more than the CIA failing to penetrate the IRA. So if I take out some low-level thugs and then go to MI-5, I think my cache as a target will increase. I have to rattle some more cages."

"You know, Striker, I'd be real careful rattling MI-5's cage. They're some of the best in the world, and they don't mess around."

Bolan knew that, too. In fact he was banking on it.

MI-5 London Headquarters

BOLAN SAT ON A FOLDING CHAIR in a "white" or interview room. It was actually a neutral beige. There were no furnishings other than a table and two chairs. Several cameras were positioned in the ceiling and a CD recording device sat on the table. The gray-haired woman sitting across from Bolan looked like a stereotypical British grandmother right down to her horn-rimmed glasses, frumpy tweed jacket and gray wool skirt. Bolan had not been offered any coffee, tea or sherry. He sat, maintaining a professional and calm demeanor while Assistant Director Heloise Finch quietly and, with a British upper-class politeness so stiff it was insulting, lit into him.

Phrases like "poor spirit of cooperation," "endangering a relationship that had thrived since World War II" and Bolan's own "temerity" were tripping off her tongue forward, backward and sideways. It appeared that the director was finally winding down.

"…and while I do appreciate the courtesy of your taking the time to call upon us, I'm really not sure in what capacity I or my department can be of any assistance to you."

Finch didn't appreciate the visit at all. She was clearly appalled by the whole situation. Bolan smiled winningly. "Would it be shabby of me if I asked for your help anyway?"

Finch steepled her hands and stared at Bolan for long moments. "You know, I believe it would."

"I can see how you'd feel that way."

"The CIA has—"

Bolan cut in before she could work up a fresh head of steam. "Director Finch, I don't work for the Central Intelligence Agency."

"You know—" Finch flipped open a thin manila folder "—I have something of a file on you, or at least someone matching your description. Much of the intel is above my pay grade and security clearance. Barely a pamphlet, actually, but it appears you have operated within the United Kingdom before, sometimes in what can loosely be described as cooperation with British Intelligence and apparently sometimes without the permission of Her Majesty's government."

Bolan saw no reason to lie. "That's essentially correct."

Finch was somewhat taken aback by Bolan's directness. "I have received a report of a disturbance over at Pub Claddagh last night."

Bolan shrugged.

"May I state that Her Majesty's government does not appreciate American citizens coming to her shores and engaging in donnybrooks and shillelagh battles in her pubs."

MI-5 clearly had informants in the London IRA infrastructure. Bolan maintained his poker face.

"However, MI-5 has received rather veiled suggestions from some very strange quarters that it would not be 'unappreciated' were my department to show you whatever professional courtesy seems appropriate." Finch leaned forward and peered over the rims of her glasses. "I have taken this to mean I should not have you immediately detained and deported."

"That would be preferable."

"However, to reiterate, I am not sure what if any assistance I am willing to provide you."

Bolan smiled.

Assistant Director Finch's cool reserve broke as she smiled resignedly. "Of course, I have already been of assistance to you. You are sticking your nose into the IRA doings, and your taking a meeting at MI-5 HQ ups your market value."

Bolan didn't bother to deny it.

"I will be blunt with you. My superiors and members of the government concerned with this organization consider this rumor of the IRA acquiring weapons of mass destruction rather something of a wild-goose chase, and your government's dogged pursuit of it puzzling if not downright ridiculous, as well as a strain on the relationship between our two countries."

"Director Finch, the fact remains that two CIA intelligence agents have been killed."

"The CIA agents in question were trying to infiltrate the Irish Republican Army's London infrastructure, and that, and I say this in all modesty, if it is attempted without the help of my department is an excellent way to commit suicide. Their loss is indeed regrettable, however, it is not totally surprising."

"I appreciate your candor. Let me blunt, as well." Bolan's smile fell away from his face. "There is something very wrong going on here, and you know it."

Finch sighed. "Other than your two dead CIA agents, what

proof do you have that the IRA is up to anything worse than usual?"

"Nothing. Just a hunch. Just like you."

Finch stared at Bolan for long moments. He knew he'd read the woman correctly. Finch knew something was wrong, as well. MI-5 was one of the top internal intelligence agencies on the planet, second only perhaps to the FBI. Like all internal intelligence agencies they had civilian oversight. The FBI was responsible to congress. MI-5 was responsible to the House of Lords and the House of Commons. Throughout their illustrious history, MI-5 was known far and wide for spending almost as much time battling English bureaucracy as they did enemies of the United Kingdom.

"You are playing a very dangerous game, and I cannot even begin to describe my feelings toward yet another U.S. citizen engaging in rogue intelligence operations under my nose."

"However," Bolan countered, "you know there is something bigger going on here, and for whatever reason your department has been told to low priority the situation or ignore it completely."

Finch's face set in stone. "For the record, you are not to engage in any intelligence operations against the IRA on English soil. For that matter, you are not to 'operate' on English soil in any capacity at all unless directly requested to by Her Majesty's government. If you are caught doing so, it would be my duty to have you at the very least detained and deported if not brought up on criminal charges."

Bolan nodded. "I understand." He glanced at the recorder on the table and Finch clicked it off. "For the record, any and all intelligence I might gather if I engaged in such a questionable activity would be immediately shared with Her Majesty's government, and done so through your offices exclusively."

"I believe we understand each other." Finch placed her business card on the table and pressed the intercom button. "Security, please have our guest escorted off the premises."

BOLAN GLANCED at his watch as he drove through traffic. His modified wristwatch was blinking at him, which meant that someone had gone into his hotel room without deactivating the security suite. Bolan drove an extra block past his hotel and then circled around to approach from the back, heading into the hotel loading dock. A man in a purple hotel jacket looked at his vehicle askance. Bolan exited the vehicle and handed him a fifty-pound note, and the man went back to overseeing the off-loading of towels from a linen truck. Bolan followed the pallets of towels into the laundry.

His watch peeped at him again. Someone had opened his laptop.

Bolan approached two men in white uniforms speaking what Bolan was pretty sure was a Nigerian dialect and smoking cigarettes. "Say, can I ask you a favor? Could you go up to the fifth floor and see if anyone strange is lurking around outside room 502?"

One of the men grinned. "Sorry. We're on break."

Bolan peeled off another fifty-pound note. "There's no way I can convince you?"

The second Nigerian snatched the note. "I am convinced." He pinched out his cigarette and carefully placed it back in the pack. "I'll be back."

His partner scowled after him as he disappeared into the service elevator.

Bolan smiled sympathetically. "I might have a job for you in a minute."

The man peered at Bolan narrowly. "This is nothing illegal, then?"

Bolan was almost positive the two men were illegal immigrants. They were probably in desperate need of money but even more desperate to have no attention drawn to themselves. Bolan shrugged. The man clapped a hand to his forehead as if he had a migraine. "Oh, man…"

Ten minutes later Bolan's scout returned. He shook his head. "This real James Bond shit, you know."

Bolan nodded. "How many?"

"Two. One big. One little. Nasty-looking white men. Lounging about. I don't know, but beneath their jackets I think they have guns." He peered at Bolan in identical suspicion as his partner. "That your room?"

Bolan held up his key. "Can I ask you gentlemen a favor?"

They blinked in unison. "Oh?"

"I need a diversion."

They stared at Bolan noncommittally.

The big American turned to his scout. "What's your name?"

"Musa Balam."

"Musa, nice to meet you." He turned to the other man. "And you?"

He stared at Bolan defiantly. "Sheriff Modu."

"Nice to meet you. I'm Matt. What I want you to do is this. I want you both to go back up the elevator. When it opens, Musa, you run down the hall to the stairs, and you? You chase him, yelling in Hausa."

Modu looked at Bolan as if he were insane. "Not for fifty pounds."

"How about a hundred?" Bolan grinned. "Each, and another hundred once it's done."

Balam peered curiously. "And after it is done, what?"

"You're better off not knowing. You just run for the stairs and keep going."

A furious exchange in Hausa ensued. Balam apparently won. "Show us the money."

Bolan peeled several bills from his money clip. Even the reticent Sheriff Modu's eyes lit up. Bolan handed them a hundred each and followed them into the elevator. Modu took a wet towel from a bin and coiled it into a rat's tail. The door pinged open on the fifth floor. Balam ran out screaming and Modu raced after him, shouting in scathing Hausa and snapping the towel like a whip. Bolan waited four seconds until he knew they had passed his door and then filled his hand with his Beretta 93-R and stepped out of the elevator.

As Balam had said, two men stood near his door. Both men had short, brush-cut blond hair and wore leather jackets. By the bulges under their left arms, his scout was right. They were packing substantial heat. The smaller man held a cell phone, obviously waiting for warning from the men watching the garage and the lobby. The two Nigerians were almost to the stairs at the end of the hall. The big man shook his head in disgust at their antics. "Agh, can you believe those bloody foreigners."

The accent told Bolan that the man was a South African. Bolan strode up to him, the big man catching the movement a second too late. Bolan cracked the slide of his Beretta machine pistol across the side of the man's face, laying the cheek open to the bone. He whipped the 93-R backhand across the bridge of the little man's nose and shattered it. The big man had bent over with pain and clutched his face. The butt of the Beretta crunched into the back of his skull and dropped him unconscious to the ground. Bolan rammed the muzzle of the Beretta into the side of the little man's neck and he fell to the carpet.

Bolan knelt over the big man and took his ID. Beneath his jacket he was wearing Threat Level II soft body armor. In a shoulder rig he was carrying a BXP submachine gun with the stock folded and a sound suppressor fitted over the barrel. The weapon was basically an American MAC-10 cleaned up and improved to South African specifications. Bolan took the weapon and checked the load. It was loaded with hollow point rounds. He took the little man's BXP, as well, and checked his watch. Someone was still messing with his laptop. That laptop had been designed by Akira Tokaido, one of Stony Man Farm's cybernetic experts. The Farm's resident armorer, John "Cowboy" Kissinger, had installed a number of security devices that had nothing to do with binary code. Bolan pumped the bezel of his watch three times and was rewarded with a scream as the right-hand speaker in the laptop's monitor frame spewed a compressed stream of pepper spray into the operator's eyes.

Bolan kicked open the door of his hotel room.

A redheaded woman was on the floor in front of Bolan's laptop clutching her face. The man who had been in guard position looked up from where he bent over her. His BXP was in his hand but on the wrong side of his body. Bolan put the red-dot sight of his right-hand weapon on the man's chest and squeezed the trigger. The BXP stuttered and twenty-two rounds of 9 mm hollowpoint ammo jackhammered into the gunner's chest as Bolan held the trigger down on full-auto. The man's armor held, but he still had to absorb the bullets' energy and his body took a beating like he was being kicked to death by a mule. The BXP clacked open on empty, and Bolan helped the man onto his back and into unconsciousness by flinging the five and half pounds of smoking steel into his face.

The redhead squirmed across the carpet, her hands clawing for her own fallen submachine gun. Bolan pressed the muzzle of his second weapon against her cheek and pinned her head to the floor. "One more move and I'll turn your head into applesauce. You understand?"

The woman nodded, her eyes streaming and wincing as her lower lip split beneath the pressure of the submachine gun.

Bolan backed the weapon off her mouth. "Who are you?"

She glared up at Bolan in red-eyed defiance. Bolan reached into his jacket and clicked open his phone. He pressed a preset number and Assistant Director Finch answered on the first ring. "You have reached MI-5. This is Assistant Director Finch."

"We spoke earlier today."

Her voice replied curtly. "Yes."

"I have something for you. In my room."

"Oh?"

"Yes, you should send a team down here. You have three suspects."

The redhead stared up in alarm. She was part of a four-man team.

"They're suffering from various broken bones and contusions," Bolan continued. "One at least appears to be of South African extraction."

"South African?"

"Yes."

"Really?" Finch registered genuine surprise. "Are you sure?"

"Pretty sure."

"I'll have a team there in ten minutes."

"I won't be here."

"I'm not entirely surprised."

Bolan was about to hang up when Finch spoke. "You're to be arrested on sight."

"I'll call you later." Bolan clicked off. He didn't have much time. "You." He pointed the BXP back at the woman's head. "You're coming with me."

CHAPTER FOUR

"Running the prints now, Striker."

Bolan had taken the woman's fingerprints and faxed them to Kurtzman. She sat on a chair with her hands cuffed together in front of her and her ankles bound to the front chair legs with plastic zip restraints. The gun Bolan had held in his hand during the ten-minute drive to the safe house had kept the woman docile. Bolan had washed out her eyes with water. They were still red-veined from the gas and still glared bloody murder at Bolan.

Kurtzman got back to him almost instantly. "I have a hit on the Interpol database."

The woman went rigid on the chair.

"What have you got?"

The computer whiz hit a key and a police photo of the woman popped up on the screen. "Sylvette MacJory, born in Aberdeen, Scotland. Attended Strathclyde University and received her degree in computer science. In 2005 she was accused and convicted of cybernetic crimes in the U.K., including identity theft and criminal hacking into the databases of several major U.K. financial institutions. Sentenced to five years, sentence reduced to two years probation and public service. Current residence in London. No further criminal record."

Sylvette's face clouded with rage.

"So who are your South African friends?" Bolan asked.

"Piss off, Yank!"

"You should try to come up with something more original than that."

"You're no cop, then." The woman's eyes narrowed. "You're holding me illegally. I want my lawyer."

"You're right. I'm not a cop, and you're not being held." Bolan clicked open his phone and punched a button. "You've been abducted."

MacJory swallowed with difficulty as her position became more clear to her.

Assistant Director Finch answered on the first ring. "Where are you?"

"Did you get the package I left you?"

"Yes," Finch admitted.

"I have another."

There followed an appalled silence. "Listen to me. You really must—"

"Her name is Sylvette MacJory. You'll have her in your files. Felony computer hacker. She was attempting to get into my laptop."

"Did you know we detected pepper spray within the room?"

"She tried to get into my laptop," Bolan reiterated.

Finch tried a different tack. "You shot one of the suspects twenty-two times. He survived only because he was wearing body armor."

"I shot him twenty-two times precisely because he was wearing body armor and I knew you would want him alive."

"Mr.—"

"The large one out in the hall is South African. Did you get an ID on the other two?"

Bolan was pretty sure she would have hung up had she not been attempting to trace the call. The NSA satellite Bolan was bouncing his signal through made that a losing proposition, but it would take the MI-5 communications people a little while to figure that out. Finch let out a long, grudging breath. "You're correct. The large one is Ruud Heitinga, South African citizen, as is the other, one Kew Timmer."

"You get a bead on the man inside?"

"He was a bit of an anomaly. His papers say he is a French citizen named Guy Diddier. All of them have clammed up, however, call it a hunch, but I found Monsieur Diddier most un-Gallic in his behavior."

Bolan was swiftly coming to the conclusion that Assistant Director Heloise Finch had earned her hunches the hard way. "So what did you do?"

"I called in a favor with French intelligence and ran the name. Diddier is a French citizen, but not by birth."

Bolan's intuition spoke to him. "He served a tour in the French Foreign Legion."

Finch seemed pleased. "That is correct. He was originally an American citizen by the name of Gary Pope. He served four years in the California National Guard's 223rd Infantry Regiment. Somewhere along the line, he got the romantic notion of joining the Legion. Once he'd been accepted, he took advantage of the Legion's opportunity of identity change and after serving his tour successfully he accepted French citizenship."

"Any line on the two South Africans?"

"Not yet, but I have every faith they are veterans of the South African Defense Force."

Bolan agreed. "Ms. Finch, these individuals are mercenaries."

"So it would seem, and how do you believe the girl fits in?"

Bolan glanced over at the hacker. "She may use a computer rather than a silenced submachine gun, but she's a hired gun, nonetheless."

"I agree."

"Director, I find it very strange that the IRA is employing mercenaries."

MacJory stared at Bolan strangely and then snapped her poker face back on. Bolan pretended to ignore the slip as Finch continued.

"It is indeed odd. It goes completely against their method of operation. By nature, mercenaries work for money and historically are notorious for switching sides. The terrorist wing of the IRA chooses its members for their absolute loyalty. They would never entrust any kind of sensitive operation to outsiders."

"So someone else is in the game."

"So it would appear."

"Any ideas?"

"None whatsoever. The appearance of mercenaries in this situation is positively anomalous."

"What's their legal status, currently?"

"Well, their visas and passports are in order, and while they weren't guests of the hotel there is currently no law in England against being beaten to a pulp in a hallway. However, we did find three automatic weapons on the premises. They are currently being held on suspicion and possible weapons charges." Finch's voice went slightly dry with sarcasm. "Since you took the liberty of kidnapping Miss MacJory, I suspect any evidence concerning her will be inadmissible in an English court of law."

"Yeah, I figured."

"So what do you intend to do with her?"

Bolan raised the BXP. "Shoot her."

MacJory started in her seat.

Finch shouted in alarm. "You can't—" Bolan clicked his phone shut and stepped forward. MacJory cringed as far as her restraints would let her. Bolan pressed the muzzle of the BXP between her eyebrows and pinned her head to the back of the chair like an insect.

"You're of no more use to me."

"No!"

The safety clicked off beneath Bolan's thumb with grim finality.

MacJory screamed. "Please!"

"Who do you work for!" Bolan roared.

The woman shook her head, crying. "I don't know!"

"You've got five seconds."

"Please—"

Bolan knew MacJory's type. She wasn't a terrorist. She was a genius. Breaking code and committing crimes in cyberspace was a game to her. Even after her conviction, she still didn't believe she had done anything wrong. He wouldn't shoot her, but he had to make her believe he would.

Nothing had prepared her for gutter-level, get-your-hands-dirty fieldwork.

"One…"

"Please!"

"Two…"

"I don't know who I work for!"

"You're working for the IRA. You're a traitor to the U.K. Three."

"I didn't know!"

"Four…"

"I don't know anything about the IRA!" The woman wept uncontrollably. "I swear it!"

Bolan read her body language and pulled the gun back. MacJory started to suck in a breath of relief and gave a strangled shriek as Bolan fired a burst into the ceiling. Plaster rained down on her, and he aimed the weapon at her again. "Okay, you're a merc. Who brokered the deal? Who pays you?"

She shuddered with her betrayal. "Aegis…"

Bolan cocked his head slightly. "Aegis Global Security?"

"Yes! I swear! I freelance for Aegis!"

That was not good news. Aegis was one of the oldest, and in the controversial world of executive VIP protection, military advisement and "solutions by other means," Aegis Global Security was one of the most respected.

Bolan clicked his phone open. Finch picked up midring. "Jesus, bloody—"

"She's still alive and unharmed. She freelances for Aegis. I suspect the other three are permanent men on the roster."

Finch was flabbergasted. "Aegis Global Security?"

"That seems to be the situation."

"Not good."

"No, it's not. I'm going to turn Miss MacJory loose in a couple of hours, and I'll let you know where you can find her."

"Listen, I need you to—"

Bolan clicked off and went back to his computer. "You get all that?"

Kurtzman nodded. "Oh, yeah."

"Get me everything you can on Aegis." Bolan already knew a lot about it. "Where's David McCarter?"

"You've got a bit of luck there. He's in the U.K. right now visiting family."

Bolan nodded. "I need him."

Guernsey, The Channel Isles

"RED-HOT WILLY." David McCarter stared at Bolan accusingly as he drove the Land Rover over the bleak, bumpy countryside of the island. "You know the man's a bloody legend."

Bolan glanced off across the gray chop of the English Channel toward Normandy. "Red-Hot" Willy was indeed a legend. The man's biography read like an adventure novel. A television series on the BBC and two lines of pulp fiction paperbacks had been loosely based on his life. Just about anyone who had ever been in the military community had heard of Colonel William Glen-Patrick. However in England, formally, he was Lord William Glen-Patrick. The Glen-Patrick line had held the title of baron in England since the Middle Ages. Like a Dickens novel, little Lord Willy had been orphaned at the age of five when his parents had crashed their Lotus Elan into the wall of a cattle enclosure. The executors of his estate had been unscrupulous and absconded with the greater part of the family fortune, and by the time Willy had reached the age of seventeen the Glen-Patrick family had been bankrupt. Unable to pay his taxes, Lord William had sold the family castle and estates and used his family name to wangle a commission in the Life Guards, the most senior regiment in the British Army. He had served with distinction in Aden and Borneo and become the British army welterweight boxing champion. In the late 1970s he had joined the SAS, being one of the few members of the English peerage to ever successfully qualify and serve in English Special

Forces. During the Falkland Island War, he had won the Victoria Cross for conspicuous bravery.

The wounds he'd received in the Falklands had forced him to retire from the British army, so he had taken his name and reputation and gone to West Africa, where he had gotten himself involved in the constant wars and revolutions. He'd come back with a personal fortune in diamonds. Throughout the 1980s Lord William had been famous for winning and losing fortunes at the baccarat tables in Monaco, reaching a respectable ranking on the Grand Prix circuit when not crashing his own personal sports cars, climbing Mount Everest and K2, sailing around the world, dating a different girl every month and even occasionally flexing his hereditary right as an English peer to cast his vote in the House of Lords. He was a nobleman, a hero, a mercenary, a professional adventurer and a dilettante. For decades he had been constant fodder for the British tabloids and earned the sobriquet "Red-Hot" Willy.

In the military community he was known most for pioneering what may have been the first VIP/executive protection mercenary outfit. In West Africa, war and violence had been and still were endemic. At the same time gold and diamonds flowed out of the area and guns and money flowed in. Glen-Patrick had seen the need not just for bodyguards for VIPs, but men who were soldiers in their own right. Developers, businessmen, African royalty and heads of state needed more than just bullet shields. Glen-Patrick had used the contacts he'd made in the army and the SAS, finding highly qualified men from around the world not just to guard VIPs, their families and business interests, but men who would act proactively. Glen-Patrick had developed a simple, three-step plan. When a threat was determined, it would be bought off. If it couldn't be bought off, it would be intimidated. If it couldn't be intimidated, it would be eliminated.

The work had been lucrative, but it was the international business contacts he had made that had made him a millionaire.

Lord William had slowed down upon reaching the age of sixty and retired to an estate on the Isle of Guernsey, living with three women, none of whom he was married to, and again, very occasionally, casting his vote in the House of Lords, usually on environmental issues. His mercenary group had gone from Aegis Incorporated to Aegis Global Security and was reputed to be less bloodthirsty in the new century. According to its prospectus, it was doing a thriving business in Iraq and Afghanistan.

Bolan took note of Lord William's service record with the Life Guards and the SAS. He'd seen service in Northern Ireland with both units. What he had done there with the SAS had been redacted.

Bolan closed the file. "I see a few red flags, David."

"Oh, I know, millionaire playboy entrepreneur moves to a tiny island in his dotage, goes quietly bloody bonkers and starts engaging in crazy politically motivated actions." The former SAS man shook his head as the Land Rover rumbled and bumped along the narrow, muddy lane between the hedgerows. "Don't think I haven't thought it."

David McCarter was the leader of Stony Man Farm's Phoenix Force and another man whose instincts Bolan trusted. "You knew him?"

"I met him. We're two different generations of SAS. He was ending his career when I was starting mine. But he's peerage and he won the Victoria Cross." McCarter glanced meaningfully at the brown gorse all around them. "That bloody well means something in these islands."

Bolan knew by "islands" McCarter meant the entire United Kingdom.

"I called him, like you asked," McCarter continued. "He remembered me and agreed to see us, but he didn't sound too happy about it. I'm— There are men in the hedgerows."

Bolan had noticed them, too. McCarter brought the Land Rover to a halt as a man stepped out into the lane in front of them.

The man was about five foot ten. White hair fell around his ears in a shag that seemed to be three weeks past due for a cut. A white mustache draped across his upper lip. He wore a tweed hacking jacket with leather patches on the elbows and a quilted leather patch on the right shoulder for shooting. His heavy wool pants were tucked into stained Wellington boots. A tweed cap was perched on his head at a rakish angle. He looked lean and fit and every inch a British squire out for a morning hunt. All he needed was a double-barrel shotgun broken open and crooked in his elbow.

Instead Lord William stood in the misting rain cradling an L-2 A-3 Sterling submachine gun.

A pair of Great Danes flanked him. One had the black-and-white markings of a Dalmatian while the other was a startling, near-hairless pink. A human argyle vest with the sleeves cut off strained at its seams to insulate the giant furless dog against the cold.

The Sterling's muzzle was not quite pointed at the Land Rover. Lord William's finger was not quite on the trigger. His men came out of the hedgerows; there were four of them, two on each side of the lane. They were dressed in heavy wool sweaters, and all carried double-barrel shotguns.

McCarter glanced over at Bolan. The Land Rover's armor package was rated up to direct hits from .30-caliber weapons.

He was waiting for Bolan's signal to run over the baron and his men.

"I say, David!" Lord William jerked his head. "Why don't you and your friend come out, stretch your legs! We'll chat a bit!"

Bolan caught motion out of the corner of his eye. The hedgerow was six feet tall, but a barn was visible above it some fifty yards away. A pair of men were atop it now, and Bolan recognized the 84 mm profile of a Carl Gustaf recoilless antitank rifle across one of the men's shoulder.

The seven-pound, rocket-assisted warhead would light up the Land Rover like the Fourth of July.

Lord William shrugged. "Of course I could just bloody well light you up like November Fifth!"

November Fifth was Guy Fawkes Day in England, commemorating the day in 1604 when Guy Fawkes had stockpiled thirty-six barrels of black powder in a cellar beneath the House of Lords and tried to blow up Parliament.

Bolan turned to McCarter. "Let's go stretch our legs and chat a bit."

"Right."

"Slow and easy!" Lord William called. He nodded at his yeomen. "Steady on, lads."

Bolan and McCarter stepped out of the Land Rover and moved to stand in front of it. McCarter grinned. "Hello, Bill!"

Bolan nodded. "Your lordship."

The two dogs quivered at the sounds of their voices. Lord William spoke soothingly. "Spot… Starkers…" Bolan looked into Starkers's colorless albino eyes and saw cold, pale murder. Only their master's will kept the giant dogs rooted in place in the muck instead of savaging the intruders.

Lord William ignored Bolan's and McCarter's greetings. "Lunk, their pistols, if you please."

The man behind them was very good. Even in the squelching mud he'd barely made any noise on his approach. Bolan and McCarter slowly opened their jackets. A huge hand reached around Bolan and drew the Beretta 93-R. The Executioner spoke quietly. "Ankle holster and right pocket." He was relieved of his snub-nosed 9 mm Centennial revolver and his Mikov switchblade.

The Executioner slid his eyes to look at the man as he moved off to disarm McCarter. Lunk had earned his name. He was huge. Not big like a bodybuilder or an athlete, but a human built to a different scale. He was running six foot six with shoulders that were axe-handle broad, from which hung arms like an orangutan. He had the pale complexion, anvil jaw, snub nose and tightly curling brown hair that fairly screamed Welshman.

He took McCarter's Hi-Power pistol, noting the shortened Argentine "Detective" slide and the chrome base plate of the Israeli 15-round magazine with one raised brown eyebrow.

McCarter kept his smile painted on his face. "Not the warmest welcome I've ever had in Guernsey, Bill."

"Can't be too careful these days, David." The aging lord stared at McCarter long and hard. "These days, in this business, it's your friends who come to kill you, and they come smiling."

"You sound like you're speaking from recent experience, Lord William," Bolan commented.

"A Yank, then?"

"Yes, your lordship. I've been having a few people coming by to kill me, as well. David was kind enough to arrange a meet so that you and I might compare notes. I think we have a few things in common."

Lord William turned to McCarter. "I haven't seen you in years, David. Then you call me out of the blue sky and tell me it's urgent and come armed with an American in tow. What's this all about?"

"Well, it's a fine, soft morning, Bill. Shall we take that stretch of the legs and talk?"

Lord William stared up into the misting rain. "Oh God, no. I'm an old man. It's worth my life to be out in this mist and muck." He slung his weapon and suddenly grinned. "Let's go inside and drink whiskey."

CHAPTER FIVE

They sat in leather chairs in front of a roaring fireplace that was large enough to double as a car port for a Volkswagen. Spot and Starkers lay curled before it on a polar bear rug. Lord William had put away his Sterling, but when he unbuttoned his coat a Browning Hi-Power pistol in a shoulder holster was revealed. He and McCarter sipped ten-year-old Laphroaig single-malt whiskey from the Isle of Islay. Bolan drank a pint of the locally brewed ale. Lunk and two of the yeomen hung back in the shadows of the cavernous hall drinking ale and keeping their weapons close to hand. They were all quiet for a few moments while Lord William observed the laws of hospitality and everyone warmed their bones.

"So, David. What's this all about?"

"Well, Bill, there's been some trouble in London."

Lord William peered over the rim of his whiskey glass. "Oh?"

"Yes, the CIA had two agents end up in the Thames. The IRA is involved."

"Well, what the bloody hell is the CIA doing mucking about with the IRA? Can't MI-5 cut the mustard anymore?"

Bolan decided to play it straight. "The operation was run without the cooperation or the knowledge of MI-5 or Her Majesty's government."

"Well, it serves them bloody right, then, doesn't it?" Lord William snorted with disgust born of long experience. "Central sodding Intelligence my flaming—"

"Lord William, it appears some of your employees are involved."

"Really."

Lord William turned to the gigantic Welshman. "Lunk, you taffy bastard! Have you been having it on with the IRA again?"

"Oh, no, m'lord." The giant grinned malevolently from where he stood drinking by the sideboard. His voice was as deep as thunder in the distance. "I haven't killed an Irish in, oh, ten years?"

"CIA?" Lord William said hopefully.

"No." Lunk finished his pint. "Not that I'd mind so much, though."

Lord William gestured with his whiskey glass at the four men bearing shotguns and drinking on the couch. "How about the rest of you lads, then? Been misbehaving in London when I wasn't looking?"

The men grinned and shook their heads in unison.

Lord William turned back to Bolan with a helpless shrug. "That's most of the men I have on staff."

"Actually, I'm thinking more along the lines of Aegis Global Security employees."

Lord William shifted uncomfortably. "Well, for one, except for some accountants, lawyers and office staff, Aegis has no permanent employees. We have stockholders, and then we have contractors—we call them associates—whom Aegis employs, contract by contract, job by job. And two, Aegis Global Security doesn't take contract work from the IRA. Indeed, on numerous occasions we've taken jobs to protect people *from* the IRA. Successful jobs, mind you, and we weren't in the business of arresting people or taking prisoners, if you get my meaning. Except for MI-5 we're the IRA's worst bloody nightmare."

Bolan opened his folder and started handing over pictures. "Do you know this woman?"

Lord William stared at the Scottish redhead with appreciation. "No, but I'd like to."

Bolan handed him the pictures of the former French Legionnaire and the smaller South African. Lord William shook his head in mounting irritation and suddenly stopped. He tapped his finger on the final picture of the big man.

"You know him?"

"I remember him vaguely." Lord William nodded. "Ruud something. Yes, that's it, Ruud Heitinga. South African lad. Reconnaissance Commando." He frowned. "Bit too fond of interrogation for my taste. Always pulled his weight, though. Had a brother, Arjen, even bigger than he was, big enough to give Lunk a run for his money. Together, the two of them were something of a terror."

"Lord William, I realize that Aegis doesn't have a standing private army, and that people who have worked for you in the past are quite capable of going off and doing private, illegal contract work without your knowledge. But you must have a roster of people who have worked for you," Bolan said.

"Well, of course, but I'm not sure how I can help you. You see, I haven't had my hand directly in the business except for shareholder votes in oh, well, probably going on ten years."

"But you are listed as the president of the company."

Lord William flushed with embarrassment. "Well, it's not something I'm particularly proud of, but about eleven years ago I grew a wild hair to sail solo around the world. It took me ninety days, a respectable time, but when I returned I'd found there'd been something of a hostile takeover at Aegis." Lord William shrugged. "I've always been good at making fortunes and starting businesses, but the trick, you see, is keeping them. Never my strong suit. It was all very polite. All very firm."

Lord William glanced up at the life-size replica of classical Greek hoplite shield hanging over the mantel. It was painted black, and a gold fist holding a lightning bolt was emblazoned in the center. It was the Aegis, the all-protective shield of Zeus in Greek mythology. "Of course they wanted to keep the logo hanging over the door and my face on the yearly prospectus. So they let me have the title of president, but it's largely ceremonial, for publicity purposes."

"I'm sorry to hear that."

Lord William shrugged philosophically. "Well, you know. Aegis turned a profit but it was never a huge moneymaker. I started it in the eighties almost on a lark to get work for some good men I knew, myself included. It's Jennings who really made the company take off. It's bigger than ever, and good men from dozens of services around the world who've been cashed out by wounds or are a bit past it physically are still making good money doing what they do best." Lord William poured himself another two fingers of whiskey. "You Yanks and your War on Terror have been good for business."

"Jennings." Bolan knew the name from the files Kurtzman had given him. "The chairman of the board."

"Indeed." Lord William made a face as though he had just tasted something vaguely unpleasant. "Rich boy. Went to Eton. He spent a couple of years in the Territorial Army Volunteers.

He made lieutenant but never served anywhere. Something of an 'intense' personality. Loved shooting guns, rolling around on the judo mat and hearing everyone else's war stories. A real 'weekend warrior,' as you Yanks would say."

McCarter had met the type before. "Sounds like a right proper Charlie."

"A right proper head for business, though," Lord William countered. "Bought stock when we went public. Then he bought more. Infused some needed cash when I was between fortunes and ended up with controlling interest in the company. A real murderer in the boardroom. Trust me, I have the scars to prove it."

"Lord William, the situation is this," Bolan said. "The CIA heard chatter that the IRA was somehow mixed up with weapons of mass destruction. MI-5 discounted them."

"Bloody right they did. What's the IRA going to do with a nuke or some ugly bloody bug? They're smart enough to know if they ever did such a damn fool thing all it would get them is a second Norman invasion. England would turn the entire island into a medieval fife again. I'm sure a few of the buggers have dreamy dreams of Parliament going up in a mushroom cloud, but that's all it is, a pipe dream."

"I agree. However, two CIA agents were killed investigating that rumor, and when I looked into the matter and stirred things up with the IRA, Ruud Heitinga and the other three in the pictures I showed you showed up unannounced at my hotel room. During interrogation, the woman claimed she was under contract with Aegis Global Security."

Lord William was appalled. "What's a woman doing working for Aegis?"

"Computer hacker."

The baron considered this strange turn of events. "Really."

"These days, breaking into enemy computer bases is almost more necessary than infiltrating their firebases," Bolan told him.

"Computer hacker. Well, that is forward thinking," Lord William admitted. "Must be one of Jennings's innovations."

McCarter saw his opening. "Bill?"

"Yes, David?"

"Not that I'm complaining, but that was an unusual welcome this morning."

"Well, there's been some trouble about."

"What kind of trouble, Bill?"

Lord William stared into the crackling fire. "Oh, you know. The usual thing. An attempt or two on my life. One was a sniper's bullet through the terrace window. Took my nightcap clean off my head." He shook his head ruefully. "Never found the bastard."

"And the other?"

"Lunk found him by the compost pile. Starkers was busy burying the poor bastard."

Bolan and McCarter stared at the mutant Great Dane.

Lord William shrugged. "Well, they always say leave the dogs outside during the day but bring them in to defend you at night. But after the sniper attack, I started leaving the dogs out after hours. Felt bad for Starkers. I had to buy him some canine Wellies to keep him warm. Poor hairless bastard. You know, I almost had him put down when he was born. Bloody runt of the litter. But my lady friend at the time thought he was cute, so I kept him. Well, then, anyway, apparently Starkers and this son of a bitch had a difference of opinion in the wee hours a fortnight ago. Needless to say, Starkers earned his kibble." Lord William leaned down and scratched the immense animal between the ears. "Who's a good lad? Who's a good lad, then? It's bloody you, Starkers, isn't it!"

Starkers thumped his tail on the polar bear carcass in agreement.

"You know, all the bastard had was knife?" Lord William turned to Bolan. "One of your Yank Bowie knives. I swear it was a foot long. You could skin an elephant with the bloody thing. Guess he wanted to get up close and personal with me." Lord William gave his dog another rub behind the ears. "Should have brought a bloody elephant gun for you, Starkers, shouldn't he have?"

Starkers rolled onto his back and shuddered like a squid.

"So then I get a call from an old comrade whom I never really knew that well from the old days in SAS. You, David, and you'll forgive me if I was a bit suspicious."

Bolan finished his beer. A bottle cracked open behind Bolan and the giant Welshman stalked forward and refilled his glass. "No harm, no foul, your lordship. May I ask you a personal question?"

"Everyone does, and I find myself far more fond of you than the average Yank."

"I assume you still have stock in Aegis?"

"Oh, a sizable chunk. Jennings wanted to buy me out outright, but that's where I put my foot down. I still get my dividends quarterly and occasionally vote in the stockholder's meetings."

"Do you still have the legal right to look into the company's doings?"

"Might be a bit touch and go." Lord William leaned back and contemplated his whiskey. "Though I suppose I could call an emergency stockholders' meeting and raise a stench. There aren't that many of us, but then again, we're scattered about the globe a bit. It would take time."

"What if you pulled a surprise visit to corporate headquarters?" Bolan suggested.

"You mean, just show up in Amsterdam, unannounced?" A devilish grin suddenly passed across Lord William's face. "Brass balls and all that."

"Something like that."

"Well, it's the last thing they'd expect, but I doubt I can get more than one guest through the door." Lord William raised an eyebrow at Bolan. "I assume you would like to come along?"

"If you don't mind."

"Not at all."

McCarter frowned. "You sure you don't want some backup?"

Bolan had already given that some thought. "Actually, I'd like you to go back to London. My name is mud with MI-5 right about now, but last I heard you're still a golden boy with British Intelligence. You're our best shot at getting real cooperation."

He took out Assistant Director Finch's business card. "Look her up. Deal with her and only her. I still have the feeling there's someone higher up trying to smother this whole situation."

McCarter scanned the card and memorized it. "Right, then." He tapped his copy of the mission file. "I don't like it, though. The more I hear, the less I trust this Jennings git."

"Oh, well!" Lord William grinned. "If you've a git problem, then Lunk's your solution." He turned to the massive Welshman. "Lunk! How's about a little jaunt to Holland?"

Lunk considered this for several long moments. "The smoked eel is delicious."

Amsterdam

LUNK WOLFED SMOKED EEL from a roll of newspaper. Bolan had learned on the flight from Guernsey that "Lunk" was short for Lynnock ap Nock, and the Cymric superman had been a Coxswain in the Royal Marines 539 Assault Squadron. The mission was rolling too fast for the Farm to arrange a full war load of weapons to await him in Amsterdam, but Bolan had gone to the American Embassy and the CIA station chief had acquired a Beretta 92 for him from the Marine Guard armory and a snub-nosed .38 from his own personal cache. Lord William was currently making a pit stop of his own, and Bolan and Lunk stood outside the Central Bank of the Netherlands. Lord William came out ten minutes later and tossed Lunk an old-fashioned canvas courier's pouch. "Hold on to that, Lunk, would you?"

Lunk tucked the canvas package under his arm, and they took a water taxi to the River Ij. Huge sections of Amsterdam were considered historical landmarks, with entire neighborhoods dating back to the 1850s. It was along the River Ij that Amsterdam had some of its most modern city developments, and freed from the constraints of historical preservation, the developers had explored their artistic sides. The neighborhood was famed for its unusual and experimental architecture. They stepped onto shore, and Lord William paused by a stand of willows. "Lunk?"

Lunk reached into the canvas bag and passed Lord William a Hi-Power pistol, and the Englishman made it disappear into his jacket. The Welshman pulled out a stainless steel .357 Magnum Smith & Wesson Model 66 and grinned at Bolan. "Traded one of your Navy SEAL lads for it, back in the day."

Lord William suddenly shot Bolan an embarrassed look. "Not to be insulting, old boy, but I gather you are armed?"

"I am, your lordship."

"Good. Jolly good. They won't do us much good, but at least we can lull them into a false sense of security. Oh, and for God's sake, drop that 'your lordship' rubbish. Call me Bill. My friends do."

"Bill." Bolan nodded. "I gather we won't get any weapons past security?"

"No, but we have Lunk in our back pockets, don't we?"

Bolan let the cryptic remark pass as they stepped out of the little stand of trees and walked a block up the canal and came to a two-story building of glass brick and pink stucco right out of an episode of *Miami Vice*. Lunk kept on walking as Bolan and Lord William pushed through the smoked-glass double doors into a teak-paneled lobby. A beautiful Dutch woman with platinum-blond hair sat behind a desk.

Lord William whispered in appreciation. "Well, she's new."

A twin of the life-size Aegis shield and thunderbolt logo in Lord William's Guernsey manor took up almost the entire wall behind her. Bolan noted the security cameras above it. The receptionist turned a blazing white smile and greeted them in Dutch. *"Goede ochtend!"*

"And good morning to you, too, my dear," Lord William replied. "Is Mr. Jennings in today?"

The receptionist switched to thick English. "Yes, but he is very busy. Do you have an appointment?"

"Tell Mr. Jennings that Lord William Glen-Patrick and associate are here to pay him a call."

"Lord William!" The woman's jaw dropped charmingly. "I will inform Mr. Jennings immediately! You may wait—"

"What is your name, again?"

The woman flushed. "Grietje."

"We'll wait in the courtyard, Grietje, thank you."

Bolan followed Lord William's lead as he walked past the desk to the hallway beyond. A chime peeped as they crossed the threshold. Grietje shot the English lord a look that was both amused and accusing. "You should know policy, Lord William."

"Sorry about that." Lord William took out his Hi-Power. There were metal detectors in the door frame. "Old habits, you know. Feel naked without it."

Grietje pushed a panel on the wall behind her that slid back to reveal a wall safe. She pressed in a combination code as Bolan took out his Beretta and the snub-nosed Smith. Grietje locked the weapons away. "Lord William, if you—"

"Would you be a dear and bring us some coffee?" Lord William continued on his way. Bolan followed. Grietje made a small noise of consternation. She had their weapons, but protocol was not being observed. However, William Glen-Patrick was a noted eccentric and the founder of the company.

"I will bring you coffee."

Lord William grinned like a schoolboy getting away with something as they stepped out into a tiny courtyard with a fountain, two small stone benches and a flowering lemon tree. "Big brass balls, then?"

Bolan smiled. "I can hear them clanking while you walk, Bill."

Lord William flushed with pleasure. He pulled out his cell phone and punched a button. "Hello, Lunk! In position, then? Right. I'm facing the north wall of the courtyard. Jolly good. Heave away, then!"

Bolan looked up into the sky to see Lord William's canvas pouch hurtling over the roof. The man clicked his phone shut and shook his head in wonder. "I swear that man could hurl a grappling iron over the Eiffel Tower. Be a good lad and catch that, would you?"

Bolan caught the package and handed it to Lord William. The little canvas bag was a handgun horn of plenty. Lord William produced a pair of Walther PPK pistols and handed one to Bolan. It was underpowered by Bolan's standards, but the pistol was reliable, a classic, and best of all, the enemy had no idea they had them. He checked the loads in the little .32 and tucked it into the pocket of his jacket. Lord William gave him a spare 7-round magazine and tossed the empty pouch behind the lemon tree just as Grietje came out with a tray of coffee, brandy and cigars.

Lord William gave his coffee a healthy watering of brandy and let Bolan light his cigar. The two men drank coffee and Glen-Patrick blew smoke up toward the sky as they waited for their host.

"Bill!" Clive Jennings threw open the door and came out grinning. "Good to see you!"

Bolan sized up Jennings. He was just a shade under six feet, and his French-cut suit was tailored to accentuate his trim physique. His blond hair had enough product keeping it in place that it would take a gale-force wind to move it. His personality was hyperintense. He practically bounced across the courtyard. Jennings shook Lord William's hand hard enough to make the older man wince. "How've you been, man! Came out of your self-imposed exile on the island, then, did you?"

"Something like that." Lord William retrieved his hand and put it in the same pocket as his PPK. "This my associate, Mr. Cooper."

Jennings slapped his hand into Bolan's. He grinned as he gave Bolan the bone crusher. "Nice to meet you, Coop!"

He'd had his suspicions, but now, shaking the man's hand and looking into his green eyes, Bolan was certain.

Clive Jennings was a sociopath.

Bolan squeezed back just enough to prevent his hand from being broken. He noted the golden Oxford University signet ring as they let go. "Heard a lot about you, Clive."

"All lies?"

"No, worse," Bolan replied. "The truth."

Jennings threw back his head and laughed a bit too heartily. He clearly dismissed Bolan as a spear-carrier. He returned his attention to Lord William. "Well, I'm surprised to see you, Bill."

"Well, I wanted to have a word, Clive, and I wanted to look you in the eye rather than talk over the phone."

"Sounds mysterious, Bill." Jennings smiled good-naturedly, his eyes unreadable. "What's this all about?"

"Well…" Lord William looked down at his shoes in embarrassment. "To tell you the truth, Clive, I'm rather between fortunes at the moment."

Jennings cocked his head. "You've been at the baccarat tables again, haven't you?"

"Nothing quite so romantic. The fact is I've never had much of a head for business. Some investments haven't panned out. Indeed, they've cost me rather dearly."

"Don't sell yourself short, old man. You've done quite well." The words were solicitous, but Jennings's body language told an entirely different story. He loved Lord William coming to the business he'd stolen from him with his hat in his hand. "You'll land on your feet and be flush again in no time. You always do."

Lord William squared his shoulders, seeming to summon what dignity he had left. "Clive, I'm not a young man anymore. The truth is, I need your help."

"Well, I suppose I could arrange a loan for you." Jennings shrugged. "I'd be willing to accept your shares in the company as collateral."

"That's generous of you, Clive, but what I really need are some good men."

Jennings blinked. "Men?"

"I'm an old man, Clive, but I think I may have one last adventure left in me. Mr. Cooper came to me with a rather hare-brained scheme. So harebrained, in fact, it sounds like it almost might work."

Jennings was clearly intrigued. "You have a mission?"

Bolan kept the smile off of his face and reminded himself never to play cards with Lord William.

"I'll be blunt, Clive. It's a treasure hunt."

"A treasure hunt?"

The old man flashed his trademark grin. "You know me, Clive. Diamonds have always been my best friends. Mr. Cooper's research is quite solid, and I've had it discreetly verified. They're there. The bugger of it is, the location is remote, and the terrain, the locals and the local government could only be described as exceptionally hostile. I need to put together a team, and I've lost contact with most of the men I worked with in the past. For that matter, most of the men I know from when I was running the company are like me, ten years past it, if not more. I'm not asking you for money, Clive. I need a few good men. Then the money will come."

"'Gold does not find good soldiers, but good soldiers are quite capable of finding gold.'" Jennings was quoting Prince Machiavelli. "Or in this case, diamonds."

"Just so, old man." Lord William grinned. "Just so."

"So…" Jennings frowned in thought. "You want me to recommend some men for you, then, is it?"

"I'd like to look at the current company roster. See who's been where, what languages they speak and all that. There will be some aspects of this jaunt that will require some very specific skills. I want to put together a short list and begin interviewing as quickly as possible."

"You need to tell me more, Bill."

"'Fraid I can't, Clive." Lord William smiled slyly. "You're

something of a go-getter. I think if I told you too much about it, you might just go off and get them yourself."

"Well, that is possible." Jennings smiled slightly at the compliment. "But our list of associates as well as recruitment are my purview, and our associates depend on our discretion and respect of their serving in anonymity."

"I believe most of the men on the roster would lose their little minds if they knew Red-Hot Willy was looking for a few good men."

"That may be." Jennings sighed in mock reluctance. "But I'm afraid I can't do it."

"I'll cut you in for ten percent."

"Ten percent of nothing is still nothing, Bill. You don't have anything yet, and treasure hunts have a habit of turning out badly in my experience. As a matter of fact, most of them don't turn up anything other than debt. It's not a good investment in men or publicity. For that matter Aegis Global Security doesn't need our associates being captured and rotting in some third-world prison."

"Clive, I need this."

"I can't help you, old man." The words were an insult coming off Jennings's lips.

Lord William stared up into the clouds for long moments and reluctantly played his ace. "I'll sell you my shares."

An ugly light gleamed in Clive Jennings's eyes. "Your shares aren't worth that much, Bill."

"Oh, I think they're worth far more to you than what they're listed at."

Jennings shrugged indifferently.

"My shares and ten percent." Lord William put a wounded look in his eyes. "It's my last hurrah, Clive. Help out an old man."

Lord William had built Aegis with his own sweat and

blood. Jennings had stolen it with ones and zeroes. It was very clear that Jennings despised the old man. It was also clear that Jennings was very capable and shrewd. He smiled at Lord William. "Bill?"

"Yes, Clive?"

"You're up to something."

"Well, to be honest, yes." Lord William dropped the act. "Clive, I really do need to have a look at the current Aegis roster of associates."

"You can bring it up at the next shareholders' meeting." Jennings's smile was sickening. "Now, I'm afraid I'm going to have to ask you to leave."

"'Fraid I'm going to have to insist, Clive."

Bolan cocked the Walther in his pocket. It was a small noise but noticeable in the sudden quiet in the courtyard. Jennings shook his head. "What? You're going to threaten me with a cigarette lighter?" He started to reach under his jacket.

Bolan took the cocked PPK out of his pocket and pointed it at Jennings's face.

The man's eyes widened. He was clearly used to being in control of every situation. Being caught flatfooted was an alien experience. He nearly made a move as Bolan reached under his jacket and relieved him of his two-tone 9 mm SIG-Sauer P-239 pistol but apparently thought better of it.

"Now, let's have a look at that roster, then," Lord William cajoled.

Jennings slowly folded his arms across his chest. "No."

"No?" Lord William took out his Walther and thumbed back the hammer. "Are you sure?"

"You're not going to shoot me, and neither is your friend."

Lord William frowned. "We're not?"

"No, you need to get into the computer and only I have the access codes to Aegis operational files."

"Hmm." Lord William scratched his jaw with the muzzle of his pistol as he considered the problem. "Guess we'll just have to beat it out of you."

Jennings looked at Bolan in speculation and Lord William in open scorn. "Try."

"Right!" Lord William cupped a hand beside his mouth. "Lunk!"

Lunk arose on the roof. It seemed he had scaled the side of the building. Jennings's mouth dropped open as the giant Welshman slid down one of the courtyard's drainpipes and landed on his feet without a sound. It was genuinely disturbing to see a man that large move with such silence. Lord William dropped all pretense of polite behavior and snarled, "Now, you listen to me, you poncey little git. I don't give a good god damn what bloody dan-ranking you have in judo. You just aren't ready for what Lunk is going to do to you, and he's wanted a piece of you for a very long time. Now you are going to give me complete access to my company, or I'm going to fucking feed you to him."

Lunk leaned down to nearly press his face against Jennings's. "Going to beat seven bloody shades of shite out of you, mate."

Jennings was reduced to stuttering. "I…I…"

Lord William prodded the man with his PPK. "Good lad. I knew we could work this out."

CHAPTER SIX

Bolan vainly wished Kurtzman or Akira Tokaido was on hand. He sat before the computer in Clive Jennings's office and knew he was a little out of his league. The room looked more like a command center than the executive office of a small, highly specialized consulting company. Lord William peered about with a frown on his face. "Made some changes then, have you, Clive?"

Jennings glared and said nothing. He sat in the chair opposite his desk with Lunk standing behind him. The Welshman held his .357 loosely in one massive paw and had made it very clear on the short walk down the hall and up the stairs to the office he would pistol whip Jennings repeatedly with the gun if he tried anything.

Lord William waved his PPK at the flat-screen monitor. "So, how are you and the old 'devil in a box' getting on, then?"

Bolan took out his PDA. Like his laptop, it, too, was a product of Akira Tokaido's cybernetic skill and would qualify as a supercomputer. "This isn't my strong suit. I can probably hack in, but I'll have to be walked through it, and it'll take time. Time we don't have." Bolan turned to Jennings. "Give me your passwords and codes."

Jennings's jaw set.

A second later his head rubbernecked as Lunk's open hand slammed against his ear. Jennings's defiant look turned into a grimace of agony. Bolan had to admire Lunk's style. It took a deft touch to box a man's ear that hard without shattering the eardrum.

Lord William sighed. "Clive, despite all you've done, this isn't personal between us. You took my company from me, but as far as I can tell you did it fair and square. Easy come, easy go, the better man won. All that jolly rot. However, to quote your earlier remark, I believe you're up to something. There's something rotten afoot, and I think you are at least aiding and abetting it if not actively involved. I dislike torture, so, let me state for the record you will not be tortured. What will happen is this—Mr. Cooper and I will leave the room for a moment, and in our absence you are going to have a fight with Lunk."

Jennings flinched and involuntarily brought a hand up to his ear.

"Keep your bloody hand down," Lunk rumbled.

Jennings's hand fell into his lap like a dead bird.

"It will be a fair fight," Lord William continued. "Bare-handed, man-to-man, as God intended. After a minute or two, Mr. Cooper and I will return to this office and ask you once more for your passwords and codes. Should you persist in your obstinate ways, you will have another fight with Lunk, and then another, and another. This process will continue until you come to see reason. Do you understand?"

Veins began pulsing in Jennings's temples. Lord William sighed impatiently. "Lunk, keep him conscious, don't break his fingers or his jaw. We'll be needing him typing and talking I should think."

Jennings snarled through clenched teeth. "What do you want first?"

Bolan considered going file by file, gleaning out the relevant information, but that would take time and despite the fear in Jennings's eyes he didn't trust the man. There could be data deletion programs infesting the computer. However good Jennings's defenses were, Bolan was willing to bet they were not up to the Akira Tokaido's standard. He connected his PDA to an open port on the computer. "Download your entire hard drive."

Jennings blinked. "Into that?"

Bolan's PDA probably had ten times the computing capability of Jennings's entire computer suite but he didn't bother explaining. "Do it."

Lunk slid Jennings's chair around the desk, rammed him in front of the computer. "You heard the Yank."

Jennings's hands hovered, trembling over the keyboard. Bolan leaned in and peered into his eyes. "Forget Lunk. Do it or deal with me."

Jennings flinched. What he suddenly saw in Bolan's burning blue eyes was far more frightening than a beating at the big Welshman's hands. He typed in letters and numbers, and files began to transfer into Bolan's PDA. Jennings jumped in his seat as Lord William punched him in the shoulder in a comradely fashion. "Good lad! I knew you'd see reason."

Grietje's voice spoke across the intercom. "Mr. Jennings? Mr. Van der Beers has called to confirm lunch this afternoon."

Lunk's huge hand covered the speaker. He and Lord William both looked to Bolan, who nodded to Jennings. "Tell her you'll be a few minutes late, but lunch is on."

Jennings spoke as Lunk uncovered the intercom. "Lord William has brought some unexpected business to my attention. Tell Van der Beers I'll be a little late, but we're a green light for lunch."

"A green light. Yes, Mr. Jennings."

The intercom clicked off. Bolan screwed the muzzle of his PPK into Jennings's temple. "Green light. That's the signal for what? Intruders? Lockdown?"

Jennings stared up at Bolan with renewed purpose. "The police have been alerted. I suggest you leave while you still can."

"Blow his brains out," Lord William suggested.

A phone to one side of the desk rang. Bolan recognized the receiver as a satellite link. Jennings jerked and stared at the sat link in horror. "No," Bolan said. "He's going to answer that phone."

"No, I'm—"

"Do it or I'll kill you."

Jennings stared once more into Bolan's eyes and whatever recidivist bravery he had summoned wavered. He and Bolan both knew he was one pound away on a cocked, two-pound trigger toward death.

"I—"

The phone chimed.

"Do it," Bolan ordered.

"But—"

"You're out of time." Bolan pulled the pistol away from Jennings's temple and pointed it at the Englishman's face.

"No!" Jennings lunged for the satellite phone.

Lunk's paws slammed down on his shoulders. "Compose yourself."

Jennings took a shuddering breath.

"Better." Bolan nodded. "Put it on speakerphone."

Jennings pressed a button on the link. A deep, British upper-class voice came across the speaker. "Clive, we need to talk."

Bolan watched Clive's face closely. He'd broken into a sweat.

"I agree," Jennings replied.

"Listen," the voice continued. "I've spoken with our counterparts in the East. We are in agreement. We need to step up the timetable."

Jennings looked like he might throw up.

Lord William cocked his head. Clearly something about the voice was familiar. Jennings got that staring-into-the-middle-distance, everything-unraveling look on his face again. He opened his mouth and then closed it again.

"I say," the voice said. "Clive, are you there?"

Bolan silently mouthed the words "keep talking" at Clive. "I…"

Lord William suddenly beamed and leaned in toward the intercom. "Parky, you old sod! How the bloody hell are you?"

Jennings's jaw dropped. Lunk shot Bolan a knowing grin. The voice on the other side of the secure link paused in shocked silence. "To whom am I speaking?"

"Why, Ian, it's Bill! Bill Glen-Patrick! Haven't seen you since I last voted in Lords! By God, when was that? Aught 2, then?"

The voice on the other end was clearly stunned. "Clive, what is going on?"

"I…" was all Jennings could manage.

Bolan subvocalized to Lunk. "Who?"

Lunk muttered under his breath, "His Lordship Ian Parkhurst, if I'm not mistaken."

Bolan had never heard of Lord Ian, but then there were close to seven hundred members of the English peerage. "Is this bad?"

Lunk's craggy brow furrowed. "Bad enough. Lord William is a baron. Parkhurst is an earl."

"Listen, Parky," Lord William continued. "Your lad Clive has cocked things up a bit. I'm doing a little spring-cleaning around the old office. I'm putting a stop to whatever he's up to. I do hope you won't be inconvenienced."

"Glen-Patrick," the voice said, "I'm afraid I'm going to have to ask you to leave my office."

"Your office?"

"Yes, William. Just who do you think it was who took your wretched little box of tin soldiers away from you? Surely not that pissant Clive?"

"Well, truth be told, yes," Lord William admitted. "Not quite cricket, Ian. Peers turning on each other like this, is it, old bean?"

"You know, I never really considered you a peer," the voice stated. "None of us ever did. You're just a jumped-up country squire who never knew his station. You spent more time on your sordid little escapades and in the tabloids than you ever did voting in the house."

Bolan listened to the exchange with interest. Whoever Parkhurst was, he was an amateur. He was gloating and monologing when he should have kept his mouth shut. Bolan silently mouthed the words "keep him talking" to Lord William. The baron nodded.

"Listen, Parky. We have dead CIA agents, the IRA, whispers of mass destruction, Aegis somehow involved. I was looking into this out of duty, you know. Queen and country and all that. But you know something, Parky? Now I think it's personal."

"Do you know what one does with toothless, barking old dogs?" The voice went utterly cold. "One puts them down. However, I've come to learn that you're not an old dog. You, William, are a cockroach. A pest that refuses to be crushed. And I'll tell you something, William. When Clive failed to kill you in Guernsey, I had a thought you might show up at the offices."

"Oh? And what might that thought—"

"Goodbye, William."

The line clicked dead.

Lunk was peering out the window toward the river. "Company, Lord William, coming to kill us quiet."

Bolan gazed out the window. Men were spilling out of a pair of Volkswagen vans. They were dressed in civilian clothing, but each one was sporting a micro-Uzi machine pistol with the long black tube of a sound suppressor screwed over the stub barrels. The gunners' torsos had the barrel shape of men wearing body armor beneath their clothing. Bolan counted ten of them and was pretty sure there would be more coming around the back. If Lord Parkhurst was telling the truth about owning the company, the killers would probably have their own keys.

He turned on Clive. "Where are the guns?"

"Your guns?" Jennings stared up at Bolan in confusion. "Grietje has them in the safe downstairs. You know that—"

"No, Clive. Where are your guns?"

"Mine? You have my—"

Bolan seized Jennings by his hand-painted Italian silk necktie. "You're a boy who likes playing with the grown men's toys, Clive. Where's your toy box?"

"I—"

Bolan's eyes flicked around the room and instinctively came to rest on the hoplite shield mounted on the wall.

Lord William's mustache lifted in a curtain of amusement. "Oh, jolly good."

Bolan nodded. "Lunk?"

Lunk happily wrapped his fingers around the edges of the shield. His knuckles went white as he pulled. Wood splintered, cracking and breaking around the hidden lock. Lunk let out a groan of effort, and the Aegis ripped away from the wall.

The shield formed the door of a recessed gun cabinet.

Lunk picked an inch-long splinter out of his palm. "Little boys with grown men's toys." The Welshman grinned. "Have to remember that one."

Clive Jennings had some toys.

"My rifle!" Lord William exploded in outrage. "My bloody fucking Falklands rifle!"

Jennings cringed.

Lord William stalked to the ruptured gun cabinet and ripped a 1980s-era British L-1 A 1 SLR rifle off the rack. He racked the action on the big black .308 self-loading rifle and peered through the SUIT optical sight. "You son of a bitch! You told me it'd been lost!"

Bolan made his choice from the cabinet. "Lunk, mind Clive."

Lunk slammed his hands on Jennings's shoulders as Bolan pulled out something a little more modern. Personally, he had little use for the SA 80 assault rifle. Despite its futuristic good looks and compact bullpup design, it had been plagued with problems. In both Iraq wars it had been found that it jammed at the slightest bit of dirt or fouling, various parts broke off or bent with frightening regularity and many came home held together with duct tape. The magazine release was so poorly designed that it often spontaneously ejected when shouldered by men wearing armor and web gear, and there was a persistent rumor that at desert temperatures, with prolonged firing, and with the right combination of British army-issue insect repellant and cam cream on the user's hands, the plastic parts would melt.

The SA 80 really only had one virtue, and that was that

the combination of rifle and its SUSAT 4X scope was one of the most accurate out-of-the-box assault rifles available.

Bolan inserted a loaded magazine and racked the action. He had hopes that the trouble-plagued weapon might hold together for one firefight in Amsterdam. He pointed the assault rifle between Jennings's eyebrows as Lunk pulled a Steyr AUG light machine gun out of the cabinet and clicked in a 100-round C-Mag double drum magazine.

Bolan's PDA cheeped as it finished swallowing the contents of Clive Jennings's computer. "We're out of here."

Downstairs Grietje let out a scream.

Lunk prodded Jennings with the muzzle of his machine gun. "Let's move."

The Executioner took point with Lord William behind him. Lunk rumbled as he took up the rear position with the machine gun. "You heard the man, blast you. Move along already— Bloody hell!"

Bolan whirled in time to avoid 280 pounds of flying Welshman. Lord William didn't and they collided in a tangle. The SA 80 rifle cracked three times in Bolan's hands, but Jennings had already risen up out of his throw and lunged back into the office. Bolan flicked his selector switch to full-auto and sprayed a burst around the doorjamb before lunging in. The eastern wall of the office had slid open, and Jennings ducked in as it began to slide shut again. Wood paneling flew as Bolan fired, but he knew it was hopeless. The door hissed shut, and he could hear the heavy mechanical bolts tumbling into place.

Jennings had built a panic room into his office.

"We've lost him."

Lunk was already up and pulling Lord William to his feet. "Oh, what I owe that one."

Lord William winced as he stood. "Do we have a plan, then?"

"Well—" Bolan could hear the thudding of boots even in the soundproofed office building "—we've lost our meat shield. I guess we'll just have to make a door and take a van."

"Meat shield…" Lunk's laugh was like distant thunder.

"Cover your eyes." Bolan raised his rifle and put a bullet into the window overlooking the river. The cracked window failed to shatter. The windows were armor glass. Bolan lowered his assault weapon. "Bill?"

Lord William shouldered his big .308 battle rifle and began squeezing off shots. Bits of glass flew like shrapnel throughout the hall. The glass was bullet resistant, not bulletproof. At point-blank range the rounds began to punch holes. Lord William lowered his rifle on a smoking empty chamber. "Bloody hell."

The window looked like the surface of the moon but seemed far from falling apart. Jennings had built himself a fortress.

Bolan heard the door to the stairwell open down the hall. "Here they come."

A cylinder skipped through the cracked door spewing CS gas.

Bolan strode forward, firing short bursts from his rifle at the door. Lunk fell into line behind him. The big man snapped open one leg of his machine gun's bipod and came forward with his machine gun in the hip-assault position and spraying it like a fire hose. Bolan held his breath, but the rapidly expanding gas began stinging his eyes instantly.

The door was riddled with bullet holes under the onslaught. Bolan roared over the sound of gunfire, "Lunk! Door!"

Lunk kept moving forward and firing. When he was muzzle distant from the door, he put his size-16 boot into it. The wood buckled beneath the blow. Two men in gas masks reeled back as the door slammed off its hinges and into them. Bolan's rifle cracked once, shattering the left-hand lens of one man's mask. Lunk hammered the second man down with a long burst. Lord William moved onto the crowded landing, racked with coughing. His spent rifle was slung over his shoulder. He scooped up the fallen men's Uzis.

Bolan calculated. He had about five rounds left in his rifle. Jennings undoubtedly had the spare ammo and supplies in his panic room, and he had said the police had been alerted. The enemy couldn't afford a siege, and Bolan and his crew didn't have the ammo to hold one off. He figured they were about to be rushed. Gas was filling the hall behind them.

The only way to go was down.

Bolan glanced back at Lord William, who was leaning heavily on the rail and limping slightly. He was an older man and having Lunk thrown on top of him had hurt more than he had let on.

But that gave Bolan an idea.

"Lunk?"

"Aye?"

Bolan nodded at the two dead men.

Lunk's eyes widened. "Meat shield, then?"

"More like meat missile." Bolan coughed.

"Oh—" Lunk shook his head and dropped his machine gun on its sling. "He's a clever dick, this Yank is." Lunk heaved up a dead man like a sack of potatoes. "On your go."

Bolan slung his rifle and took Jennings's commandeered 9 mm pistol in two hands.

A voice shouted out downstairs in command. "Go! Go! Go!"

Another gas grenade clattered onto the bottom landing.

"Now!" Bolan boomed.

Four men spilled into the stairwell spraying their silenced weapons upward. Lunk used the military press to raise the dead man over his head with a grunt and then dropped him over the rail. The stairs were narrow, and there was no cover to be taken. The two-hundred-pound corpse fell on its comrades, and two of them fell ugly beneath it. The other two barely kept their feet, as limp arms and legs clubbed them. Bolan was already moving. His pistol barked twice, and both men went limp from the head shots. The Executioner kept firing as he moved down the stairs and into the gas cloud. More men leaped into the stairway to meet him. They didn't know what had happened, but they charged in depending on gas, body armor, numbers and firepower to win.

The second corpse fell onto the two lead men like a ton of bricks as Lunk gave the cadaver the bum's rush from above. Lord William fired bursts from his Uzi. Bolan reached the ground floor grimacing into the gas. He was right on top of the grenade. Gas sprayed from the crevices between the piled bodies in gray geysers. Bolan stuck the SIG-Sauer pistol around the corner and fired it dry. He dropped the spent pistol and picked up a pair of Uzis for himself.

"Move! Move! Move!"

Lunk came halfway down the stairs and then leaped over the rail. Lord William came down the stairs as fast he was able. Bones broke and living men screamed as the giant Welshman landed on the pile. Lunk fell back against the wall and began firing bursts from his machine gun into the downstairs hall. "Go!"

Bolan rolled into the hall with an Uzi in each hand.

A voice was shouting in near hysterics. "Heavy resistance! Repeat! We are encountering heavy resistance! Automatic weapons! Request—"

Bolan could barely see the man down the hall crouched

behind the reception desk. Bolan thrust out his Uzis and held down the trigger. Wood stripped and splintered and the man behind the desk screamed and fell. Bolan dropped the spent machine pistols and pulled his PPK. He moved to the court-yard door and scanned the outside.

It was blissfully clear of gas or men with Uzis.

Lunk ushered Lord William forward. The older man was gagging and clutching his face. Bolan himself could barely see or breathe. He took the baron's arm, led him to the foun-tain and shoved his head under the water. Bolan let him go and rammed his own head under the surface. A few startled koi huddled in terror as Bolan swept his head back and forth and washed out his eyes. He surfaced to hear the strident sound of European police sirens in the distance. Lord Wil-liam came up a second later with a gasp.

"Well…that's a bit…better, then." He sat heavily on the side of the fountain.

Lunk stood in the doorway, his eyes a solid red of in-flamed blood vessels, and tears streaming down his cheeks. He held his eyes open and focused as he scanned down the hall through some superhuman act of Welsh willpower.

Bolan eyed the drainpipe Lunk had used to make his en-trance and then glanced at Lord William. The old warrior wouldn't make the climb and even Lunk wouldn't be able to scale the slick iron carrying him. Even if he could, the two-story drop on the other side would be problematic.

"Lads." Lord William was reading Bolan's mind. "Just go. I can deal with the law, as well as Clive or any other bastard still running hot around the premises."

Lord William would be facing weapons charges, unex-plainable firefights, the use of war gas and possible multiple murder counts at a business that he was still officially the president of. Jennings was still in his panic room, and Bolan had a pretty good idea who would win in a "his word against mine" situation in a Netherlands courtroom.

Bolan grinned. "The hell you say."

They were just going to have to go out the front door.

"Lunk?"

"I see movement in the lobby."

"Let's go."

Bolan threw Lord William's arm over his shoulder. He passed him off to Lunk at the doorway and the three of them moved down the hall. Bolan had counted ten out front before the engagement and had figured maybe the same number out back. They'd taken a terrible toll. There couldn't be more than two or three fighters left among the enemy.

Lunk groaned. "Wait…" He dropped his weapon on its sling and propped Lord William against a wall. The Welshman ripped the 18-liter reservoir out of the lobby water cooler and upended it overhead his face. Lunk washed, gargled, snorted, spit and finally dropped the keg-size cooler with a thud. He shrugged sheepishly. "Sorry about that, but I haven't been gassed since basic."

Bolan caught movement outside. Two men were running for one of the vans. One of them had Miss Grietje Van Jan. Bolan threw open the glass doors and roared. "Freeze!"

One man whirled and the PPK snapped four times in Bolan's hand. Two shots took the man in the chest and the second double tap took him in the head. Lunk and Lord William fell into formation on either side of Bolan. The second man kept his Uzi rammed into Grietje's side. "I'll kill her!"

"Let her go!"

"Drop your weapons!"

"I said let her go!"

"I'll cut her in two!"

Bolan didn't doubt it. He dropped the Walther to the pavement. "Lord William?"

Lord William dropped his Uzi and shrugged off his rifle with an exhausted sigh.

"Lunk."

"The bloody hell I—"

"Lunk!" the baron snapped.

Lunk unslung the AUG light machine gun and dropped it in disgust. He glared, red-eyed, at the assassin. "I'll see you in—"

Bolan blurred into motion.

He spun the SA 80 rifle around on its sling and shouldered it. The assassin's face instantly filled the 4X scope and Bolan squeezed the trigger. The killer went limp as the bullet traversed his skull, and Miss Van Jan screamed anew as she was sprayed with blood and bone.

Bolan whipped his rifle around and aimed at the man behind the wheel of van with the engine running. The man screamed and dived out the driver's door. "No! Please, God, no! Please!"

Bolan flung the spent SA 80 into the river and scooped up his PPK and reloaded. Lunk scooped up his machine gun by the barrel. The driver screamed as the giant stomped forward. "Please! God! No! I—"

"Shut your cakehole!" Teeth flew as Lunk swung the light machine gun by the barrel like a cricket bat. The man dropped unconscious and drooling blood. "Bloody hit men." He tossed the AUG into the river, then helped Lord William into the van as Bolan slid behind the wheel.

"Bill?"

"Yes, Cooper?"

"We're going to need some men."

The baron smiled wearily as Bolan pulled away from Aegis. "Oh, I have a few in mind."

CHAPTER SEVEN

Guernsey

It had taken two days to get back to Lord William's manor in the Channel Islands. Bolan had assumed both the British and American embassies were being watched, so they had simply driven to Belgium. At the U.S. Embassy Bolan had used their satellite link to download his PDA into the Farm's computers. Lunk had started making phone calls. Lord William had rented a French turbo-charged Socata Trinidad aircraft and flown them to the neighboring island of Jersey. From there he had hired a fishing captain he knew to sail them to Guernsey in the dead of night.

They sat in front of the fire and compared notes and files. Lord William had filled Bolan in on his peer. Lord Ian Parkhurst was a hereditary earl, a senior member of the House of Lords, and sat on the Appellate Committee of Law Lords. As a teenaged lieutenant in World War II he had won two wound stripes and the Victoria Cross in desperate rear guard actions during the terrible withdrawal at Dunkirk. He'd twice been a British ambassador, and he'd been knighted for his philanthropic activities in former British colonies. He was a very wealthy man with international business interests and despite being a Lord he was very active in the liberal British Labor Party. He lent his name, money and political clout to a number of British environmental and political activist groups.

None of which explained why he'd sent men to kill Lord William in Amsterdam.

Bolan knew that with a man of Lord Ian's wealth, influence, title and popularity he could put a smoking gun in his lordship's hand and still get zero cooperation from MI-5 or any other British law-enforcement agency. Bolan would have to gather the evidence himself. No one would help him, no one would thank him, and indeed he would be resisted all the way if not arrested and deported.

Most of the news was bad.

McCarter had phoned from London. Assistant Director Finch had been cordial but had little new information to offer. The barristers of Sylvette MacJory, Ruud Heitinga, Kew Timmer and Guy Diddier had arranged for their clients' release on bail, and all four had promptly dropped off the face of the planet. MI-5 had no idea of their whereabouts.

Lord William was wanted for questioning in the Netherlands regarding his role in the firefight at the Aegis offices in Amsterdam. Clive Jennings was wanted for similar questioning. According to Dutch authorities and Interpol, Mr. Jennings's whereabouts was currently unknown.

The first thing to come out of the stolen files from Aegis was the current roster. There were 315 men and seven women on it, each with an accompanying personal file. The majority of the contractors were former soldiers in the British and American armed forces with a sprinkling of other nationalities. Most of the active ones were working as VIP protec-

tion contractors in Afghanistan and to a lesser extent Iraq and
Pakistan. A few were doing similar work in Central and South
America, mostly Colombia. Again there was a sprinkling of
strange and out-of-the-way destinations but all could be clas-
sified as world "trouble spots" where above-average men of
above-average martial ability could expect to be paid top
dollar for their skills and services.

That was one of the problems. The mission profiles were
not matching up with reality. Ruud Heitinga and Kew Timmer were supposedly in Afghanistan at the moment. According to the files, Guy Diddier and Miss MacJory were currently
on jobs in Vietnam.

The next problem was that neither Lord William nor
Lunk knew very many of the men on the list. They'd been out
of the game for a decade. Most of the names they did know
were on separate inactive and reserve lists of old soldiers like
themselves. Nevertheless they knew a few, and Lunk had
been making some calls. Lunk swallowed a pint of ale in a
gulp. "Well, the good news is Partridge is in and ready for
anything. He got hold of Layland and Layland got hold of
Lovat. Lovat thinks Thapa might be in, but only if you ask
him personal."

"Thappy!" Lord William straightened in his chair. "By
God, we could use that little bugger!"

Bolan glanced at files. Alvin Partridge was a fellow Welshman and fellow Royal Marine of Lunk's. He'd made Mountain Leader Grade 2 in the Mountain and Arctic Warfare
Cadre. Nick Lovat had been a corporal in the U.K.'s 5th Airborne Brigade and a sniper. Scott Layland was a former Australian SAS sergeant.

Bolan paused at the next file. Thapa Pun had been a member of Queen Elizabeth's own 6th Gurkha Rifles and gone on
to join the Gurkha Independent Parachute Company. He'd

served on detachment to the Sultan of Brunei, returned to Nepal and then joined the Indian army's 8th Gorkha Rifles and reached the Indian NCO rank of subedar. He'd been decorated in all three services, and had seen heavy counter-insurgency fighting in Kashmir.

"Ah, Thappy." Lord William sighed into his whiskey. "I swear the man has the power to turn himself bloody invisible. We had some trouble in Africa back in the day with some locals. They called themselves revolutionaries, but they were hill bandits, pure and simple. Knew the jungle, though. So Thappy goes walkabout, lurking as is his wont, for a couple of weeks. I swear, it got to the point all he had to do was carve his sign on a tree, and the jungle emptied like a bloody vacuum."

Bolan smiled. The "happy warriors" of Nepal had earned a fearsome reputation as jungle fighters in their centuries of service in the British military. Many legends had sprung up around them, many of them specifically about the huge, curved, kukri knife. Rumor had it that once a Gurkha drew his knife it could not be sheathed until it had drawn blood. That wasn't true, but the Gurkhas themselves had done nothing to discourage it. Throughout British military history, riots and even small unit engagements had ended abruptly or resulted in panicked routs at the sight of Gurkha riflemen drawing their foot-long knives.

"A wizard with a bloody wok, by God!" Lunk enthused. The giant Welshman's life seemed to revolve mostly around his stomach. "One always eats well with Thappy about. We'll be lucky to get him."

Bolan was about to take on a knight and lord of the realm with God only knew how many professional mercenaries and the Irish Republican Army in his back pocket. He'd take every Gurkha rifleman he could get.

"Got hold of Otto." Lunk shook his head. "He's back in bloody Nigeria. He says he'll come, but he's broke. We'll have to send him a ticket."

Bolan scanned the list. Otto Owu had been born in England of Yoruba parents. He had spent a great deal of time shuttling back and forth between the U.K. and Nigeria before enlisting as a teenager. He had made corporal in the Royal Welch Fusiliers. Bolan noted he'd earned his expert rating in rifle, pistol and light machine gun and had served a tour in Northern Ireland. It also mentioned that he'd currently been spending time as a hunting guide in Africa, which meant he was a tracker. "Is that a problem?"

Lord William stared into his whiskey. "Well, Cooper…"

"Bill? Call me Matt."

"Matt, do you remember that story about being between fortunes for Clive?"

Bolan sighed. "You weren't making it up."

"'Fraid not, old boy." He gestured around the manor. "This bit of sod is just about all I have left. Well, and Lunk. But he's strictly a volunteer. The rest of the men will come out of loyalty, and face anything, but they'll expect to see something for their trouble at the end of it."

Bolan considered his money belt. "Will a hundred thousand pounds get the ball rolling?"

The baron waggled his snowy eyebrows gleefully. "You know, it just might."

Lunk grinned. "I want mine up front."

Bolan reached into his gear bag and pulled out the money belt. He placed approximately fifty thousand-pound notes in varying denominations into Lunk's hand. "Lunk, I'll leave recruiting up to you. You decide who you want and how to pay, but I want every man to have a good chunk of change in his pocket up front."

"Not to worry, then."

"You'd better tell them up front we're going up against a Lord of the realm, and that arrest and incarceration for life are a real possibility."

"I know, I'll—"

"And you'd better tell them we may be going up against Aegis employees." Bolan locked eyes with the Welshman. "If they aren't salty for any of that, then we don't want them."

"Aye." Lunk nodded slowly. The enormity of the undertaking hadn't escaped him. "I will."

"Well, I'm to bed, then." Lord William rose with a wince. "Bring the dogs in, will you, Lunk? And have Tommy and Carrick spelled by Rooney and Todd. They've been in the weather for hours."

"Aye, m'lord."

Bolan watched Lord William limp toward the stairs. He'd been limping since Amsterdam. Worse, he'd been coughing since the gas, and it occasionally descended into an ugly, wet rattle. "He's not well."

"No. He's not." Lunk's face went stony. "Damage accrues."

Bolan was all too aware of the accumulation of battle damage. He'd had access to the very best doctors, surgeons, physical therapists and alternative medicine the planet had to offer. But he'd still been strenuously warned by all and sundry against suffering any more of the battering that was unavoidable in his profession. In the end he was a soldier in a war that was everlasting. The war would take his life. He'd accepted that long ago. But in the dark of night, in those contemplative moments, he sometimes wondered what he would do when even he himself had to admit that time, tide and damage had reduced him to ineffectiveness.

He watched Lord William pull himself up the stairs one

stair at time and knew the old man wouldn't accept being sidelined, and that was the rub. He needed the old soldier. He needed his connections both military and with the English peerage. Bill could open doors. Bolan grimaced. There was another thing Lord William had told Clive Jennings that wasn't a lie.

This was his last hurrah.

BOLAN AWOKE to the tube noise. His feet were in his boots and the folding stock of the Sterling snapped open and the bolt racked on a live round heartbeats before the first mortar bomb struck. By the sound Bolan figured it was a pair of 81 mm's firing in tandem. He was surprised not to hear the blast and shake of high explosive. Instead he saw a flash. Outside the window yellow-white fire snapped and hissed in the rain and streamers of gray smoke fell in arcs. The enemy was hitting them with white phosphorous. Shotguns roared downstairs in quick double booms and were met by automatic weapons fire. The enemy's plan was fairly obvious. They were going to burn down Lord William's manor and shoot anyone who came out. Anyone who stayed inside would be burned alive.

Bolan slung a web belt with six spare magazines around his shoulder and charged out into the hall. Lunk was pounding up the steps with a Sterling in hand. "We're afire!"

"Get the baron!"

"The baron is here." Lord William was shrugging into his hacking jacket and had his Sterling. "Lunk, go find our friend Carl."

Bolan knew Glen-Patrick meant the Carl Gustav recoilless rifle.

Lunk pounded back down the stairs.

The yeomen had made a strategic retreat into the manor.

Spot and Starkers were lunging on their leads and almost out of control. The blond man Bolan only knew as Todd was breaking open his shotgun and plucking out spent shells as he shouted up the stairs. "Tommy's dead! Carrick's injured."

That left four yeomen.

Bolan cocked his head as the mortars thumped again in tandem. They were close, by the sound. The lag time between firing and detonation implied they were firing nearly straight up, which meant a lot of hang time. "They're right on the other side of the hill. The riflemen will be in the hedges front and back, waiting for us to make a break for it when the fire drives us out."

Lunk returned with the antitank weapon hanging from one hand and a crate of rounds perched on one shoulder.

The second salvo hit the manor. They all crouched as rifle fire began cracking in a steady stream outside, punching out the windows.

Bolan nodded at the Carl Gustav. "Who's your gunner?"

"Tommy." Lunk grimaced. "And he's dead."

Bolan drew the No 1 Mark V bayonet from the web gear Lord William had given him and pried open the crate of ammo. It was a standard NATO six-pack for the Carl Gustav. Four HE antitank HEAT rounds, one illumination round and one smoke.

Lunk shrugged. "There's more in the pantry."

"This will do." Bolan turned to a fireplug of a man named Hargreaves. "You, you're the new gunner. Todd will be your loader."

Smoke was beginning to fill the air as the manor began to burn in earnest.

Bolan quickly showed the two men how to break open the weapon and load it. "We need to cross the killzone between here and the hedges. So I'll put the smoke round where I want it. Once we're outside, you're going to load the illumination round. When I give the signal, I want it straight up in the air over the hill. Then drop it and come running, shotguns at the ready. Can you do that?"

Hargreaves and Todd nodded in unison.

"Good. Load up it up." Bolan took the bayonet and clicked it onto the muzzle of the Sterling. He glanced at Lord William. "You up for a stretch of the legs?"

"You know, I've been a soldier for nearly fifty years and never once fixed a bayonet in anger." Lord William fixed his bayonet. "This will be one for the memoirs."

"Good. Lunk? Hold the dogs."

Lunk took Spot's and Starkers's leads from the yeoman.

"When the smoke hits, let them loose. It doesn't matter which way they go, but hopefully two of the riflemen in the hedges will get an unpleasant surprise."

Hargreaves and Todd held up the recoilless gun. "Locked and loaded."

Bolan shouldered the weapon and took a knee facing the shattered window. "Cover your ears." He aimed for the middle of the dead ground and fired.

The Carl Gustav blasted fire from both ends. The last of the window glass blew out, and a twenty-yard cone of fire filled the cavernous hall behind him and set fire to the drapes and couches. The five-pound warhead streaked out into the night. Bolan dropped as rifle fire answered. "Sorry about the interior, Bill!"

Lord William shrugged. "Well, technically, the house was afire already!"

The smoke round hit a fold in the ground and detonated with an almost inaudible thump. The titanium tetrachloride smoke compound ignited instantly and began laying out a massive cloud of gray smoke, completely oblivious to the rain.

"Loose the dogs!"

Lunk dropped the leads. "Attack! Attack!"

Starkers and Spot leaped out the window like scent-guided antipersonnel weapons. Bolan followed them. "Go! Go! Go!"

Lunk bodily shoved Lord William up and out the window and leaped to follow. The three of them ran straight for the hill and were almost instantly engulfed in smoke. It wasn't as ugly as the CS gas had been in Amsterdam, but it still burned, and they would suffocate if they stayed in it long. The wind was in their favor; it drove the sleeting rain and the gas cloud straight at the hill.

A man let out a thin, wailing scream in the hedgerow to Bolan's right. An automatic rifle stuttered on full-auto. Bolan continued forward. He could hear Lunk's boots smashing into the muck and Lord William laboring behind him. Bolan caught the orange flare of a rifle shot that seemed to float in the air thirty yards ahead and ten above him.

He had reached the base of the hill.

The Executioner dropped a knee. "Shoot and drop!"

Lord William and Lunk both rattled off a burst and hugged mud. A pair of rifles shot in response, aiming at the strobing flash of the Sterlings. Bolan put his front sight on the muzzle flash and fired a burst. He was rewarded by a cry as he swung his muzzle around and fired on the second. He knew he'd missed and threw himself down as the rifle blasted at him and the supersonic crack of a bullet passed over his head.

Lord William and Lunk both fired while prone to put the rifleman in a cross fire. The rifle fell silent, and a second later Bolan could hear a body rolling and sliding downhill through the mud. The soldier stripped his nearly spent magazine and shoved in a fresh one. He crept up the hill on knees and elbows. The mortars had stopped firing, and men were shouting on the other side of the hill. Bolan froze as he heard a voice speaking in an urgent whisper a few yards away.

"...don't know! Tyler and Franks are down! The enemy has laid smoke! They're close! Give me HE on my position! I'll break cover as soon as I hear tube noise! I—"

Bolan rose. He became aware of the shape hunched in the smoke and lunged his bayonet. The man's cry never left his throat as it was stopped by seven and a half inches of Sheffield steel. He collapsed facedown in the muck. Bolan heard the voice calling on the other side of the man's tactical link. "Repeat! I say, repeat last message!"

Bolan stripped the night-vision goggles off the dead man's head and pulled them down over his face. He crawled forward to the top of the hill and struggled not to cough as his lungs tried to burn their way out of his chest. The smoke was crawling down the other side of the hill like a bank of malevolent fog. There were seven men below, two three-man teams manning the two mortars and someone commanding. Two men had broken off and were running at a crouch toward the hill with compact rifles shouldered. Seven riflemen at fifty yards. Not good odds with a submachine gun.

Bolan ignored the men and aimed at the little pyramid of 81 mm bombs.

Shooting high explosive was a very poor way of trying to detonate it. It required the heat of the detonator rather than the slam of a bullet to set it off. However, mortar bombs also had fuses, primers and the increment charges that hurled them into the air. They were more susceptible.

Bolan fired off a burst and was rewarded with sparks flashing off the bombs. Men below shouted in consternation, and the two approaching riflemen swung their weapons toward the stuttering flash at the top of the hill. Bolan kept his sights on the ammunition pile and fired a second and third burst.

The riflemen were set on full-auto and muck erupted in a line a foot to Bolan's left.

The Executioner fired his fourth burst.

Below, a sharp flash snapped like a firecracker in the bomb pile as an increment fired. There was no tube to contain the propellant gas, so rather than rocketing skyward the bomb leaped like a fish. It was a tiny explosion, but the propellant gas was briefly several thousand degrees and it washed over the bombs that Bolan's bullets had perforated.

The HE bomb detonated and set off the two beneath it and the two white-phosphorous bombs beside it. Bolan squeezed his eyes shut as the mortar emplacement exploded.

Lord William and Lunk were instantly beside him. The old man, hacking and choking, held a handkerchief over his mouth. He stared down into the smoking, burning, hissing crater. It looked like an opening to hell. "My God."

Bolan glanced at the two riflemen who'd been approaching. They'd been flung like rag dolls but appeared to be physically intact. "Strip them of their night-vision gear. We still need to sweep the hedges."

There was little need.

Engines snarled into life, and the taillights of a pair of vehicles bounced like red eyes a quarter of a mile down the road. With the mortar position gone, the shooting party had pulled out. The yeomen came slogging up the hill, shotguns at the ready.

"Bill, why don't you stay here with the men and catch your breath. Lunk and I will check the hedge."

Lord William didn't protest.

Bolan and Lunk descended toward the hedgerow. They found the spent brass of the riflemen and the holes they'd cut in the hedge to fire through. They found Spot lying on his side, whimpering, with a bullet wound traversing his hips.

"There's a good dog," Lunk rumbled, and scratched the dog behind its ears. Spot thumped his tail happily and went limp as Lunk put him down with a squeeze of his trigger. They found Starkers a few yards down the hedgerow. A burst had taken him down. An Israeli TAR-21 assault rifle lay in the mud near him.

Starkers still held a human hand and most of the arm below the elbow in his massive jaws.

Lunk's lower lip trembled as he knelt. "You got some, boy, didn't you?"

"Lunk." Bolan lifted the hand slightly with the tip of his bayonet and stared at a bloody, glistening gold band. "The ring."

Lunk shrugged sadly as he stroked the dead dog. "You can have it."

"No." A hard smile crossed Bolan's lips beneath his goggles. "It's an Oxford University signet ring."

Lunk stared. "It's Clive's."

Lunk's face went savage with triumph. "I'm going to pray a dozen rosaries for that dog."

"We need to get out of here." Behind them the manor was going up like a torch. "Even a baron is going to have a hard time explaining this away."

Lunk pulled off the ring and pocketed it. "Wanted in Amsterdam, now wanted in Guernsey. England is going to be a bit hot for his lordship. Where should we go?"

"The last place anyone would expect."

"Where's that, then?"

Bolan rose. "London."

CHAPTER EIGHT

London

"God, I love this car!" Lord William hit the town like exiled royalty. Which in a way, he was. Lunk sat behind the wheel of the brick-red 1980 Rolls-Royce Silver Shadow and tore through the streets of London as if he were at Le Mans, while Bolan and Lord William sat chauffeured in back. They weren't keeping a very low profile, but both Bolan and Lunk were relieved to see Lord William seeming stronger and invigorated. "Bought it back in the eighties one year when I was flush, you know."

They'd dropped off the wounded yeoman at the Guernsey hospital and then taken a boat back to Jersey. Bolan had used some help from the Farm to file a flight plan under an alias and they'd flown the Socata Trinidad to Heathrow. A cab had taken them to a car storage unit in Staines. Lunk had spent about an hour prepping the Rolls, and then they had rolled back into London proper in style, if not concealment.

"How are we doing on recruiting?"

Horns blared in strident alarm. Lunk changed lanes as if

transporting royalty gave him divine right of way. "We've got everyone except Owu and Pun. They're all bunking in a suite at the hotel you mentioned. Owu's on a plane from Lagos and should arrive in London tonight. Pun is at his restaurant and still having a bit of trouble believing all this. He may be a hard sell."

"Well, Matt—" Lord William watched London flash by "—here we are in London. MI-5 probably wants a word with me, and Aegis, the IRA and God only knows who else may be keeping an eye on my flat. Have you any ideas?"

"I do. We pick up Pun, go visit MI-5 HQ and then go to your flat."

"Really."

"Brass balls, Bill," Bolan said. "Big brass balls."

"Jolly good!"

Lunk rumbled approvingly from the front.

"Well then, Lunk, let's pick up some barbecue."

Lunk swung the Rolls about to horns of outrage and screams of terror and headed for the Great Portland Street tube stop. Londoners called the area "Banglatown" for its enclaves of Indians, Pakistanis and Bangladeshis. More horns blared and fists shook as Lunk double-parked outside the Katmandu Vegetarian BBQ House. Horns and insults ceased as Lunk emerged from the Rolls, folded his arms across his chest, leaned against the car and glared at all comers.

Bolan and Lord William strolled into the restaurant.

The room was a typical diner style with Formica-topped tables and booths along the walls. What was remarkable were the smells coming from the kitchen. Nepali cuisine was an ancient fusion of Indian, Chinese and Tibetan tastes. The scents of ginger, cumin, coriander, nutmeg and Szechwan pepper filled the air, as well as the unique Nepali smells of frying yak butter, mustard oil and jimbu leaves from the Himalayan Mountains.

Bolan and Lord William were the only Caucasians in the room. Everyone else was South Asian of one flavor or another. Eyes flicked to them, but no one ceased slurping noodles or eating curried vegetables and cabbage rolls.

Bolan admired and puzzled over the cuisine. "I thought this was a barbecue joint."

"Well, Pun really only barbecues one thing," Lord William admitted, "and that's white rabbit."

Bolan considered this. "I thought this was a vegetarian barbecue."

"The white rabbit is paneer cheese."

"He barbecues cheese."

"Bloody fantastic, too. Lunk will run amok if we don't bring him five orders or so."

Faces peered from the service window and a moment later a man came out from the back. He wore little more than an apron, a white T-shirt and khaki shorts. A paper cap was tilted to one side of a head nearly as round as the moon, and his head was shaved to military stubble peppered with gleaming bits of silver. He barely cracked five feet, but his forearms and calves were the size and shape of bowling pins. His facial features were nearly flat. Long slitted eyes stared out from thick eyebrows that veered off like hawk's wings. The nearly malevolent eyes were startlingly offset by a permanent, lopsided grin. The Gurkha wiped his hands on his apron and saluted smartly. "Colonel."

Lord William returned it. "Subedar."

The two men stared at each other for long moments.

"Pun?"

"Yes, Colonel."

"I need you."

Thapa Pun nodded. "I'm yours."

"Jolly good." He handed the Nepali a card from the hotel where the team was going to meet. "Oh, and Lunk is outside. Give me all the white rabbit you've got."

Pun went back into the kitchen and began shouting orders.

"Well!" Lord William said, grinning. "That was simple enough. Let's go see if MI-5 is as agreeable."

MI-5, London HQ

BOLAN AND LORD WILLIAM walked into the lobby. Lunk was outside with the Rolls, gorging himself on marinated, stuffed and barbecued half-pound slabs of cheese. Bolan and the baron had agreed that a surprise visit would be in their favor. They walked up to the man behind the reception desk, and Lord William removed his cap. "We would like to see Assistant Director Finch, if you please."

The uniformed man behind the desk stared blandly. "Do you have an appointment, sir?"

"Kindly tell the assistant director that Lord William Glen-Patrick and an American of her acquaintance named Cooper beg a moment of her time."

The man's face went blank with shock. "I'll…" He visibly shook himself. "Right away, your lordship."

"Much obliged."

Assistant Director Finch appeared within a minute. Her slightly disheveled hair and her breathing implied she'd run all the way from her office. "My lord, I—"

Lord William bowed formally and took Miss Finch's hand. "Madam Director."

Finch flushed. One didn't reach the rank of director in MI-5 without being as hard as nails, but Heloise Finch was still an upper-class British woman of two generations back, and the word *Lord* still rang with meaning. She seemed to be fighting the compulsion to curtsey. "Um…please. Do follow me, won't you?"

Finch led them down the hall. Bolan was relieved that she took them into a small conference room rather than an interrogation cell. Finch put on her game face as they took their seats. "My lord, you have put me in a very awkward position."

"Director, myself and Mr. Cooper are here to assist and cooperate in any line of inquiry you may have."

Bolan weighed in before Finch could react. "You undoubtedly have questions about the incident on Guernsey. We believe that at least some of the men who attacked Lord William's estate are mercenaries who were once or are currently employed by Aegis Global Security."

"What leads you to believe that?"

"The attack was lead by the current CEO of Aegis, Clive Jennings."

"Can you substantiate that allegation?"

"We found his hand on the premises."

Finch blinked. "His hand?"

"I took fingerprints off it. I believe you'll find they match his service records with the Territorial Guards."

"And where does this…hand currently reside?"

"It should be in the Guernsey morgue with the rest of the bodies."

"I—"

Bolan held up a CD. "You're probably aware of the disturbance at Aegis corporate headquarters in Amsterdam. Lord William and I managed to download Jennings's hard drive. We believe it has files on all past and present Aegis associates. We haven't had time to confirm it, but I believe your agents will find a number of the men on these files to be a match for the bodies in the Guernsey morgue. It will also give you and Interpol a list of people who need to be contacted or watched."

Finch took the CD.

Bolan laid out the kicker. There just wasn't any getting around it. "One other thing."

Finch looked at Bolan as if there was nothing more he could do to surprise her. "And what would that be, Mr. Cooper?"

"Lord Parkhurst is intimately tied up in all of this."

Finch stared in utter surprise. "Lord Ian Parkhurst?"

"Yes."

"Mr. Cooper, am I to understand that you've coopted Lord Parkhurst into your little renegade operation?"

"No, I'm telling you he's actively aiding and abetting the enemy."

Finch just stared.

"He was the silent partner in the hostile takeover of Aegis from under Lord William. He ordered the attack on Aegis HQ in Amsterdam."

"I don't believe you."

Lord William sighed. "I'm afraid it's true. I was there."

"Director, you and I both had the feeling that someone higher up was suppressing any investigation into the chatter linking the IRA with weapons of mass destruction."

"I had such a thought, but we've received no order to stand down."

"And you won't. What I suspect is that MI-5 has received very reasonable suggestions as to the allocation of their valuable time and resources to pursue more concrete domestic terror leads." Bolan's instincts spoke to him. "Some hot leads have fallen into MI-5's lap in the past few weeks, haven't they?"

Finch stared at Bolan, convinced he could read her mind.

"The enemy doesn't have to stop the investigation," Bolan continued. "Just put it on the back burner long enough for whatever they're planning to go into motion. My question to you, Director, is this—would Lord Parkhurst have the power to make something like that happen?"

Finch chose her words carefully. "He's not part of any committee that could order such a thing, but yes, he has connections in government that he could call upon were he so motivated. Though I find the entire idea incredible. However, what you've said is true. Given some of the rather remarkable leads we've recently found, MI-5 has put any investigation into what is being described as the IRA/WMD goose chase on very low priority."

Lord William weighed in. "Madame Director, it is my intention to go after Lord Parkhurst."

Finch looked like she getting a migraine. "Go after him, my lord?"

"Yes, I intend to confront him, peer to peer as it were, and find out just what he's up to."

"Lord William, Lord Parkhurst is currently under no compulsion to speak with you, much less MI-5. As for his involvement, all I have is your word, substantial as that is, and that will not stand up in court."

"Yes, which is why I intend to force the issue."

"Force the issue?"

"Let me be candid, Director. I am going to break the law."

"My lord, if you—" Finch seemed startled at the words coming out of her mouth "—attack Lord Parkhurst, and are caught, notwithstanding your title and previous service to your country, you will undoubtedly spend the rest of your life in prison."

Lord William drew himself up, instantly turning from rakish mercenary adventurer to a peer of the realm. "You are undoubtedly correct. However, the Irish Republican Army, highly qualified mercenaries in my former employ and Lord Ian Parkhurst all wish me dead. The fact of the matter is that I really do not expect to survive the rest of the week. My only option is to go on the offensive. My only hope is to stop whatever is happening. Failing that, I hope to blow it open so wide that you and MI-5 can finish the job. If any actions I take result in my being killed or captured, so be it. Should they result in my arrest, public shame and imprisonment, then I will pay that price gladly, having done my duty to queen and crown."

Bolan had to admire the old boy. It was a hell of speech, and it was clear he meant every word of it. The effect on Finch was galvanizing.

"My lord—"

"Madame Director, Mr. Cooper and I are on a very tight timetable. We believe whatever the enemy is up to is not just a plan, but an operation, and it is happening now. If you wish to detain or arrest us, now is the time."

Bolan rose and stood shoulder-to-shoulder with Lord William.

Finch turned the CD in her hands. "As far as I am concerned, you and Mr. Cooper came here to answer my questions and deliver information of interest." She glanced up from the CD and her face was an iron mask of resolve. "If I detect even the slightest indication that you have engaged in illegal activities, as much as it pains me, Lord William, I'll have you in irons."

"I would expect nothing less."

Bolan turned as he and Lord William went to the door. "Director, I want to assure you that any information we come across will be forwarded to you immediately."

"Thank you, Mr. Cooper."

"Oh, one other thing, if you don't mind."

Finch waited helplessly. "Yes, Mr. Cooper?"

"Can we have some guns?" Bolan asked.

Finch's face went blank. "Guns."

"Yes, guns."

"You want me to give you guns."

"We've been hopping from Amsterdam to Guernsey to London and right now we're between armament," Bolan said. "I'd rather not go to the U.S. Embassy. I suspect it's being watched. I can arrange things through alternate channels, but that may take a little time."

"Mr. Cooper—" Finch was clearly having a crisis of credulity "—if you think I am going to issue you weapons from MI-5 armory, you're mad."

"Yeah, but you must have some confiscated firearms in the evidence room?"

Finch looked like her head might explode.

Bolan frowned. "Madam Director, two attempts have been made on the life of a peer of the realm. One on English soil."

Finch walked stone-faced out of the room. Bolan nudged Lord William and they followed. They went to the elevator and down two levels. The director led them along another corridor and key-carded a steel security door. A tiny lobby lay within. At the far end was a service counter shielded with bulletproof glass. A balding, bespectacled man dropped the football scores and shot to attention behind the counter.

"Director Finch!"

"Mr. Howard, can you tell me what firearms you currently have in inventory? Specifically, pistols or automatic weapons."

Howard tugged his nose in thought. "Well, Director, the fact is the last big lot was inventoried and declared 'no longer evidence' by the courts. We slated them for destruction as per usual. They've been taken downtown to the smelters and should've been sawed up and melted down, oh, yesterday at the latest. I'm waiting on the paperwork."

"Have you received anything since?"

"Some sporting shotguns that were confiscated from a robbery ring. We're still trying to trace the original owners, so they're—"

"Bring them."

Howard disappeared into his catacombs of racks and came back with four ancient-looking, double-barrel sporting shotguns in various states of repair. "Just these."

Bolan nodded. "We'll take them."

"Mr. Howard, I need you to release these weapons to me and any ammunition that came with them."

"This is most unusual, Director."

"You have no idea how aware of that I am, Mr. Howard."

Howard reluctantly held up a clipboard and slid it through the slot. "You'll have to sign for them, of course."

"Of course." Finch stiffly pulled out a pen and signed the clipboard. She looked like she was signing over her soul to the Devil. Howard stared at her signature, clearly bewildered by this strange turn of events. "Well, I'll fetch the ammunition, then."

Bolan glanced at the weapons behind the glass. "Howard?"

Mr. Howard stopped and regarded Bolan warily. "Sir?"

"You got a hacksaw back there?"

Finch's pen snapped between her fingers.

LUNK DID A LAP around the block and then stopped the Rolls. "Seems quiet, then."

Bolan looked up at the curtained windows of the Hyde Park flat. "When was the last time you stayed here, Bill?"

"Going on two years, I should think."

Bolan cocked back the hammers on his shotgun. He'd cut the barrels right down to the forend, and they were barely a foot long. The muzzles were ragged and shiny from the saw. "Open the garage and drive by."

Lunk hit the remote clipped to the visor and pulled past the flat. The little one-car garage was vacant save for a small workbench and a pegboard holding tools.

"Pull in."

The Rolls pulled into the garage.

"Leave the door open and the engine running."

They slid out of the Rolls. Lord William took out his keys while Lunk took position behind the driver's door and Bolan took a position by the tool bench. Lord William plastered himself against the wall beside the door and slid in his key. He turned the knob, shoved the door and jumped back. A narrow, steep, white-carpeted stair led to the main flat. He leaned in and flicked on the light above it and looked back at Bolan. The soldier eyed a shop coat hanging off a peg and liberated the wire hanger.

"Give me your key."

Bolan stripped the hanger straight and threaded it through the key and crimped it shut between his fingers. He bent the other end to make a handle and walked up the stairs, several of which creaked beneath his boots. Lunk filled the doorway at the bottom. He'd cut off the butts of two of the shotguns as well as sawn down the barrels, and he held one in each hand like giant handguns. Bolan reached the landing and crouched. He spit on the key to lubricate it and extended his makeshift key arm until the tip pressed against the keyhole. He glanced back at Lunk. The big man nodded in readiness.

Bolan shoved the key into the knob.

The door vibrated and twin lines of bullet holes magically

appeared in the door at gut level. The silenced weapons made no noise save for a smacking sound as the bullets tore through the wood.

Bolan threw an elbow into the wall and dived flat on the stair with a convincing thud. The door kicked open on its hinges and a lanky man in a coverall filled the doorway. A suppressed Stechkin machine pistol with a wire stock filled his hands.

Bolan and Lunk fired their weapons in the same instant, and the twin loads of buckshot smashed the man back like a fist, forcing him into a man behind him. The Executioner dropped to a knee and emptied his second barrel. The second man's face smeared away beneath the cloud of lead and the two men fell in a dead heap.

A third man inside was screaming something. Bolan didn't know what the words were, but he knew they were in Russian. The soldier broke open his shotgun and plucked out the smoking empty shells. He was nearly fluent and shouted in Russian, "Surrender! Surrender now!"

A short burst stripped paint and paneling off the stairwell wall.

Bolan pushed in two fresh shells, snapped the shotgun shut and spoke low to Lunk and Lord William. "Cover me!"

Lunk rushed up the stairs with Lord William right behind. He stood high enough to hold his shotguns at door level and fired off his remaining two barrels. He instantly crouched and Lord William let off both barrels at once in a deafening double detonation.

Bolan lunged through the door.

Glass broke in a room facing the street. Bolan charged forward for the bedroom. The third man had thrown a chair through the bedroom window. He whirled as he heard Bolan, but he was a second too late. The Executioner's shotgun boomed twice and the man screamed as his knees collapsed horribly beneath him.

Bolan lunged back behind the doorjamb as the man squirted off a long burst as he fell. Bolan shucked in fresh shells and pulled out a choice Russian phrase.

"Russian?" the attacker asked.

Bolan decided to play a wild card blind and shouted around the door. "*Da!* SPETSNAZ!"

Bolan had told the killer he was Russian special forces, and that seemed to give him further pause. He began shouting back in rapid-fire Russian Bolan couldn't understand, but his voice sounded shaken and confused. Bolan roared with the unmistakable timber of command. "Surrender! Surrender now!"

A weapon clattered to the floor in the bedroom.

Bolan motioned Lunk and Lord William forward and entered the room. It was right out of an Austin Powers movie, with a round bed, satin sheets and mirrors on the ceiling. Lord William's swinging decor wasn't Bolan's primary concern. The third killer lay on a fur rug moaning and clutching at his legs. At this distance Bolan's buckshot had almost no time to spread and had hit the man's knees in fist-size patterns. Only strings of tendon and jellied flesh held his upper and lower legs together. The Stechkin lay a few feet away where the assassin had thrown it. He stared up into the sawed-off barrels of Bolan's shotgun uncomprehendingly.

"SPETSNAZ? SPETSNAZ?"

"No." Bolan shook his head. "American."

The killer paled in horror.

Bolan knelt beside him. A very strange new player had entered the game. "Lunk, hold him while I bandage his legs. Lord William, I think you should call Director Finch."

CHAPTER NINE

A roomful of more dangerous men would have been hard to imagine. They were swilling pints of beer as if it were soda pop and apparently had been doing so for the last forty-eight hours. Little empty cardboard boxes of Nepalese take-out delights and empty bottles covered nearly every flat surface. Clouds of cigarette smoke slowly crawled in banks across the ceiling. A mostly ignored cricket match played on the television. David McCarter and Jack Grimaldi sat among the other men. Grimaldi had flown overnight from the U.S. He was red-eyed but at least seemed relatively sober. Bolan's favorite bellhop in Britain, Sheriff Modu, stood and waited as Bolan handed him a wad of money, then passed out three key cards to Bolan. "Anything else you need? You let me know."

Otto Owu waved a half-empty pint glass at Modu. Owu was big, black, bald and had a mouthful of silver and gold teeth. Ritual tribal scarring marked both of his cheeks like sergeant's chevrons. Three on the right pointed up and two on the left pointed down.

The Nigerians spoke rapidly back and forth in a common dialect. Modu winked, nodded, made an okay sign and shot a thumbs-up before leaving. Owu turned a somewhat bleery glance on Bolan. "You are the Matt-man?"

"That would be me," Bolan confirmed.

Owu nodded. "We have guns. What do you want?"

Apparently the black-market machine was booming. "What can you get?"

"This is England." Owu shrugged elegantly. "Russian, what else?"

England had some of the most draconian firearms legislation in the world. Not surprisingly, gunrunning and gun crimes had been skyrocketing nonstop for a decade. Russian black-market weapons were cheap, reliable and came by the container vessel across the channel.

Bolan took a pen and a hotel notepad from the writing desk and wrote out a list.

Owu raised his eyebrows as he scanned it. "You got the coin for this?"

"If you boys don't drink it all."

A round of laughs met this.

"Are we really going to have a dust up with Lord Parkhurst, then?"

Bolan recognized Alvin Partridge from his file photo. Facially, the Welshman could have been Lunk's brother, but rather than a six and a half foot human tombstone Partridge had the size, build and cocky attitude of a bantamweight boxer.

"I know some of you may have reservations about going after an English peer."

Nick Lovat, the sniper from Blackpool, snorted. "Some of us have waited our entire bloody lives for the opportunity."

The men laughed, but Partridge stayed on topic. "So it's true? And he's caught up with WMDs?"

"We have confirmation that Lord Ian tried to kill our good

friend Bill in Amsterdam. Then he burned down his house and shot his dogs in Guernsey."

This was met with angry muttering around the room.

"The WMDs are unconfirmed, but that's what brought me to England, and a hell of a lot of people are dying whenever they inquire." Bolan glanced meaningfully around the room and played a motivator card. "We also know it was Parkhurst who financed Jennings's takeover of Aegis."

"Clive?" Scott Layland scowled over his pint. The Australian was clearly a little drunk. "He always was a right wanker."

"The good news is Lord William's dog took Clive's arm off at the elbow, so he'll be a left wanker from now on."

The men roared.

"The bad news is this. We were attacked this afternoon at Lord William's flat, and we think it was by a Russian assassination team."

Owu seemed to sober up instantly. "So, for the record. IRA, Aegis, a British lord and Russians."

"That's the mix, but we're still not sure about the players."

"Shouldn't MI-5 being taking care of this? Or SAS?"

"No English authority is going to act against Lord Parkhurst without damning evidence. We can't give them any."

"So." Thapa Pun sighed. "We're expendables. Damned if we win, damned if we lose."

"That's it." Bolan didn't need to sugarcoat it for men of this caliber. "We go after Parkhurst, we go after the IRA, we go after Aegis, and we go after the Russians and any other target of opportunity. We follow the trail until we find out what's going on or the last man on the team is arrested or killed. MI-5 has a vague idea of what we may be up to. So if we blow the thing wide open and they swoop in to pick up the pieces? We did our duty. I won't lie to you. It won't be easy. At the enemy's hands, all you can expect is torture and death. The only thanks you'll get from the British government is probably life in a supermax prison facility."

"Job's a piece of cake, and the perks sound fantastic," Layland opined.

Bolan shrugged. "There are perks."

The men stared.

"Each and every one of you has his dear old Uncle Sam standing behind him."

Bolan knew some of the men in the room didn't have a whole lot of use for Uncle Sam, but they all intrinsically grasped what that statement meant. Bolan spelled it out anyway. "The CIA already has two agents dead. The United States can't intervene directly with men or material. However, for all practical intents we have an unlimited budget. We'll also have access to any pertinent CIA or Pentagon files requested as well as satellites tasked to our requirements. As for pay…"

The team members leaned forward expectantly.

"I want each man down for this, hard-charging and no questions asked. I have a thousand pounds and a plane ticket to anywhere for any man who walks away now, and thank you for your time. For those who stay, I have one hundred thousand."

The men just stared.

Bolan's War Everlasting had pitted him against drug lords, mafias and terrorists with vast financial backing. During his war, he had confiscated or seized entire fortunes. Huge sums were stashed in his war chest. That money was slated for situations exactly like this.

"I'll have an offshore account in the Cayman Islands set up for each man who's in. In the event of your death or incarceration your families will be given the money. Each one of you needs to write me out a short statement as to how you want that to work."

Stunned silence reigned.

Bolan scooped up a can of stout and cracked the tab. "So who's in?"

EVERYONE WAS IN. The team had spent a day sobering up and now was running inventory. The Nigerian smugglers had gotten it mostly right. The team began taking out equipment and checking it. The majority of the men would be armed with 9 mm AS "silenced" assault rifles. They were short, stubby weapons with folding metal stocks. Silent was a misnomer. The AS was far from silent. However, it was quiet, and even Special Forces veterans who had not heard an AS fired before would not recognize the sound signature as a weapon.

Bolan took a 9 mm VSS silenced sniper rifle out of its case. It was almost exactly the same weapon as the AS, except that it had a solid, polymer skeleton stock and its action, trigger and barrel had been specially chosen and tuned for accuracy. A 4X PSO-1 optical sight was mounted over the action. The Russian nickname for the weapon was "Vintorez" or threadcutter. The name had a double meaning. Not only was the weapon supposed to be accurate enough to cut a hanging thread, but also in old Scandinavian and Slavic mythology each man's life was a thread unrolled from the skein of the world and measured out by the Fates.

The Vintorez had been designed to cut that thread.

The long, heavy subsonic bullets were only precision accurate out to three hundred meters, so the VSS wasn't really a sniper rifle as such, but the fast, accurate and deadly weapon of a sharpshooter on the move.

Bolan looked around at his team. He basically had a nine-man infantry squad, and that was how he intended to play it.

They would break up into two sections, one led by himself and the other by Lord William. "All right, David, Pun, Owu, you're with me. The rest of you are with Lord William." Bolan tossed the VSS to Partridge. "I'm the designated marksman for my team, you're the sharpshooter for Lord William's section."

Partridge caught the weapon and nodded.

Bolan levered open a crate and pulled out a revolver.

Scott Layland's eyes went wide. "Balls!"

It was huge and all strange, futuristic angles raking forward and back.

"Russian UDAR 12.3 mm, that's .48-caliber to anyone who's counting. It's a five shooter." Bolan held up a 5-round cassette of ammo. "These are SP-9N less-lethal munitions, your basic rubber baton round. Each cartridge has a payload of three rubber buckshot. Maximum useful range is around fifteen meters. We need to be surgical on this op. IRA, Aegis, Russians—anyone with a gun, you're a green light with the rifles. However, groundskeepers, servants, guests and most especially Lord Ian himself—any of them that resist, any that refuse to drop or freeze when you tell them, you give them the UDAR. Just try to keep your shots low. The baton rounds are supposed to be nonlethal, but at short range they can still crack a skull."

Lunk picked up one of the two-pound revolvers and examined it thoughtfully. He finally seemed to have found a weapon that didn't look puny in his hands. Thapa Pun grinned and happily took two.

"Night-vision and tactical communications are all Russian. They're solid kit, but bulky and a generation behind what you may be used to. Take a little time to get familiar with it. Again, we're trying to go in and get out as soft as possible. Grenades will be flash-stuns and CS. Two of each for each man. The gas masks are British S10s. Make sure yours fits, and remember it won't be compatible with your night-vision goggles. So be careful where and when you deploy gas."

Bolan kicked a box at his feet that rattled. "Our Nigerian friends were kind enough to throw in a crate of Type 3 bayo-nets. They won't fit on your weapons, but anyone who needs a knife take one." Bolan raised a knowing eyebrow at Pun. "Of course, some of you may have brought your own from home…."

Subedar Pun drew his thirteen-inch kukri and waggled it to the whistles and catcalls of the rest of the men.

"You bring enough for the rest of the class, then?"

"Compensating for something, are you then, Pun?"

"Thappy, you dizzy bastard!"

The mirth rolled around the room as opinions about Thapa Pun and his knife grew increasingly revolting. Bolan sup-pressed a smile. Despite facing desperate odds, the team was salty and committed to the task at hand.

Scott Layland brought things back to business. "I hear Parky lives in a fucking castle."

Bolan laid out a schematic and some satellite photos. "Ac-tually he lives in a fortified Edwardian manor."

Layland made a rude noise.

Partridge shrugged hopefully. "Well, that's good news, then."

"It is." Bolan had been in a few battles in medieval for-tresses around the world. With modern armament like hand grenades, flamethrowers, thermobaric weapons and war gas, the thick stone walls and narrow corridors of a castle could easily be turned into death traps for the besieger as well as the besieged. "Parkhurst's place was built more for show than fortification. Lots of windows cut into the stone to let in light. No moats or walls. We have multiple options for assault and extraction. Even though Parkhurst lives there, the castle is an official English Cultural Heritage site so we have blueprints for the whole place."

Pun peered over the blueprints. "How do we go in?"

"We jump." Bolan indicated Grimaldi. "Jack here has acquired us a plane and logged a flight plan. That will get us past the gates, the hedges and any perimeter security." He tapped the blueprint. "The place is a castle only in name, but it does have an attached tower in the west corner. It was actually built for astronomical purposes by the first Lord Parkhurst. It's not big but the top is flat, and it's a bit bigger than the targets most of you aimed for in jump school."

Lunk cleared his throat. It was the first time he'd seen the big Welshman uncomfortable. "Beggin' your pardon, but what if we never went to jump school?"

"That's been taken into consideration. You and Owu will jump tandem."

"Ah." Lunk sounded utterly unconvinced. Owu stared into the middle distance and shook his head in resignation at the idea of being smashed like a bug.

"We jump in two teams. My team will be hitting the top of the tower. Lord William and his men will land on the grounds and assault from the front door. They'll act as the diversion for the top team." Bolan nodded at McCarter, Owu and Pun. "Should any of us miss the tower top, then just land on the grounds and link up with Lord William."

Lovat put his VSS rifle back in its case, apparently satisfied with the Russian kit. "How do we extract?"

"Once we've jumped, Jack is going to fly straight for the airfield outside Carlisle. The CIA has been kind enough to arrange a civilian Eurocopter BK117 to be waiting. Lord Parkhurst's manor is only fifty kilometers from Carlisle and the helicopter will be hot on the pad, but Jack will still have to land, switch aircraft and fly back. We're looking at a twenty-minute turnaround time, best case. From there we have a flight plan for Ireland with a CIA safe house waiting for us in Dublin."

Owu still stared into that terrible place where he was going to jump out of a plane. "And worst case?"

"Worst case, we extract on foot. The Lake District National Park is thirty kilometers south of the castle. Each of you will be issued a map with two alternate extraction points. If we somehow lose Jack, then we lose ourselves in the mountains and escape and evade due west. The good news is Cumberland is some pretty wild country, and sparsely populated. Towns are few and far between. It will take the local authorities time to respond to our incursion and far longer to mount any kind of manhunt. Even if we have to extract on foot, I'd say our chances of getting away clean are fair to good. There will be boats waiting for us on the coast in the towns of Whitehaven and Seascale. From there, Pentagon satellites and CIA contacts will apprise us of the pursuit, and we'll extract to the Isle of Man, Scotland or Ireland, depending on which looks most viable."

Bolan glanced around at the men. "Gentlemen, this is a snatch. Lord Parkhurst is our primary target. We want him alive, and assuming J.G. arrives safe and we're all still alive, we'll also have room for two more individuals of interest. Tolerance for civilian casualties or collateral damage is at zero. Any questions?"

Partridge snorted. "Yeah, who do I—"

"Have to screw to get out of this chicken-shit outfit?" Bolan inquired.

"Yeah." Partridge stared into Bolan's eyes. Every man in the room was a battle-proved veteran and Special Forces of one stripe or another. They all looked to Lord William as their natural leader. Somehow, an unknown American had come and usurped command. It was something that had gone unspoken until now, and despite the apparent goodwill, Bolan had felt the undercurrent during the past twenty-four hours; Partridge's challenge was suddenly real, and all eyes were on the two of them. The little Welshman looked Bolan up and down. "Tell me, Yank. Just who would I have to screw?"

Bolan shrugged. "Lunk."

Lunk nodded and cracked his knuckles.

Partridge blinked.

Bolan suddenly loomed over Partridge. "And you know? I have no idea what would happen if you tried to bugger Lunk." Bolan suddenly grinned. "But I'll tell you this—people will be talking about it for years to come."

The men roared. The situation defused as colorful metaphors regarding the immanent destruction of Alvin Partridge's rear contact point flew back and forth. The message was clear. Bolan had Lord William's confidence, and if Bolan was in command of this strange little legion, Lunk was his centurion.

Partridge rolled his eyes as every orifice in his body became a source of humor. "All right, all right, then. Let's go bloody bugger old Parky for the nice Yank and be done with it."

CHAPTER TEN

The DeHavilland Twin-Otter soared over the Cumberland Lake District. Grimaldi spoke over the intercom. "Five minutes!"

"Lights!" Bolan shouted. "Check night vision!" The cabin lights dimmed and Bolan's world turned a flat, grainy-green in the Russian lenses. In the crowded cabin eight men gave Bolan the thumbs-up. "Weapons and rigs!" The men checked each other's straps a final time. Bolan leaned into the intercom. "Jack, we are go."

"Roger that, Sarge. One minute."

Bolan would have preferred a few days of mission preparation. They'd had neither time nor opportunity to practice with their weapons. Russian kit was nothing if not reliable, but every weapon had its quirks and the team had had no time to learn the ins and outs of the silenced assault rifles or baton-round-spewing handguns.

The jump was going to be interesting.

Every man in the plane except two had earned his jump wings the hard way, but some of the men hadn't jumped in a decade, some considerably longer. Owu and Lunk had never jumped at all. Scott Layland was busy hooking himself up to Lunk and McCarter was rigging up Owu. Lunk looked genuinely nervous. Owu maintained a very stoic sense of doom.

"You look good, Otto!" Partridge grinned. "You look good with a white man on your back!"

Owu shook his head and continued to stare out the window into the dark below. "White man been on my back since my mother dropped me."

The men laughed.

Grimaldi's voice came over the intercom. "Gentlemen, you have the green light!"

Partridge yanked open the door and Lord William roared at his team. "Go! Go! Go!"

Lunk and Layland toppled out of the door followed by Partridge and Lovat. Lord William shot Bolan the thumbs-up and stepped into space. Bolan raised his voice over the howling wind. "Go! Go! Go!"

McCarter and Owu stepped out and Pun jumped right after. Grimaldi's voice came over the intercom. "See you in twenty!"

Bolan dropped into the void.

It was a fairly simple jump. Ten thousand feet was plenty high enough so that the airplane would neither be seen nor heard on the ground, and low enough so that no oxygen bottles or special equipment would be required. The castle grounds were a big target, and all Lord William's team had to do was spiral downward. Hitting the top of the tower was the only technical part, but Bolan and McCarter had both made more jumps than they could count and Pun had risen to the rank of noncommissioned officer in the parachute regiment.

Bolan checked his altimeter and pulled his rip cord. His straps cinched against him as his chute deployed. He was suddenly floating rather than falling, and he pulled on his right toggle to start his slow spiral downward. A glance down showed him the castle directly beneath him and the two canopies of McCarter and Pun beneath him. The men of Red Team were vague gray spots in the distance beneath his boots. "Red Leader, what's your status?"

"Red Leader" stood for Red-Hot Willy, and he was leading Red Team. Bolan's team was "Striker."

Lord William came back across the link. "Red Team is go, Striker Leader. No malfunctions. Maintaining formation."

"Copy that, Red Leader. Striker Team, sound off."

"A-ok, Striker Leader," Pun responded.

McCarter paused before answering. Bolan peered down at the Briton's larger tandem chute. "Red Two, you're descending too fast."

McCarter's voice came back. "We're heavy, Striker Leader. Don't know why, but we're going down and going down quick."

"Copy that. Forget the tower. Land on the grounds."

"We'll hit the bloody tower, Striker Leader."

Bolan trusted McCarter's judgment, but the Englishman was spiraling down awfully fast despite repeatedly flaring his canopy. The earth swung up swiftly to meet them. Red Team began sounding off.

"Red One, down."

"Red Two and Three, down."

"Red Four, down."

"Striker Leader, this is Red Leader. Team is down and deploying. No enemy sighted."

"Copy that." Bolan watched as McCarter and Owu swiftly outstripped him and Pun. "Striker One, suggest you join Red Team on ground."

McCarter snarled as he fought his chute. "We'll make it, Striker Leader."

The Englishman swirled down in a hard, tight spiral toward the top of the tower. He was going in much too fast for such a small, hard drop zone, and he knew it. "Bloody hell! Strike Leader, we're not going to make the drop zone!" McCarter abandoned his spiral maneuver and passed the tower roof by a scant few feet as he flew downward in a harsh, high diagonal for the ground. Bolan didn't speak any Nigerian dialects, but Owu was clearly praying.

McCarter snarled as he fought to slow them. "Shut your gob, Otto!"

Bolan winced as they hit. "Striker One! Striker Two! Respond!"

It took McCarter several seconds and all that came across the link was profanities. Owu was making vomiting noises.

"Striker One, status."

McCarter reined in his anger. "Striker Leader, I bolloxed it."

"Status."

"My ankle is balls-up."

"Is it broken?"

"Can't tell. Don't think so."

"Striker Two?"

Owu came back weakly. "We're down. I'll take care of him."

"Striker One, can you move?"

A few seconds passed. "I can hobble. It's not broken."

"Find cover somewhere along the castle's frontage. You're covering fire for the extraction. Striker Two, get him in place and then link up with Red Team."

"Roger that."

"Copy."

Bolan focused on the tower rushing up at him. Pun flared his chute and landed with just two running steps. The Gurkha scooped up his chute and went to the edge to make as much room for Bolan as possible. The Executioner hit his toggles and filled his canopy with air. He braked, but his heel bones rang against the stone hard enough to rattle his spine and seemingly loud enough to wake the dead. Bolan gathered up his chute and clicked out of his harness. "Striker Team on the tower. Red Team, wait for my signal."

"Roger that, Striker Leader."

Bolan caught movement and crouched. "All units! Hold position! Hostile sighted!"

The small, sudden, unmistakable flare of a match lit up Bolan's night-vision goggles. There was a man on the other corner of the castle. He was smoking and carried a Steyr AUG rifle slung over his shoulder. The sentry wasn't wearing night-vision equipment and appeared to be oblivious to the invasion of County Cumberland. The Steyr rifle was Irish-army issue. Bolan doubted the Irish Defense Force was stationing troops at Parkhurst Castle. On the other hand, in light of recent events, the Irish Republican Army just might, and much of their equipment was stolen or "donated" Irish-army issue. Bolan raised his VSS rifle to his shoulder and took aim through the scope.

The sentry abruptly squatted behind a chimney.

"Damn." Bolan kept his weapon trained. "Red Four, do you have the shot?"

Nick Lovat came back. "Negative, Striker Leader. Target between the chimney and an air-conditioning housing. I can try to maneuver for it."

Bolan grimaced. That would put Lovat out in the open directly in front of the target. "Negative, Red Four. Hold position. Striker One, do you have a shot?"

McCarter responded from the fountain near the gate. "I have line of sight, Striker Leader, but shot is long without optics."

They were going to have to fix the situation from the top. Bolan turned his head at a low rasping noise behind him. Thapa Pun had drawn his khukri. He waggled the gleaming blade in question.

Bolan nodded at Pun. "Go."

Pun unzipped his boots and stepped barefoot onto the stones. A long, narrow stone catwalk separated the tower from the roof corner where the sentry was smoking, and the little Gurkha scampered down it making less noise than the patter of cat feet. He held his giant knife low along his leg so there would be no telltale gleam. Pun scurried up to the chimney and the khukri gleamed as he raised it on high. The khukri flashed as Thapa Pun dealt a killing blow. Even from his position on the tower Bolan could hear the splintering of skull. Pun didn't bother with the com-link. He just shot a thumbs-up as he ran back.

"All units. Hostile down. Take your positions and hold. Striker Team going in."

Pun sheathed his blade and slid his feet back into his boots. "No door over there."

The sentry had come up through the tower and chosen his concealed cubby behind the chimney to smoke out of the wind. "Let's do it."

The door to the tower roof was a wooden hatch. Bolan's solid pull revealed it wasn't locked. Pun covered him as he lifted the hatch. The wood screeched horribly, but there was supposed to be a man on the roof. Bolan swept the room with the muzzle of his weapon. The tower attic was filled with telescopes, some modern and some brass antiques. He descended and Thapa followed.

"Red Leader, we're in. Cut the power and begin assault."

"Copy that, Striker Leader," came back Lord William. "Assaulting now."

Bolan and Pun descended the spiral stairs to the top floor of the castle. Bolan pushed open the door and found himself in an opulently appointed hallway with Persian carpets on the floor and antiques and paintings along the walls. The hallway suddenly went dark as Scott Layland cut the power line. Down the hallway, Bolan heard someone swear at the sudden power outage. It had been a long time since Bolan had seen a man wearing a nightshirt, but an ancient-looking man swearing in a thick Northern accent came down the hall with flashlight in his hand. Bolan pressed himself alongside a standing suit of medieval armor as the servant approached.

The Executioner stepped out and pressed the muzzle of his weapon into the old man's cheek. "Quiet."

The old man nearly had a conniption but suddenly thought better of it.

"Drop the flashlight."

The flashlight thudded to the carpet.

"Where is Lord Parkhurst?"

The old man's lower lip trembled. "He's with his guests downstairs. In the main 'all."

"Pun."

Thapa Pun hog-tied the man with plastic restraints and muted his protests with duct tape. Bolan thumbed his throat mike. "Red Leader, status."

"Striker Leader, we are inside. Two hostiles down, one is definitely Irish. The other was that Yank Legionnaire who used to work for me, Guy Diddier."

Aegis and the IRA were definitely on the premises. God only knew where the Russians might be lurking. Bolan froze as the lights flickered several times and came on. The castle had an emergency generator. He'd been afraid of that. Another advantage lost. "Copy that. We have reason to believe target is downstairs in the main hall."

"Roger, Striker Leader. We have lights and sound coming from that—" Downstairs someone began shouting. The shouting was instantly followed by the crackle of gunfire. "Striker Leader! We've been spotted!"

Pun looked at Bolan expectantly. The little Gurkha wanted to be in the action, but the enemy still didn't know that Striker Team, even if their numbers had been cut by half, was above them. They'd been detected earlier than Bolan had wanted, but the plan was still vaguely working. The gunshots below ceased. "Status, Red Leader."

"Two hostiles down. More in the main hall," Lord William advised. "Numbers unknown. At least half a dozen with automatic rifles."

McCarter broke in. "Team leaders, I have men moving toward the castle from the grounds."

"Numbers?"

"Two on the frontage."

That was another thing Bolan had been concerned about. "Guards or groundskeepers?"

"They have automatic rifles."

"Do you have the shot?"

"Roger, Striker leader. I have the shot."

Bolan nodded. "Green light."

McCarter came back in three seconds. "Hostiles down."

"Copy that, Striker One. Red Leader, what's the status on the hall?"

"Hostiles have barricaded themselves in. Doors to the main hall are substantial. Do you wish us to key them?"

Both Bolan and Lunk had retained their sawed-off 12-gauges for "master-keying" the hinges of any offending door. Bolan peered at a sliding mahogany shutter set into the wall in front of him. "Hold on, Red Leader." Bolan opened the door and found an ancient-looking, rope-pulley dumbwaiter. He mentally reviewed the manor's floor plan. The kitchen would be directly below them, and it was attached to the main hall. "Red Leader, I am inserting from above. I need a diversion. Use the UDARs on the door."

The big revolvers would give Bolan covering noise, and the rubber bullets would hammer the doors without ripping through and possibly hitting him and Pun or Lord Parkhurst. Bolan unslung his VSS and handed it to Pun. He glanced at one of the UDAR revolvers Pun wore on each hip like a gunslinger. "Let me see one of those."

Bolan drew his pistol and took Pun's in the other. He folded his frame into the dumbwaiter compartment. There wasn't an inch to spare. Pun braced a foot against the wall and grabbed the pulley rope. "Ready."

The soldier thumbed his mike. "Red Leader, start your diversion."

Below, UDAR revolvers began booming dully. Automatic rifles fired back in response.

Bolan nodded at Pun. "Go." The little elevator creaked as Pun lowered it hand over hand. Bolan cocked back the hammers on both UDARs as he descended in the cramped compartment. He was heavier than the average coffee service and Bolan came to a halt with a thud. He waited for the little elevator car to be riddled with rifle fire, but nothing happened. Hooking the lip of the door with the muzzles of his UDARs, he slid the shutter up. The lights in the kitchen were on, but no one was inside. The big American climbed out of the dumbwaiter and grabbed the rope to send it back up. "Striker Three, come ahead." The dumbwaiter creaked as it took Pun's weight, and Bolan lowered it. Pun was half Bolan's size and his rifle's stock folded, so he popped out grinning and fully armed.

"Red Leader, we're in the kitchen. Wait for my signal, and

then key the door and assault. Use the flash-stuns. Kitchen will be on your left."

"Roger that, Striker Leader."

Bolan and Pun crept toward the kitchen entrance to the main hall. They could hear people shouting and an occasional burst of gunfire. The nice thing about a castle was that the doors all had old-fashioned keyholes. Bolan knelt and peered through. There were eight men that he could see, all in civilian clothing. Four had AUGs, while the others had handguns of various descriptions.

Bolan leveled his revolvers. "Hit it."

A shotgun boomed twice, and the main door flew away in ruins beneath Lunk's boot. The gunmen in the hall sent a storm of lead through the shattered portal. A black-and-yellow metal cylinder the dimensions of a tall-size beer can looped into the room. A sound like the blast of a 105 mm howitzer rattled the kitchen door and was swiftly followed by a second. Bolan kicked the kitchen door open. The main hall was filled with the swirling fireflies of the flash-stun grenade's pyrotechnic aftereffect.

A man with an AUG caught Bolan's motion, but he was deafened and half blinded by the flash. Bolan's UDAR revolvers rolled in his hands as he printed six rubber buckshot bullets into the man's chest and knocked him back over an overstuffed chair. Pun's AS assault rifle hissed and clicked on full-auto, taking down another two men.

Lunk and Layland came through the main door with their rifles shouldered. The weapons were unheard beneath the crack and boom of gunfire, but their bolts hammered back and forth and their chambers sprayed smoking brass as they came on. They dropped to one knee as Lord William and Owu moved into the room firing. Bolan's UDARs boomed twice again, and the last man staggered backward beneath the hail of buckshot.

The gunfight had taken less than three seconds.

Pun moved at a crouch to the back of the hall and nodded. "Clear!"

Bolan peered at a massive oak door to the side of the hall. Lord William pressed a fresh magazine into his weapon and racked the bolt home on a fresh round approvingly. "Russian kit. Who knew?"

Bolan pressed fresh cassettes of ammo into his UDARs and holstered them. He unslung the sawed-off 12-gauge from behind his back. "The hired help said Lord Parkhurst was downstairs with his guests." Bolan gestured at the dead and wounded littering the floor. "These men are soldiers and guards." Bolan peered at the door. "That leads to the library. I think Lord Parkhurst and his guests are in there."

"Sounds about right. Any other way out?"

"Back when this place was built people wanted as much natural light as possible. Recon photos showed a lot of windows on this side of the castle, but the floor plan doesn't show any doors." Bolan thumbed his link for McCarter. "Striker One, be advised of possible break out imminent on west side of building, corresponding to the library."

"Roger that, Striker Leader. I have clear line of fire on library."

Bolan gestured at the door with his sawed-off. "Lunk, I'll take the hinges. You hit the knob. Lovat, you throw the flashstun. Layland and Partridge? You're our point men. Owu, you go in with me, then Lunk. Bill, you and Pun cover our six just in case anyone we missed comes sneaking up."

The men quickly fell into position as Bolan and Lunk stood on either side of the door. Bolan nodded. "Now." The sawed-off shotgun yanked in Bolan's hands like a bucking mule as he blasted the top and then the bottom door hinge with solid slugs. He whipped back as Lunk blasted the lock.

The cotter lever of Lovat's grenade pinged away. Layland put his boot into the twisted and broken lock.

The door exploded.

Splinters scored Bolan's face. Lunk toppled like a tree as a chunk of iron-bound door hit him in the face. Layland and Lovat were blasted backward with the door and flew into Owu and Partridge. Lovat's grenade fell to the carpet.

"Grenade!" Bolan shouted.

He felt his eardrums compress and his eyelids light up from the flash as lightning and thunder cracked in the hall. Bolan opened his eyes to pulsing purple pinpricks, thousands of pyrotechnic butterflies and hellish ringing in his ears. Lord William and Pun were out of range of the blast and their silenced rifles instantly clicked and hissed in a steady stream pouring fire through the shattered portal. Bolan dropped his shotgun and slapped leather for his UDARs. He snaked the pistol around the doorjamb and fired off three random rounds. Layland jumped up. He'd lost his rifle but held his UDAR with both hands.

Lord William's voice rose above the cacophony of carnage. "Down!"

Bolan whipped himself back as something big began thumping in rapid semiautomatic fire. Layland went stiff as a fireplace poker and fell like a tree. Lovat had barely gotten to his hands and knees and he dropped belly down twisting and screaming beneath the barrage.

Everything suddenly went quiet except for the moans of the wounded.

Bolan yawned to clear his ringing ears. His blue eyes went arctic.

Lovat lay in full view of the doorway clutching his sides and screaming. Blood welled up under his hands. Layland lay flat out on the floor. His eyes had been miraculously spared but two dozen thin steel slivers filled his face like a pincushion. None of the projectiles had penetrated his skull deeply enough to kill. It was the dozen or more .17 darts ice-picking his throat that had killed him. His rigid body told Bolan that one or more of the darts had punctured his spinal cord. The enemy in the library had a semiautomatic 40 mm grenade launcher, and it was loaded with antipersonnel fléchette rounds. The rest of the team had managed to roll out of the arc of fire. Bolan pulled a flash-stun and jerked his head at Lord William. Both of them pulled the pins and the cotter-levers pinged away.

A sheet of brutally hot flame hosed forth from the library like the breath of a dragon. Nick Lovat howled like the damned in hell as the jellied jet fuel of the flamethrower eclipsed his body. The hairs on the backs of Bolan's hands singed as he flung his flash-stun through the sheet of fire. Lord William's grenade detonated prematurely as it passed through the jet of fire and the stream pulsed and blew outward in all directions, spattering bookcases and tables. Partridge rolled on the floor trying to smother his burning left arm, and Owu pounced on him. Lunk lay on the ground clasping his head.

Lovat was encased in flame and screaming in agony. The UDAR boomed once in Bolan's hand, and Lovat's agony ended as the rubber buckshot rebounded off his skull at point-blank range.

The Executioner filled his left hand with steel and went through the door.

The flash-stun had taken its toll on the flamethrower and grenade man. The broken doorway to the library was burning all around the door frame, but the blast had made the flamethrower man lean back and the ceiling was on fire where he had sprayed. The grenadier blinked and fired half-blind.

His six-chambered grenade launcher thudded three times into a bookshelf and clicked on empty.

Bolan's revolvers barked in either hand as he shot the grenadier and the flame man in the face.

Five more men were in the room.

Two were clearly guards who had abandoned their duty. They had smashed open windows and were crawling out onto the grounds. First one and then the other fell with a silenced rifle round through his skull courtesy of David Mc-Carter. A skinny young man with long hair and a bad suit tossed away a small automatic pistol and fell to his knees screaming in Russian. The little South African, Kew Timmer stood with a bandage over his nose, which Bolan had broken and a 9 mm Vektor automatic pistol in his hand. Lord Ian Parkhurst stood in a beautiful red-and-gold brocaded silk smoking jacket behind the library's desk. He looked every inch a British lord.

Timmer gasped and flew back against a bookcase as Bolan shot him in the chest. The pleading Russian howled and fell squirming to the floor as Bolan's rubber shot cracked his clavicle. Bolan swung the front sights of both UDARs on to Lord Parkhurst. Taking out the other two had taken him a second too long. Lord Parkhurst raised a revolver in his right hand. He wasn't aiming for Bolan. The .38 banged once as Lord Parkhurst assassinated the Russian with a bullet to the back of the head. He whipped the revolver toward Timmer.

The man was plugging leaks.

Bolan's revolver spit flame and Lord Parkhurst violently sat back down into his reading chair. He wheezed and tried sit himself up straight.

The Executioner cocked back both hammers. "Drop the pistol."

Outside Lord William barked orders. "Owu! Lunk! Sweep

the rest of the building before it burns down around our ears. Partridge! Get those bodies extinguished and bagged!"

Lord Ian stared into the smoking 12 mm muzzles of Bolan's guns and struggled to catch his breath. His hand still rested on the British .38 on the desk. Lord William came into the library with Pun beside him. The room was starting to burn in earnest. He'd slung his rifle and his UDAR was in his hand.

Bolan kept his eyes on the earl. "I said, drop the pistol."

Lord William nodded. "Come along, Parky. There's a good gentleman."

Parkhurst's pale face reddened at the familiarity. "Don't you 'Parky' me, you jumped-up son of a whore."

The two men stared at each other over their pistols.

Lord William shrugged. "So, Ian. What's this all about?"

Lord Ian regained some dignity. "Nothing a common fool like you could possibly understand."

Lord William cocked his revolver. "What I understand, Ian, is that two of my men have just kicked it off on the hard end of a bloody fucking flamethrower, and I just don't think I'm ever going to forgive you for that. Now you're going to tell me what you're bloody well up to, or I'm going to take Pun's khukri and chop the information out of you one joint at a time. Don't you bloody doubt it."

"Oh, I don't doubt it, William." The old man smiled savagely. "I'm sure you learned the torturer's trade quite well during your little adventures in Africa. You were such a good little dog for the mining consortiums. Just like England is America's faithful little dog. Just like the Americans themselves are slaves, slaves to their own—"

"I don't have bloody time for this." Lord William cut the earl off. "Pun!" Pun drew his khukri and presented it to Lord William. The baron took a step forward. "Now drop the gun and start talking, Ian, or it's going to go hard on you."

Lord Ian's pistol still lay on the top of the desk. He'd been unwilling to lift it as he stared down both of Bolan's barrels. But something changed. Lord Ian Parkhurst smiled and Bolan didn't like it at all. He'd clearly come to a decision. The wrong one.

"The good news is, gentlemen, the world as you know it is about to—"

Both of Bolan's UDARs roared simultaneously. Beneath the hammering rubber buckshot Lord Ian still snatched his pistol upward. Lord William's round hit the earl a second later and two more rounds rolled out of Bolan's pistols. Despite the horrific hail of Russian baton rounds Lord Ian pressed the muzzle of his Enfield No 2 Mk 1 .38-caliber revolver beneath his chin and pulled the trigger.

Lord Parkhurst collapsed face-first onto his desk with his skull open to the sky.

Lord William let out a weary sigh. "Well, that was damn obstinate of him."

Bolan reloaded his UDARs with fresh cassettes. Heat rolled in waves through the castle. The ceilings of the library and the main hall were burning out of control. "Striker Flight, what's your ETA?"

Bolan could hear the rotor noise on the other side of the link as Grimaldi responded. "Ninety seconds, Striker Leader."

"M'lord." Alvin Partridge limped into the room. His left arm was wrapped in gauze. "I got…" Lord William bent over and had a coughing fit as he breathed in smoke. Partridge turned to Bolan. "Coop, I got Nick and Scotty extinguished, then."

Bolan nodded toward Lord William. "Get his lordship outside. Bag Layland and Lovat in their chutes. Take Lord Ian outside, too. Pun, help him."

Owu trotted in with the bound servant from upstairs over

his shoulder and passed him off to Pun. "Rest of the castle is clear. Seems Lord Ian sent most of the servants away for this meet. What do you want to do?"

There wasn't much to do. Lord Ian Parkhurst's head was blown off, and a British national landmark was burning to the ground. Bolan suspected whatever cache he might have had with MI-5 was just about spent. The mission was a goatscrew, except for one thing. Bolan turned his attention and the muzzle of one of his revolvers to the corner where Kew Timmer was cringing. "Bring him along, would you."

Timmer yelped as Owu yanked him up by the hair. He marched the South African outside with repeated boots to the backside. "Move your bigot ass along! I said scamper!"

Bolan thumbed his mike. "Red One, respond."

Partridge and Pun ran in and grabbed Lord Ian's body. They all retreated to the hall as the library turned into an inferno. The hall wasn't much better.

"Red One, respond," Bolan repeated. "Lunk."

Lunk tottered into the hall. He couldn't respond because he was reclining beneath a load almost too heavy even for him. The giant dropped what looked like a small aircraft engine on the huge dining hall table. The wood creaked beneath its weight. Lunk's right eyebrow hung down in his face where the flying chunk of door had torn it. "Found this, in a workshop like, near the north end. It was surrounded by smaller bits and papers in foreign scribble."

Bolan looked long and hard at Lunk's find. Wires trailed from it and parts were obviously missing. Parts of the metal were green, powdering away and deeply corroded. Bolan had seen the like before. The main component was shaped like a lopsided dumbbell. It wasn't an engine. It was a gun. The bigger end contained the propellant charge; the smaller end was the target. The foot-long cylinder in between was the barrel. The "gun end" fired the bullet, which was a mass of uranium 235 down the barrel to the target. The target was a similar mass of uranium. When the bullet slammed into the target, fission occurred and you had an explosion.

Lunk had scrounged up a thermonuclear weapon.

"Lunk?"

Lunk wiped blood out of his eyes. "Yeah, guv?"

"Let's get this away from the fire."

CHAPTER ELEVEN

"Striker, you're the most wanted man in England," Kurtzman stated. Bolan sat in a chair in the CIA safe house while the rest of the team was sleeping.

"Good thing I'm in Ireland."

"Yes, the IRA wants you dead, so you and Striker's Stompers go and hide in their happy hunting ground."

"I've only got two leads left, Bear, and Ireland is one of them."

"Are you going to burn it down, too?"

Bolan pressed a cold Harp lager against his brow. He still had a headache from the grenade blasts, and good men had died.

Kurtzman relented. "What's your other lead?"

"We have Corporal Kew Timmer."

"The little South African? He was at the castle?"

"Yeah, we haven't squeezed him yet. I was considering giving him to MI-5 as a peace offering." Bolan took a pull on his beer and looked over at the nuclear bomb on the bed. "You get the pictures I sent you?"

"Oh, yeah."

"What did you make of it?" Bolan had seen a number of nuclear weapons in his day, but this one wasn't configured like a backpack nuke or a nuclear demolition charge. It was too large for an artillery shell, and the casings were much thicker than any missile warhead he'd encountered.

Kurtzman instantly warmed to the prospect of technical talk. "That's the interesting part. The weapon has clearly been partially dismantled. It was a little difficult working from pictures alone, but I think we have it nailed."

"Russian?"

"Oh, it's Russian, all right, and it's naval."

Given the thickness of the casings Bolan had considered that. "A depth charge?"

"No. Actually, due to the size and shape, I'm betting it's the warhead for a torpedo."

It was Bolan's turn to be surprised. "Oh, yeah?"

"Yeah. It was part of the old Soviet Cold War mentality. No matter what they said to the contrary, their entire naval strategy was based on first strike. Their ships, even the smallest ones, were massively armed. Their philosophy was to make one, huge, overwhelming strike the U.S. Navy would never recover from. You've been on some of their ships. Some of their battle cruisers actually have giant missiles in unarmored tubes above deck. One hit from an enemy missile or a cannon shell, and the whole thing would go up like pack of firecrackers. Safety, crew comfort, operational range, efficiency and sometimes even seaworthiness were sacrificed to give them that one big punch. Nuclear torpedoes were part of that plan, and were designed to knock out one of our fleet carriers or battleships in one go, and hopefully damage some of the surrounding battle group, as well."

"We never went in for that?"

"Not to my knowledge. It looks good on paper, but there are a lot of problems involved. The blast wave would change depending on depth, so firing sub to sub, your firing solution would change from depth to depth, and you always have to make sure you're out of range of your own weapon. On the surface, the blast would be much bigger, and again, you would have to fire from maximum range to keep yourself out of it. The U.S. Navy looked at it. We did develop nuclear depth charges, but we decided that the nuclear torpedo route was more trouble than it was worth. Naval Intelligence tells me they believe the Soviets came to the same conclusion in the 1980s and gave up the program."

Bolan looked back at the weapon on the bed. "So why does that look like salt water corrosion to me?"

"Because it probably is. I did a little research and came up with an interesting story. About two years ago, the Italian weekly *L'Espresso* reported that the Italian rescue services had acquired a secret Russian dossier. The dossier stated that twenty nuclear torpedoes had been deposited off the coast of the Gulf of Naples by a Soviet submarine sometime in the 1970s. The U.S. Mediterranean fleet spent a lot of time in Naples, and the Marine Corps had units stationed there, as well. It's believed that if the gloves came off, the Soviets would remotely detonate the weapons all at once and hopefully cripple U.S. operations in the Med."

"I gather the Russians deny all of this."

"Categorically, and so far, searches by the Italian navy have come up empty."

"If the weapons have been buried underwater for over thirty years, that might explain the corrosion. You think this might be one of them?"

"I could tell you more if I could get my hands on the weapon. However, if you can give me some scrapings of the corrosion and a sample of the casing, I could probably get a metallurgist to tell me something about the salinity and the mineral content of the water that did it. That could give us a tentative location."

"I'll have it on a jet today."

"I can also tell from your photos that the detonator has been removed, so the weapon is currently inert, even if the corrosion hasn't reached the inside of the mechanism."

"Good to know." The team had given the nuclear weapon in their midst some mighty long looks. "So the question is, what was Lord Ian Parkhurst doing with a Soviet nuclear torpedo warhead?"

"That's a very good question." Kurtzman looked at Bolan unhappily across the video link. "You think there are more?"

"He had a really smug look on his face right before he blew his head off."

"Well…fudge."

"Yeah, and he shot the only guy speaking Russian in the room before he did it."

"Well, I've got good news and bad news."

"What's the bad news?" Bolan asked.

"The bad news is MI-5 isn't talking to us."

"You know, I kind of figured that one out on my own."

"Yes, but I'm thinking if you turn the weapon over to them they're going to have to talk to us whether they like it or not," Kurtzman stated.

"Yeah, I figured that, too. David is going to contact the SAS detachment in Northern Ireland and arrange for them to pick it up once we clear out. My team is busted up pretty bad. I've got two KIA, one man with a badly burned arm and David is on crutches. I'm going to leave him here as our liaison with British Special Forces and hope MI-5 doesn't step in and arrest him. I'm down to five people, including myself."

Bolan frowned. "Lord William isn't well, but I need him. Your good news had better be good."

"Well, before MI-5 refused all contact with us, they provided some information on the men who ambushed you at Lord William's flat. The one you captured isn't talking, but they have a positive ID on him. He's someone they've had their eye on in London. His name was Igor Barranikov. He's a cultural attaché with the Russian embassy. Of course, they suspect he's a Russian Federal Security Service agent."

The FSB and its international branch, the SVR, was the old Cold War KGB by another name. "What else does MI-5 suspect him of?"

"The usual, assassination and kidnapping of people the FSB is interested in or irritated with in the London area. Mostly fellow Russians. The other bad news, of course, is that he has diplomatic immunity. MI-5 can't hold him or question him with any rigor. As soon as he is medically fit, he's being deported. He's been in private contact with Moscow and personally with Russian embassy personnel. We have to assume Moscow knows everything."

Bolan considered that one. "I don't think the Russians were working with Lord Parkhurst. I don't think they even knew he was involved. I think somehow they found out some of their weapons had surfaced, and somehow they knew Aegis was involved or running security. Lord William may have been forcibly retired from the firm, but he was still president of Aegis in name and his face was still on the cover of the prospectus. I think FSB wanted to have a long ugly talk with old Bill. That also explains why the agent in his flat freaked out when he thought I was Spetsnaz. If he was renegade, he just would've kept shooting, but if he was on official business for the Federal Security Service, he would have wondered what the hell military intelligence was doing showing up. It actually made him surrender."

"And that," Kurtzman said, "is the good news."

"How is that?"

The computer whiz played his trump card. "We've received a rather oblique message from the Russian Foreign Ministry."

"The United States has, not MI-5?"

"Not as far as we know."

Bolan could see where this was going. "Let me guess. They want to sit down and have a powwow."

"They say, and I quote, 'We wish to speak to the individuals involved in the regrettable altercation at London residence of Lord William Glen-Patrick.'"

For Russians, that was tantamount to saying they were desperate.

"Bear?"

"Yes?"

"Set up a meet."

"Where? You can't show your face in England at the moment," Kurtzman stated.

"Dublin's nice."

BOLAN QUIETLY WATCHED the two Russians approach. It was a beautiful spring day in Ireland, sunny, but with a cold snap in the air to bring color into your cheeks. It was a fine day to be sitting on the edge of a flatbed truck at the Dublin farmer's market sipping a cold one. All around the market square, people were selling vegetables and flowers, and tourists shopped for handicrafts. Local musicians played traditional Irish music. It was a very unlikely place for the Russians to try anything. If they did, Lunk was Bolan's guardian angel. In the early hours of the morning, the Welshman had secreted himself and one of the VSS assault rifles in the bell tower of the church across the street. Bolan was wearing what appeared to be an MP3 player, and the mike of the com-link was taped against his throat under his black turtleneck.

"You see what I see?"

"Oh, I do," Lunk rumbled low in Bolan's earpiece, "and I want to switch places."

Nearly all intelligence agencies kept a few beautiful women on the payroll. Men would let slip things to a woman they would never divulge even under torture to a man. Russian female agents, in particular, had a reputation for amoral ruthlessness. They would sleep with suspects or foreigners they needed information from and strangle them in their sleep with equal facility.

Russia had sent him one of their heavy hitters.

The Russian woman gave Bolan a charmingly tentative smile. She was short and slender, and wore a fisherman's sweater several sizes too large and faded jeans with holes in the knees. The look was adorable rather than sensual. Her face offset the cuddly look. Her black hair was long on top, and fell carelessly into her face but was cropped off short at the neck. Her huge brown eyes slanted upward ever so slightly. The woman's eyebrows were sculpted arches. One was set almost imperceptibly higher than the other, and it made her look as if she was either questioning or challenging whatever she laid her eyes upon. Her skin was very pale, and her ruby-red lips were bee-stung full. Her exotic looks were clearly the result of some highly successful cross-pollination going on in the southern Russian republics.

She stuck out her hand and spoke excellent English. "Hello, I am Yuliya Tymosh." Bolan shook hands with her as she motioned to the man beside her. "This is Ruslan Shust."

Most foreign intelligence agencies also had a brute squad on hand for intimidation duty. Shust was six and a half feet of blond, blue-eyed, bullet-headed Viking invader. Neither Russian gave off the vibe of spies or infiltration operatives. Both the man and the woman carried themselves like soldiers. The man's bearing screamed sergeant, and Bolan was willing to bet somewhere back in Moscow the woman had a brown uniform with lieutenant's bars on it. Bolan suspected a lot of suspects had given up everything they knew after being brutalized by Shust and then soothed by Tymosh. It was an act as old as interrogation. They were the good cop/bad cop team. Beauty and the Beast.

"Nice to meet you." Bolan held up a beer he'd been sipping. "You guys want a beer?"

Ruslan spoke in a voice that was a dead ringer for Darth Vader's long-lost twin Russian brother. "*Da,* that would be pleasant."

Tymosh smiled winsomely. "I am preferring stout."

Bolan pulled a bottle of ale and a can of stout out of his bucket and cracked them open. Any negotiation with Russians was fraught with multiple hidden agendas and endless jockeying for the tiniest bit of information. If the Russians thought they had a ringer in front of them, they either stonewalled or circled endlessly until their opponent in the negotiations tired. Bolan found the best way to deal with them was to shock, awe and short-circuit with the unexpected.

Bolan held up his bottle. Russian toasts tended to be long and notoriously sentimental. The Executioner cut to the chase. "Well, here's to the GRU. I'm glad I'm dealing with soldiers instead of FSB pussies. Cheers."

Tymosh and Ruslan blinked and looked at each other. The jig was up and Bolan's instincts had been correct. The two Russians weren't Russian Feds. They were Russian military intelligence. They nodded dutifully and slammed their beers into Bolan's.

"To GRU. Cheers."

"Here." Bolan took a slug of ale and pulled up a tarpaulin in the back of the truck. "This is yours."

Shock and awe went into full effect. The Russians goggled at the partially dismantled Soviet-era nuclear warhead. Tymosh grasped for a response. "This is…"

"Yours," Bolan agreed. He'd decided getting information out of the Russians was more important than MI-5's goodwill at the moment, so he would give them back their bomb. Bolan kicked-tapped the wheelbarrow behind him. "Yeah, and it's heavy. You can take the wheelbarrow if you like."

Ruslan cleared his throat. "We thank you."

Tymosh's eyebrow arched slightly. "And where were you finding this device?"

"I took it from Lord Ian Parkhurst's castle in Cumberland."

The Russians were shocked by the brazen admission and the gigantic clue Bolan had thrown in their laps. The assault on Lord Parkhurst's castle was international news, but it was pretty clear they'd had no idea of Parkhurst's involvement. They pressed their heads together and whispered in rapid Russian. Bolan decided to play another hunch. "This one wasn't one of the weapons your navy buried in Naples. Where do you think it was extracted from?"

The Russians put their heads together again. The American knew too much and was giving too much away.

"So." Bolan kept up the pressure. "How many more are you missing? Ten, twenty?"

The Russians grimaced in unison and the words they passed between them flew faster.

"How many have you recovered?" Bolan grinned infuriatingly. "However many you have, I bet I've found one more than you."

Tymosh's beautiful eyebrows formed a vee in anger. It

took Shust a second to process the sarcasm and then his hands closed into fists like wrecking balls. "Perhaps, Yankee-boy, you and I talk. Privately. Man to man."

"I don't think so." Bolan shrugged. "I like it right here."

Shust took a step forward and smiled unpleasantly. "No, I think you and I—"

Bolan cut the Russian off with a useful word in his own language. "Vintorez."

Thread cutter.

Shust stopped in his tracks. Bolan stopped smiling. "Pointed right at your head, big man," he said in Russian.

Shust's knuckles creaked and popped, but he didn't move any closer. Tymosh spoke soothingly. "We are getting off on wrong foot." She spoke a few words rapidly and jerked her head. Shust purpled with rage and went for a walk. Yuliya sat on the tailgate and pulled out a pack of cigarettes. "You have light?"

Bolan's butane lighter flared, and she cupped his hands. Her touch was electric. So were the huge, brown kitten eyes that peered unblinkingly into Bolan's as she dragged on the cigarette. Yuliya Tymosh was a woman who clearly knew how to get things out of men. Even Bolan had to admit the slight sense of loss as her hands fell away from his. Her lips pursed artfully as she blew smoke. "So."

"So."

"Do not anger Shust. He is sambo champion. He will break your bones like kindling."

Sambo was the Russian equivalent of judo, only several degrees more brutal. Like judo, it had become a sport; but unlike the Japanese martial art, it had never become a spiritual path, and the Russians had never lost the sense that it was still a method for their soldiers to kill people. "I'll keep that in mind."

"Best you do."

"So what should I keep in mind about you?"

Tymosh's face went from kitten to erotically charged predator as she smiled. Bolan had been in the crosshairs of a number of seductions. The Russians had sent a genuine secret weapon. "I am helpless woman, with only my charms to protect me."

Bolan tossed back the rest of his beer. "I'm a dead man."

The Russian tossed back her head and laughed.

"So how did you find out about the involvement of Aegis?"

"How did you?" the Russian countered.

"I think you owe me," Bolan told her.

"Very well, the CEO, Jennings. He has employed some ex-Russian Special Forces operatives for jobs in Eastern Europe.

"And one of them was loyal, and when he somehow became aware of Russian warheads, he contacted the Russian government."

"Except he contacted the Interior Ministry rather than military intelligence."

"Yes, he was former FSB paramilitary, so he contacted his former superiors." The arch of her brow told Bolan Tymosh firmly believed that if the GRU had been contacted in the first place, the situation would already be contained.

"And the FSB dropped the ball."

"Yes, FSB, pussies—" Tymosh wrapped her lips around the word "—drop ball. Aegis informant disappear. Assumed compromised and executed. Then they go in shooting at flat of Lord William and get caught while Jennings disappear without trace."

"I may have a line on Jennings."

Tymosh tilted her head slightly. "Really?"

"Yes."

"Where?"

Bolan reached back and lifted up another tarp. "Here."

Kew Timmer was roped like a calf at the rodeo and gagged with duct tape. He blinked into the sun and his eyes rolled blearily. The Russian eyed him. "He is drugged?"

"Five milligrams of sodium pentothal. Just to keep him quiet."

Tymosh peered into the man's eyes with clinical detachment. "You have not pressed him."

"Not yet."

Tymosh eyed Bolan in speculation. "He, too, is…gift?"

"No." Bolan dropped the tarp. "And you're going to have to give me a lot more."

The beautiful eyes narrowed and went from sexual predator to carnivore. Bolan sensed only the threat of his having a sniper was preventing her from whistling Shust back on the double, or maybe just taking matters into her own hands right then. Instead she changed tactics. "You ask me to divulge secrets of state security of Russian Federation."

"Listen, Lieutenant—" Tymosh's pale cheeks colored slightly, and Bolan knew he'd guessed her rank correctly "—the Cold War is over. The United States considers the Russian Federation a valuable ally." Bolan nodded at the defunct weapon behind them. "That device is probably thirty years old and represents no technology my government is interested in. What we are interested in is that an unspecified number of these devices are currently in the wrong hands. My government's number-one priority is to secure the weapons. We realize the political situation. The Cold War is over, but if the former Soviet regime violated the national boundaries of a foreign nation and mined their harbor with nuclear weapons, there will be a political uproar. My government is prepared to use the utmost discretion in this situation. The weapons must either be destroyed or placed in the hands of Russian Military Intelligence. Whichever is more expedient."

"Yes, and this discretion will be…bargaining chip…in future."

"The United States can only hope that any aid and assistance we can render our friend and ally during these circumstances may be returned someday in the future in the same spirit of goodwill."

Tymosh clicked her can against Bolan's bottle. "You are charming man."

"We can discuss that later. But right now I want to know how many weapons we're dealing with."

Tymosh finished her stout and hopped off the truck bed. She put her thumb and forefinger between her lips and gave three piercing whistles. Shust came back at the double. A few words passed between them, and Shust offloaded the wheelbarrow, veins pulsing out of his temples as he manhandled the warhead out of the truck bed.

Tymosh turned and reached into her pocket.

Lunk spoke in Bolan's ear. "I can take her."

Bolan subvocalized into his mike. "Wait for it."

The Russian beauty produced a cell phone and tossed it to Bolan. "I will be in contact."

Bolan caught the phone. It was undoubtedly bugged and had a tracking unit inside, but he was confident it would not pass the mobile electronic screening unit in the cab of the truck. Tymosh walked another five steps, putting a slow sway in her hips for Bolan's benefit before turning once more.

"We are now missing nineteen weapons." Her voice floated back over her shoulder as she and Shust walked away with their warhead. "They were embedded in English Channel."

"THE ENGLISH CHANNEL. That was pretty bold." Kurtzman was impressed. "God only knows how the Soviets managed to embed that many weapons without being detected."

Bolan had thought about that, too. "I'd suspect midget subs equipped with caterpillar tracks creeping along the bottom and putting them in place, maybe one or two at a time."

"Could work," Kurtzman conceded. "Though I admit I'm shocked the GRU would let that much slip after just one meet."

"Yeah, well, I gave them a lot to think about. They know they need us now. Speaking of the Russians, what have you dug up?"

"Ruslan Shust was indeed, as advertised, the All Russian Federation sambo champion, one-hundred-kilo-plus category, years 1997-1999. He made Sergeant 1st Class in Spetsnaz, was a hand-to-hand combat instructor and was decorated for bravery in Chechnya before becoming a GRU asset in 2001. After that, his activities become, shall we say, hazy, at best."

"What about the woman?"

"You'd better be careful with that one, Striker."

Bolan saw what was coming. "Let me guess. No records."

"That's right. No military service records we can access. As a matter of fact, no such woman exists in Russian public records. She's a ghost. However, I pulled in a couple of favors. In Israel, a woman matching her description is wanted for questioning in the disappearance of a rather highly placed MOSSAD director. Interestingly enough, a woman matching her description is also wanted for questioning by Interpol for the deaths of several businessman and diplomats in the Ukraine. The Ukrainian Security Service doesn't know who she is, either, but they have a death warrant out on her."

There was only one explanation for beautiful Russian

Military Intelligence agents who didn't exist yet left an international trail of the dead and disappeared. She fell under the category of "in case of uncomfortable political emergency, break glass."

Yuliya Tymosh was an assassin.

The Russians were angry and wanted their weapons back.

"I'll try to stay on her good side."

"Oh, and how are you going to do that? She probably has orders to kill you the moment you cease being useful."

Kurtzman was undoubtedly right, but at the moment Bolan needed the Russians as much as they needed him. "I don't know." He shrugged. "She likes stout."

"I see. Beer versus the assassin's bullet."

"It's a start," Bolan said. "But the real question is, how did Lord Ian Parkhurst come up with the weapons?"

"We've been breaking into every business file we can involving Lord Ian's financial operations. They're extensive, and as you know he is one of the richer men in England. However, our best bet is that a construction firm he has an interest in was involved in building the Channel, particularly some of the early exploration, survey and feasibility studies. Assuming someone gave Lord Ian the locations, he would have had the financial and technical wherewithal at his disposal to extract the weapons."

"I'll buy it. So now the question is why?"

"We can find two things. One, Lord Parkhurst made a lot of his money in the import-export business. He was doing some fair business with Iran."

"Really."

"Well, the U.S. has slapped a lot of trade embargoes on Iran, but the rest of Europe, including the U.K., is still engaged in thriving trade with them, and not just in rugs. Iran exports oil, agricultural products, iron and steel."

They also exported terror and were currently dedicated to the destruction of Israel. "Refresh my memory, Bear. What kind of subs is the Iranian navy sailing these days?"

Kurtzman clicked a few keys on his end. "They currently have three ex-Russian Kilo-class submarines. They're reported as having serious operational difficulties, but it's rumored the Chinese are helping the Iranians with spare parts and upgrades."

"What kind of armament?"

"Six tubes for Russian standard 21-inch torpedoes."

"Are the warheads compatible with 21-inch torpedoes?"

Kurtzman saw where this was going. "It is believed they were specifically designed for interchangeability with standard torpedoes. For example, a Kilo only carries eighteen torpedoes in her magazine. It makes a lot more sense to hold the warheads separately in store and then swap them in on a mission-by-mission basis rather than having part of your magazine useless with dedicated nukes you may never use."

"Where are the Iranian subs now?"

"As far as I know, all three are with the Fleet Maintenance Unit at Bandar-e Abbas receiving those upgrades I was talking about. If any of them had moved, U.S. Intelligence would know about it."

"Bear, the Iranians would give their left testicle to get their hands on those tactical nuclear weapons. There's an angle here."

Aaron Kurtzman had to agree. The Iranian government was in a race to develop its own homegrown nuclear arsenal. Seventies vintage Russian tactical nuclear weapons wouldn't help them much in developing their strategic nuclear ambitions, but they could be very useful in their political strategy. Their subs were old, but diesel-electric subs were quiet and famous for their ability to lurk undetected in shallow coastal waters. Armed with nuclear torpedoes, their fleet would be in a prime position to threaten the Persian Gulf and the fleets of international oil tankers that sailed out of it. Such weapons would also be a very ugly threat to Israel's major coastal cities like Tel Aviv and Haifa, and capable of wiping out her small navy in a matter of seconds.

Bolan was right. The big men currently running Tehran would love to get their hands on the weapons. Just the threat they posed, alone, would be an immense bargaining chip.

Bolan broke in on Kurtzman's ruminations. "We still don't have a why. Why would a lord of the realm want to give nukes to a state that sponsors terrorists and is an avowed enemy of his country?"

"Well, he always was on the radical left of the Labour Party."

"This goes beyond party politics. Something pushed him over the edge. Give me something to work with."

Kurtzman's face looked uncomfortable across the link. "Well, Lord Ian never married or had children."

Bolan shook his head. "I don't believe a winner of the Victoria Cross is going to betray crown and country over his sexual preference."

"It goes a little deeper than that."

"Better explain yourself, Bear."

Kurtzman hit a few keys and brought up a cover of *The Times of London*. The headline was five years old, and read, Scandal!

Bolan scanned the article. "Lord Ian was a member of a gentleman's club?"

"One hell of a lot more than a gentleman's club. It was a highly exclusive—" Kurtzman searched for a proper word "—after-hours society."

Bolan vaguely remembered the scandal. He scrolled

through the file. Every British rag from the respectable to the reprehensible had published multiple stories on it. It was comparable to the Hollywood Madam scandal in Los Angeles. Only rather than beautiful girls, the London Pleasure Dome had catered to a clientele whose tastes were widely varied. Royalty, lawmakers, sports figures and rock stars had all been implicated.

"Lord Ian was involved?"

"It was widely rumored. But here's where it might be relevant." Kurtzman shot Bolan another file.

Two police photos appeared on the screen. One was a lushly beautiful, dark-haired, dark-eyed young woman. The other was a disturbingly handsome young man with almost the exact same features. They both smiled into the police camera with the jaded condescension of Siamese cats.

"Fereydoon and Khatereh Nekounam."

"That's right. A brother and sister act out of Iran. Feyd and Kiki, as they were known, rose up from London club scene glitterati to social entrepreneurs. They ran a place called the Pleasure Dome. They actually built it up inside one of the old London clubhouses. Their philosophy was anything the client wanted at any time. Rumor was they stopped short of animals and small children, but anything else was fair game."

"So they ran a bordello."

"No, that's how they escaped prosecution. They threw parties. Money exchanged hands weeks in advance or well afterward and was strictly an offshore proposition, and if you didn't know how to get an invitation then you weren't invited. Rumor is Lord Ian spent a lot of time there. Unsubstantiated rumor is that Feyd and his sister spent more than a few holidays separately and in tandem at Lord Ian's castle."

"What happened to them?"

"They have a mansion in Wales and are still throwing parties. They avoided any kind of prosecution, but they got smart. They got classier. They lost their clubbing attitude and ditched the rock stars, athletes and wannabes. Now they cater exclusively to politicians, foreign diplomats, barristers, the filthy, landed rich. People with reputations to protect and the power to protect their investment in their personal…pro-clivities."

Bolan smiled.

Kurtzman raised a wary eyebrow. "What?"

"Bear?"

"What?"

"I need to get into one of those parties."

"And how are you going to do that?"

Bolan grinned. "Well, they cater exclusively to the filthy, landed bourgeois."

"And?"

"We'll just put out the word that Lord William Glen-Patrick wants to party."

"And what am I supposed to do on my end?" Kurtzman queried.

"You can find me a sub."

"You want a submarine?"

"No, I want you to find the sub that's transporting the weapons."

"You think it's a sub?"

Bolan's instincts said yes. "Boats and planes are risky. They have to put in to ports, pass inspections. If you're going to transport nuclear weapons from London to Iran, you want them all to arrive safe and at the same time. A sub is your best bet."

"Striker, the Iranian sub fleet is in port for refits. Who the hell else would involve one of their subs?"

"That's the question, Bear. Find me a sub."

"While you…?"

"Me? I'm going to a sex party."

CHAPTER TWELVE

Cardiff, Wales

"So, you take me to sex party." Yuliya Tymosh shook her head at Bolan in bemused disgust.

Lord William steered his Rolls-Royce at breakneck speed through the Welsh hillside. "No, my dear. I'm taking you to a sex club. The Yank's just along for moral support."

Tymosh snuggled into Lord William. "Better." She turned her head to look back at Bolan over the seat. "I am still not sure how sex party is relevant."

"Rumor is Lord Ian was very involved with these two."

Tymosh wrinkled her nose. "Yes, Nekounam siblings. I received file you sent. I am still not sure. I cross-reference with GRU files. For long time, it is believed Lord Ian was homosexual or bisexual. Cold war KGB tried blackmailing him with handsome boys on several occasions. He was clever and rebuffed seductions. KGB approach him anyway and threaten him. Lord Ian is quoted in KGB file as saying, 'Do your worst.'"

Bolan considered the old man in the burning library,

beaten half to death with rubber buckshot, who had resolutely pressed a revolver beneath his chin and pulled the trigger. "I don't think it was blackmail. Right before he blew his head off he had that true-believer look in his eyes."

The Russian's eyes narrowed. "You think he was converted to cause?"

"It's not that hard to imagine. An old man falls in love with a beautiful woman, or a beautiful young man, or both. They cater to his whims, make him feel young again and important. They whisper in his ear and over time give him a cause to believe in, one that jibes with his own political leanings. At a certain point, he crosses the line and no longer cares. He has something new in his life, he's invigorated, reenergized. He feels like he's doing something in his last years that makes a difference, and he's loved, supported and admired. It's a fairly straightforward seduction."

Lord William sighed in rueful agreement. "There's no fool like an old fool."

Bolan looked deep into Tymosh's brown eyes. "You could do it."

"Standing on head. I agree with your logic. What is state of security?"

"Unknown. It's a members-only club. We have to assume that alcohol and drugs are involved, so they must keep a few big men around to take control of any situation that gets out of hand. Probably not up to Lunk's or Ruslan's standard, but I'd bet on at least two if not four men on security."

"Here we are." Lord William pulled onto a circular drive in front of a Victorian mansion. There were about a dozen other vehicles, mostly high-end sports cars and sedans, as well as half a dozen limousines. Lord William pulled out his cell phone and put it on walkie-talkie mode. "Thappy, old man. How you doing back there?"

Thapa Pun was curled up in the trunk of the Silver Shadow with one of the Russian AS rifles and a knapsack of other assorted weapons. "A-ok, Colonel."

"Jolly good." Lord William popped the lock on the trunk. "Well, let's join the party."

The three of them stepped out into the night. Bolan wore an impeccably tailored Saville Row pinstripe suit. Lord William wore his casual tweed. Yuliya Tymosh was nothing short of stunning in a black cocktail dress, a sable stole and pearls. Bolan surveyed the mansion. Tall hedges surrounded it on all sides except the front. All of the many windows were shuttered, but tastefully placed outdoor globe lamps shed a warm and homey glow. They walked up the steps and Bolan knocked on the door. It opened at once and was immediately filled by a massive man in a suit wearing a turban. He bowed graciously and spoke with a Turkish accent. "Your presence honors us, my lord."

"Not at all, my good man. Not at all."

The Turk nodded at Tymosh but put up a hand like a catcher's mitt before Bolan as he started to walk in. "You will not require a bodyguard here, my lord. We shall attend to your safety in all things."

Lord William arranged a pained look on his face. "He's not just my bodyguard, he is my—" he looked away, unable to meet the big Turk's gaze "—assistant. My personal assistant, in all things."

The Turk nodded. It was clear that having worked there for some time, very few things could faze him. "I will require his firearm. None is allowed here."

Bolan opened his jacket and removed his snub-nosed 9 mm Centennial revolver by the butt. The Turk slipped the pistol in his pocket and gave Bolan a proficient pat-down.

"Do you wish masks?"

Lord William shook his head. "I think not, thank you."

The Turk stepped back and bowed them in.

Kurtzman's recon had been right. The Nekounam twins had become a strictly class act. There was no dance floor, blaring music, slave boys wrapped in rubber or naked women walking their pet cheetahs. Smooth jazz played at almost a subliminal level, and several dozen people sat on couches or stood by the fireplace at the long bar, which was manned by another large individual of Middle Eastern persuasion. It looked more like the cocktail hour before a very swanky dinner party rather than an orgy. The only nod to the purpose of the place was that a few of the men and women scattered around the room wore masks to hide their identity, though most did not.

A man detached himself from the cluster of people around the fireplace and walked toward them with liquid ease. In the police photo, his dark hair had been in a ponytail. Now, it fell around his face to his shoulders. He was classically handsome with an aquiline nose and strong chin. He wore a black silk suit with no shirt beneath to show the thin line separating his pectoral muscles. The arch of his eyebrows gave Tymosh's a run for their money. He looked like a satanic Yoga instructor.

"Lord William." Fereydoon Nekounam's accent told Bolan that English was neither his first nor second language. "Such a dashing adventurer, such a star in the firmament of Albion. I cannot believe it has taken you so long to come unto us."

"Better late than never, old bean. Mr. Nekounam, is it? Forgive my pronunciation."

"Call me Feyd. My friends do, and I do hope you and I shall become friends. Allow me to introduce my sister, Khatereh."

Khatereh Nekounam seemed to float across the room like some dark angel and took Lord William's hand. "My lord." She was luminous in black silk. But while Feyd gave off a faint aura of jaded evil, his sister gave off a strange air of innocence. Bolan suspected both of them had spent a great deal of time cultivating their acts.

One couldn't have asked for two better ringmasters of depravity.

"Please, call me Kiki."

Lord William smiled gallantly. "I prefer Khatereh. It's a lovely name. Whatever does it mean? I must know."

Khatereh seemed to glow at Lord William from some beautiful interior lamp meant only for him. "It means *memory*." She let that hang between them with a thousand untold secrets that a man would give his soul to know. Bolan kept the smile off his face. Kiki was good. He also reminded himself that the two were master manipulators. They might not be Special Forces operatives, but they would be consummately skilled at reading people.

Lord William remembered his manners. "Oh, and this is my dear friend, Julia, and my personal assistant, Mr. Striker."

"Julia." Feyd favored them both with a smile. "And Striker. Such a bold, American name."

"And your name, Mr. Nekounam?"

Nekounam's dark eyes drank in Bolan's frame. "The name comes from the *Shahnameh,* the Persian Epic of Kings. Fereydoon did battle with the demon Zahak and imprisoned him forever in Mount Damavand."

Bolan smiled. "A demon slayer."

"Yes." Fereydoon smiled back and extended a languid hand about him. "But the only demon I seek to slay is desire."

"By satisfying it utterly."

Feyd gave Bolan a glow of his own. "I believe you and I understand each other."

Lord William looked back and forth between them. "Good, jolly good." Lord William suddenly looked down and flushed. "I mean—"

Feyd captured Lord William's eyes and held them. "You would like Mr. Striker and I to be friends?"

Lord William stared at Feyd like a moth into a flame. "Yes, I should like that. I should like that very much. I would like us *all* to be…such very good friends."

Lord William, Bolan thought, could have had a career in the theater.

The spider stared at the fly with immense satisfaction. "My sister and I must act the gracious hosts, at least for a while longer, but come, avail yourself of the small pleasures of our parlor, and soon you shall be our lord in all things."

Lord William flushed bright red. "Oh, for heaven's sake. Call me Bill."

"Bill." Feyd let the word and his smile linger on his lips as he and Khatereh turned away toward their other guests.

Tymosh gestured to a servant and ordered drinks for them. The man returned almost instantly with a whiskey for Lord William and a pint of bitters for Bolan. Tymosh accepted a champagne flute full of Czech absinthe and tossed off a third of it without blinking. "Woman is in control but pretends otherwise." She took another long slug of absinthe and smiled at Bolan. "She is suspicious of you."

Bolan trusted Tymosh's intuition. He reached into his pocket and pressed a preset on his cell phone without taking it out of his pocket, sending Pun the signal to start lurking. Bolan settled in to wait. They spent a happy hour by the fire sipping their drinks, exchanging nonclassified anecdotes from three very different lives and fending off the occasional perverted advance from their fellow partygoers.

Tymosh leaned away from a French businessman and shook her head as she took Lord William's arm. The Frenchman sighed sadly and walked back to the bar. Lord William watched him go. "What did he want?"

"All he say was…schnauzer." The Russian wrinkled her nose. "Is this code word or request?"

Bolan shrugged. "I don't know, and I don't want to know."

Feyd Nekounam came gliding across the room and his manicured hand alighted on Lord William's shoulder. "Bill, my sister has arranged an intimate little party to get acquainted with one another. Will you and your companions join us?"

William beamed with pleasure. "Why, it's more than I dared hoped for. We would be delighted."

Feyd slid his arm into William's and led the man toward the stairs. Lord William followed with a dazed "take my hand, I'm a stranger in paradise" look on his face. Feyd smiled like a shepherd taking the lamb to the slaughter.

Tymosh leaned into Bolan's ear. "I do not trust him. He is up to no good."

Bolan didn't doubt it.

They followed Feyd and Lord William upstairs, and Bolan punched the 2 key and pound symbol on his cell phone. Pun would know they were on the second floor and to begin his infiltration. They entered a room set up like a tale from *1001 Arabian Nights*. Swathes of scarlet fabric fell from a central point in the ceiling, giving the room the feeling of a Moroccan tent. Incense burned in braziers and stylized erotic tapestries hung from the walls. Numerous low couches were set around a central table laden with fruit and wines, and a hookah water pipe burned with the unmistakable sweet smell of marijuana. Bolan noted the couches were designed so that they could all be pushed together to form a massive round bed.

Tymosh glanced around, clearly wondering behind which door the plastic tarp, the carbonated hot oil and the schnauzers were lurking. Bolan kept his eyes appreciatively on Kharateh Nekounam's lush beauty, but his initial survey and his instincts told him all he needed to know.

They were not alone in the room.

Khatereh awaited them reclining in Roman splendor and beckoned them enter and take their ease. Lord William sighed happily as he looked around the room.

Feyd went and took a seat beside his sister, and Bolan heard the door lock behind them. Lord William pretended not to notice, and he gestured for Bolan and Tymosh to sit with him. Khatereh poured them wine, while Lord William continued to beam. "Thank you for making such…special arrangements on such short notice."

"Oh, my lord, you intrigue us." Feyd smiled. "For example, in the last hour I have learned your home on Guernsey was attacked and burned to the ground."

"Bad bit of luck, that," Lord William conceded.

"I also learned that your flat in London was the site of a gunfight." The limpid dark eyes became suddenly piercing. "Then there was the very unfortunate fate of Lord Ian Parkhurst."

"Yes, very sad," Lord William agreed. "I hear he was quite friendly with the two of you."

"Yes, he was quite toothsome, despite his decrepitude. I can forgive a few wrinkles for a man who is impassioned." Feyd's smile was reptilian. "The three of us had such glorious days and nights in his castle."

"Yes, I'm sure the three of you wiled away many a happy

hour unscrewing nuclear warheads from torpedoes." Lord William smiled. "Sorry I burned the place down, old man. Hope you'll forgive me."

Feyd's smile died on his face.

"Indeed, I brought my good friend Mr. Striker here to speak with you about this whole torpedo-screwing-and-unscrewing business, specifically."

Bolan dropped the friendly banter. "Feyd, when was the last time you saw the warheads?"

Khatereh clapped her hands. Men began appearing from behind the tapestries. Bolan recognized the doorman and the bartender, and knew that there were hidden passageways throughout the old Victorian building. It seemed the Nekounam siblings had relieved the nations of the Middle East of their super-heavyweight Greco-Roman wrestlers and jammed them into silk suits and turbans. Feyd slid his hand beneath a cushion and produced Bolan's confiscated 9 mm revolver.

Feyd gestured at the doorman and the bartender. "Of course, you have met Attaturk and Orhan. You haven't yet had the pleasure of Rasoul, Yahya, Nagi and Nur's company, but that shall be remedied. What shall happen now is the three of you become their very intimate friends. I have been advised by reliable sources that your recent actions bespeak that you are currently running renegade, as they say. The governments of the United States and the United Kingdom are intensely interested in anything that you might learn, but you are operating outside the law, without sanction, and you are most likely considered expendable and deniable."

He turned to Tymosh. "I am sure you are very active in Russian Intelligence of one stripe or another, but, regardless, your country's assets in Wales must be thin, to say the least. I advise all of you to start speaking now. I am most motivated to punish you for your insolence in coming here, but any compliance you display may mitigate the horror of your ultimate demise."

Bolan rose. The cat was out of the bag and playtime was over. "Feyd?"

"Yes, Mr. Striker?"

"Screw you."

Feyd blanched.

The Executioner yanked at the shoulder of his suit and the sleeves of his jacket and shirt came away. The three throwing knives taped to his inner forearm ripped away into his hand. Bolan had fully expected to be disarmed at the door. He had expected a metal detector in the frame of the doorway. The three knives were made of titanium, which was a nonferrous metal. They would beat an airport walk-through metal detector but not a dedicated security wand. Bolan had been betting that the Nekounams would not subject their VIP guests to such an indignity, and he had been right. The sensor in the door frame had detected his pistol, and it had been confiscated. Bolan had been patted down, but the doorman had been looking for concealed firearms in the usual places rather than flat leaves of sharp titanium along the long bones of Bolan's body.

Bolan pivoted and threw his first knife as Attaturk charged him.

Titanium was lighter than steel, and getting a throwing knife to punch through a human rib cage was problematic under even the most ideal circumstances. Humans also had the tendency to put up their arms and jerk their heads aside when something was flung at their face.

Bolan threw hard, threw overhand and released low.

The parkerized black titanium blade hit Attaturk an inch below his belt buckle, and all seven inches disappeared into his bladder. The big Turk groaned horribly and fell clutching his groin. Feyd shoved Bolan's pistol out at arm's length and pointed it at the Executioner's face.

The pistol clicked three times in his hand.

Bolan had known he would be disarmed at the door, and there was no way he would give the enemy a weapon that could be used against him. Feyd pulled the trigger twice more on prepierced primers, but just because the gun was loaded with duds didn't mean Feyd didn't have a weapon of his own somewhere near to hand. Bolan turned and flung his second knife. Feyd screamed as the blade sank into his bicep. The revolver fell from his nerveless fingers, and he fell on top of his sister.

Throwing a knife was a circus trick and no soldier's best bet on the battlefield. But as a surprise tactic in the boudoir, Bolan had succeeded beyond wildest expectations. Bolan took his third knife into his hand. On the few occasions he had found the need to carry a throwing knife, he had insisted that rather than being just a dart it have a sharp, serviceable edge on one side. The knife was coated in nonreflective black finish, but one thin edge gleamed like quicksilver. The Executioner dropped to one knee and put his thumb on the blade as Rasoul came for him with a stun-gun sparking in his hand.

Rasoul gasped as the titanium whispered underneath his kneecap and severed his patellar tendon from one side of his tibia to the other. The big Iranian's right leg turned to rubber beneath him, and he fell prone across the couch. The bloody leaf of metal spun in Bolan's hand into an ice-pick grip. Rasoul screamed in agony as Bolan plunged a good four inches into his right kidney.

Yahya closed on Tymosh. Bolan yanked his blade free and flipped the weapon around in his fingers for the throw.

The Russian snatched the strand of pearls from over her head and snapped it against the center table. The ceramic fakes cracked apart like clay to reveal the tensile steel wire beneath. Yahya's hands closed around the agent's throat. The necklace fastened with an oversize loop and toggle. Tymosh ignored Yahya's crushing hands and crossed her own as she dropped the hoop of wire behind his head with practiced ease. She yanked her hands in opposite directions, and the tungsten wire sank through Yahya's carotid nerves and arteries, only stopping when it reached his spine.

Bolan turned as the bartender bore down on Lord William. The baron skipped back a step and flicked three fast jabs into the Turk's chin and then threw a right cross to the jaw with everything he had behind it. The Turk ate all four blows without blinking and sent his adversary hurtling backward over the couches with a massive fist to the chest. Orhan turned with a cruel grin on his face only to swallow Bolan's blade as it hissed through the air and crunched through the cartilage of his trachea.

Nagi charged at Tymosh like a bull, hands extended to protect his neck from the Russian's garrote. The woman snapped the garrote taut between her hands and rammed it into Nagi's clawing hand. The razor wire sheared through the webbing between Nagi's middle and index fingers and stopped on the bones at the base of his palm. He stopped short and screamed at the state of his filleted hand. Tymosh crossed her hands again and looped the wire around Nagi's wrist. She heaved backward and the Iranian's hand noosed off in a spray of crimson.

Nagi stared at his stump in shock while the Russian snapped her foot up between his legs and dropped him to the floor.

A pistol crack froze everyone place.

"Enough." The smoking blue steel of a Turkish 9 mm Zigana pistol seemed huge in Khatereh's hands but it did not waver as she pointed it at Tymosh. "Cease, or I will shoot the bitch in the stomach."

Bolan was out of knives.

Feyd got to his knees on the couch and moaned as he pulled the throwing knife from his flesh. He pointed it at Bolan while his face purpled with rage. "Oh, how you shall suffer! I will—"

"Empty your pockets," Khatereh interrupted. "Now."

Tymosh dropped her killing wire. Bolan very slowly reached into his pocket and took out his cell phone. His thumb depressed the star key before he dropped it. Khatereh jerked her head at Lord William where he lay sprawled. "Nur, search him and—"

Yellow fire hissed around the doorknob and the door imploded under a boot. Five feet of Gurkha in grease paint and black raid gear dived into the room and rolled up into a rifleman's crouch. He instantly tracked his VS assault rifle toward the man bending over Lord William, and the weapon hissed and clicked. Nuri fell, and the little Gurkha instantly swung his weapon onto Khatereh.

Bolan almost shouted that they needed her, but Khatereh had a gun and Pun was already shooting. The Gurkha's burst dropped Khatereh, shattered, to the couch. Feyd screamed as he was sprayed with his sister's blood. Smoke oozed from the black tube of Pun's suppressor as he pointed it at Feyd. "Drop the knife."

Feyd shook. His knuckles went white around the throwing knife as his pupils dialed down to pinpricks of insane rage. Feyd was losing it. His dark eyes slid to the bloodstained pistol lying next to his sister.

Bolan shook his head. "Don't do it."

"Drop the knife," Pun repeated.

Feyd dropped the knife. His hand shot for the pistol. His head jerked up as Lord William suddenly stood.

"Colonel!" Pun snarled. "Down! Down!"

Bolan charged.

Feyd raised the gun, then his nose broke beneath Lord William's left jab. His jaw unhinged under a wicked right hook. The Iranian collapsed in a bloody heap. Lord William bent forward and put his hands on his knees to try to catch his breath.

"Thappy...good lad. Right on time." Tymosh went to give Lord William an arm to steady him. Bolan looked into Khatereh's blown pupils. They didn't call them Gurkha riflemen for nothing. Thapa had printed a neat 5-round burst over Khatereh's heart you could fit inside a teacup.

Lord William stood and looked at the blade in bartender's throat and then back at Bolan guiltily. The baron knew that Khatereh would never have reached her pistol if Bolan hadn't expended his third knife to save him. "Sorry about that, Matt. Didn't get my man. I'm afraid that Orhan fellow was—" Lord William took a ragged breath and put a hand to his chest "—a bit out of my weight class."

"No worries. Pun, how did you get in?"

A happy grin split the tapestry of green, gray and black camouflage paint. "Scaled the wall and jimmied the window."

"Nice work." It was, but it wouldn't serve their purpose now. They needed to extract Feyd Nekounam and get out without alarming the guests. The room was soundproofed as was the hallway, and the only sound the people downstairs might have heard was Pun's cutting charge. Flexible charge didn't sound like a gun or an explosion, but someone might get curious. Bolan walked to the tapestry Attaturk had appeared from behind and ripped it down. There was nothing but Victorian paneling behind it. Bolan's foot crashed through the panel to reveal the narrow passage concealed behind.

"Pun, go down the way you came and start the car. Yuliya, help me with Feyd. Bill, you're on point."

Lord William squared his shoulders with effort and accepted the UDAR that Pun pressed into his hand. "Right. Let's bid this place our fond farewell."

Tymosh's eyes burned through Lord William's back like an X-ray as he took point in the concealed passage. "He is not well."

"No." Bolan took up one of his knives and slung one of Feyd's arms around his shoulder. Lord William held his pistol low and level as he found the secret stair, but his hand shook and he needed to put one hand on the wall to keep himself from falling over. "He's not."

CHAPTER THIRTEEN

"I have your sub." Kurtzman looked pleased with himself.

Bolan sank back wearily into his chair. "That was fast."

"Well, there were only a limited number of possibilities. You needed a sub to transport nuclear weapons all the way from England to Iran. That ruled out any private submersible. So it came down to a government willing to use one of its submarines to give the Iranians nukes or a sub skipper gone renegade. That ruled out European or South American nations and a quick look at their captains' lists ruled out any renegades. Neither Russia nor China particularly want to see Iran go nuclear, so again it comes down to renegade captains. Both China and Russia are very wary about that kind of thing. Only navy men who have earned the highest levels of trust are inducted into the submarine fleet. Same with India. Pakistan was a possibility, but again, even though they're a Muslim nation, the armed forces are rigidly secular. One of their captains stealing a sub is unlikely, and their government would be likely to enlist our help in tracking it down."

"And?" Bolan pressed.

"With the Iranian fleet in port, that pretty much left everyone's favorite culprit and usual suspect."

"North Korea." Bolan could read the smugness behind the political lecture. "But you're not buying it."

"I'm keeping them as Culprit B."

"So who's Culprit A?"

"Egypt."

Bolan mulled that one over. "I find it hard to believe that the Egyptians would buy into this, Bear."

"Oh, not knowingly, certainly, and certainly not willingly. But how about a ghost?"

"A ghost."

Kurtzman clicked keys and a window opened on Bolan's screen to reveal a news article. It read that the Egyptian Romeo-class submarine *Halqa* had fired a distress buoy and was believed to have sunk with all hands while on maneuvers in the Gulf of Aden. The estimated depth of the wreck was four thousand meters. Far below the crush depth of the aged Russian-built submarine. A slow smile spread across the Executioner's face. No rescue had been attempted and no salvage effort was expected anytime in the future.

"You buying the story?"

"Well, it's certainly possible, if not downright to be expected. The Russian- and Chinese-built Romeo class is just about the oldest sub still afloat, and throughout their service their safety record has been less than stellar. Most nations scrapped their Romeos a long time ago, and those that are still afloat generally hug the coast for dear life. There are trenches in the Gulf of Aden that dip below five thousand meters. It's a recipe for disaster."

"Or a sub-jacking." The story had been only a small blip in the news. It wasn't like a Russian sub going down with its nuclear engine polluting the ocean and a cargo of thermonuclear missiles for the taking. The Romeo was an aged, obsolete, shallow-water submarine that only carried torpedoes. It was a tragedy for the Egyptian navy, but the world at large hadn't even blinked.

However, it was a tailor-made scenario for the nuclear crisis at hand.

"Tell me about the captain."

Kurtzman pulled up another window. A man with a shaved head and a mustache stared starch-stiff into the camera in full naval dress uniform. "Captain Wael Goma. The most interesting thing about him is that he's Shia Muslim."

That gave Bolan pause. "The Shia minority in Egypt is pretty damn small."

"That's right, but in almost all Arabic nations the Shia minorities tend to be highly educated and generally successful in business. Goma passed through the Egyptian naval academy with flying colors, and his family holds significant interest in several shipping companies."

Bolan hit a key on his laptop and brought up a geopolitical map of the planet. His eyes slid along the African coast. "So from point anywhere in England to Iran, hugging the coastlines of Africa, that's what? Seventeen or eighteen thousand miles?"

"Approximately, depending on your exact route."

"What's the cruising speed of a Romeo, assuming it's in decent shape?"

"Twelve knots surfaced, maybe eight to ten submerged, but this is a very old sub. It's a long cruise and he wants to be quiet, so I'd halve that. He's going to have to come to snorkeling depth at regular intervals to recharge his batteries, but catching him at that would be pure dumb luck. Goma's Achilles' heel is fuel. The *Halqa* is a medium-range vessel. Under ideal conditions, she has a range of seven thousand nautical miles if she maintains her ideal speed of five knots. But then again, the *Halqa*'s not as young or efficient as she used to be. He'll also be hugging the coast to be less detectable, which submits the sub to tidal action and makes travel much less efficient. I predict Goma will have to refuel at least twice, possibly three times. Another thing to think about is this. Along most of Africa, he has no worries from the local navies, but when he hits the cape he's in the cruising ground of the South African navy. They have a tidy little fleet of modern vessels and five subs of their own. Even if they're not on alert, he still has to sneak past their regular patrols. Those kind of hide-and-seek games can take time and take him off his regular course. He'll want to be topped off before he gets there."

Kurtzman was right. There was a window of opportunity here. Bolan stared long and hard at the west coast of Africa. "A strange sub pulling into port is newsworthy anywhere in the world. They're going to need a designated refueling area under friendly control, with several more as backup. We need to plot Goma's course. Project me a timeline from the supposed sinking of the *Halqa,* and give me a round-trip estimate. Then I need to you tie in any connection with Lord Ian's business interests in Africa, as well as Goma family shipping, as well as anyone who's even laid eyes on a member of the Nekounam family. Every CIA and MI-6 agent along the African coast needs to have his or her eyes peeled, and frankly I'd be tempted to involve French Intelligence. They still have a lot of assets in West Africa and this affects them directly."

"You don't think I'm already on that?" Kurtzman brought his hands to his chest in false pain.

"Another thing, this hunt has to be low profile."

Kurtzman's brow furrowed. "Mack, once the President sees my report he's going to want to send in the entire Atlantic Fleet, which, by the way, has the most sophisticated sub location and tracking ships and planes in the world."

"I know, but Captain Goma is in a Russian Romeo with twenty-one-inch torpedo tubes. Six in the bow and two in the stern. If he's smart, and you said he was the Egyptian navy's best and brightest, he'll have gone hot and swapped eight of the nukes onto his ready load."

"And he won't be afraid to use them."

"No, and like you told me in your last lecture, diesel electrics are slow and sneaky. Just because the U.S. Navy didn't find nuclear torpedoes an efficient option doesn't mean that given the right circumstances they don't work. If Goma can get close enough, a full spread from his bow tubes would vaporize the USS *Ronald Reagan* and probably take part of the Carrier Support Group, as well."

"Yes, but once he floods his tubes and fires, we have him. He'll get a spread of torpedoes and depth charges from every ship, plane and sub within range. Goma has to know that if he fires, he's dead."

"That's right, but if he's doing this because he's a fanatic, then destroying a major U.S. naval surface combatant would be a victory worth martyrdom."

The computer expert had to admit that Bolan was right. "And if he's doing it for money?"

"Then he won't want to die in an exchange of fire with the Atlantic Fleet, but he still has options."

"Like what?"

"Nuclear blackmail." Bolan glanced along the political map on his screen. "He's going to be creeping along the coastline of Africa. Many African nations along the coast really have only one major city. It's their capital, and it's always on the water. It's their one political, industrial and import-export center. The fire and fallout wouldn't be as bad as Hiroshima or Nagasaki, but a sixty-kiloton spread fired into the harbors of say, Dakar, Freetown or Accra would be a blow that would kill tens of thousands and take decades to recover from. Politically, half the nations in Africa have active or simmering revolutions going on. With their nation's capital suddenly devastated, any number of them would instantly plunge into civil war."

Kurtzman stared at his own map and knew Bolan was right. Captain Goma had cards to play. "Mack, we don't have a lot of satellites tasked to watch the west or east African coastlines. U.S. Intelligence has always been centered around the north and the northeast facing Israel and the Middle East. It will be a miracle if we manage to spot the *Halqa* when she surfaces."

"I know."

"So you want me to get Hal to tell the President that and then tell him not to send in the Atlantic Fleet?"

"Yeah."

"And Hal is going to tell the President that you're going to find this nuclear armed sub creeping below the surface through…"

"Footwork."

"You're going to find a submarine through footwork."

"Yeah."

Kurtzman picked up his phone and dialed Hal Brognola's number. "This is going to be good."

"No," Bolan said wearily. "Convincing the Russians, now that's going to be good."

Cardiff Castle

"WE WANT SOUTH AFRICAN." Yuliya Tymosh had come to play hardball. "We want Nekounam woman."

So had Bolan. "You can't have them."

Bolan, Tymosh and Shust stood to one side on the greens of the ancient Norman castle as tourists piled out of buses. "United States has been rumored in past to have given prisoners to third party to extract information," Tymosh suggested. "This can easily be arranged now."

"That may have happened in the past, but that wasn't me."

A response clearly came to Tymosh's mind, but she looked into Bolan's eyes and thought better of it. She went back to bargaining. "We have deal."

"We have nothing. I gave you back your bomb, and we exchanged information. Then we took down the Nekounams." Shust was with her, but Bolan kept his eyes on Tymosh. She was clearly the more dangerous of the pair. "And I said you need to give me a hell of a lot more. I don't think you have anything more. You're tapped out, and I owe you nothing."

The Russian's eyes flashed.

Bolan smiled suddenly. "But…"

The Russians blinked in unison.

Bolan pulled a file out of his jacket. "I'll give you this."

The Russian assassin took the file and flipped it open contemptuously. Her eyes widened as she quickly scanned the contents. It was bare bones, only three pages, but it was enough. Kurtzman had boiled down the hypothesis he and Bolan had come up with, and the Pentagon's best Russian translator had been up late tidying it up. It gave the basic information on the supposed sinking of the *Halqa* and Captain Goma's résumé. The second page was a map of Africa with likely surfacing points along the coast that Kurtzman had come up with as well as a possible timeline based on the date of the sub's sinking and what they knew about Romeo-class submarines. The third page was a terse bulleted list of notes, including recommendations against involving wide naval action and the possible results.

Tymosh snapped the file shut and handed it to Shust. She regarded Bolan with renewed respect. "Interesting."

Shust read the file at glacial pace. Second by second, his brows drew down and then knitted together until they formed a bunched mass of radiating lines and scar tissue. He handed the file back to Tymosh, and the former Russian naval marine grunted at Bolan grudgingly. "I agree with American assessment. Fleet-wide action against Goma would be perilous. Subtlety and human intelligence are best option." Shust tapped the file into one callused paw. "Give me South African and Nekounam woman. I will press them."

"No."

Shust stared at Bolan as if the American before him was some dangerous breed of animal he had never seen before and whose behaviors he didn't understand. "Yet you will not press them?"

"I'm going to give them to MI-5."

"Give to English?" Shust spat on the ground between them. "Foolish."

Bolan shrugged. "You in or out?"

Shust scowled. "In…or out?"

"Human intelligence, subtlety and footwork. From Morocco to Ethiopia. I have resources you don't. You have resources the U.S. and U.K. don't have access to. We need to work together."

Tymosh flipped through the file again. "American goal remains same? Return warheads to Russia?"

"Return or destroy, whichever is most expedient."

Shust grunted in approval. Bolan didn't like the look in Tymosh's brown eyes. The Russian woman sighed and snapped the file shut. "You realize I must give file to superiors."

"I knew that when I gave it to you."

"You realize GRU must pass file to highest echelons of

Russian Federation government. I cannot guarantee that Russian fleet will not descend."

"I know that." Bolan held the woman's eyes. "But we both know that we stand a better chance of working together and using human intelligence." Bolan lifted his chin at Shust in acknowledgment. "Doing it our way."

"*Da.*" Shust nodded at Tymosh. "You must make superiors understand."

"You need to make them understand fast. It's three thousand miles to Mauritania, and I've got a plane waiting on the runway at Cardiff International."

Tymosh arched an eyebrow. "Mauritania?"

There were a few more desolate, nations-only-in-name spots on the planet, but Mauritania had its hat in the ring. Other than the flood plain of the Senegal River, the vast majority of the nation's 397,000 square miles consisted of the Sahara Desert. Ethnic violence had been flaring between the original Africans and the Arab invaders for four hundred years. Vast numbers of the population were still pastoral and desert nomads. However, they did have some of the world's largest fishing grounds off their coast. "Lord Parkhurst was involved in a sustainable fishery project in the capital. Floating docks, diesel fuel, everything a submarine captain could want in a clandestine stop."

Tymosh handed the file back to Shust. "I will require several hours to alert my superiors, send file and receive confirmation for mission."

Bolan checked his watch. "You have forty-five minutes."

CHAPTER FOURTEEN

Nouakchott, Mauritania

It had been a slaughter. The bodies of the Russian team lay stripped and bloated on the beach. Crabs and gulls had their way with the mortifying flesh, but scavengers alone did not explain the gaping wounds. Bolan saw that more than a few of the dozen corpses had distinctive bruising and abrasions on the wrists and ankles and bore visible signs of severe physical torture. The bodies had been here twenty-four hours, and the local authorities had yet to bother to remove them.

Shust surveyed them bitterly. "Fools."

"FSB." Tymosh shrugged as if that explained everything. She had faxed the GRU the file and gotten on Bolan's plane. In the intervening forty-eight hours it had taken them to get to Mauritania, somehow the Russian government had scraped together a team and sent it in. Most likely, they were FSB intelligence analysts with a few embassy guards for backup. They'd been outmatched by whatever they had run into and had died in agony for their trouble.

"This requires revenge," Shust grated.

Owu sidled up. He took a leery look at the corpses and nodded. "News."

"What have you got?"

Owu was fluent in both French and Arabic, and he had spent the past hour down on the docks handing out packs of cigarettes for information.

"No one's denying anything." Owu shook his head in disgust. "People are bragging about it on the docks."

Shust's jaw muscles clenched and unclenched. "Who has done this?"

Owu leaned back slightly from the enraged Russian. "Mandé gangs."

That was a new one even for Bolan. "Who?"

"Soninke tribe. They're Mandé people from the south. Non-Moorish. After independence from the French? Many indigenous people come to Mauritania. Soninke, Haalpulaar, Wolof, Bambaras. All want a better life in a new country. Now they're in Mauritania."

"So the Mandé gangs rule the shantytowns?"

"They try." Owu shrugged. "But you want someone dead? Mandé gangs a real good bet. Violent, and on the ground floor of booming new drug trade. Soninke are big men, so many get jobs working on the docks. Plenty of opportunity for drug smuggling."

"What kind of drugs?"

"Crystal meth. Used to be only poor Yankee white trash dumb enough to do meth. Now it's the poor man's drug of choice all over Africa."

Bolan knew all about crystal meth. Heroin addicts were pathetic, cocaine fiends crazy, but at a certain point meth heads stopped being human.

"So who's doing the bragging?"

"Word is Michael Jackson Taha and his brothers did it."

"Michael Jackson Taha?"

"Yeah."

Every once in a while, Bolan had to remind himself that outside of the United States Michael Jackson was still considered a living god. Lunk gazed northward toward Wales for strength. "Oh, for Christ's sake."

Owu pursed his lips and pointed an accusing finger at the Welshman. "I'll hear none of your tabloid drama about the King of Pop, taffy. The man is a genius." Owu sighed. "A smooth criminal."

"I'll tell you what, Otto." Lunk cracked his knuckles. "You start moonwalking, and I'll smash your face in."

Owu looked like he just might.

Bolan intervened. "How are Taha and his gang armed?"

"They're African street criminals. If it's old, it's English or French. If it's new, it's Chinese or Russian. Pistols, submachine guns and AKs, mostly. An RPG or two lying about would not surprise me."

Drug gangs were the same the world over. Heavily armed but lax on security. People were afraid of them, and the corrupt local constabulary would be bought off. Their greatest fear would be drive-bys by rival gangs.

They weren't ready for a raid by professionals.

"How were the Russians taken?"

"Pretty straightforward bait and kill. Russians started poking around. Someone paid the local gangs good money to take notice of anyone poking around and give them a false lead. When they showed up? Ambush."

Bolan handed the bribe money back to Owu.

"Find me the Taha brothers."

BOLAN AND PUN SLID into the water. The ocean was sweat warm and absolutely filthy beneath the pilings. Both men were naked except for steel. Bolan swam with a Russian bayonet strapped to his leg. Pun swam with his khukri between his teeth. Taha and his gang hadn't been hard to find. After Owu's reconnaissance, Tymosh and Shust had gone to the constable's office and made a fuss and then down to the docks offering bribes and asking questions about the killings and anything suspicious happening on the floating dock a hundred yards offshore. The Mandé gang members working the docks had been only too happy to go for a double on slaughtering unsuspecting Russians and fed them a lead.

The storehouse was an ambush.

There was only one approach from the dock, and when Tymosh and Shust walked down the pier they would be funneled into a killzone. Taha and his men would have them in cross fire. Bolan suspected that the gangsters would want to have their fun with them first, particularly Tymosh, and that was to their advantage. In fact, it was part of the plan. As the Russians made their approach in civilian clothes looking unarmed and slightly lost, Lord William, Lunk and Owu would be following them thirty yards back, silently moving from shadow to shadow. Bolan and Pun were the ace in hole. Michael J. Taha just wasn't expecting an amphibious assault tonight.

They passed beneath the storehouse and Bolan could hear the murmurs of the waiting gangsters. The limp evening tide made small splashings against the supports and masked whatever noise Bolan and Pun made during their passage. They swam on another twenty yards, and Bolan stopped at a piling. The timber was wrapped in heavy coils of hemp rope to act as a bumper for docking boats. He gripped the rope with callused hands and jammed his feet into crevices between the coils. The rope was wet, but the fiber was frayed and rough and the short climb wasn't hard. Bolan emerged from the ocean slicked with oil and filmed with filth. He crouched in shadow and removed the rubber surgical tubing holding the Russian bayonet to his calf. Pun appeared beside him.

The enemy had left no one guarding the back door. That was to be expected. The majority of people, even fisherman and those who actually lived on boats out on the water, didn't know how to swim. There were no boats docked down this far and none currently out on the water. Taha thought he was safe, but he was wrong. Bolan and Pun crept down the dimly lit pier. Pun pointed ahead, but Bolan had already seen the two men. They were hunkered down beside a pile of pallets, and each one had a rifle. Both men were looking the wrong way. Their job was to cut off the quarry if they ran for the water. One put his hand on the other's shoulder and pointed. His comrade nodded and stubbed out his cigarette.

Tymosh and Shust were on approach.

Bolan and Pun separated and moved in for the kill on either side. Paper rasped and scraped beneath Pun's foot. The two men turned, but the first thing they saw was Bolan, and both gangsters took a fatal second to gape at the naked, knife-wielding white man. Pun took two running steps and sank his khukri into his man's throat. The second man brought his fingers to his mouth to whistle in warning. Bolan put his thumb on the blade of the bayonet and thrust up. The alarm died on the gangster's lips as the Russian steel slid underneath his sternum, perforating his diaphragm, deflating his lungs and invading his heart. Bolan caught the rifle before it could clatter and eased the dead man against the pallets.

Pun pulled the crushed, empty cigarette pack from the bottom of his foot with a rueful shake of his head. Other than the scrape of paper, the scuffle had been nearly soundless, and in other small ways Fortune was smiling. Bolan picked up the AK-74 rifle and his bayonet fit perfectly. Pun reluctantly slid his khukri into the pallet for later retrieval and picked up the other rifle. Bolan took point as they slid along the wall of the storehouse. They kept moving as the commotion began. Harsh laughs rang out, as well as gutter-level words spoken in French.

The ambushers had risen from their positions. There were ten of them. More than half had rifles like the ones Bolan had commandeered, and he suspected the weapons were spoils taken from the slaughtered Russian team. The most interesting thing was that Guy Diddier and Ruud Heitinga were with them. Heitinga had a line of fresh stitches from his ear to his nose where Bolan had pistol-whipped him. It was interesting that the two mercs were here in Mauritania working with gangsters, but the two men had the qualifications for the job at hand. Diddier spoke French, and according to Lord William, the South African enjoyed interrogations a little too much.

The gangsters ringed Tymosh and Shust. Michael J. Taha stood in front of them in the full regalia of his namesake. He wore a white commodore's jacket with a purple sash and a white glove on one hand. Despite the dim light on the dock, he wore wraparound sunglasses. However, he was six foot three and had been forced to cut off the sleeves of the jacket to allow the passage of a massive pair of biceps. In one hand he held a stubby AK-74 carbine. Tymosh shrank before him. Shust stood rigidly with his fists clenched as one of the men took the machine pistol from the shoulder holster under his jacket. Taha reached under Tymosh's shirt and relieved her of her snub-nosed revolver.

Tymosh cried out as Taha relieved her of her shirt and bra with a single brutal yank.

Shust lunged and was reward for his chivalry with an AK-74 barrel in the guts and a brutal butt from behind to the kidneys. The big Russian fell gasping to one knee. A butt to the side of the head dropped him, and two more gangsters began giving him a professional stomping. Taha slung his carbine. It took him several yanks, but the buttons on Tymosh's skirt popped and the garment came away. The woman tried to cover herself with her hands, but Taha slapped them away.

Diddier said something in French. The gangsters ceased booting Shust and yanked him, bleeding, to his feet. Taha grabbed Tymosh by the hair, and they began dragging the Russians toward the storehouse. Bolan and Pun stepped out of the dark.

Heitinga gasped at the sight of the dripping, naked American. Bolan shot him five times in the chest. The gangsters were caught flatfooted. Pun shot two of them before they remembered they had rifles. Others jerked and shuddered as if they were being beaten from behind, and blood blossomed from their chests as Lord William, Lunk and Owu hit them from the rear with their silenced rifles.

Shust roared like a bull and shrugged out of the grip of his captors. He kicked the legs out from one and drove his foot into his adversary's face with all of his might. Shust's heel only stopped when it hit the back of the man's skull. The other man tried to wrestle Shust back into his clutches, and it was the last mistake of his life. It took the sambo champion two heartbeats to get behind his man. It took immense strength to break a man's neck even under the best of circumstances. Shust's arms wrapped around the Mauritanian's head and neck like pythons. The gangster let out a thin scream that stopped as his vertebrae snapped.

Taha yanked Tymosh close to him to use her as a shield as he clawed her pistol out of his pocket. The woman yanked her head away in an act of self-brutality. Taha stared at the fistful of hair in his hand. He screamed as Tymosh's thumb rammed through the left lens of his sunglasses and violated the eyeball beneath.

Lord William, Lunk and Owu came out from the shadows.

Guy Diddier stared down Bolan's and Pun's rifles in sick horror. His pistol fell from his limp hand. Taha fell to his knees screaming and clutching his face. Everyone else was dead. Tymosh grabbed Taha by the hair. Bolan shook his head. "I need him alive."

Tymosh stared at Bolan for a moment and then deliberately reached down and took Taha's other eye with a twist of her thumb and forefinger. The gangster howled like the damned in hell and fell kicking to the dock. She flung the eye into the ocean. "He does not need eyes to talk."

Bolan kept his reaction off his face. But with nuclear war on the table, her atrocity would serve Bolan's purpose. "Guy?"

Diddier's lip was trembling. He took his eyes off Yuliya Tymosh with effort.

Bolan nodded as he gained Diddier's full attention. "Actually, we're both Americans. How about I just call you Gary?"

The former Gary Pope just trembled and waited.

"Maybe you've already picked up on this," Bolan continued, "but the Russians are really pissed. So I'm going to make it real simple. You're going to talk to me, right here, right now, and you get out of this alive. If you don't spill for me, we're going to take a walk while you go in the storehouse with the Russians. Shust will hold you down and God only knows what Yuliya will do, but she will have her way with you. Do you understand? And one way or another, you'll talk. Which is it going to be?"

Shust smiled through mashed lips and missing teeth. Tymosh simply stood beneath the bare overhead bulb wearing nothing but a thong with blood dripping from her fingers. She looked like a she-demon sent from hell.

Diddier's voice was barely a whisper. "I'll talk to you."

"Did the *Halqa* refuel here?"

Diddier's jaw dropped again, and Kurtzman's theory was confirmed.

"I asked you a question. Did the sub refuel here?"

"N-no. It was supposed to, but after the Russian team arrived we waved them off. If the Russians were here, then there was too much chance of a satellite watching. They'll be going to an alternate refueling point."

"Where?"

"I don't know."

Bolan nodded to Tymosh and turned away. "He's all yours."

The woman's fingers curled into claws as she took a step forward.

"No!" Diddier shrieked. "No! I swear! Jennings kept us in cells! Only he knows who's stationed where and the sub's possible stops! Nouakchott was my and Ruud's security sector! Our job was to make sure the refueling went smoothly or warn them off if anything seemed suspicious. After the Russian team arrived, we waved them off! That's it! That's all I know and all we were told!"

It was exactly how Bolan would have planned it. "Where's Jennings?"

"He's...on the sub."

"How many working warheads do you have?"

Diddier couldn't stop shaking. "I...don't know. I was never told. It wasn't part of my purview. I'm just the Mauritania control agent! Believe me! I swear to God! You've got to believe me!"

Bolan did believe him. "How do you contact the sub?"

"I don't! Once they passed our sector, Ruud and I were to stick around for seventy-two hours! To see if anyone came looking and take care of them."

"And then?"

"We go to the Caymans and…collect our money." Diddier couldn't meet Bolan's eyes.

"You're a traitor to the United States, Gary, and a traitor to your adopted nation of France. What do you think the Iranians are going to do with those weapons?"

"I—I didn't know they were going to the Iranians, I swear I—"

"You knew they were going to someone, Gary, and it wasn't the Red Cross. If you were a fanatic, I could forgive you. But you did this for a paycheck."

Guy Diddier hung his head in shame. "I didn't know what was going on. When I did, it was too late to turn back, they would have killed me, gone after my family—"

"The way I see it, you only have one option."

Diddier stared.

"You were a California National Guardsman once. Infantry. The 223rd. Guy Diddier has two ways to die tonight. One is at the hands of Russian intelligence. The other is Gary Pope finds some testicular fortitude and decides to serve his country again."

"I'll—"

"Think about it. God help you if Iranian Intelligence or your friends at Aegis get hold of you. I hear Ruud's brother Arjen is half his size and twice as sadistic." Bolan stared down at Diddier. "You know something? I lied. You have two options. Maybe your best bet is to run. You'll be a hunted animal for the rest of your short life, but maybe there's some hole in the wall in Greenland or Tierra del Fuego where you can hide."

Gary Pope reached into the collar of his shirt and pulled out two pairs of dog tags. One was round and French and the other pair U.S. military rectangles. The ball chain snapped off in his hands and he held up his California National Guard tags like an icon. The young man met Bolan's eyes. "Gary Pope, Corporal, 223rd."

"We'll talk again tomorrow." Pun grabbed Pope and dragged him away.

Shust clapped his hands once, twice, three times in contempt. "So, traitor begs and you give absolution."

"He's an asset. My asset. Tomorrow he's going to identify every Aegis employee he knows who's involved. Then he's going to buck up and be a soldier. I've lost men. We need replacements, and he has skills."

"Vengeance is required." Shust cocked his head and spit a loose tooth out into the Atlantic. He looked Bolan up and down in challenge. "I am not sure I am taking orders from American not wearing pants."

Lunk stepped in front of Shust and loomed from his three inches of advantage. "If you're wanting to see who wears the pants in the family, sunshine, I'll bloody well show you."

Shust glared up. The Russian was clearly ready to go.

Tymosh draped the remnants of her shirt around herself. "Shust."

The Russian turned.

"Yankee traitor is intelligence asset until I say otherwise."

Shust turned on his heel and scooped up his machine pistol without a word.

CHAPTER FIFTEEN

U.S. Embassy, Mauritania

Bolan, Kurtzman, Tymosh and Shust had a four-way conversation over the satellite link. The computer wizard was clearly skeptical. "You trust this Pope-Diddier character?"

"As a matter of fact, I do. Pope drifted into this. He was bored as a guardsman and joined the Legion on some romantic notions. Working for Aegis was the dream job he'd always wanted. By the time he knew he'd crossed the line, he was in too deep. If he tried to get out, he knew he'd be killed, just like the Russian who contacted the FSB. If he did get a running start, he knew Jennings would go after his family. For that matter, I don't think he was going to run. Whatever else you can say about him, he's a soldier, and soldiers don't run out on their comrades, no matter how distasteful the job is."

Shust made a disgusted noise. His face still looked like hamburger from the previous night's beating.

Kurtzman seemed to agree. "A lot of Nazis made the same argument at the war tribunals at Nuremberg."

Bolan shrugged. "Last night I gave him a choice. This

morning Lord William gave him a father-son type talk, and he's already given us a list of the Aegis employees he knows that are in on the mission."

"How many?" Kurtzman asked.

"Without Pope or Heitinga, he has forty-five."

"A platoon," Tymosh said.

"Yes," Kurtzman agreed, "a platoon of seasoned mercenaries."

Bolan had given that a lot of thought. "Some will be on the sub with him, others like Pope will be acting in pairs as security controllers around Africa and any other possible ports of call, probably based on experience and language skills. But if I were Jennings, I'd be keeping ten or twelve men in reserve as a strike team in case he needs backup. We didn't meet them in Mauritania because the *Halqa* had moved on, but I'm betting they're somewhere in Africa, shadowing the sub's course by plane, ready to descend at any critical juncture."

Tymosh nodded. "This I would do, also."

Kurtzman pulled up a map of Africa. "Critical juncture is the key word. It's interesting that Goma was planning to refuel in Mauritania. That's a pretty short leg of the journey. Either he was topping off, or for some reason he didn't refuel in England."

"Bear, I'm starting to think maybe he didn't. England has a fleet of submarines patrolling her waters. Maybe collecting the weapons and refueling had to be done at two different points and Goma considered it too much exposure. A diesel electric sub takes what? Tens of thousands of gallons of fuel? Without using a commercial dock, that much fuel being transported could attract notice, and the refueling itself could take up to twelve hours. Doing it in some lonely port in Africa actually makes a hell of a lot more sense."

Kurtzman nodded. "So if Pope and Heitinga waved off Goma without refueling in Mauritania, the *Halqa* is going to be one thirsty submarine." The computer wizard ran his eye down the map, ticking off countries. From Senegal to Gambia, most of the African nations had only one major port where tens of thousands of gallons of diesel fuel were to be had. He nodded to himself and clicked a key. Nigeria rose up out of the map and the coast was highlighted.

"Nigeria is his best bet. It's the largest and the most modern of the West African nations. It has multiple ports and is a major oil and fuel exporter. A few hundred thousand dollars in the right hands, and he can buy a clandestine refueling."

Bolan stared at the map as his instincts spoke to him. "That's the problem. It is the most obvious choice. Jennings will know that Lord Parkhurst was taken down. He and Goma know they're being hunted. They're probably surprised that they haven't heard a U.S. or Russian fleet humming above them yet, but they know we're looking for them."

"Well, it may be the obvious choice, but it also may be the only choice. I mean, how many backup secret submarine refueling points can he have? I recommend you head to Nigeria, and now."

Tymosh tapped the screen with her finger and traced the coastline from the city of Lagos to the southernmost city of Calabar. "Major ports, and in between hundreds of offshore oil rigs. It will be his best opportunity. *Halqa* will be needle in haystack. I agree with Bear. We should go to Nigeria, now."

Bolan was looking at Shust. *"Nyet."*

Tymosh's face darkened. "No?"

"Yankee is right. Nigeria is obvious choice," Shust said.

Kurtzman looked at the bruised and beaten Russian

askance. "Forgive me, Sergeant, but what other choice does he have?"

Shust's eyes were burning holes through the screen. "Angola."

Kurtzman and Tymosh looked at Shust blankly.

Shust nodded, becoming more and more sure of himself. "During Angolan civil war United States, South Africa, they support rebels. Soviet Union support Marxist government, mostly through Cuba, as proxy. Soviet Union officially deny, but Russian soldiers, Spetsnaz, engage in clandestine operations. This was before my service, but I hear old-timers talk of covert actions undertaken in Africa. In last century." The Special Forces soldier stabbed his finger at the map decisively. "There will be submarine base, small, hidden, but there for sensitive insertion and extraction. Angola has no submarines. Base probably abandoned, but it will be there!"

Tymosh pulled out her cell phone. "I will have location in ten minutes."

"Okay, we have our window," Kurtzman said, "but there's a wrinkle."

Bolan felt the rub coming. "We've heard from Jennings."

"Or Captain Goma. We don't know. NSA tracked the transmission to Amsterdam, but all the CIA team found on the site was an empty room with a melted satellite rig. Anyone could have sent it, but the message was this—'I'll nuke any ship or sub I detect. If cornered I will nuke a city.' If Shust is right, the sub base will probably be near or in the capital-city port. Goma and Jennings will have men waiting to give the all-clear. If we attack the submarine or he detects a trap at the base, the city of Luanda goes up in flames. For that matter, if he does smell a trap, he can just backtrack for Nigeria and play hide-and-seek with us."

Bolan considered the two men. "Jennings and his men won't be big on suicide. What's your take on Goma?"

Kurtzman didn't look happy. "We ran a psych report based on everything we could learn about his life. NSA believes he was doing this for God, not money. They believe he'll take anyone and anything with him if he's cornered."

Tymosh clicked her phone shut. "GRU will be sending me full file on submarine base in next few minutes, but Shust is correct. It is currently abandoned. I say we send sub. It gets there before *Halqa*. Hide on bottom. Torpedo *Halqa* as soon as it is detected."

Kurtzman hit a key, and blips appeared in the Atlantic Ocean. "Those are U.S. submarines operating in the Atlantic." It was clear to everyone at the table that they were several inches too far away from the west coast of Africa. "Does Russia have anything closer?"

Tymosh bit her lip. "I do not know, but I doubt it."

A plan began to form in Bolan's mind. "We could fly in a minisub. An American military transport would cause an uproar, but Angola receives weapons and aid from Russia all the time. They just might get away with it."

"Da!" Shust shot to his feet. "Yankee is right! Russian AN-124 Condor heavy lift aircraft could airlift midget sub from Russia in time to beat *Halqa*. Tracked infiltration sub lurk on bottom at periscope depth, uncomfortable, I have been in, but doable. When we detect *Halqa?* Deploy divers with limpet mine!" Shust smacked his fist into his palm. "Boom!"

"No." Bolan shook his head. "I don't trust Jennings. If I were him, I would've kept one warhead aside and told Goma it was corroded like the one we found at Parkhurst castle and inoperable. Then I'd have left it some nice place like London with orders to detonate if Jennings doesn't check in at regular periods. I think when the *Halqa* gets within twenty-four hours of its refueling area, the NSA is going to get another message to that effect."

Shust raised his hands in defeat. "Then what point infiltration sub?"

"Sergeant Shust?" Bolan smiled again. "I didn't say I wanted a Russian infiltration sub."

A few seconds of processing passed and then Shust smiled to reveal the upper canine and two lower incisors that had been kicked out. Kurtzman frowned on the screen. "Then what kind of sub do you want?"

"I want a Russian rescue submersible. I want something with a docking ring compatible with a Romeo-class submarine. I've been reading up on Romeos. They only have one main deck, and one of their hatches is right above the torpedo room."

Tymosh grinned as what Bolan proposed dawned on her.

"I don't want to sink the *Halqa*," Bolan concluded. "I want to take it."

Angolan coast

THE CONDOR'S ENGINES HOWLED in protest. The AN-124 was a massive plane with a maximum takeoff weight of 392 tons. The Russian Bester rescue-recovery submersible had been specifically designed to fit inside the Condor's hull and be flown to a submarine disaster anywhere in the world. However, the pilot of the Condor was being asked to fly his giant transport mere yards over the surface of the ocean at near stalling speed and then ditch his plane.

The skipper of Bester *One* wasn't too thrilled, either. He hadn't had a lot of practice backing out of sinking airplanes.

A yellow light came on in the hold. It was time to board

the sub. Bolan's team shouldered their equipment and climbed up the side and descended down through the sail into the belly of Bester *One*. The Russian sub was normally painted in huge pink-and-white stripes for high visibility. Within the past twenty-four hours, it had been repainted black. Bolan stayed up top while the Condor's copilot climbed in. Bester *One*'s skipper, pilot and two crewmen climbed down. The skipper was a small, bearded man. He paused in the hatch and regarded Bolan the same way he would a Martian who had dropped into his company, and he spoke with an accent you could cut with an ax.

"I am told this idea is being yours."

Bolan shrugged.

The skipper shook his head. "Americans."

The word seemed to explain everything in the skipper's mind.

Bolan glanced at Grimaldi where he was drinking some ferociously bad Russian military coffee and gazing out the window at the spectacular rooster tails the Condor was hurling up. "You coming?"

Grimaldi crushed the paper cup in his hand. "They should have let me do this."

"The Russians are already upset that my plan calls for the trashing of a forty-million-dollar aircraft. They're not about to let an American have the fun of doing it."

"I'm a little worried."

It was an unusual remark coming out of Jack Grimaldi. "You're not sure about the pilot?"

"Chichkin? Nah, he's good. It's the rest of the crew I'm worried about."

There was reason to worry. The normal crew of a Condor was six plus a loadmaster if the aircraft was carrying cargo, but once the plane ditched, the crew would have to board the submersible, so the crew had been stripped to the pilot, co-pilot, loadmaster and one airman. "What's their problem?"

"Fact is, with a load this heavy the Condor may break apart when it hits, and it may break apart only enough to snag the submersible and drag her to the bottom. The chalks have to be removed for the sub to back out the loading ramp once the cabin floods. There's a real good chance that the airman and loadmaster will be crushed or drowned and then sub doesn't go anywhere but down."

"So we need more men."

"I'd say at least four, and count on losing some of them."

Gary Pope's head appeared in the hatch. "I'll volunteer. I was scuba certified in the Legion."

Bolan looked the man up and down. He seemed in deadly earnest. "All right. Get me some C-4. Jack, get in. I'm going to stay up top with Gary and make myself useful."

"Actually, I thought I might do it."

"Swimming was never your specialty, Jack. Get in the sub."

"I'm a gettin'." The pilot started to climb up into the minisub.

The pilot's voice came over the intercom. "Mr....Jack?"

Grimaldi grinned and leaned out to press the intercom in the side of the hold. "Yes?"

"You—" the pilot took a long, unhappy pause "—expressed willingness to—"

"On my way!" Grimaldi gave Bolan an insufferable grin and hopped back down to the deck. "Sarge, I'm going to drop this bird as lightly as possible, but you still won't have much time."

"I know." Bolan felt the plane lurch as the pilot wrestled with the controls. "You'd better get up there."

Grimaldi sauntered away and disappeared into the cockpit. Within moments, the howl and throb of the engines changed and the plane flew a little more steadily. His voice crackled across the tactical link. "Sarge?"

"Yeah?"

"This plane?"

"Yeah?"

"It's a pig."

"Oh, yeah?"

"A pig that swallowed a brick."

Grimaldi could almost always find something to like in any plane he flew. The fact that he was calling the Condor a pig with a brick in its belly didn't exactly bode well. "We're gonna hit hard."

"Oh, yeah, we're going to hit hard," the pilot said. "Beginning my descent. Opening ramp door now." Hydraulics whined and daylight blazed in as the giant ramp below the tail opened. Wind and spume blasted into the cargo hold. The entire plane lurched forward grotesquely as the ramp dipped into the water and the plane threw a wake like a giant hydrofoil. The loadmaster and his lone airman screamed from their seats near the cockpit.

"Boy, we're going in fast!" That was as close to an admission of stark-raving terror Bolan had ever heard out of Jack Grimaldi. Outside the ramp, the world was a kaleidoscope of rainbows and vortices in the prop wash as the aircraft skimmed bare feet above the ocean. The plane shuddered and moaned as Grimaldi fought the throttle. "Here we go!"

Bolan shouted down the sail. "Brace for impact!"

God reached out His hand and slapped down the Condor.

Bester *One* tilted sickeningly beneath Bolan as the aircraft met the sea. The Condor skipped like a stone, and on the second bounce the starboard wing folded and tore away in a scream of rending metal. Bolan hunched in the sail as debris flew through the hold like shrapnel and the sun flared in from above.

The Condor ceased its skipping and began trying to smash its way through the sea. The fuselage made a sound like a dying beast as structural integrity was lost and the plane snapped in two. The remaining wing tore away, and Bester *One* tilted all the way off of its chalks and thudded against the hold. Water began flooding the hold as the dying bird came to a rest.

"Jack!"

"We're all right!"

The Condor wasn't resting. It was slipping into the sea. Bolan looked back to find the ramp was in ruin and had twisted upward. Ahead, a huge flange of fuselage was bent against the rescue sub's bow. *One* was blocked on both sides. The Condor's tail tilted downward as the hold flooded and the little sub tipped with it. "Pope! Ten seconds on the charges!"

Bolan leaped from the sail and grabbed webbing straps on the fuselage, and Pope jumped after him. Behind him, the hatch to *One* slammed shut and locked behind them. There was no way to climb to the nose of the sub. Bolan was going to have to wait until the water reached him. He didn't have to wait long. The broken Condor was sinking fast. Water rose up around Bolan's shoulders, and *One* went buoyant, bobbing up against the metal flange with a screech of metal. Bolan pulled the adhesive strip on the block of C-4 and swam for the razor-sharp flange that held the sub. The ocean closed over his head as the section of fuselage sank below the surface and dragged the sub with it. Bolan pointed at an obstructing section of wing root above. Pope nodded and kicked upward. Bolan drew his knife and cut a one-quarter portion of the C-4 and abandoned the rest of the brick to the depths.

He pressed the lump against the base of the flange and pushed in the detonator pin. Bolan gave the pin a twist and banged his fist against the thick glass portal where the sub's captain stared unhappily upward.

Bolan held up ten fingers and the captain nodded behind the superthick glass. He looked upward as the water darkened and the pressure began to press against his ears. Pope looked down and gave Bolan the thumbs-up. The soldier pushed in the tip of the detonator like a ballpoint pen and swam upward for his eardrums. He didn't want to be under the water when the charges blew. Part of his mind was counting the seconds as the bright roof of the ocean loomed closer and he saw Pope hit the surface.

Seconds later the Executioner surfaced. A moment later a mushroom of water seemed to push up against him, and the ocean roiled like a hot tub. Bolan took a deep breath and dived a bit. The fuselage of the Condor was a murky and disappearing hulk trailing bubbles. The hulk lit up as *One* hit its lights. The fuselage slid away from the sub like a sheath as the skipper hit his thrusters.

Bolan resurfaced.

The nose, cockpit and a good section of the front part of the Condor were standing straight up out of the ocean like some miraculous oceangoing obelisk. Grimaldi, the pilot, the loadmaster and his airman were holding on to seat cushions, kicking their way over.

"That was fun!" Grimaldi called. "Let's do it again!"

One surfaced a few yards away. Bolan swam over as the skipper stood up in the sail. He held out a hand as the Executioner clambered up the side. He was sweating bullets but grinning as he looked at the bobbing hulk of the Condor. "Americans!"

"Is everyone all right inside?" Bolan asked.

"Everyone all right. Damage…minimal. Vessel still worthy."

Bolan climbed back into the sail and held out a hand to Grimaldi. The pilot was still grinning, but his hand shook slightly as Bolan grabbed it and hauled him aboard. "So what now?"

Bolan gazed at the distant shoreline of Angola. "Now we wait."

CHAPTER SIXTEEN

"The *Halqa,* she comes," the sub captain said.

Bolan shrugged into his armor and clicked into his web gear, careful not to let anything bang or clank against the hull. "All right, by twos, gear up."

The Russians had brought weapons. In the narrow confines of the *Halqa*'s steel corridors there would be no need for silence or telescopic sights. What was needed was compact and overwhelming firepower. Bolan checked the load in his Groza short assault rifle and clicked a 40 mm antitank grenade into the built-in launcher. Both the Groza rifle and the Gurza pistol holstered on his thigh were loaded with needle-nosed, armor-piercing bullets. Bolan started hanging grenades and flexible charge about his body like Christmas ornaments.

The interior lit up in a dim red glow as the skipper turned on the emergency lights. He came down out of his tiny conn and had a brief exchange with Ruslan Shust before addressing Bolan. "*Halqa* come. Coming slow, hugging bottom, but on predicted vector."

They had caught some luck on that one. The GRU had

given Yuliya Tymosh complete diagrams of the concealed, Cold War-era sub station. The underground dock had facilities for two submarines. It had been designed for the delivery and extraction of Special Forces units as well as deployment of the specialized Russian midget subs with caterpillar tracks. The little cove the Russians had chosen was ideal. Rock formations on the shore and out in the water obscured the base from direct observation from both land and sea, however, the rocks and the shallow water had forced the Russians to dredge a three-hundred-yard-long trench so submarines of Kilo class or larger could approach and not have to surface until they were safely inside. The trench was the key. It gave *One* a perfect vector on the *Halqa*'s approach, and the insane possibility of dropping down on top of it undetected until the very last second.

The skipper squared his shoulders. "Crewman Zaur and I wish to volunteer for boarding party."

Shust shook his head. "No."

The skipper was a small man, but he stared up at Shust resolutely. "Romeo class has complement of fifty-six officers and crew, plus expected mercenaries. You are down to ten men."

"Tell me, little captain," Shust said with a sneer, "just what is it you think you and Crewman Zaur can do?"

"Zaur and I can stop bullet as well as any man."

Even Shust had to respect that.

"And warheads must be secured," the captain concluded.

Bolan had to admire him. It wasn't bravado. The skipper was Russian navy through and through. He considered this his duty, and he was prepared to die doing it. "What about *One?*" Bolan asked.

The skipper shrugged. "Crewman Kharkov will stay with *One* and try and maintain lock with *Halqa*. Failing this, he will send out distress signal and then scuttle *One* in trench in attempt to block *Halqa*'s escape."

Shust shrugged. "We have no weapons to spare you."

The skipper didn't bat an eye. "Perhaps there are weapons on *Halqa*."

The two men stared at each other and an understanding passed between them. The Russian navy was playing hardball today. Shust nodded. "Very well."

The big Russian glared around the hold at the team of soldiers, sailors, airmen and assassins, and gave a last-minute review. "I am in command. Should I be killed, Yankee is in command. He falls? Then Colonel Glen-Patrick. Taking *Halqa* is optimum outcome, but stopping *Halqa* is premium. If we fail to break out of bow section, if we are overwhelmed?" Shust held up a pair of remote detonators. "Then survivors will detonate conventional torpedo warhead and sink *Halqa* in channel. Russian navy will then come and scavenge hulk for surviving nuclear warheads. Questions?"

There weren't any.

Twelve people were going to storm a hostile submarine at six-to-one odds, and if they failed, suicide was the only acceptable option. The skipper spoke very quietly. "Once I turn on engines, *Halqa* will hear us. We will have seconds to match speed and dock. *Halqa* will most likely shake off *One*, and then torpedo room will flood."

The skipper's meaning was clear. Once the attack began they would have to keep moving forward or drown. He returned to the conn and took the controls in hand. Crewmen Kharkov and Zaur took their position at the docking ring. Shust was in command, but he said nothing as Bolan crouched beside Kharkov and took point. The Executioner took a premeasured hoop of flexible-shaped charge and pushed in a detonator pin. The cutting-charge was triple thick to burn through a submarine's exterior hatch rated to a depth of five hundred yards, and it was going to burn hot.

The skipper flipped a switch and ocean lit up around *One* as the powerful underwater rescue lights sent out their beams.

Aboard the Halqa

"BRING US TO PERISCOPE depth." Captain Wael Goma stood on the bridge. He was an imposing figure even without the Helwan automatic pistol holstered on his hip. Not all of the crew had been as pious as they should have been or been willing to martyr themselves in the name of Jihad against the infidel. After Goma had personally martyred the cook, the second engineer, the medical orderly and the Torpedo Technician First Class, the crew had become much more attentive in their duties to the *Halqa* and God. All the officers carried sidearms, and Goma's loyal cadre of crewmen carried submachine guns from the armory to make sure those duties remained unswerving. With no naval duties to attend to, Jennings's little band of mercenary bodyguards roamed the sub peering at every unarmed crewman with extreme suspicion.

Captain Goma slid his gaze toward Jennings. He did not like the Englishman. Twice he had contradicted Goma in front of the crew. His breath stank of the whiskey that he mixed with the bottle of painkillers that was never far from his remaining hand. Goma stared at the bandaged stump in its sling. The startling rumor that Jennings's hand been eaten by a dog did nothing to raise the mercenary in Goma's estimation.

The *Halqa*'s hull ticked slightly as the planesman began bringing her to periscope depth. The sonar man clapped a hand to his earphones. "Contact!"

"Tarek!" Goma stalked to the sonar station. "What do you detect?"

"Unknown! Very faint!" Petty Officer Tarek clicked keys on his computer. The *Halqa* was a Chinese-built copy of an ancient Russian design, but the Egyptians had updated their ancient subs with some very modern American electronics. Tarek ran the noise through his computer's sound catalog. "Captain! The contact matches nothing in the catalog!"

"Bearing!" Goma snarled.

"Faint! And above us! It is hard to get exact bearing!"

"All stop!"

The *Halqa* went to full stop and lay in the water listening.

Jennings leaned over the sonar man's shoulder. "Fishing boat?"

Goma restrained his angry retort. It wasn't a bad guess. Fishing off West African waters was still overwhelmingly artisanal rather than commercial, and squid and sardinella often ran at night. "Bearing?"

"Still faint, but above us, and getting closer."

The captain considered. Faint, unknown, above them and getting closer. He didn't like it at all. "The contact is still anomalous?"

Tarek frowned. "Captain, I am tempted to say screw-noise, but if it is a craft and this close, we should hear his engines, as well."

Goma turned to his XO. "Mr. Moteab, flood forward torpedo tubes one, two, three and four, and both stern tubes. Mr. Tarek, ping the contact five times."

The bridge went silent. Flooding the tubes was an act of war, and everyone in the sub knew that two of the torpedoes forward and one of the aft were loaded with nukes. Going to active sonar would alert anyone listening for miles of their location.

Tarek cleared his throat. "Captain—"

Goma's hand went to his holster. "Do you question my orders, Mr. Tarek?"

"No, sir!" Tarek pulsed the active sonar. Every man on the bridge went as silent as a statue as the sonar "pinged" five times.

"Captain!" Tarek's face paled with sick horror as the reflection of the active sonar pulses gave him exact information. "Contact is directly above us! Ten meters away and closing! Collision course!"

"Full reverse! Mr. Tarek! Give me a firing solution on contact!"

"Captain! He is on top of us! He is—"

The hull of the *Halqa* rang like a bell and then echoed with strange and distant knocks forward.

"Tarek! What is happening?"

Tarek was undoubtedly the best sonar operator the tiny Egyptian submarine fleet could ever have hoped to have and while nothing that had happened fell into his training or experience, the instincts of a sonar operator were a strange and wondrous thing.

"Captain, I believe the contact has docked with us above the torpedo room."

Goma drew his pistol and gave orders that were almost unthinkable to a sub-driver. "Mr. Moteab! Mr. Jennings! Send your men forward. Prepare to repel borders!"

THEY'D CAUGHT A BREAK. Predictably, like any good submariner, when confronted by the unknown, Captain Goma had gone full stop and silent. That had given *One* precious moments to sink like a stone and use her electric motor only for the smallest maneuvers. The magnetic docking collar had attached *One* to the *Halqa,* and by the time they had reacted it was too late. The lip of *One*'s titanium umbilical had sunk into the counter screws of the *Halqa*'s red-and-white-painted hatch. Crewmen Zaur and Kharkov hurled their strength against the locking levers, and steel had mated with steel as the docking ring and the *Halqa*'s hatch spun together and mated.

Bolan ripped the adhesive off the hoop of shaped charge and pressed it around the circumference of the hatch. "Fire in the hole!" The hoop of charge cracked like a whip and for one second a halo of fire filled the umbilical. Bolan squinted against the smoke and brimstone stench. The hatch hadn't fallen.

"Zaur! Kharkov!"

One's crewmen raised their sledges like pile drivers and rammed them down the umbilical. The hatch clanged and half tore away from the scorched metal still holding it in place.

"Again!" It had taken too long. Bolan pulled the pin on his flash-stun grenade as the sledges slammed down once more. The *Halqa*'s hatch tore and fell into the torpedo room. Bolan dropped his grenade. "Back!"

A submachine gun ripped into life below them. Sparks screamed off the walls of the umbilical and ricocheted off the ceiling of *One*'s main compartment. Crewman Kharkov fell, clutching his face. Bolan's grenade detonated below and cut off the automatic fire. The pyrotechnic effect funneled up the umbilical like a fountain of fireflies. Bolan leaped down the umbilical and landed in a crouch on the floor of the torpedo room. The submachine gun burned back into life as a blinking crewman in a grease-stained T-shirt cut loose. The bullets tore over Bolan's head and sparked against the interior torpedo tube hatches. The Executioner's return burst stitched the man from belt buckle to collar. A man with a pistol tried to fire past his stricken comrade. Bolan held down his trigger. The Russian armor-piercing SP-6 ammo punched through the torpedo man, as well as the man behind him, then shattered apart on the bulkhead behind.

There were two more men in the room. One was trying to jam himself beneath a rack of torpedoes while the other knelt rocking back and forth and shaking his clasped hands in supplication while he screamed in Arabic. It was as Bolan had suspected. Not every crewman was happy about deserting the Egyptian navy and becoming a terrorist.

Lunk and Otto dropped down behind Bolan.

Bolan moved to the bulkhead as more of his team dropped into the torpedo room. "Otto! Find out what he knows!"

The Nigerian grabbed a fistful of the man's shirt and yanked him up nose-to-nose.

Shust dropped down and immediately affixed an explosive charge to the gray-painted warhead of one of the torpedoes racked along the wall. He flicked a switch on his detonator box and a tiny red LED light blinked on as the charge armed. He glared about the room grimly. "We go forward."

Owu dropped his informant. "He says the captain executed four men to keep order. Jennings has four men of his own with him."

Bolan scooped up the fallen submachine gun. The Egyptian weapon was a knock-off of the old Swedish K-gun. Bolan calculated. Subs didn't usually carry enough weapons to arm the entire crew. Most only had a dozen or so outdated weapons to arm men guarding the sub in port or in the strange and unlikely event the captain felt it necessary to arm a shore or boarding party. It was clear that Goma did not consider all of his crew reliable. Bolan made it twenty-four men at most with automatic weapons, and in all navys it was traditional to have a sidearm for each officer. "Owu, ask him how Jennings and his men are armed."

Owu inquired in Arabic and then looked back at Bolan disgustedly. "He says they have 'fancy' guns."

That meant modern assault weapons of one variety or another, and Jennings had expensive tastes. Bolan handed the old subgun to *One*'s skipper as he dropped in and gave Zaur the fallen officer's pistol. The Russian navy men took the weapons and fell into rank behind Shust. Bolan nodded at Lunk and pulled out a frag grenade. The Welshman spun the heavy iron wheel on the torpedo room door and shoved it open a crack. A storm of submachine-gun fire met the intrusion. Bolan flinched as a bullet spalled off the bulkhead and hit him in the chest. The cotter pin pinged away as he shoved the grenade through the door and Lunk slammed it shut again. The detonation rang dully through the metal door and the hull echoed with the sound of muffled screams. Lunk flung the door open and Bolan dived through firing.

He rolled up into a crew compartment. Bunks lined the walls and more torpedoes were racked beside and between them. The dead and dying littered the floor. The lethal radius of the Russian frag was ten meters. The crew compartment was a killing box that offered no cover whatsoever. Lunk strode past as Bolan dropped his weapon on its sling and pulled another fragger. Owu and Shust came in behind them.

The enemy suddenly decided to return the favor.

The far door cracked open and a dull gray iron sphere came rolling across the floor of the compartment at them.

"Grenade!" Bolan shouted.

Lunk hurled himself on top of it.

The grenade detonated. Smoke and sparks squirted out from beneath the giant and his body lifted like a horse had bucked him. Bolan had no time to help him. He knelt and raised his rifle. "Owu! With me!" The Nigerian dropped to one knee beside Bolan, and Shust and Lord William leaned in overhead, leveling their weapons. The far door flew open and the four of them opened up like a full-auto firing squad.

In the confines of the compartment, it was easier to hit than miss.

The point man fell forward, shuddering as he took dozens of hits, and so did the man behind him. Weapons blasted back in response. Bolan grunted as he suddenly took Shust's weight across his shoulders. He shrugged off the fallen Russian and continued to fire. Owu groaned and fell face-first to the deck. Lord William dropped to one knee, still firing as Pun and Pope stepped forward to replace the fallen. Someone in the far compartment managed to slam the door shut, and the wheel spun to lock.

Bolan rolled Owu over. His pupils were blown and his body was as limp as a rag. The Executioner glanced at the dead attacker. He was blond, wearing civilian clothes, and the weapon lying on the deck was a Belgian P-90. Its ice-pick-like bullet was rated to penetrate up to forty layers of Kevlar body armor and had distinct propensity to tumble once inside the body. The Russian titanium-and-fiberglass armor weave they all wore stood no chance against it, and the Nigerian tracker had taken ten through the chest.

Shust had taken five through the face.

Pun and Lord William had Lunk sitting up. He stared dazedly. The fabric of his armor had been burned and blasted open to reveal the dented and scored titanium plates. His nose was bleeding, and his jaw worked up and down as he struggled to get air into his lungs.

"Get him back!"

Pun and Pope yanked Lunk up by his straps and passed him back to the skipper and Crewman Zaur. Lord William knelt beside Bolan. "How do you want to play it?"

Bolan glanced at the bulkhead in front of them. "The next

compartment is the bridge. It'll have more space, enough for a dozen or more men to be aiming at the door and there will be some stations for men to take cover behind. We can use flexible charge to cut through it, but God help anyone who goes through."

"Or?"

"Or we can cut the door and play a game of toss with hand grenades."

Lord William stared at the bulkhead grimly. "But again we get the hard end of it."

"Third option." Bolan tapped the grenade launcher beneath the barrel of his rifle. "We hit the door with antitank grenades."

The shaped-charge warhead grenades would burn through the door just as they would a light-armored vehicle and send jets of molten metal and superheated gas into the compartment beyond. Lord William did some calculation of his own. "They're meant to kill men inside a tank. There's a lot more space on the bridge of a submarine, and cover."

"That's right, so we do all three. We hit the door, cut it and then attack. And we'd better do it quick before Goma gets ideas of his own."

"Bloody hell." Lord William stared back the way they had come, clearly wishing he had Lunk beside him.

Tymosh stared at Bolan and held up her detonator. Her meaning was clear. They had just lost their three best men. One more exchange of grenades and armor-piercing bullets, and there would be nothing left of the assault team. It was time to consider Plan B. "I will go back into torpedo room with Lunk and lock door. You will knock three times. I hear anything else? I tell *One* to break contact and then detonate."

"Do it."

Tymosh gave Zaur her gun, and the rest of the team filed

into the crew compartment. The skipper suddenly began waving his arms and talking so excitedly he lost his English. Tymosh's expression went from quizzical to predatory as she listened.

Bolan pressed flexible charge around the circumference of the next hatch. "This had better be good!"

"Skipper says Romeo is old! It will have tunnel!"

"Tunnel?"

"He says modern submarines more efficient, have access hatches at critical junctions. Romeo is old. It will have tunnel."

Bolan nodded. The skipper was trying to tell him the *Halqa* had a crawlspace. She was an old sub and a single-decker. Nearly every square inch of ceiling and wall space was taken up with tubes, pipes and ducts. The crawlspace would allow critical access to junctions throughout the submarine. "Does it access the bridge?"

Tymosh and the skipper had a quick exchange. "He thinks not. It is more for accessing ballast tanks, air induction system and masts. Access will most likely be forward in torpedo room and in machinery room near engines." The woman's eyebrow cocked. "But he says perhaps you could cut your way into bridge as you did torpedo room."

Pun grinned at Bolan. "You and me. Again, like tunnel rats."

The Executioner had to agree. If he and the little Gurkha could invade a castle in England through a dumbwaiter, then a crawlspace should be cake. "All right. Bill? When you hear my flexible charge go off, you hit the door with two grenades and then the cutting charge. After that, everyone goes through."

"Right."

"I'm bloody well coming along!" Lunk reeled into the door and promptly sat down again.

Tymosh handed him the detonator. "You will stay and detonate torpedo if we fail." She smiled at Bolan. "I come through tunnel with you. I am quite limber."

Bolan was already stripping off his armor. "You think you can handle that, Lunk?"

The Welshman didn't look good, but his eyes were steady. "Like the lady said, three knocks. Anything else and I blow the bloody boat to hell."

"Good." Bolan took a hoop of charge, his pistol and his knife, and went back to the torpedo room with Pun and Tymosh in tow. It took a moment gazing up through the rat's nest of pipe, but they found a panel in the ceiling sealed by four heavy bolts. A quick search of the torpedo compartment yielded a wrench, and Bolan heaved on the bolts until they turned. He slid the panel aside and climbed up. The crawlspace was octagonal, and while narrow, it was more spacious than Bolan had hoped. There had to be enough room for a man to crawl along it as well as carry and use tools. "Flashlight."

Pun handed over a light and climbed up as Bolan started crawling. The *Halqa* was seventy-seven yards long. There wouldn't be any signs that read Bridge Below, and even if there were, they would be in Russian. The periscope tubes would be the giveaway. Twenty yards in the round bulge in one side of the passage announced the periscope shaft. Bolan crawled a few feet past it and pressed his hoop of flexible charge into the floor.

Bolan crawled back a few feet and pressed the detonator. "Fire in the hole!"

They were inside the pressure hull, so the metal was nowhere near as thick as the exterior hatch. The flexible charge flashed yellow and burned through clean. The ragged circle of steel fell onto the floor of the bridge with a bell-like clang.

A pistol shot instantly sparked up through the hole and was

followed by the buzz-sawing of half a dozen automatic weapons. Bolan kept back as Armageddon erupted on the bridge below. Burning metal hissed and screamed as Lord William's first antitank grenade hit. It was instantly followed by the second, and Bolan felt the heat wash up through hole. Burning men screamed and howled.

The Executioner dropped down into hell.

Anything on the bridge that could burn was on fire, including human beings. Goma's gunmen had been packed tight on the bridge, and the jets of molten steel and superheated gas had wreaked hideous devastation. Bolan was forced to fight upon a burned, bleeding carpet of human horror. A man crouching by the planesman's station rose and shoved his pistol forward. The Gurza automatic pistol in Bolan's hand barked three times in rapid succession and sat him back down. The big American slid to one side and then shot the man by the sonar station as Pun dropped down with a pistol in one hand and his khukri in the other.

A ring of fire lit the forward hatch, and the door fell from the bulkhead.

Two of Jennings's men rose from behind the conn, and Bolan shot them both down before they could spray into Lord William and his team as he came in. Tymosh dropped down and began shooting men trying to get out the open door at the back of the bridge. Lord William stepped to one side and joined her, spraying his rifle at the far door to keep anyone from closing it. Captain Goma loomed out of the carnage. He clutched the burned ruins of one half of his face. His remaining eyed glared bloody murder as he swung up his pistol at Lord William. *"Allah akhbar!"*

God is great. The call of Jihad.

Gary Pope hit Goma in a flying tackle that sent both men in a pinwheel over the burning charts on the plotting table.

The shooting suddenly stopped. Grimaldi and the gaggle of Russian sailors and airmen piled in. Bolan could see men in the next compartment. None had guns. They had dropped to their knees and were pleading for their lives. Pope sat on Goma's chest and held him pinned with a pistol to his forehead. Bolan rose from his crouch. They had the bridge. The *Halqa* was theirs.

Then he froze.

Clive Jennings's voice was a hiss of rage. "That's right, you bloody son of a bitch! You stand right where you are." The former CEO of Aegis Global Security was underneath the desk of the communications station. His remaining hand was hooked over the edge and his finger was on a red switch on the console. He slowly rose, his hand never leaving its position. "Drop your gun. Or I release the buoy."

Bolan stared at the man. His eyes were slightly glassy and he didn't look completely rational. "And that will be the signal to…?"

"To blow up bloody London, that's what."

"You kept a warhead behind."

"Too bloody right I did! Now drop your pistol!"

Bolan dropped it.

"And you, Billy-boy." Lord William unslung his rifle and let it fall. He nodded at his team, and they began disarming. Bolan slid his glance over to Pun. The Gurkha was closest. Pun met Bolan's eyes, and then the Executioner looked meaningfully at the stump protruding from Jennings's sling. Pun held the khukri low along his leg.

Jennings jerked his head at Pun. "And you, you slant-eyed bastard!"

Pun tossed his pistol aside.

Bolan shouted. "Hey!"

Jennings turned in surprise. Pun's blade scythed through

the air, and the former head of Aegis Global Security gasped as he was relieved of his remaining hand. Pun put himself between Jennings and the communications console and prodded the Englishman in the chest with the point of his blade to keep him and his stumps away from the red switch. There was no need. Jennings collapsed, keening, to his knees among the charred bodies.

Bolan went to the console and found the intercom. With Owu dead they were out of Arabic speakers, but English was the second language of most Egyptians. Bolan's voice rang throughout the vessel. "I have the bridge and the torpedo room. I have Captain Goma. Surrender. You will not be harmed."

Bolan turned to Grimaldi. "Take Chichkin and Airman Valery, round up the guns and prisoners. Yuliya, ask the skipper if he thinks he and Zaur can bring the *Halqa* to the surface."

The Russians spoke for a few moments and Tymosh shrugged. "Skipper says there is a great deal of damage to controls. He believes he can bring submarine to surface, but even with willing help of crew, he does not believe *Halqa* will sail anyplace fast or far."

"That'll be enough. Pun, go give Lunk the all-clear. If Kharkov isn't disabled, give him the signal to detach *One* and surface. Then get Lunk out and seal the torpedo room. It's going to flood once *One* breaks off. Then come back here."

Pun sheathed his knife and trotted out of the room.

Bolan scooped up his pistol. Jennings flinched as the Executioner stood over him. "Clive, who controls the warhead in England? One of these fanatics, or someone from Aegis?"

Tears streamed from Jennings's eyes. "One of…mine."

They'd caught another break. Mercenaries could be reasoned with. "When we surface, you're going to communicate with MI-5 and tell them who has the warhead and where it is, along with any detonation codes or failsafe procedures."

"N-no. You are going to get me a doctor and let me go, once I'm in a— No!" Jennings flinched in terror as Bolan suddenly crouched with him face-to-face. The Executioner's arctic-blue eyes bored into the mutilated mercenary unblinkingly.

"Clive, for days now I've been preventing the Russians from torturing people. I'm tired. I'm tired of you. We're going to surface and you're going to turn over the weapon." Bolan jerked his head at Tymosh. "Or we're going to surface and she's going to make you do it, and when she's done, your hands will be the least of what you miss most, and as God is my witness I won't lift a finger to stop her."

"I...no...you—"

"Now, where are the warheads on this sub?"

"Two are loaded on torpedoes forward. One is loaded in one of the starboard tubes aft."

"Where are the rest?"

"In the storeroom."

"Yuliya, you're with me." Bolan strode over to Captain Goma. The wounded man snarled as the big American took a set of keys from his belt. Bolan and Tymosh walked aft. Grimaldi, the Russian pilot and his loadmaster were stripping guns and emptying chambers. The remaining crewmen of the *Halqa* seemed overwhelmingly relieved rather than rebellious. Bolan found the storeroom. Behind the stacks of food and supplies, red-and-yellow-painted torpedo warheads were stacked and strapped into place with heavy webbing along the far wall.

Bolan grimaced. Tymosh said something very unladylike in Russian. Bolan walked as cold as stone back to the bridge. He stood over Pope and Goma. "Captain, where are the other four warheads?"

One half of Goma's face smiled in triumph. "God is great."

The captain suddenly surged upward. Pope's cocked Gurza pistol went off inadvertently in his hand. Goma went limp and the steel deck beneath the back of his head puddled red.

Pope gasped in shock. "Jesus! I didn't mean to… I mean…"

Bolan turned away. A lot of good men were dead. The hunt was still on. He was fresh out of leads. The Russians would be here soon, and they were going to be pissed.

CHAPTER SEVENTEEN

U.S. Embassy, Kinshasa, Democratic Republic of Congo

Bolan sat back, exhausted. The Russian navy had arrived in the form of the Akula-II class nuclear attack submarine *Pantera*. Yuliya Tymosh and the remaining Russians had been ordered off the boat, and *One* had been given a new Russian crew. Bolan knew the captain of the *Pantera*'s orders were to kill anyone associated with the incident. The fact that four weapons were still missing threw things up into the air. Bolan had refused to disarm his team. He'd also explained the situation to the *Halqa*'s remaining crew, and the Egyptians had decided unanimously that going down with their ship fighting was preferable to interrogation and execution by the Russian Internal Security Services. Bolan had armed every one of them and put them to work. He'd refused the captain's demand to hand over Jennings or Pope. Then he'd refused to hand over the nuclear warheads unless the captain of the *Pantera* received Bolan, his team and the entire compliment of *Halqa* aboard the *Pantera* under arms.

The captain, whose English had not been that good to

begin with, had become incoherent with rage, but through an interpreter had suggested that a spread of torpedoes into the *Halqa* with Bolan and all aboard would satisfy his superiors. Bolan had countered, suggesting that all of the *Halqa*'s bow and stern torpedo tubes were loaded, flooded and had firing solutions on both the *Pantera* and *One*.

In the end, the crew of the *Halqa* had been inserted onto the Angolan coast near the capital. Bolan had given each man a hundred U.S. dollars, and in ones and twos they had taken taxis or buses and made their way to the Egyptian consulate. The *Pantera* had taken possession of the warheads, towed the *Halqa* out to sea and scuttled her. Bolan and his team, along with Jennings, had been clandestinely inserted onto the Congo River delta, acquired a boat and made their way to Kinshasa where the CIA had a presence.

Tymosh had stepped off the *Pantera* with them and Bolan hadn't stopped her. He suspected the woman had done some fast-talking with her superiors. The fact remained that four warheads were still missing. The Russians needed Bolan and his team, and he needed them. Bolan needed food and twenty-four hours' downtime.

Sleep he would undoubtedly have to catch on a plane. He was going to have to settle for food.

A helpful embassy intern brought Bolan a piece of newspaper wrapped around a dozen *suyas* or West African stick meats, which he wolfed down.

Lord William and Tymosh entered the secure communications room, and each took a seat.

"Hello, Bill. How's Lunk?"

"Resting comfortably. He's got a cracked sternum and a few ribs in similar condition. Throwing himself on top of bloody grenades. Nothing for it but tape, painkillers and rest, and mind you he's going to have to settle for two out of three." Lord William feigned disgust, but his eyes shone with pride. "Papist bastard, ought to say a dozen rosaries for Russian titanium armor while he's fumbling with those beads of his."

Bolan grinned. "What about Jennings?"

Lord William's eyes twinkled. "Well, now, the young lady and I had a chat with him while you were dealing with the station chief."

"Bill…"

"Oh, nothing untoward happened. I adopted a kindly, rather grandfatherly tone with him."

Bolan looked over at the Russian. "And her?"

"She found a scalpel and lifted up his hospital gown."

"What'd Clive do?"

That "schoolboy getting away with something" look appeared on the baron's face again. "Well, not much. He doesn't have any hands, then, does he? Couldn't really resist. Can't even press the bloody buzzer for the nurse, actually."

"Tell me you didn't cut him."

Tymosh shrugged as if the matter was of little importance. "Colonel Glen-Patrick prevailed upon me not to."

"But you got something."

"Just this, old man. I grilled him about every action of the *Halqa* once it left England. He swears he was there on the bridge when Pope and Heitinga waved them off from the scheduled stop in Mauritania. But he says seventy-two hours earlier they paused to surface and recharge the batteries. It took about six hours, and Goma insisted all nonessential personnel stay in their quarters. Something about leaking fumes."

Diesel electric submarines had to at least go to snorkel depth to recharge their batteries and exchange out the fumes. In an old sub like the *Halqa*, that would be better performed on the surface so all hatches could vent in fresh air. It was perfectly plausible. Bolan wasn't buying it.

"Give him eight knots traveling speed, seventy-two hours from Nouakchott, call it six-hundred-odd miles." Bolan did some quick calculations as he backtracked the *Halqa*'s most likely path and ended up frowning. "That puts the weapons on the beach somewhere along the middle of the Western Sahara."

"That's what I got, as well. Not a lot out there. Only two airports in the region, and by my timeline he'd placed the weapons hundreds of kilometers from both."

"So why there?" Bolan mulled it over, looking for the missing piece.

"Well, I'm sure I don't know." Lord William sighed. "I've been out there a time or two, and there's nothing between the Western Sahara and Egypt except about five thousand kilometers of desert. Anything of any note in Africa is either north or south of the Sahara. The interior is big, empty, nothing but a bloody sandbox."

Bolan had been in the Sahara a time or two, as well, and except for Antarctica it was the most hostile terrain on Earth. "The English have always been fond of it."

"Well, yes. Mad dogs and Englishman and all that." The baron smiled. "When I was out in it, I must admit I was taken by the grandeur. A man could get lost out there."

"Maybe that's what the weapons are doing out there."

"Getting lost, you mean?" Lord William stroked his mustache in thought. "So you think Goma going around the Horn of Africa with the *Halqa* was a feint?"

"No, not a feint. I'm sure the Iranians wanted to see him make it all the way and deliver all the weapons, but by the same token, Goma was willing to die with his ship. If the *Halqa* was sunk with all hands by the U.S., Russian or South

African navy, no one would ever know four of the warheads were still missing."

"Right, but then, are four warheads enough to shift the balance of power in the Persian Gulf?"

That was bothering Bolan, as well. "I'd rather have all twenty. But four would certainly be a viable threat."

"Or enough to start a war if placed in the wrong hands."

Bolan had been considering that, as well, and it brought terrorism back to the table. "Yeah, you light one or two off in Israel, and all bets are off in the entire region."

"So!" Lord William sat up happily. "We go to the Western Sahara, track the warheads inland and take them."

"That sounds like our best bet. Except that neither the U.S. nor England has a whole lot of assets in the Sahara. The only people with anything out there are the French, and I doubt their field agents leave the air-conditioned offices of the embassies very often."

"Oh, well! We've a spot of luck there!"

"We do?"

"Yes, I have an asset in the Sahara."

"What kind of an asset?"

Lord William Glen-Patrick waggled his eyebrows.

Bolan clicked open his phone, and Grimaldi answered on the first ring.

"Yo!"

"Jack, we need a plane and flight plan to the Western Sahara."

Awsard, Western Sahara

THE SUVS GROUND to a halt. It was literally the end of the road. They had landed in Mauritania's northernmost city of Nouadhibou and crossed the border into the Western Sahara.

The road simply stopped, and then nothing but desert and dunes stretched out beyond the horizon. There were some sights on this Earth that took a human's breath away. The Grand Canyon was a sentimental favorite. The Himalayas brought a man high enough into the ethers that he might catch a glimpse of God. The Sahara Desert stretching out into infinity challenged man's claim to very the planet.

Man's claim to the Western Sahara had always been troubled.

The land had been conquered by the Arabs, colonized by Spain and then forcefully annexed by Morocco. The United Nations in their inimitable wisdom currently defined the Western Sahara as a "non-self-governing territory" and let the brushfire war burn.

Bolan pulled his shemagh scarf from around his nose and mouth and surveyed the town. Clay huts and cubes mixed strangely with a few French colonial homes and buildings. The dusty town was basically a square built around the bazaar and the mosque. At the edge of town was a 1960s vintage European-style gas station with a hand-painted sign that read, Last Water/Gas for 500 km. The Western Sahara was a disputed territory, but for adventure trekkers looking to cross the great Saharan expanse from the Atlantic to the Suez, the town of Asward was one of the major jump-off points. At the nearer gas station rested two khaki-painted civilian conversion Unimog 4x4 fire trucks and between them a gleaming white modern Unicat.

Lunk, Pun and Pope began pulling their meager belongings out of the SUVs. Tymosh stared at the vast dunes stretching eastward with the easily identifiable awe of a Saharan first-timer.

Lord William coughed and cleared his throat. "Those trucks must be ours."

Three men dropped down out of the cab of the Unicat. Two wore the blue-and-black-striped robes of Tuareg nomads. The fifth man was clearly the leader. He wore khaki pants and a khaki travel shirt with dozens of pockets. His skin was the color of an old penny, and his hair was a spectacular riot of brassy blond curls. He smiled as he came forward, revealing a mouth full of gold and silver teeth. His eyes were a startling gray. His sleeves were rolled up, and he wore multiple gold and silver amulets that Bolan knew contained scraps of the Koran. A gold earring dangled from each ear, every finger wore a ring and jammed between his amulets on one wrist he wore an expensive top-of-the line watch. A short, gold-hilted dagger was strapped to his left arm, and a Heckler & Koch VP-70 pistol was casually thrust under his belt.

His eyes roved up and down Tymosh in open piratical appreciation, and then he gave Lord William a graceful bow and spoke his English with a French accent. "Lord William, do you remember me?"

The baron started slightly. "Good Lord, don't tell me you're little Zayid! You have grown into quite a man!"

The Berber smiled in false modesty. "My lord is too kind."

Lord William grew animated. "Matt, I would like you to meet Zayid Hakmoun. His father, Oumu, was the greatest desert tracker I ever met and one hell of a soldier, as well. He and I worked together, oh, thirty years ago or more, doing something I'm probably still not allowed to talk about." The baron smiled in happy memory. "Tell me, Zayid. How is the old man?"

"My lord, it pains me to say he passed on several winters ago. The cancer of the lungs."

A little wind seemed to fall from Lord William's already flagging sails. "I'm sorry to hear that. He was a good man."

"Yes."

Bolan took in the trucks. There were few better vehicles for traversing the desert than the Mercedes-Benz Unimog. The two converted fire trucks looked old and hard-used but well maintained. The Unicat gleamed like it had just driven off the cover of an outdoor-adventure magazine. Bolan also took in the two men by Hakmoun's side. "These are your drivers?"

"Indeed."

Bolan would have preferred to drive his own rig, but driving in the Sahara Desert was an art unto itself and if these men did if for a living then he would leave it to the experts and only break up their team if he had to.

Lord William regained his composure. "Good men, then?"

Hakmoun deigned to notice his flunkies for the first time. "Oh, good heavens, no, my lord. Aksil is a sneak-thief and wanted for murder in Morocco." Hakmoun cuffed the second man hard enough to skew his turban. "Thuf? He is the son of a slave, and both would slit your throats for a handful of dirham notes. However, children of Satan that they are, they are also children of the Sahel, rather than useless townsmen."

Tymosh eyed the two men. "Yet you trust them?"

The metal filling Hakmoun's mouth gleamed as he smiled at the Russian. "Aksil and Thuf will obey my will implicitly because…" The Berber searched for a phrase in English. His smile turned brutal as he found it. "They know what is best for them, no?"

Bolan knew all he needed to know about Zayid Hakmoun. He was a pirate. Only rather than the sea, he roved the shifting sands of the Sahara. He would run before superior forces, trade in a position of parity and take from those weaker than himself. "You have the guns?"

"Indeed." Hakmoun led them to one of the Unimogs and opened up a side storage panel. A few contemptuous blows set Aksil and Thuff to pulling out wooden crates with French markings. Resupply for the Russian special-purpose weapons was nonexistent in the Western Sahara. Bolan's own closest contact would be the U.S. Embassy in Marakesh, and they didn't have the time to wait. The local black market would have to do. Thuf cracked open a crate.

Bolan pulled out a MAS 49 rifle. It was old, and old school. The weapon was three and a half feet long and made of wood and forged steel rather than high-impact plastics, aluminum and steel stampings, and chambered for the equally old and heavy French WWII 7.5 mm cartridge. It was an overly large and ugly rifle and weighed in over ten pounds, loaded. It made up for these shortcomings by being accurate, powerful and utterly reliable.

Bolan racked the action and was pleased to note that while the rifle stock was dinged and the steel was missing most of its finish, the action itself was well broken in and smooth.

Hakmoun spread his hands. "Will it suffice?"

Bolan clicked in a 10-round magazine and chambered a round. "It will."

Lord William picked up the rifle and seemed to sway beneath its awkward weight. He put it back and reached into a separate crate, choosing a lighter and equally ancient MAT 49 submachine gun. Hakmoun's eyes narrowed and he smiled. Bolan could see the Berber calculating, judging the old man's weakness in the already terrible heat of the morning.

Hakmoun would bear watching.

The Berber sensed Bolan's gaze and turned his own to the sky. He gauged the relentlessly rising sun with the eye of a man born of the desert. "Come, my lord. Embark your servants. We have many kilometers of desert to cross." A strange smile passed across his lips. "And your daughter awaits you at the oasis."

CHAPTER EIGHTEEN

Zikr Oasis

Zikr was Arabic for "Remembrance of God." After the eight-hour hell run in the Unimogs, the oasis was a remembrance that there was something else on the planet besides sand, rock, dust and 115-degree temperatures. It was little more than a hectare of land, but suddenly there was shade beneath the sheltering fronds of the palm trees, and the searing wind cooled as it blew across the ponds fed by the artesian wells in the rocky substrata. Goats and chickens browsed for fallen dates and figs, herded by children with sticks. Lemon and pear trees laden with fruit seemed incongruous in the little golf green of life surrounded by the harsh, ovenlike horror that was the Sahara Desert in summer. Striped tents and lean-tos were huddled among the palms like a tiny circus at rest. Women in all-concealing robes crouched in front of cook fires made of twigs and dried fronds, heating pots of mint tea.

A small mob of children laughed and screamed and chased one another around the trucks and then laughed and screamed and ran away as Bolan climbed down out of the overheating

Unimog. The two fire trucks had been converted into fuel and water transports and had been doing regular business along the desert fringe. They were the team's fuel, water and supply vehicles. The Unicat "Terracross" had folding bunks, cooking facilities and even a tiny shower stall as well as modern climate control. It was literally a family RV that had been designed from the ground up to withstand whatever the Sahara Desert could dish out. It had been purchased from a coastal adventure/eco-tour outfit at four times the retail asking price.

A man in the full robes and face veil of a Tuareg came forward and offered Bolan a copper dipper of water. Bolan took it and drank. The water was cold and had the heavy mineral tang of water that came out of the earth. The man bowed happily and backed away to offer water to the rest of the team. In the desert, the laws of hospitality were scrupulously observed.

Lord William took the dipper and several of the veiled men clapped their hands as the baron exchanged a few pleasantries with them in the local Tachelhit language. The dipper fell forgotten to his side as a woman came forth from the nearest tent. Contrary to most other Muslim communities, among the Berber peoples it was the men who wore veils rather than women. The woman's hooded dark blue robe concealed her body, but the way it flowed as she came forward was an art unto itself. Like Tymosh, she was exotic-looking, but where the Russian's skin was vampire-pale hers was the color of cinnamon. Tymosh exuded cruel sensuality. The huge dark eyes of the beauty before them were as mysterious as the desert itself.

She brought a hand to her chest and cast her gaze downward as she bent a knee to the baron. "Father."

"Emma." The baron stared in obvious shock at the beauty

he had wrought. Very clearly he had not seen her in some time.

The woman rose and spoke with an English accent. "I have done as you asked. Riders have been sent out, and a caravan has embarked for the deep desert during the timeline you specified. I have also learned that many dollars have flowed in the caravan's wake, spreading from oasis to oasis. This money has filled the hands of the worst of men that roam the Sahel. The caravan does not wish to be followed, and I fear you will find few friends upon your journey."

Bolan had suspected as much. "The caravan, is it a motorcade or are they traveling by camel?"

The woman looked long and hard upon Bolan. "Camel."

That was to their advantage. In the Unimogs, they stood a good chance of overtaking them. The bad news was there would be hundreds if not thousands of strings of camels moving goods across the Sahara. Satellite tracking would be useless. They would need human intelligence, but human intelligence that Bolan had harvested with his own hands was the kind he trusted the most anyway.

The men who would come to kill them would probably know something.

"We should start as soon as possible."

"Your man is correct. The more time we wait the more men your enemies will be able to raise against you." The woman extended a hand at the sizzling cook pots and boiling tea. "You and your men should take refreshment. I shall gather my things and we shall go."

The Sahel

"EMANUELLE MARYAM NERA." Tymosh was busy text messaging on her own satellite link as the equipment and spares

Unimog rumbled through the rocky terrain. She, Bolan and Pun were pulling rearguard duty in the convoy, driving in the equipment and spares truck. Lord William and Hakmoun led from the Unicat at the front with the water and fuel truck in the middle. Bolan rode shotgun beside Thuf while Tymosh sprawled out on the backseat bench of the cab.

The air of the desert was freezing cold at two in the morning and the moon was a tiny silver sickle of ice above. Despite this, Hakmoun wound the caravan through the rock formations as if he were threading a needle, and he did it without the benefit of night-vision equipment.

Bolan clambered into the backseat. "You have information on her?"

"A little, from old KGB file. During Cold War, Soviet Union supported Socialist Libyan leader Colonel Muammar Khaddafi. He wished, with Soviet urging, to spread socialism in North Africa. Fueling terrorist cells and inciting separatist insurgencies in nominally western friendly nations was common tactic. Colonel Glen-Patrick's friend, Oumu Hakmoun, was apparently great warrior and caravan master. He travel from Dakar to Cairo and know every oasis in between. Have friends in every major city in North Africa. KGB believe Oumu Hakmoun also British agent. I believe Colonel Glen-Patrick's friendship with him confirm this."

Bolan knew what was coming. "And old Oumu had a sister."

"Hakmoun have fifteen sisters, but I believe your hypothesis is correct. Dashing British soldier, beautiful Berber woman, moonlit night over oasis, a secret tryst, it is not difficult to imagine. Then dashing soldier must leave to fight other wars, and child is born behind him. He fights many wars, meets many women in many places. He is absentee father at best, and it is source of strain between himself and Oumu. Perhaps friendship ended over it." Tymosh shrugged. "Bold of him to come requesting aid now."

"Asking for aid was the excuse he needed. He wanted to see the old man one more time and see his daughter, and to take his lumps if necessary."

"Repentance and atonement, yes." Tymosh's lips pursed delightfully. "But why now?"

"Because he's dying."

The Russian agent was quiet for several moments and watched the dunes grind by. "She went to school in England. A degree in Cultural Anthropology and Women's Studies at Cambridge. Then she return to desert. Reason unknown. File on her ends."

Bolan stared out across the endless ergs of the Sahel. Emanuelle Nera's haunted beauty was a mystery. He'd be a liar if he said it didn't intrigue him. "So that makes Zayid Emma's cousin."

"Yes." The predatory smile twitched across Tymosh's lips. "And he is utterly untrustworthy. He also hungers for Emma. I can tell."

Bolan smiled slightly. "She looks at Zayid like he's a bug."

"Yes. She prefers you."

Bolan hadn't caught that particular vibe, but then again he'd had a lot on his mind lately. "She didn't look particularly happy to see me, either."

"Her father has returned. She is conflicted. I watched her while we ate. You are dangerous man of the West who has suddenly appeared in life, which she considered, settled, and settled for less. It is kismet. Fate. She will make the same mistake as her mother. I will wager you any sum of money you care to name."

"You're sure about that."

"Sure enough to know that I must have you now if I am to have you at all."

Bolan laughed. "I'm not sure if now is the perfect time."

"Now is perfect time. In camp, one must be on guard, working, or best, sleeping."

It seemed the Russian was serious….

"WE WILL CROSS into Mauritania before sunset," Hakmoun said.

Bolan stood with their guide. Unimog 2 was steaming. Lunk and Thuf had their heads under the hood and were wrenching away. Anyone not on guard duty or working was busy sleeping in the air-conditioned comfort of the Unicat. The sun had dropped past its zenith, and the temperature had dropped to a more bearable 110 degrees. It would be time to move soon. Hakmoun seemed oblivious to the brutal conditions, though his one nod to the open Sahel was that he now wore a white, ten-gallon Stetson hat and a red bandanna around his neck. His desert cowboy-pirate look was complete. He had also clipped on the plastic holster-stock of his VP-70 pistol and wore the weapon slung at the ready over his shoulder.

Crossing into Mauritania was good news. The Western Sahara was claimed by Morocco, and money in the hands of the right governmental entity could send Moroccan Mirage F-1 fighters or helicopter gunships sweeping the desert for a strange caravan. Mauritania was one of the poorest nations on Earth and had almost no infrastructure outside the few cities. By the same token, the lawless, roadless, northern interior would be the most likely place for the ambush to happen.

Hakmoun was thinking the same thing. "Soon, no?"

"Yeah." Bolan pulled his scarf down around his shoulders

and replaced it with a very battered khaki boonie hat. He tilted his MAS 49 rifle across his shoulders and scanned the desert. The rifle had cleaned up well. It had not been particularly well cared for, but it had been built solidly in the first place. The good news was that while the dry desert climate and sand might have stripped the finish and bleached out the stock, it also kept the rifle free of rust and the bore fairly clean. Bolan had oiled and tuned the action, and just a little bit of file work on the trigger group had brought the trigger pull to a smooth, clean break. Bolan had stared sadly at the sight bar and wished vainly for an optical sight to mount on it, but the ancient diopter iron sight still graduated from 200 to a somewhat optimistic 1200.

A few French AMEX rifle grenades would have been welcome, as well, but they, much like snow, were in short supply in the Sahel this day.

Bolan looked back at the Unicat. Lord William came out to eat and that was about it. Again Hakmoun and Bolan were on the same frequency.

"It is not the heat, or the sand, but the dust that kills. It scars the lungs. In my father's day foreigners refused to wear the veil. The British had to maintain their foolish dignity."

Bolan smiled tiredly at the raider. "I don't see you wearing the *shesh.*"

Hakmoun showed his metalwork like a shark and cocked his hat at a rakish angle. "I have my own foolish sense of style to maintain, no?"

"Very chic," Bolan acknowledged. "Where's the next well?"

"A day, and half another more. It is in the middle of a range of hills. A perfect place for an ambush."

Bolan shrugged. "Yeah, but where would you set the ambush?"

Hakmoun laughed. "I would ambush me now. It may be

the enemy has the money and power to buy the allegiance of an entire oasis, but, tactically, it would still be best if we never lived to reach it, no?"

"That's what I'm thinking, as well."

Among many things, Gurkhas were famous for the sharpness of their eyesight. Almost on cue Pun barked from his position on top of the Unicat, "Striker! A rider approaches!"

The team spilled out of the Unicat and took position around the trucks.

Something shimmered out in the salt flats. Bolan pulled his shades down over his eyes, and a man on a camel became visible. Lord William came forward, snapping out his weapon's folding stock and squinting into the glare.

Hakmoun grinned. "I know this man! He is Ali ibn Baly."

"A bandit?"

"When the situation warrants. A trader in salt when it does not."

Bolan raised his binoculars. The rider rolled forward on a groaning, swaying camel. His head and face were swathed in dark indigo and he wore a long robe in a bright electric-blue. Peaking from the beneath the hem were canvas French desert combat boots. Long minutes passed as he crossed the salt flat between them. Above his scarf, his eyes were heavily blackened with kohl against the unceasing glare.

Bolan nodded to him. "Zayid, ask him if he will take tea or a cigarette."

"Ah." Hakmoun and Baly exchanged a few words. The Berber sighed. "He thanks you for your gracious hospitality, but he is on a pressing errand and he does not have the time."

"And that errand is to kill us."

"I am afraid that is the case."

Lunk threw a long shadow across the salt flats. The big

man stood with a French AAT general-purpose machine gun cocked on his hip like a sporting shotgun. The rider gaped openly at the giant Welshman. "So why don't I twist his bloody head off, then, and be done with it?"

"I am afraid that would not do," Hakmoun replied. "He has come to parley. Even having refused our hospitality, he must be allowed to leave the same way he approached. The code of the desert must be observed. Without it we are but beasts, no?"

Lord William smiled up at the rider. "So, the bugger's come under a flag of truce to count our guns and examine our disposition."

Hakmoun shrugged. "He would be most foolish not to."

Bolan kept his rifle tilted casually across his shoulders, but his finger was not far from the trigger. "This isn't a false parley. He's offered terms, hasn't he, Zayid?"

Hakmoun grinned. "Oh, indeed, he has. The son of Baly has told me that I may take the trucks, weapons and gear and leave the desert alive if I arrange to deliver yourself, the baron and the baron's daughter into his hands."

"And what says the son of Oumu Hakmoun?"

"I must admit I am tempted." Hakmoun let out a heavy sigh. "And yet, my heart still bears what some might say are unreasonable ambitions toward the baron's daughter. I would not see his hands upon her."

"Tell him I'll pay him and his men double."

Hakmoun relayed the information. "He says it is a gracious offer, but he can take whatever you have once the desert is bleaching your bones."

"Then tell him to go the way he came, and to go with God."

Hakmoun spoke a few words. Baly pulled his scarf down enough to show Bolan an evil smile and then switched his camel. The Executioner watched as the raider rode off toward the dune in the distance. "How many men?"

"A good question. Money will have undoubtedly swollen his ranks. I would dare say twenty, perhaps forty, and perhaps a handful more."

Bolan turned to Lord William. "What do you think?"

"You don't want to know what I'm bloody thinking."

"Yeah, Bill, I do. You've fought these people before."

"Well, Ali Baly and his forty thieves? They're just that. Raiders. Your 101st Airborne Division loses a platoon? They send another. But Baly and his men? They're tribal. They'll all be brothers and cousins and affiliated families. Unless they're defending the faith in holy war, casualties are their worst nightmare. If they lose many of their adult males, the tribe is dangerously weakened, and other enemy tribes will start circling like sharks smelling blood in the sand."

Bolan nodded. "And Ali ibn Baly is dictating terms from strength."

"Yes, and I don't like the bloody sound of it. It makes me nervous."

Lunk's voice rumbled angrily. "He's bluffing."

Bolan didn't speak Berber, but he had looked into the raider's eyes. "He isn't bluffing. We're about to get pounded."

Lunk scanned the dune; everything else was salt flats in all directions. "Pound us with what?"

There was no place for Baly and his men to be except behind the long dune. Bolan estimated it was slightly more than a thousand yards off, far beyond RPG range, and he wasn't expecting a cavalry charge. "Zayid, any chance he has mortars?"

"It is unlikely."

Desert raiders were unlikely to have anything heavier than

light machine guns and RPGs. That did not preclude them having some form of foreign assistance.

The baron read Bolan's mind. "You think Baly may have some of Jennings's Aegis boys with them?"

"It's crossed my mind."

Pun shouted from his perch atop the Unimog. "Cannon!"

In the distance, Ali ibn Baly had thrown himself down from his camel, yanked it to its knees and hidden behind it.

Hakmoun was outraged. "The dog! He attacks while parley is in effect!"

Bolan raised his binoculars. Pun was mostly right. It was a Moroccan army-issue 106 mm recoilless rifle, but no one on the wrong end of it would care about the technicality. Two robed men had set it on top of the dune while a third loaded it. A man in desert camouflage fatigues crouched behind the sights while a second military man slammed in a round.

"Get away from the trucks! Lunk, covering fire!"

Lunk dropped to one knee and the machine gun began rattling off short bursts. A puff of smoke rose from the top of the dune, and Bolan saw the tracer from the M-40's spotting rifle streak across the intervening distance and unerringly punch a hole in the Unimog beneath Pun. Water spewed from the ruptured storage tank and the salt beneath it drank it up instantly.

"Pun! Move!"

Pun sprinted across the top of the truck and vaulted into the air. Flame and black smoke exploded from both ends of the recoilless rifle. Pun hit the salt, tucking and rolling like a trained paratrooper, and bounced to his feet and continued sprinting for his life. The water and fuel Unimog went up in an explosion of smoke, fire and steam behind him as the 17-pound, high-explosive shell hit the diesel tanks and detonated.

Lunk sprayed away but he was firing offhand, and the range was too long.

"Zayid! Take a knee!"

"What? I—"

Bolan rammed Hakmoun down to one knee and laid his rifle across his shoulder. "Cover your ears!"

The Berber cringed and clapped his hands over his ears.

Lord William stood with his binoculars raised. "He's traversing!"

Bolan shoved the slide on the rear sight all the way forward to 1200 and the diopter rose up in the air to a ridiculous height. Bolan seesawed his front sight up across Hakmoun's shoulder to match it. Bolan had keener eyesight than most people, but hitting an individual target at more than a thousand yards with an open sight was beyond even his skills. However, the four men were clustered around a crew-served weapon in a convenient lump.

A tracer streaked from the top of the dune and sparked against the side of the Unicat. The 106 mm tube belched fire and the round hit the Unicat broadside and detonated within. The Unicat wasn't full of hundreds of gallons of diesel fuel, but the damage was done. The blow rolled it over onto its side, cracked it open like an egg billowing smoke.

Bolan put his front sight in the middle of the crew on the dune and began squeezing the trigger as rapidly as he could bring his sights to bear after each shot.

"He's traversing!" Lord William roared.

Bolan kept squeezing his trigger. A tiny figure in the distance fell away from the gun crew and began rolling down the dune. Bolan's rifle racked open on a smoking empty chamber.

The remaining Unimog belched smoke as it revved into life. Hakmoun started to rise. "Aksil! You coward! I will see your entrails opened to the sky!"

Bolan vised his hand into the side of Hakmoun's neck and yanked him back into place. He slammed in a fresh magazine as the Unimog's gears ground and it began to roll westward. A tracer round streaked in a line of smoke from the top of the dune and hit the Unimog squarely between the taillights. Bolan rammed his action forward on a fresh round and began firing as fast as he could pull the trigger. The recoilless rifle boomed from atop the dune.

The shell struck the Unimog squarely in the back bumper. Flames exploded out of every window, and the truck flipped end over end.

Bolan's rifle racked open on empty.

Lord William lowered his binoculars. "They've retreated behind the dune."

Bolan rose and surveyed the situation. The damage was total. The satellite links and radios were wrecked. He had already tried and found no phone service this far into the desert on his cell. They had no food, no water except for a few canteens, no shelter and no transportation.

In the morning the sun would kill them.

"We need to—" Bolan stopped as Lord William made a terrible noise and broke into a run.

Emma lay in the sand and it darkened around her head with blood.

Bolan charged past him and knelt beside her. A shard of truck had hit her like shrapnel. A bare corner of it stuck out from her temple but the wound in the side of her head told Bolan most of it was within her skull. She was still beautiful. Her death mask was serene, but her pupils were blown and her sightless eyes stared straight up into the sun.

Lord William fell to his knees beside her with a groan.

Lunk's hand fell lightly on Bolan's shoulder. "Let me."

Bolan rose as Lord William fell to his hands and knees and wept. Lunk took a knee beside him and spoke softly.

Hakmoun took in Emma's body and then turned to stare out toward the dune. Baly had recovered his camel and ridden to safety during the firefight. "The dog shall wait, far away in his camp, drinking tea and eating dates while he lets the sun slay us."

The man's callousness did not surprise Bolan. He had met men of the desert before. The Sahara took and only infrequently gave. Survival was always the first priority, then revenge. Mourning was more often than not a luxury. Bolan reloaded his rifle. A rescue mission into the deep Sahara would not be coming in any useful time frame. The answer to their predicament was obvious. "Baly has water, food, camels and tents."

For once Hakmoun was at a loss for words. "You wish to attack him? He will be thirty kilometers away! If not more!"

Bolan surveyed his team. Lord William was destroyed. Lunk had cracked ribs. Tymosh was an assassin, not a soldier. Thuf was a noncombatant. "Pope, Pun, gear up. Water, rifle and ammo, that's it. We head out once the sun sets."

Hakmoun was incredulous. "You will march thirty kilometers across the desert, and attack Ali ibn Baly with three men?"

"No, with four. You're going to track them for us."

CHAPTER NINETEEN

Bolan sized up the enemy from atop the mountain of sand. Their camp was a cluster of low tents. Men huddled around tiny camel dung fires against the morning chill, drinking mint tea. The sun was just starting to rise. The night trek had taken longer than expected. Pope was out of shape, and while Hakmoun was a powerful man, he had probably not run anywhere since he was a small child. After they had both thrown up twice, the run had turned to a forced march. Bolan counted a score of men including the bright blue figure of Ali ibn Baly and the two men in fatigues. There would be at least twenty more probably still in their tents. However, the day started early in the desert. They wouldn't be there long. Bolan examined the two men in uniform. Neither bore any insignia. They appeared Middle Eastern or North African.

Bolan passed Pope the binoculars. "You know these guys?"

"Nah, they aren't Aegis. Least, none I've ever met."

Bolan took back the binoculars and handed them to Hakmoun. "Any ideas?"

The desert pirate scowled in disdain. "They are not Ber-

bers. Nor are they even men of the desert. They sit, eat and talk like Arabs, and city Arabs at that."

"Egyptian commandoes?" Bolan suggested.

"Perhaps."

They crabbed backward down the dune, out of sight. Pun stayed up top watching. "All right, I'm betting they're the rearguard of the caravan carrying the warheads. They probably debarked with the weapons or met them. I want at least one of them alive." Bolan took out his half-full canteen, and the four men passed it around until it was empty.

Pun spoke quietly from his station. "Striker."

Bolan crawled back up followed by Hakmoun. Two men had mounted camels and were ambling around the dune. "Scouts?"

"I believe they go to see how we are doing. They will not get close, and will give the ambush site a wide berth. They will have binoculars, but knowing we are afoot they will not be particularly alert."

The question was how to sneak up on them when, other than the dune, there was no cover. "Zayid, we need a diversion. Go back about thirty meters and start walking toward the camp. When they see you, fall to your knees, plead, whatever, but keep them focused forward. We'll come up behind them."

Hakmoun peered at Bolan for long moments. "Very well."

Bolan put down his rifle and drew the Russian bayonet he'd retained. "Gary, Pun and I are going to take these guys. I want to do it quiet. I want you to stay at the top of the dune. If we miss and either of them starts to ride away, you take them, then start shooting at the men in camp and don't stop."

"Copy that."

Hakmoun moved down the dune and back, while Bolan and Pun hurried to its foot and swiftly began digging a shallow declivity with their knives to hide themselves for a few precious seconds. A fold in the dune helped, and soon Bolan and Pun were huddled in a shallow, slanted grave. They didn't have long to wait. The two riders came at a leisurely pace, laughing and talking.

They pulled up short as they caught sight of Hakmoun.

The Berber staggered forward. He tossed his machine pistol into the salt at the sight of them and waved his arms, obviously pleading. He pointed back the way he had come, and Baly's two men never noticed Bolan and Pun in the sand cleft as they passed. Hakmoun was good. He drew his arm dagger and fell to his knees. With both hands, he plunged it into the ground in front of him and spread his arms in abject, weeping surrender.

Bolan and Pun rose and raced forward.

Camel riders did not use stirrups. They simply crossed one leg over their saddle horn. Bolan vaulted up and grabbed his man by the sleeve of his voluminous robe and yanked him out of the saddle. The raider thudded to the salt and wheezed as the breath was knocked out of his body. He never drew another as Bolan sliced Russian steel across his throat.

Pun wasn't quite tall enough for the maneuver, so he grabbed his man by his trailing robe and scuttled up him like a monkey. He drove his fist into the Tuareg's face and the two of them tumbled out of the saddle. Pun drew his khukri in midtumble, and it crunched into the man's skull as they hit the ground.

The camels ran honking and groaning in alarm into the salt flats. Hakmoun retrieved his dagger and his automatic weapon, then followed the beasts, making a strange kissing noise and beckoning. The camels ceased their flight and peered at him.

Bolan began stripping the Tuareg of his scarf and robe. Pun

did the same. The men were wearing two layered robes each against the morning chill. A few minutes later, Hakmoun returned with the camels in tow. They took one of the water skins and passed it around and quickly wolfed salted strips of dried goat from the pannier.

With slaked thirst and food in their bellies, the team looked a little more ready for action.

Bolan pulled on the nomad's robe. "Help me with the scarf."

Hakmoun swiftly wound fabric around Bolan's head and rummaged a khol stick from one of the dead men's belongings to darken Bolan's eyes. "Very handsome."

"Do Pun and then yourself."

In a matter of moments, they all looked like desert raiders, except that Pun's robe was about five sizes too large. Until one got up close, he looked like a kid dressed up for Halloween. Hakmoun adjusted Pun's hem with his dagger and shrugged. "He will not pass but the most casual inspection."

"With any luck, he won't have to. He'll hang on the side between us. We head straight for the strings of camels and drop him off. Then you and I infiltrate the camp. Pun goes for targets of opportunity, and if the shit hits the fan, then Gary gives us support fire from the top of the dune."

Pun nodded.

The Berber considered that. "And what is our objective?"

"Kill people. Break stuff, and I want one of the men in uniform alive."

"Ah." Hakmoun peered back and forth at Bolan and Pun and then at Pope at the top of the dune. If he was going to betray them, this was going to be his golden opportunity. The Berber clucked at the camels, and with a couple of tugs on the reins they knelt to be mounted. Bolan had ridden a camel before but it had been a while. The gigantic beast groaned beneath him and swayed like a ship in a gale as it rose. It craned its neck around to bite Pun as he hauled himself up onto its left side but seemed to think better of it as Bolan took up his switch. Pun reached out to Hakmoun's camel as it rose and hung between them like a spider.

"Hut! Hut! Hut!" At Hakmoun's urging, the camels lurched into a slow walk. They ambled along the edge of the dune and came back into sight of the camp. "This plan is, how do you say, thin?"

"Maybe. You hungry?"

"Famished."

Bolan watched the camp. No one had seemed to take much note of their return. "The food is there."

"Ah."

They gave the camp a fairly wide berth and moved to the strings of camels. There were close to seventy of them, as most of the raiders brought a spare with them as a remount or a loot carrier.

"Who's going to be watching the camels?" Bolan asked.

"Boys or slaves. If this were a caravan, I would lean toward boys of the tribes. Since this is a military venture, I do not believe they would risk their sons. I believe they will be slaves from enemy tribes."

They slowly approached a group of a dozen men and boys in brown robes of inferior cut. Other than working knives on their sashes and camel switches, they were unarmed. They sat around a tiny dung fire and passed a battered copper teakettle between them. They didn't wear face scarves, and they were clearly black Africans from the south. Two of them rose to take Bolan's and Hakmoun's camels. They came to a startled halt as Pun dropped down and swung up his rifle.

Bolan pulled down his scarf so the drovers could see his

face. "Zayid, tell them I will give them each a thousand U.S. dollars and their freedom."

Hakmoun was appalled. "A thousand—"

"Do it."

The Berber started speaking low and quick to the wondering drovers. Bolan reached under his robe and pulled out a clip of cash as thick as a deck of cards. Excitement rippled through the circle of men. A grizzled old man who was clearly the leader listened to the exchange. His eyes flicked to the encamped Tuaregs a few dozen yards away and then made some pointed comments.

Hakmoun turned back to Bolan in irritation. He was clearly outraged to find himself bargaining with slaves. "This man's name, which is of no importance I can imagine, is Kante. He says he says he and his men will not fight the Tuaregs. They would be slaughtered."

"Tell them they don't have to."

Hakmoun relayed this. "Kante is intrigued by the fact that there are only three of us and forty Tuaregs, and wonders why he should not raise the alarm."

"Tell him we are more than three and there is a rifle pointed at his chest from concealment."

Kante appeared to give this the weighty consideration it deserved before speaking. Hakmoun sighed. "He wishes to know exactly what they must do."

"Tell them I wish them to drink tea, and enjoy the show."

The Berber stared at Bolan for long moments and then translated. Kante stared even longer and a very slow smile crept across his ancient face. He shrugged and nodded to the man next to him to refill his teacup. *"Inshallah."*

Bolan smiled. It was Arabic, and meant "If God wills it."

"Pun, take one of the young men's robes that fits, and let me have your submachine gun. Take a water skin or some other burden and go from tent to tent. Take out as many as you can as quietly as you can."

Pun scooped up a carpeted water bag and handed off his weapon. "Yes, Striker."

Hakmoun shook his head bitterly. "And we are to slaughter the rest of them?"

"No, just convince the majority to surrender."

"I was not aware that you are a sorcerer," Hakmoun observed.

"It's amazing how a 106 mm recoilless rifle can change attitudes."

The Berber looked at Bolan slyly. "You wish to approach the weapon."

"I do, indeed."

That was their best piece of luck so far. The weapon was only a few feet away from the circle of men containing both Baly and the Egyptians, and was mounted on its tripod and apparently ready for action with a crate of 106 mm projectiles open beside it.

"Then let us approach it."

The two men began to walk a circular route, talking low and approaching Ali ibn Baly's little group. Pun ducked into a tent. Bolan and Hakmoun kept walking. He glanced back as Pun came out of the tent. The water skin was still across his shoulder. He held his bloody khukri low at his side. He casually held up four fingers and headed for the adjacent tent. The two men walked behind Baly's tent, and when they came around the other side, Pun shot them another hand sign.

Three.

Their luck couldn't keep holding. "I'm going to the weapon. When I start shooting, grab an Egyptian and get him out of the way without killing him."

"Very well."

Bolan broke off from Hakmoun and walked straight up to the 106 mm gun. Baly was laughing and talking with the Egyptians in Arabic. Around ten of his cronies sat with him, armed to the teeth. Bolan glanced at the spotting rifle mounted parallel to the main tube. The 5-round magazine was in place and the rifle appeared to be cocked and locked on a loaded chamber. The ammo crate had spaces for four projectiles and one appeared to be missing.

Bolan flipped the safety off the spotting rifle.

One of the Egyptians noticed and snarled something at Bolan in Arabic. The Executioner knelt as if examining the weapon, and the man shouted in angrier French. Bolan flicked the lever for free traverse and brought the tube in line with the snarling commando. His snarl turned to a shout of alarm as Bolan swung the weapon in line and triggered the spotting rifle. The .50-caliber tracer round smashed the man off his feet and dropped him in the fire. The nine-foot tube was awkward to maneuver, but most of the men were still leaping to their feet. Bolan shot down four more and then stood as he spun the weapon backward.

Zayid appeared behind the second Egyptian and his twisted scarf looped around the commando's throat and yanked him backward. Baly had leaped to his feet and yanked a pistol from his robe, and his men were leveling rifles and submachine guns.

Bolan squeezed the trigger on the 106 mm rifle.

The principle behind the recoilless rifle was simple. Every action had an equal and opposite reaction. When a gun blasted something out of its barrel, the force of it smashed backward. That was why guns recoiled. The recoilless mitigated recoil by venting a large portion of the propellant gas backward.

It made them very dangerous to stand behind.

The range was four meters, and the six-meter cone of fire

was lethal at five. Flame spewed from the 106 mm weapon at both ends. Baly and his men disappeared in a blast of superheated gas and smoke, and the tent behind them instantly caught fire. Though almost drowned out by the din, Bolan managed to hear Pope firing from the sand ridge, and men were falling down all over the camp. Pun had his pistol in one hand and his khukri in the other and slaughtered the milling and screaming raiders. Bolan stepped away from the recoilless weapon and began firing short, rapid bursts from his submachine gun.

Four Tuaregs ran, screaming, toward their camels. Kante and his men rose and pulled them from the saddles as they tried to mount, falling upon them with their knives. Another three saw what happened to their comrades and ran straight into the desert. Of Ali ibn Baly and his forty thieves, Baly was roasted meat and only ten of his men had survived the initial onslaught. Bolan knew a few choice words in Arabic and his voice cut above the screaming and shouting.

"Surrender!"

The remaining Tuaregs stared around themselves at the horror. The burned and the shot lay everywhere. Surprise had been total. None of their comrades had come from the tents to help them. Pope had stood on the dune with his rifle. Baly was dead, and the remaining Egyptian had Hakmoun's machine pistol screwed into his temple.

Behind them, the drovers were coming forward, chanting and holding their bloody knives high.

"Zayid, tell them to drop their weapons or I let the drovers have them!"

The Berber related this with obvious relish, and the remaining raiders dropped their weapons, fell to their knees and began to wring their hands and plead for their lives. Hakmoun shook his head in wonder. "You are, indeed, a sorcerer."

"Tell Kante and his men that I've defeated their masters, that I own them by right and that by that right, I free them. As soon as the camp is secure, I will give them the money I promised, and each man may take two camels, whatever guns, food and water he needs, and go wherever he wishes. Tell them the Tuaregs and the Egyptian are my prisoners and under my protection."

Hakmoun nodded and shouted over the moans of the wounded. The drovers shouted in elation. Several shook their knives angrily, demanding payback, but Kante calmed them. Pope walked slowly down the dune. A few warning shots had corralled the few raiders fleeing on foot, and he marched them back into camp.

"Zayid, we're going to camp here for the day. I want you to take a couple of the drovers and a string of camels. Load them up with water and food and retrieve the rest of the team. When you get back, you and I will have a conversation with the Egyptian and the most senior survivor."

"Very well." Hakmoun pushed the Egyptian to the sand and shouted to Kante. Every drover shot his switch up into the air and shouted to volunteer. The Berber lifted a lip derisively. "You have an army. Albeit an army of slaves."

"They're free men, Zayid. Don't forget that, and get a move on. The sun is rising, and no one back with the trucks has had any water in twenty-four hours."

Hakmoun stalked off toward the camels like an angry cat.

Bolan frowned. "Pun?"

The Gurkha had shed his robe and was cleaning his knife with it. "Yes, Striker?"

Bolan watched Hakmoun pick four men from the shouting throng. "Go with him."

Pun tested the edge of his knife and sheathed it. "Yes, Striker."

CHAPTER TWENTY

Lord William was resting comfortably in a tent. Lunk was sticking to him like glue. The team had been in pretty bad shape and suffering from exposure when they had arrived. Bolan was loath to do it, but they were going to have to take twenty-four hours downtime at the Tuareg camp. He needed the rest himself, but there was still work to do. "Zayid."

The Berber rose from beside the fire. "Yes?"

"Let's have a talk with our guest." They entered a tent where the commando lay tied up on a carpet with Pun watching over him. "You speak English?"

The man glared at the wall of the tent and said nothing.

"Zayid, tell him he can speak English with me or Arabic with you."

The Berber drew his dagger and relayed the information with a smile.

"I will speak English," the man responded.

Bolan made a shrewd guess. "You're 130th Amphibious Brigade?" The man flinched, and Bolan knew he'd hit pay dirt. They were often involved in Egyptian naval operations, and it was a logical place for Captain Goma to recruit soldiers. "Where are the warheads headed?"

The man returned to staring at the fabric walls.

"I understand that you were quite abusive to the drovers." The man's cheek muscles flexed against his will. "They want me to hand you over to them." The Executioner cocked his head as the man squirmed. "For a holy martyr about to achieve Paradise, you seem quite agitated. I wasn't aware that profuse sweating was a sign of divine—"

A stream of Arabic invectives spewed from the man's mouth. They ceased as Hakmoun knelt happily over him with his dagger.

"You seem more like a soldier than a martyr," Bolan continued. "So let's talk, soldier to soldier. Name and rank."

The man peered at Bolan. "I am POW?"

"Name and rank, or the knife. Don't make me ask you again."

"Hossam Hamza, Lieutenant."

"Good. Lieutenant, I'm going to make you a deal. You tell me what I want to know, and I give you water and a camel and the desert decides your fate."

The man glared up at Bolan bitterly. "To be hunted by bandits and the scum of the Sahel? Hundreds of kilometers from any city? It is not a mercy."

"You don't deserve mercy, but you are an Egyptian Special Forces officer, trained in desert warfare. What I'm giving you is a chance."

"And if I do not accept this chance?"

"Then I leave you here with no water and no camel, and the desert still decides your fate." Bolan shrugged. "Or you can anger me, and I give you to the drovers. Decide."

"I do not know where the weapons are headed. I was not told. For security."

"Which way did they go when you parted directions?"

The man's jaw clenched again.

"I'm going to count to one. One…"

"East! They headed southeast!"

Bolan consulted his mental map. They were headed for Mali and the middle of the Sahara. "What is the final destination?"

"Other than God's glory, I do not know."

Bolan believed him. "How many men are with them?"

"Ten such as myself, and a score of foreigners."

"Aegis?"

The man blinked. "I do not know what that means."

"Mercenaries, mostly Western and armed with the latest weapons and equipment."

"Yes, they appeared to be mercenaries."

"They're on camels?"

"The last I saw of them, yes."

"How many more rearguard teams like yours?"

"Four, but they are spread out north and south. You have pierced the net."

"But money is paid at each oasis to see that we don't see our way out of the Sahel."

"Yes, that is so."

Hakmoun knelt, ready with his knife. "He knows no more?"

"Nothing of current interest to me."

"So I shall slay him."

The Egyptian recoiled.

Bolan suddenly loomed over the Berber. "You'll put him on a camel at dawn."

Hakmoun stared up at Bolan as if he had just dropped in from Mars. "You confound me."

"Stick around, it's only going to get better." Bolan went

outside and clicked on the satellite link he'd found among Hamza's belongings. He clicked keys and tuned to a current Farm secure frequency. "Bear?"

"Right here, Striker. Where are you? You didn't check in at the regular interval."

"We were attacked, and the trucks got totaled. We had to acquire some alternate transportation. Listen, I think the warheads are moving southeast."

"Interesting. I was betting on north into Algeria."

Bolan flipped open his map. "Going southeast into Mali, there are only two airstrips of any notice. One in Timbuktu and one in Goundam. I want you to get Jack on a plane to Timbuktu, and see if you can dig up a helicopter big enough for the whole team. I also want a doctor on site in both towns for Lord William when we come in."

"I'll get Barbara on it immediately."

"What's our satellite situation?" Bolan asked, though he suspected he already knew the answer.

"Striker, we just don't have anything high-imaging tracking the Sahara. I've been told we're a priority, but shuffling satellite orbits is a big undertaking. It's going to take time."

"All right, keep on it and let me know. I'm heading out at dawn. Striker, out."

Bolan stood as Kante approached with three men. Hakmoun frowned as Kante spoke. "He asks if you head south with the dawn?"

"Tell him I do."

Kante stared back at the strings of beasts and grinned at Bolan slyly.

The Berber rolled his eyes. "He says that even despite your generosity, you have an excess of camels."

Bolan nodded. "I do."

"And most of your people are not used to riding camels."

"Tell Kante that is true."

"He thinks you might require the services of experienced camel drovers. He says the three men with him, Yoro, Afel and Hamidou, are not totally incompetent."

Yoro, Afel and Hamidou nodded vigorously.

Bolan stared at Kante frankly. "Tell him I ride into terrible danger."

Hakmoun quirked an eyebrow at the response. "He says to ride across the Sahel is to ride into terrible danger, and you pay better than the Tuaregs."

"Ask him if he's ever fired a rifle."

"Kante says, quite rightly, that such things are not allowed to slaves."

"Well, he's a free man, and we ride into danger." Bolan glanced over to where Pope was stacking confiscated weapons. It was quite a pile. "Gary, grab four rifles, the pick of the litter. We've got about two hours of daylight left, and I want Kante and his men able to hit a man-size target at a hundred yards before dark. Zayid, you're translating."

"You're going to give them guns!"

"Yeah, and I'm running out of money. Tell Kante he and his men will have to settle for a hundred dollars a day until we get to a major city in Mali."

Hakmoun was outraged. "A hundred dollars a day!"

"Yeah, and ask Kante if he will pick me out a camel." Bolan eyed the dozens of groaning, honking, smelly beasts in the coffles. "A good one that doesn't spit."

El Mryeye Desert, Mali

THE CARAVAN RODE in the cool of the morning. They had crossed Mauritania's empty quarter without incident, and as far as Bolan was concerned, Kante and his men were worth their weight in gold. Kante sat his camel like it was a throne and he was the Prince of the Desert. He had been stolen from his family and made a slave. Now he returned with a string of camels to call his own, a fine blue robe taken from Baly's tent, his sash full of dollars and armed like a Balkan warlord.

Bolan's head snapped up and he held up his fist for the caravan to halt. Pope scanned the dunes ahead. "What is it?"

"Gunfire."

"I don't hear any—" The distant pop of guns became plain. "Oh, okay. I heard that."

"Everyone form up! Zayid! You're with me!" Bolan spurred his camel forward to the top of the nearest dune. Kante had set his man Hamidou riding forward as scout, and the Malian was charging back toward the caravan as fast as his camel would carry him. Behind him were roughly twenty horsemen firing long strings from their weapons and hitting a lot of sand. Hamidou's camel lumbered up the dune, and the man grinned at Bolan as he breathlessly gave his report to Hakmoun.

"He says he has run into men with guns."

That was pretty obvious. Bolan raised his binoculars and scanned the new threat. "If they're on horseback, then water must be close."

"Indeed," Hakmoun agreed. "Unfortunately, my knowledge of the Malian oases is not complete."

The men were equipped with the usual desert hodgepodge of small arms bought, stolen or traded throughout North Africa. The horsemen stopped on an opposite dune approximately six hundred yards away. They dismounted and began to raise their weapons.

"Back down!" Bolan wheeled his camel and took it down the face of the dune as the enemy opened up. They fired on full-auto, and at six hundred yards they could barely hit the side of the dune, but the way they were expending ammo the golden bullet was out there and looking to hit somebody. Bolan, Hakmoun and Hamidou knelt and hobbled their camels, then crawled back up to the top of the dune when the fusillade had ended. Bolan and the enemy leader examined each other through binoculars. The Malian on the opposite dune was tall enough to play forward in the NBA. He was robed but wore no scarf. He lowered his binoculars and began to shout. The acoustics of the desert were strange. Despite the distance, the sound of the man's voice was loud and clear. "What is he saying?"

"He says his name is Sogolon, son of Musa." Hakmoun gave Bolan a wry look. "I know this name. You seem to attract all the best sort out of the Sahel."

"Is he offering a deal?"

"He is bragging about his exploits regarding rape and murder."

Bolan watched as the men around Sogolon cheered and shook their weapons. The Executioner didn't want a running cavalry fight with these men, nor did he want the caravan stalked or the camp probed at dawn and dusk. He also wanted to avoid open battle. A display of precision marksmanship seemed to be in order. The Executioner took a prone shooting position.

"He says by dawn he shall be staking us out in the sand, removing our eyelids so that we may enjoy the rising sun more completely."

Bolan slid his sight slide forward to six hundred meters and took note of the wind playing across the sand.

"Now I believe he is addressing you. He says your mother was a transvestite and so was your father, and thus your crusader religion was born from the rectum of a donkey."

Bolan wasn't quite sure of the math on that one, but he was

sure of the range and windage. Sogolon was silhouetted at the top of the dune, his tall, brown-robed frame with nothing but nicely contrasting blue sky behind him. The sun was behind Bolan and the post of the front sight showed up crisply against Sogolon's chest as Bolan aimed for high, center body mass. The Executioner slowly began taking up slack on the trigger.

"Now he says your—"

The French 7.5 mm weapon bucked against Bolan's shoulder. A second later dust flew from the front of Sogolon's robe, and he rocked back onto his heels. Sogolon fell to his knees and then onto his face where he lay unmoving in the sand. The Sahara was suddenly very quiet except for the echo of the rifle shot as Sogolon's men stared in stupefied awe.

Hakmoun regarded Bolan with renewed respect. "You are an excellent shot."

Bolan stood and raised his rifle over his head. "Translate what I say exactly."

The Executioner hurled his voice across the Sahel like Moses preaching from the mountain.

"I am the Master!"

Hakmoun shouted after Bolan delightedly.

"In the Sahel, I hold the life of anything within a thousand meters of me!"

The men on the opposite dune cringed slightly as a unit.

"I come to the oasis!" Bolan raised his binoculars. "I have noted your faces, and I will kill any of you I see!"

The Malian bandits hurried to their mounts and leaped into their saddles.

"But!" Bolan changed his timbre slightly. "Should any man among you have information useful to me, I will pay in American dollars."

Touerat Oasis

BOLAN HAD A CONVERSATION with a Malian bandit named Souleye. It seemed Souleye had immediately assumed Sogolon's position and was far fonder of American greenbacks than French bullets in the chest. Souleye didn't have much useful information. He, too, believed the caravan of foreigners was heading south and east. There was one scrap of information that Bolan paid for—Souleye had heard one of the foreigners, who appeared to be African, speaking on the radio in Hausa. Hausa was a language common in many areas of West Africa, but it was the native language of Niger.

Niger was four hundred miles and directly southeast of their current position.

Bolan clicked on his commandeered satellite link, and Kurtzman answered instantly. "What have you got, Striker?"

"No one showed up in Timbuktu or Goundam, did they?"

"Our assets are thin, but we had people looking for camel caravans coming into the city or stopping near it. Nothing suspicious came in that we detected. How did you know?"

"I need you to tie Lord Parkhurst to Niger somehow, and I don't care how thin it is, and then get me a location."

"Niger? You know, Niger is arguably the poorest country on Earth. It makes Mauritania look like Club Med. I think the only industry they have is uranium mining, and its all located way up in the north about a thousand miles from where you are now. Given Lord Parkhurst's reputation for being green, I doubt uranium would have been his thing."

"So find me something more southerly. I've got a gut feeling on this one. Speaking of finding things, did you manage to scare up a ride for Jack?"

"Barb set it up. He's in Timbuktu as we speak, holding down a helicopter hot on the pad for you."

"Good, and what's the chance of getting me that satellite?"

"Slim to none, at least for the next twenty-four hours."

"How about the chances for full war loads ready at the U.S. Embassy in Niamey when I arrive?"

"About the same as getting that satellite."

"All right, have Barb get in touch with the embassy. Tell them I'm going to need to borrow some items, but I don't want to be seen there. Tell Jack I'm at the Touerat Oasis, about a hundred miles due north of Timbuktu. I need immediate pickup, and we need a flight plan to Niger."

"We're on it."

"All right, I'll check in once I'm across the border. Striker out." Bolan glanced over to where Hakmoun sat trying to charm Tymosh. "Zayid, I'm going to Niger."

The Berber lifted his nose. "Niger is the flea-bitten armpit of the Sahel."

"I need a man who speaks Hausa."

"I take it you are still paying in American one-hundred-dollar bills?"

"Handsomely."

"Then I am your man." Hakmoun's eye slid toward an approaching figure. "Speaking of your men..."

Kante began talking avidly.

"Kante says he has sold his share of the camels you generously gave him to Hamidou and Yoro, and they are going to go into business for themselves and Thuf wishes to join them, but Kante says he is old and no longer wishes to be a drover. He heard you speak of Niger, and wishes to go with you. He says he has traveled through it several times in his life. He knows the people and speaks Hausa and some Djerma, as well. He says your friend, Monsieur Pope, has already made a him a good rifleman, and he will work hard to become better."

Bolan looked the wizened old man up and down. He seemed to be in earnest, and assets were where you found them. "Tell Kante I am honored and will be happy to take him on at the same rate of pay."

Hakmoun shook his head at the reply. "Kante says he has more money now than he knows what to do with. He says you are the man who broke his chains. He will serve you, until death, as long as you remain in the Sahel."

Bolan held out his hand and Kante seized it in both of his, pumping it furiously and smiling wide enough to expose his missing front teeth.

The Executioner retrieved his hand and steeled himself as he ducked into the tent where Lord William was resting. The baron was propped up on some cushions and smoking a cigarette with Lunk hovering in attendance.

"Lunk, I need a moment with Lord William."

The baron let out a long sigh. "Lunk can stay. I know what you've come to say. You want to drop me off at the British embassy in Timbuktu."

Bolan didn't deny it. "You're not well, Bill."

A tiny, wry smile crossed Lord William's face. "I'm dying, actually."

"And you've taken too many shots, physical and otherwise."

"Well, old son, my first instinct was to tell you that if you drop me, I take Pun and Lunk with me, but that was selfish. I admit it. But I'll tell you something, something even you haven't run into quite yet. A man reaches an age. A man sees his mortality." Lord William's face reflected his anguish. "He buries his child in the sand and knows it's his fault. He sees nothing but the darkness staring back at him and realizes he has nothing left."

Bolan looked down at the broken old soldier and felt his chest tighten. "You still have Lunk."

"I do, but that's the thing, I have more than that. I have one last thing."

Bolan took a long breath. It was something no mission to stop a nuke could afford. "Revenge."

"No." The dying old man's eyes shone with a steely light. "I have duty. Lunk had to remind me, but I am a knight and a lord of the realm, and my duty to queen and crown isn't quite finished yet. I'd planned to kill myself when things got bad enough. I give you my word as a knight, that the moment I become a burden to the team I'll put the gun in my mouth myself."

One look told Bolan that Lord William was deadly serious.

"And I'll tell you another thing. I still have connections. I'm still an asset. You need me, as broken and enfeebled as I am."

Bolan measured the man before him. There was no pleading, no desperation. Just the facts. "The helicopter will be here in half an hour. You're in."

CHAPTER TWENTY-ONE

Niamey, Niger

Bolan checked the action of the M-4 carbine. One of the few benefits of the war on terror was that the United States Marine Corps was taking its job as embassy guards very seriously, particularly in Muslim countries, and they were arming accordingly. The Marine captain in charge of the embassy guard was kind enough to give Bolan the keys to the kingdom. They had M-4 carbines, squad automatic weapons, grenade launchers, shotguns, designated marksman rifles and every other useful flavor in the Marine Corps candy shop. Still, Niger was far from the most fancy embassy the United States had, but then again, in this instance that was to Bolan's advantage. The embassy didn't have any Hummers. The Marines were still driving jeeps, and the 106 mm recoilless rifle's tripod mount had been designed from the get-go to clamp into a Jeep's back bed.

A couple of young Marine privates had spent the past half hour gleefully changing their conveyance into gun-Jeep configuration. They had even gone so far as to mount an M-60 machine gun onto the hood for the man riding shotgun.

All in all, it was a very hostile-looking vehicle.

There was only one 106 mm recoilless rifle in Niger at the moment, but the Marines had been nice enough to mount a .50-caliber machine gun on a second Jeep with a similar M-60 mounted on the hood. Bolan had a two-Jeep section and a well-armed fire team. Maybe things were slow in Niger these days, or maybe Yuliya Tymosh in a tank top had something to do with it, but despite having no idea what was going on, every one of them had volunteered for whatever the duty might be. It was with a heavy heart Bolan had turned them down. All hands on this mission had to be expendable and deniable, but he would have dearly loved two squads of U.S. Marines backing him up.

They were in a warehouse in the outskirts of the city and waiting for any word from the Farm. Bolan set the carbine back on the table full of weapons and ammo as his satellite link began peeping at him urgently. "What have you got for me, Bear?"

Kurtzman's voice was smug. "Gold."

"Where?"

"Well, like I said. The only real industry Niger had is uranium mining. And peanut plantations. The uranium market has been in a slump for the last decade, and people can eat only so much peanut butter."

"But gold always glitters."

"That's right, and there have been significant gold strikes along Niger's border with Burkina Faso. There's a Canadian mining firm involved in one of the mines."

"And Lord Parkhurst had an interest."

"It's not that easy to pin down, but you said you wanted anything, no matter how thin. I can vaguely tie businesses Lord Parkhurst had interests in with businesses that have interests in the Canadian mining outfit."

"Where's the mine?"

"Not far, about fifty miles from where you are right now."

"Good work, Bear."

"I have more good news. I got you your satellite. It's not geosynchronous. Our observation window will be for six hours between 10:00 a.m. and 3:00 p.m. but I figure that's when bad guys do most of their bad deeds, anyway."

"Bear, you rule the school."

"I know," Kurtzman replied modestly.

"The Marines have set me up with a couple of gun-Jeeps, but driving them out of the capital and out to the mine might cause a stir. So I'm going to have Jack ferry the Jeeps by helicopter into position tonight after dark. Before then, I'm going to need satellite maps of the mine and the surrounding area. After that, it's hurry up and wait. With any luck, we leap-frogged ahead of the nukes and we can arrange an intercept."

"I'll have Hal inform the President. I'll have the maps and all pertinent information on the mine faxed to you in fifteen minutes."

"Good enough, Bear, and thanks. Striker out." For the first time in a while, things were going their way, but they would still be fighting Aegis employees and Egyptian commandoes and be outnumbered at least three to one. In their favor, they had surprise and gun-Jeeps. Bolan picked up a Squad Advanced Marksman Rifle and nodded as he checked the oil on glass-slick action.

And when all else failed? There was always precision marksmanship.

Sundiata Mine, Burkina Faso border

BOLAN'S SCOPE SWEPT the target area. Grimaldi's Russian Mi-8 helicopter was old and cranky, but it could lift a cabled

Jeep with little effort. Both Jeeps were now in a clearing half a mile from the mine. There wasn't much to it: a shack, a truck park and a small airstrip. Despite the heavy equipment in the truck park, the mine was more like an exploratory hole.

A hole in the ground in Burkina Faso wasn't the worst place to hide some nukes.

Other than people going in or out in ones and twos, neither Bolan nor the NSA satellite had detected any activity around the mine.

Some dollars spread around at the local level had revealed the interesting fact that some poachers had seen a string of camels being moved through the forest near the mine twenty-four hours earlier. Camels were not an unknown sight in Burkina Faso. It wasn't that far from where the forest met the desert.

Creeping through the forest at night this far south was more than a little unusual.

"Zayid, tell Kante it's time."

Hakmoun gestured, and Kante came forward. The little old man had shed his desert garb and now wore the local, long parti-colored tunic with a matching tall cap, and rather than a camel, he was mounted on a horse.

The two Africans came forward. Hakmoun translated while Bolan spoke directly to Kante. "I want you to run a recon on the mine. Ride through the forest about a kilometer and then approach the mine from the direction of town. Ride right up to the front gate. Tell anyone you run into exactly what we heard—that there is a rumor they have camels. If they ask how, tell them we heard from poachers who came into town. Yesterday. Tell them you are willing to buy all they have. Kante, there's also a good chance they'll just shoot you, so if you want out, now is the time to say so. This job is on a volunteer basis. I won't hold it against you."

Kante grinned and began to wave his hands. "He says he is your servant in this," Hakmoun said.

"Good. If they say yes, insist on looking at the animals, see if you recognize any of them. Bargain hard. Bargain in Hausa and bargain in CFA francs. If they brush you off, let them, but remember everything you see."

The little Malian brought his hands over his heart and spoke seriously. "Kante says he has been around the buying and selling of camels all of his life. He says do not fear, he can do this. If they shoot him, he dies a free man."

The only language Bolan and Kante had in common was a smattering of French. Bolan reached up to shake the old man's hand. "*Bon chance,* Kante."

Kante shook Bolan's hand solemnly. "*Bon chance,* Striker." He clucked at his horse and rode off through the forest.

The Executioner gathered the rest of his team together. "Depending on what Kante comes back with, we may be assaulting tonight at dusk. Maybe immediately. Lunk, Pope, move the Jeeps into position. Everyone else armor up, gear up, check weapons and ammo."

Bolan put down the Marksman's rifle and picked up an M-4 Benelli Joint Service Combat Shotgun. He would be taking point in the attack, and close-quarter combat in a mine shaft might well suit a semiautomatic 12-gauge shotgun.

Lord William racked a round on a Colt 633 submachine gun. The baron was looking better, but Bolan also knew he had asked for morphine and stimulants from the embassy medical supplies and gotten them. Bolan kept his reservations off his face. Chemicals were a short-term miracle in combat, but they exacted a terrible price. Lord William had taken the short, remaining stub of the candle of his life and lit it from both ends. The baron read Bolan's mind and gave him the old devil-may-care grin. "Better living through chemistry, old man, but tell me, how do you want to play it?"

"That depends on what Kante comes back with. If they play stupid, that complicates things, and we may have to mount a clandestine insertion to make sure we have the right boys. On the other hand, mercs are always looking to make a little something on the side, and camels, particularly dozens of them, add up to some real coin in this neck of the woods."

Pope and Lunk drove up in the gun-Jeeps. Everyone was armed and ready to go.

Pun spoke quietly from his side near the road. "Striker, I have Kante in sight. He makes his approach."

"All right, everyone in the Jeeps except me and Pun. Get ready. Lunk, if Kante goes down, light up the shack with the 106. Gary, you get on the 50 and your Jeep crashes the gates. We'll all pile in behind you."

Everyone nodded in agreement.

Bolan moved to the side of the road. Kante was riding at an easy walk toward the mine gate. He stopped his horse and called out, waving his horsehair switch. Several minutes passed before someone came out of the shack.

The man wore a civilian, khaki work jumpsuit, suitable for mining, Bolan had to admit, but FN 2000 modular assault rifles were pretty few and far between in West Africa and not standard mining issue. Kante made a few bold gestures with his switch, and the man at the gate motioned back at the shack. A similarly armed and clad black man came out and began to talk with Kante. The two mercs stepped back and had a brief conversation, and then the black man stepped forward and he and Kante made a few involved hand gestures. Kante nodded and turned his horse back for the road. Bolan pushed the safety off his shotgun and waited for the Malian to take the bullet in the back, but instead the two men high-fived and walked back to the shack.

Someone was making a little something on the side.

Long minutes passed while Bolan and the team waited. After a quarter of an hour Kante came back through the trees, and he was all smiles. He and Bolan shook hands again. "Zayid, what has he got?"

"Kante says he saw nothing, but he says the black man he spoke with spoke Hausa like a European rather than a native. He says he was surprised that he knew they had camels and was interested to know that they had been spotted by poachers, as if it had not occurred to him."

"Are they selling?" Bolan asked.

"Kante says they told him to come back in two days' time, and they could make trade. Kante asked how many he had, and he said sixty. Kante asked for a price and they said again, come back in two days' time. Kante believes the two men do not know how much a camel is worth in Niger at the moment and intend to find out. Kante told them he intends to send a caravan to Morocco and must leave soon. They were firm on waiting two days, and told him not to mention this to anybody if he wanted a good price. Kante agreed."

"*Merci,* Kante." Bolan turned to the team. "All right, we're going in at dusk unless they move first. I want—"

"Kante also says that keeping sixty camels in a dark, wet mine shaft for days on end is a crime against God. He doubts they are being watered, fed or hobbled properly, and these men should all be killed."

"Tell Kante these men will be forced to reckon with their misdeeds," Bolan said solemnly.

CHAPTER TWENTY-TWO

Sundiata Mine

Bolan dug. At the far perimeter of the chain-link fence he was outside of the floodlights. The Sundiata mine hadn't been set up particularly with security in mind. That would come when and if there were a major gold strike. The question was, had anyone come along and done any unseen upgrades. The first thing Bolan had found was that the fence was electrified. At two feet, he found the alarm wire connected to the fence and bypassed it. At three feet, Bolan set aside his U.S. military folding entrenching tool and squirmed up from his entry trench like a man emerging from his own shallow grave. Once inside the compound, he extended the telescoping stock of his shotgun and affixed the bayonet.

Bolan stayed where he was and took in his surroundings. The stench was the first thing he noticed. Camels were normally one of the most digestively efficient animals on earth, but if someone put them in a dark, dank hole in the ground and gave them too much hay and water they would get upset and start eliminating out of every orifice. Even at the far end of the perimeter fence, the Sundiata mine smelled like unhappy camels. It was no wonder the men from Aegis were eager to sell them off as soon as it was safe. Lights were on in the shack, and Bolan could see some movement behind the reinforced glass.

The Sundiata mine seemed to be on a low state of alert, but looks could be deceiving.

Bolan signaled Tymosh, and the Russian scuttled out of the dark and slid her frame through the hole beneath the fence. Bolan thumbed his walkie-talkie. "Entry team in. All units wait on my signal."

The gun-Jeeps came back.

"Copy that," Pope said.

"Roger, Striker Leader," Lord William acknowledged. "Awaiting your signal."

Bolan slung his shotgun. There had only been one junior and very bored CIA intelligence analyst at the U.S. Embassy in Niamey, but he had happily loaned Bolan his elderly Smith & Wesson Model 39 silenced "Hush-Puppy" pistol. Bolan moved into the glare of the floodlights and crept past the shack. He could hear voices inside, and the few words he could make out were in English. The pair of air conditioners humming in two of the shack's windows ensured no one would go outside into the wet, African heat unless they had to.

Lord William spoke across the tactical link. "We have movement on the roof, Striker. Armed sentry."

"Copy that." Bolan knelt and raised the Hush-Puppy. A man walked out onto the edge of the shack's roof. He was armored and carried an FN 2000 rifle. The sentry raised the weapon to his shoulder and peered through the night-vision optic, but he was sweeping the road beyond the fence and not the interior of the compound. He lowered his weapon and picked up a clay pot in both hands and took a sip. It was probably a pot of the local millet beer. Bolan lowered his pistol. Side deals in camels and drinking on duty. Aegis wasn't what it had been under Red-Hot Willy. "Red Leader, I'm going to sneak past him. I don't want to risk raising the alarm. Keep a rifle on him. Green light on your discretion."

"Roger that, Striker leader," Lord William replied.

The mine gaped like a black hole at the foot of the hill. Bolan waved Tymosh forward, and she came to his side as silent as a cat. The two of them faded into the shadows outside the floodlights and made their way to the shaft.

"Red One, we're at the entrance to the mine. I want the 106 aimed at the shack, and the fifty on the mine shaft. We may be coming out in a hurry." Both gun-Jeeps acknowledged, and Bolan and Tymosh moved to the mouth of the mine. The Executioner could hear the weird, muted lowings and groans of the unhappy beasts coming up from the depths like the sounds from some dromedary purgatory. Several large piles of dung formed low pyramids off to one side, but the stench coming out of the mouth let Bolan know the dromedaries were still purging away.

The main shaft itself was small, but with the clean edges of being dug by machine rather than human sweat. A narrow-gauge track led down into the earth for carts of ore samples. Tracks of fluorescent lighting lined the roof, but it was turned off except for the dim glow of safety lights every ten yards. The shaft took a fifteen-degree decline into the earth. Bolan and Tymosh descended toward the sounds and smells of camel. They came to a large cutout in the side of the shaft that had been leveled out and was intended for parking excavation machines. Rather than parked machinery, the area had been cordoned off with storm fencing, and dozens of camels pressed up against the fence shoulder to shoulder. Some recoiled into their brethren as Bolan and Tymosh passed and others pressed forward, but the fence prevented any kind of stampede.

They kept moving down into the earth, and the light got brighter ahead. Bolan smelled cigarette smoke, and people were talking in Arabic. He crept toward a second cutout and peered around the edge. Ten men in desert fatigues were distributed around a makeshift living area. The area was sparsely furnished with a kitchenette, cots and a water cooler. The main activity was four men sitting around a folding table playing a game of backgammon. Two more stood over their shoulders watching, while four more were sprawled out on cots, one of whom was sleeping, the three others reading. All of them had pistols strapped to their thighs, and AK-103 rifles with optical sights were leaned in every corner. Bolan was most interested in an ore cart parked at the rear with a tarp across it.

He leaned his lips close to Tymosh's ear. "You know any Arabic?"

"I have operated in Arabic countries."

"What are they saying?"

"They speak with Egyptian accents. Much of it I cannot follow, but they mostly complain about the quality of the food, the cigarettes, the coffee, the smell, the drunken, untrustworthy Western soldiers and the quality of one another's play."

"Anything else?"

"I miss much, but they speak and behave like bored soldiers on guard duty."

Bolan subvocalized into his mike. "Red Leader, I have the Egyptian team down in the mine. Ten hostiles confirmed, possible location of nukes. We're about to go active."

"Roger that, Striker Leader. Waiting on your move."

Bolan took the Smith & Wesson pistol in both hands and nodded at Tymosh. "Don't fire unless you have to."

The Executioner stepped around the corner. The silenced pistol made about as much noise as an air gun as Bolan began pulling the trigger. The two standing men were the immediate threat, and they both got a bullet through the brain before they knew what was happening. Bolan strode forward, swinging the muzzle from target to target and shooting as he came. The slow, subsonic bullets did not particularly have a lot of stopping power, but Bolan was going for head shots and at spitting distance the 9 mm hollowpoint rounds crushed skulls. None of the Egyptians got off a shot. Only two managed to clear leather before the Executioner ended them. On the ninth round, Bolan's pistol clacked open on a smoking, empty chamber, but he was already standing over the bed of the sleeping man. The rudely awakened commando had just enough time to blink in confusion before Bolan pistol-whipped him back into unconsciousness.

Tymosh stood with her submachine gun shouldered, covering Bolan's six. She perked an appreciative eyebrow. "You are very fast."

Bolan reloaded and moved back out into the main shaft and had a listen. There was no noise except for the camels, and their level of misery didn't seem to have changed since the firefight. "Red Leader, this is Striker. We have ten hostiles down. What is the situation up top?"

"No movement, Striker," Lord William replied. "Single sentry on top of shack. No change in status."

"Copy that. I'm going to check for the nukes. Maintain position."

"Roger that, Striker."

Bolan went back to the bunkroom.

The urn of coffee in the kitchenette was lukewarm, so

Bolan poured it on the unconscious man. The Egyptian sputtered and choked as he came awake and his eyes rolled. "You speak English?" Bolan demanded.

"Huh…what? What has happened? Who are—"

"Good to know." Bolan turned his head so he could look at the mine car and pressed the pistol into the man's temple. "Are the nukes in there?"

The commando paled as he suddenly realized what was happening.

"Last time I'm asking." Bolan pressed the muzzle down hard. "Are the nukes in that cart?"

"Yes!" he gasped.

"Is the cart booby-trapped?"

"What? I do not—"

"Is it alarmed? Will the nukes go off if it's tampered with?"

The man struggled to focus through his shock and trauma. "I do not… We were told not to—"

"He doesn't know." Bolan knocked the man unconscious, then walked over to the cart and walked around it. The tarp over the top was tied down with twine, and there didn't appear to be anything untoward beneath the car or behind its wheels. He clicked the bayonet off his shotgun and began to cut the tarp. Tymosh leaned over his shoulder and peered expectantly.

Bolan cut around the grommets, leaving the twine taut and intact in case any booby trap beneath was pressure sensitive. Bolan finished his square. "Here we go." He eased off the tarp, and he and Tymosh stared at the contents. Bolan sighed wearily. "Are you sure about your numbers?"

The Russian let out a dejected sigh. "Director of GRU was adamant."

Two Russian nuclear torpedo warheads lay in the bottom of the ore cart.

"Check them, make sure they're legit." Tymosh half climbed into the cart and began peering at the warheads. Bolan clicked his com-link. "Red Leader, this is Striker. We have two warheads secured. Two are still at large. Maintain position."

"Roger that, Striker."

Tymosh rose from the cart and blew a lock of hair out of her face. "Serial numbers are matching. If these devices are forgeries, it is beyond my ability to discern."

Bolan didn't think they were fake. What he did think was that the enemy was playing a very deadly game, and he was being played. Bolan sheathed his blade. "Let's check the rest of the mine."

There wasn't much more to check. The shaft continued down another hundred yards and became rougher. Holes honeycombed the walls where ore samples had been taken but none were large enough to house a nuke, and all the remaining carts were empty. Unless they were in the shack, two nukes were missing. They returned to the bunkroom. "Red Leader, this is Striker. We're coming up."

"Roger that, Striker."

The cart holding the nukes squeaked as Bolan began pushing it toward the main track. Almost instantly, the intercom in the wall crackled as someone in the shack snarled in English. "Tell your goddamn men not to touch the merchandise!"

Apparently there had been some sort of motion sensor on the cart. "Red Leader, we may have tripped an alarm."

"Roger that, Striker."

Bolan began pushing the cart faster up the shaft. Behind him, the man's voice turned from anger to alarm. "Respond! Shawki! Taleb! Anyone! Mine shaft! Respond!"

Lord William spoke across the link. "Striker, be advised. Roof sentry is now looking your way."

"Green light," Bolan ordered.

Lord William came back instantly. "Sentry is down."

Tymosh grabbed an edge of the cart and heaved her weight into it. "Situation is not good."

The Russian was right. The mine was a natural bullet funnel, and if he ordered the gun-Jeeps to attack the shed, this was where they would come streaming. What they needed was a diversion. "Red Leader, wait on my signal."

"Roger that, Striker."

Bolan stopped in front of the camel enclosure. He unslung his shotgun and blasted off the padlock. The camels groaned and recoiled at the noise, but when Bolan flung open the fence they surged forward and up the shaft toward the smell of fresh air. The ones in the back lowed and reared and shoved those in front. Bolan stepped back, keeping the cart between himself and Tymosh and the surging beasts.

The Russian quirked an eyebrow. "Cavalry?"

The camels kept streaming out of the enclosure, nipping and spitting at those in front of them. Bolan shrugged. The stampede was shaping up nicely.

"Striker, be advised. Hostiles exiting the shack. I count ten, heavily armed and heading in your direction."

"Copy that, Red Leader. Be advised, the camels are coming up."

There was a brief pause. "Say again, Striker?"

"You'll see in about five seconds." The last camel lumbered out of the enclosure in full, knock-kneed charge. Bolan and Tymosh abandoned the nukes and followed them on the run. At the mouth of the mine a thin, high scream tore out and was cut off almost as quickly as it started. The sixty-odd camels were squirting out of the mine shaft like water from a fire hose. At twelve miles per hour and each averaging over a thousand pounds, the stampeding beasts of burden wouldn't be able to stop and probably didn't want to.

"Bloody hell, Striker!" Lord William was impressed. "We have three hostiles down, the other seven scattering!"

Bolan trotted to the mouth of the cave. Camels were running in all directions. Some of the Aegis men were waving their arms and shooting their rifles in the air, but the camels weren't in the mood to be herded and the mercenaries didn't know how. The rest of the Aegis team came spilling out of the shack.

"Red Leader, how many hostiles did you see come out?"

"Nineteen by my count, Striker."

The Aegis count accompanying the nukes across the Sahara had been estimated at about twenty. With the sentry on the roof down that accounted for most of them. "Red Leader, hit the shack."

"Roger that, Striker. Firing now."

Bolan heard the harsh crack of the spotting rifle, and the tracer round was a red fire streak that punched a hole in the shack. A split second later the tree line on the far side of the road lit up in an orange glare as the 106 mm rifle belched fire from both ends. The high-explosive round hit the side of the shack and blasted it open. The windows blew out, and the air-conditioning units launched away borne on plumes of black smoke. Bolan and Tymosh moved out of the glare of the floodlights. "Red Leader, hit the mine before they start heading for it.

"Roger that, Striker."

One Aegis mercenary was already barreling for the mine as fast as he could. Bolan's Hush-Puppy clicked twice and the man neither saw nor heard the bullets that took him down. A tracer streaked out of the trees and sailed down the shaft of the mine. Fire erupted a second time as the 106 mm rifle cut loose and the cannon shell followed the flight of the tracer. The round impacted within the cave and fire and smoke rolled out.

Jennings hadn't been hiring fools. The veteran mercs fell back toward the burning hulk of the shack, firing toward the trees.

"Red Leader, show them the fifty."

"Roger that, Striker."

The unmistakable sound of a .50-caliber machine gun hammering on full-auto tore into life out of the trees. Tracers streamed into the wreckage of the shack and drew geysering lines in the soil around the retreating mercs. A second 106 mm round detonated against the shack and dropped the roof. Flames licked up and out as the generator caught fire. The mercs retreated from the smoking ruin and milled about for a moment. In their split second of indecision, the baron stepped out of the trees and onto the road. The two gun-Jeeps rolled forward and flanked him like bodyguards, with smoke oozing from their heavy weapons. The baron had been on a parade ground or two in his lifetime of soldiering, and his voice boomed out across the African night like God on High.

"I'm bloody Lord William Glen-Patrick, aren't I?"

That was good for a brief moment of shock and awe.

"Clive Jennings is my prisoner! And as the new sodding CEO of Aegis I am declaring this mission over! Now throw down your weapons or I'll bomb the bollocks off the lot of you!"

One man was all it took. An FN 2000 rifle clattered into the dirt, and the rest swiftly followed.

"On your bloody knees! Hands behind your heads!"

The Aegis men knelt. Bolan fixed his bayonet back onto his shotgun and stepped out of the shadows with Tymosh on his tail. The Jeeps ground forward, and Pope tore apart the gate with the .50-caliber gun. The vehicles rolled into the compound, and the camels scattered in their wake. Lord William walked into the mining compound at a leisurely pace. Several of the Aegis men recognized Pope and called out to him. Their pleas were silenced as he swung the smoking muzzle of the fifty onto the line of prisoners.

Lord William walked up and clapped Bolan on the shoulder. "You know, old man? I believe that may have been the most bloody significant use of camels in small-unit tactical history."

"Bill, once we have the scene secure, I want you to give the Aegis team here the same forgiving-father speech you gave Pope, and then I want to start conducting interviews. They probably don't know where the other two nukes are, but they may have inadvertently picked up some clues."

"Jolly good."

Bolan lifted his chin at Hakmoun where he sat behind the hood-mounted M-60. "Zayid! You and Kante corral and hobble the camels. At dawn, you can sell them in town and split the profit."

"As you say, Striker."

CHAPTER TWENTY-THREE

U.S. Embassy, Niamey, Niger

The Russians took their leave and took their warheads with them. The armored embassy limousine left for the Russian consulate flanked by a pair of SUVs bristling with armed guards. No one had said thank you. Indeed, veiled accusations that the U.S. had the other two weapons were leveled. Yuliya Tymosh had engaged in a furious conversation with the head of the Russian consulate, and in the end she had stayed with Bolan. The Russians had once again wanted the heads of the surviving Aegis operators, and again Bolan had refused. The only good news was that Lord William had made the magic happen, and Bolan had a nine-man squad of professional soldiers who wanted a shot at redemption.

Down in the lounge, Bolan found Lord William smoking a cigarette and reading a newspaper. "How are you doing this morning, Bill?"

"Right as rain, old man! After all that mint tea, it's good to finally get a decent cup of coffee. I think your embassy is buying its beans from Zimbabwe."

"Where's Lunk?"

"Laying siege to the embassy kitchens, last I heard. Now I, myself, don't mind a bit of goat meat and gruel now and again, but Lunk is something of a gourmand. Mentioned something about steak and eggs."

Bolan glanced at the packet of unfiltered French cigarettes. "You know, those things'll kill you."

"So rumor says."

Bolan got a cup from the urn and took a seat. "How are you holding up, Bill?"

Lord William looked Bolan straight in the eye. "I'm tired."

"There's going to be at least one more leg on this trip."

"You know, she always wanted to come live with me in England."

Bolan went with the shift in conversation. "You didn't get her killed. She volunteered."

"I know."

"You were a busy man. Sometimes being a legend is hard."

"Indeed, too busy. Perhaps a bit afraid, as well. I mean, what was I going to do with a daughter? I always provided for her, saw to her education. In the end, I guess I believed she must have hated me."

"But she loved you instead."

Lord William gazed long and hard at the cigarette in his hand. "I'll tell you something, old man. Those four days we spent in the Unimogs? She and I crossing the desert together? Those were the best days of my life."

Bolan knew something about losing people. "Then take them, Bill. Take them with gratitude."

"I know, I…" Lord William squared his shoulders. "Thanks. I knew that, but I guess I needed to hear it."

"No problem."

"So, where does the next leg on our little jaunt take us?"

"I spoke with my people last night. We don't have much to go on. You ever been to Oman?"

"Been in Yemen. The coffee's better. What's in Oman?"

"It's pretty thin, and our last lead. Lord Parkhurst had some interest in natural gas production up in the north, near the border with the United Arab Emirates."

Lord William consulted his mental map. "Well, from there, it's just a hop to the coast and a skip across the Gulf of Oman to Iran. If the weapons are there, then the weapons are already most likely gone."

"I know. We're going to have to hope the weapons are en route and, with luck, intercept them. Parkhurst is dead, but so far the enemy has continued to use the machine he set up."

"So far, they've all been wild-goose chases."

"Bill, it's not a wild-goose chase if you retrieve live nuclear weapons."

"Point taken, old man, but you know what I'm saying. If our count is right, and our lovely Russian traveling companion insists it is, they're down to two tactical nuclear torpedo warheads. That just isn't enough to shift the balance of power in the Middle East. If they intend to use them for a terrorist attack, why haven't they lit them off in London already and been done with it? Why all these circuitous attempts to the get them to Iran?"

The baron had a point, one that had been bothering Bolan, as well. "That's what we have to go and find out. There's a sheikh who has shares in the same natural gas development company that Lord Parkhurst did, Sheikh Shaban al-Lawati. He's a real firebrand against Israel and the West. The CIA suspects he's a financial backer of several terror groups. He also is heavy into shipping, doing a great deal of trade back and forth across the Gulf of Oman."

"Sounds like a likely lad, given the circumstances. So when do we leave?"

"Tonight, if you're up to it."

"As long as it's not in a bloody submarine or sodding camel-back. Can we book first-class this time? Something with stewardesses? I'd take it as a personal favor."

"We'll be going first-class on this one, Bill. Private jet. I don't know about stewardesses, but I think I can convince Yuliya to wear something sexy."

"Brilliant." Lord William finished his coffee. "You know, I've been thinking."

"And?"

"And I think it's just about time to hand over the reins of Aegis. Jennings is out, and I'm just about past it."

Bolan shook his head. "I'm honored, Bill, but I've got a lot on my plate these days."

"Not you, you bastard. Pope."

"Pope?"

"Well, he speaks four languages, he's been around the block, and he's proved himself."

"What about Lunk?"

"Lunk is neither suited for the job nor wants it, but he can whip Pope and our renegade squad into shape. Use them as the nucleus of a new Aegis, and God knows we have some bloody rebuilding to do. It's surely better than raffling off the business to some cretin like Jennings whom I don't even know." Lord William looked at Bolan seriously. "And I'm still not sure what exactly your job description is, but a man like you just might need the president and CEO of the world's foremost legitimate mercenary outfit to be a man who owes you a few favors."

"You have been doing some thinking."

"Indeed."

Lunk came wandering out of the kitchens. "So what's happening?"

"Lunk, I'm going to turn over Aegis to Pope, but I'm leaving you my shares. Keep him on the straight and narrow."

Lunk didn't even blink. "Right."

"Oh, and we're leaving for Oman tonight."

Lunk gave this far more weighty consideration. "The fried okra is delicious."

Muscat, Oman

"WHAT HAVE YOU GOT for me, Bear?" Bolan sat in a CIA safe house overlooking the Gulf. Kurtzman had something. Bolan could tell by his self-satisfied look.

"I may have a way in on Sheikh Shaban al-Lawati."

"I was hoping you might say that."

"Some years ago, Sheikh Lawati's youngest son, Khalil, was going to school in Sydney. He met an Australian girl named Bronwyn Monahan who was mostly majoring in surfing. They had a month-long whirlwind romance and married, much to his father's objections. Despite their difference about blondes, Khalil and his father still shared the same convictions about radical Islam. Khalil went to go fight with the Taliban against the Coalition Forces in Afghanistan. Got himself shot up and rather ironically captured by an Australian coalition unit. Khalil supposedly died of his wounds, but the strong rumor is he was given to U.S. intelligence, who shunted him off to a secret prison in Tajikistan where he died under interrogation."

Bolan saw which way this was going. "Our way in is the girl."

"That's right. Right about nine months after Khalil went off to war and never came back, Bronwyn gave birth to Khalil's son."

"And the sheikh had the child kidnapped."

"That can't be confirmed, but both the girl and the child disappeared from their apartment in Sydney with definite signs of a struggle. The Australians protested strongly, but the sheikh and the government of Oman denied any knowledge of the Monahan woman or the child's whereabouts. On the other hand, the CIA has been keeping tabs on the sheikh for years because of his activities, and there have been persistent rumors of a blond Western woman in his compound outside of Sur and a child. Rumor is she tried to escape twice."

"All right. So I go in, make contact, offer to get her and the boy out in exchange for her giving us information."

"That's the best plan I've been able to come up with so far, but I'm open to suggestions."

"Bear, if she takes the deal, she's not low priority." Bolan had seen the wrong end of these kinds of missions before. "We get her out."

"You know?" Kurtzman said. "You wouldn't be you if you didn't talk like that."

"You keep talking like that, and you're gonna get yourself a date to the prom. Now fax me the details, and give me an insertion vector on the Lawati family compound outside of Sur."

Adam Oasis

BOLAN CREPT THROUGH the palms. The sultan of Oman enjoyed friendly relations with the United States and let the U.S. military use port and base facilities in his country. It was also a quiet Plan B deployment center for U.S. Special Forces in the Middle East, and Bolan had been offered the pick of the litter in special weapons and equipment. This was a recruiting drive, so his equipment was sparse. He had a satellite phone linked to an NSA secure communications satellite lurking in space overhead, night-vision goggles, a silenced SOCOM pistol and an Mk 3 navy knife.

Sheikh Lawati's oasis was a paradise. Rounded clay white-washed walls, blue doors, blue-tiled roofs and even a tiny minaret for the call to prayer. The sheikh also had the modern amenities of satellite dishes, an airstrip and electrical generators. A six-car modular carport protected an equal number of Mercedes-Benz automobiles against the elements.

Thankfully, security at the oasis was lax and mostly consisted of a few bored men with FN rifles wandering around the outer walls, smoking. Another bonus of the mission was that the U.S. had a lot of observation satellites peering at Iran and its neighbors. A good satellite photo of the compound had been immediately available along with enough evidence to tell Bolan the location of the women's area.

Bolan stopped at the edge of the date orchard and waited for his opportunity, and in seconds he was over the wall and inside the compound. The soldier crouched in the darkness in the main courtyard. Two men sat talking by the fountain. The crepe soles of Bolan's boots made no sound on the tiled floor as he moved deeper into the Lawati holding. He passed smaller courtyards and potted trees. The holding was a typical Arabic manor, with the house consisting of cubes all facing an inner courtyard. Bolan moved toward the kitchen and then headed upstairs. Once above, he took another pair of stairs that led to a smaller half story with a single door at the end of a narrow hall.

It was traditional to lock a princess in the highest tower.

Bolan ran his hand over the ancient-looking lock and confirmed that it was locked from the outside. He opened his wallet and pulled out a pair of picks. Defeating the century-old lock took only a matter of moments. He took a tiny bottle of dry, silicone-based lubricant and gave each ancient hinge a good spritzing and waited long seconds for the lube to sink in. A long, slow creak was not to his advantage. Bolan swiftly pushed open the door just enough to admit his body and closed it behind him with little more noise than a quick rasp.

The room was fairly large but lit only by a single open window facing west toward Mecca. The bars across the window were clearly visible. Bolan pulled down his night-vision goggles and took stock. There was very little in the room other than a chest of drawers, a table with a washbasin and a jug of water. A rug adorned the floor and there were a few tapestries on the walls. Near the window was a narrow, military folding cot with a woman lying on it. Bolan took in the woman for long moments. Her mouth was slightly open and her eyes closed, but her shoulders were tense, her breathing slightly shuddering. She was awake, but pretending to be asleep.

Bolan spoke very quietly. "Miss Monahan, I—" He caught movement in the corner of his eye and whirled. A vast shape came from behind the tapestry near the door. A soft, spatulate hand clamped onto Bolan's arm with immense, rubbery strength while the second hand shot for the other arm. Bolan took a step back, going with the power of the charge, and then turned. The man's momentum kept him moving forward and then down as Bolan kicked him in the back of the knee. The man made a strange wordless sound as the Executioner leaped on top and wrapped his arms around his adversary's thick neck and applied the strangle. Bolan's forearms vised through multiple chins and dense muscle beneath to shut off the carotid arteries. The mountain of flesh surged beneath him, but his struggles inexorably weakened.

The single lamp on the table flicked on. Bronwyn Monahan stood in a thin cotton shift with a knife that she had clearly stolen from the kitchens held in a trembling hand. She spoke with an Australian accent. "Don't hurt him."

Bolan stepped away from the big man just before his struggles ceased, and took a couple of prudent steps back. "Miss Monahan. I'm an American."

The woman took in Bolan's black clothes and gear and collapsed to her knees. "My God…you've come. After all this time. You've come."

"That's right." Bolan kept an eye on the big man as he pushed himself to hands and knees. He was as big as a sumo wrestler but with strangely feminine features. "Who's he?"

"That's Saleh. He's my…" Tears came to the woman's eyes. "He's a bit hard to explain."

The giant rose and rubbed his throat. His rolls of fat bulged against the seems of his dresslike tunic. It had been some time, but Bolan had seen the atrocity before. "He's a eunuch."

"Saleh is a Khurd. He was sold into slavery as child, as a harem boy, but then he got his growth. He kept growing, as you can see, so they…" Fresh tears spilled down the Australian's cheeks.

"So they castrated him," Bolan finished.

"Yeah, there were some UN investigations here about some years back, investigating rumors of slavery going on in the Arabian Peninsula. So they cut out Saleh's tongue, too, to make sure he would never be able to tell anyone what happened to him."

It was a horror as old as civilization, and something most citizens slept better at night thinking had ended centuries ago. "So he's your guardian here at the Lawati oasis."

Monahan's lower lip trembled. "He's the only friend I have. But yes, he's my guardian. My husband has many brothers and cousins, and I'm considered something of a fallen woman hereabouts. Over the years some of them have snuck into my room to…" She shook with the memory. "The sheikh didn't want any more of his clan's lads messing with Western women, so he put Saleh in my chambers. That's why Saleh didn't try to kill you. He thought you were one more family member looking to…get a little something in the night."

"Where's your son?"

The woman stared at the floor. "He's here, but I don't see him often. The sheikh had us kidnapped after Khalil was captured. He didn't want his boy raised by infidels. Alex is six now. But everyone else calls him Ali. They've been sending him to the Madrasah school this year. He's supposed to be learning the Koran." She shook her head bitterly. "But mostly he seems to be learning to hate everybody and everything on my side of the family."

"Tell me, Miss Monahan. How's your Arabic?"

The woman pushed the tears away from her cheeks and managed a tremulous smile as a little bit of the former surfer girl shone through. "Full immersion, mate. Best way to learn a language."

"Do they keep you in here all the time?"

"No, I'm expected to work for a living. Cooking, cleaning, laundry, waiting on the men and such."

"Miss Monahan, I need to ask you a favor."

The smile died on her face. "So, here comes the rub, then."

"Not a rub, just a request. I'm tracking two stolen nuclear weapons. The trail led here. I want you to keep your ears and eyes open for the next week. Tell me about anything you hear, any strangers who come to the compound."

"And then?"

"And then I extract you, whether you have anything for me or not. You and your boy."

"And if I refuse?"

"Then I'll bring in my team tonight and have them on

standby. We'll make a plan to acquire Alex, and I'll extract you both within the next forty-eight hours."

"Fair enough, but on one condition."

"So here comes the rub?"

"No rub, then. But this freedom train of yours. I want a ticket on it for Saleh, as well."

"Miss Monahan, Oman is an ally of the United States. I need to extract you as quietly as possible. It will be hard enough to sneak you and the boy out, particularly if he doesn't want to go. You're starting to stack the deck against us getting out without a firefight."

"You know, you seem pretty clever. You've probably already figured out the sheikh's got a bit of the sadist in him. You can't imagine what Lawati'll do to Saleh if he lets me escape, and he will, but I'm not going to let him make that sacrifice. Saleh comes along or the deal's off."

Bolan could tell by the set of her jaw this one was nonnegotiable. "All right, Miss Monahan. Party of three." Bolan took out a satellite phone that matched his own. "This phone can't be traced. I'll be monitoring it 24/7, and my team is putting in an observation post within binocular distance due west, near the rock formation. Do you know where that is?"

"Yeah, I do."

"Report only if you think have something important. Any questions?"

"What if I get discovered, or I think I'm in trouble?"

"If you think you're in trouble, just hit the pound sign on the phone."

"And then?"

"Then my team and I come for you. We come for your boy and Saleh, and we come in hard."

CHAPTER TWENTY-FOUR

Observation Post, Al-Wahirah Dunes

A very important man was coming. That's what Bronwyn Monahan had told Bolan the previous night. Her report had been confirmed by the arrival of a caravan of SUVs. Bolan lay on an old Army blanket and sipped water. The observation post was a shallow excavation covered by more blankets stiffened with lime and covered with dirt and sand to look like a natural fold in the ground. Bolan's team was in position in the rocks a dozen yards away. He watched the oasis through his laser range-finding binoculars and clicked on his satellite link. "Bear, you got anything on these guys? I got one leader, his two attendants and twenty armed men with them."

"Satellite picked up the caravan leaving the city of Sur some hours ago and tracked them to your location, but all the vehicles are rentals."

"Could you hack the rental agency computers?"

"We did, all we got was the code 'courtesy rental' with no names attached to the file."

It certainly sounded suspicious. "Any chatter on who the VIP might be?"

"No, but we're working on—"

Bolan's phone rang. "Hold on, Bear, I might have something. I'm going to link you in." He clicked the phone open and connected it to the link. "Are you safe?"

Bronwyn Monahan spoke. "I'm in my room. Saleh is watching the door."

"We're in a three-way conversation with an associate of mine." Bolan checked the readout on the link. "You getting this, Bear?"

"Loud and clear," Kurtzman replied. "Go ahead."

"Bronwyn, you have anything on your VIP?"

"Just a name. Mullah Vahid Ali Roudbarian."

"That name's Iranian, not Arabic. Mean anything to you, Bear?"

"It sounds familiar. I'm running it now."

Bolan could hear the keys clicking and the gears in Aaron Kurtzman's mind turning. "Bronwyn, how are you holding up?"

"All right. Scared out of me wits. Strange thing to have hope again."

"Keep it up. You're doing fine."

Kurtzman came back. "Mullah Vahid Ali Roudbarian, Iranian national. The CIA has a file on him as long as your arm. Runs a string of Orthodox Shia Masdarah schools, in Iran, Iraq, Turkey and Azerbaijan that are known to be a recruiting ground for extremists. Outspoken proponent of jihad against the West and the initiation of a worldwide Muslim caliphate, by force of arms, if necessary. Embraces the absolute annihilation of Israel, with nukes."

"Nice guy. Bronwyn, you've seen him. Anything else you can tell us?"

"Yeah, they've been having a big feast since noon. Talking about jihad and how it's going to start."

Jihad. Bolan shook his head. Holy War in defense of the faith. "How is it going to start?"

"They haven't said exactly how, at least not while I've been in the room, but they keep saying it starts with the martyrs."

That wasn't anything new, either. From the streets of Baghdad to the Twin Towers, Islam's radical jihadists had proved themselves willing to die for their cause again and again. "Anything else?"

"Well, that's the queer bit. They keep saying it will start with twenty thousand Holy Martyrs, and the final conflict shall be born in the flames. They bloody love saying it, and every time someone does, the *bismillahs* get louder and more frenzied."

Bolan's instincts spoke to him. "Bear, you got that?"

"Oh, I got it, all right."

"Twenty thousand Holy Martyrs."

"And two tactical nuclear warheads."

"Bear, Sheikh al-Lawati and Mullah Roudbarian are going to detonate the weapons on Iranian soil."

Kurtzman saw it all too clearly. "And no matter what anyone says, no matter how much evidence can be provided otherwise, the Muslim world will think either Israel or the United States used nukes to try to stop the Iranian nuclear program. It will be war across the entire region. Every Muslim community across the world will erupt."

"Bear, tell the President I'm going in. I'm going in now."

"You don't know if the weapons are there."

"It doesn't matter. We need to take Lawati and Roudbarian now and interrogate them before they have the opportunity to disappear. I'm going in. Bronwyn, find your son. Have Saleh grab him and take him to your room or anyplace else safe you can barricade yourself in, and then tell me where that is. When I hear you and your son are together, I'll be coming in hard. Bullets will start flying. Do you understand?"

"I understand."

Bolan clicked his phone over. "Jack?"

"Right here, Striker. Hot on the sand one hundred klicks from your position."

"Get airborne. I want you and Bill assaulting on my signal."

"Copy that. ETA five minutes on your signal."

Bolan slid backward out of the observation post and crawled along the slit trench to the encampment in the rocks. "Listen up! We're assaulting now! Gear up!" Half of the men in the fire team were the new inductees from Aegis and were little more than names, Ticotin, Banf, Joseph and Heck, but from Bosnia to Baghdad to South America to South East Asia they were all veterans. Bolan also had Lunk, Pun, Pope, Tymosh and Kante rounding things out. Lord William and the other squad were twenty miles in the desert interior with Grimaldi and were going to form the helicopter assault section. Bolan slung his shotgun across his back and picked up an MGL grenade launcher. He clicked on his tactical link. "Control, do you have us in sight?"

Barbara Price came back. "Affirmative, Striker. Satellite is tracking. We have visual on you and your team. All links are active and functioning normally."

"Copy that. We are advancing to the palms and then waiting on Miss Monahan's signal."

"Copy that, Striker. You are go."

Bolan would have preferred to go in at night, but the heat of the day was just starting to fade and almost everyone would be inside the compound. There was a good chance they could make it to the orchard unspotted and keep the trees between themselves and the compound, but a mile of open ground in daylight was still a mile and a free killing zone for the enemy. Bolan chopped his hand forward and broke into a trot with his team fanning out into an arrow formation behind him.

Monahan's voice came frantically across the link. "I've got him! I've got Alex!"

"Where are you in the compound?"

"I'm back in my room! I think someone saw Saleh take Alex! I think they're coming, I—"

Bolan could hear the sudden pounding on the door on his end. "Listen! You're son is explainable, but get rid of the phone!"

"Please come! Come now!"

"Bronwyn! Lose the phone! Throw it out the window!"

"Oh God, they're here! Come now!"

Bolan heard the door break, someone yelling in Arabic, and he had long ago memorized the sound of an AK-74 firing a burst. Then the phone went dead. "All units! Full assault. We go in now! Jack, attack now!"

"Copy that, Striker! Inbound!"

Bolan broke into a run. It took two more vital minutes to cross the open ground and hit the rows of palm trees. The Stony Man mission controller spoke urgently across the link. "Striker! We have activity in the compound!"

Bolan didn't doubt it. The sheikh and the mullah were bugging out. "Copy that, Control." The squad swarmed through the trees past stone wells and racks of drying dates. Gunmen were spilling out of the compound ahead like a kicked-over anthill and running for the line of parked vehicles. Bolan brought his 40 mm MGL to his shoulder and began squeezing the trigger. Pale yellow flame burst from the barrel, and the huge cylinder clacked and turned. Windshields shattered and the SUVs shuddered as the vehicles were shredded. Bolan clicked open the giant six-shooter's smoking empty cylinder and began reloading. "Pope! Give me suppressive fire on the front!"

Pope dropped to one knee and raised his Squad Automatic Weapon. The light machine gun ripped off short bursts and cut down men streaming out of the compound. Tymosh knelt beside him, festooned with spare belts of ammo. The rest of the fire team moved forward shooting. Bolan slammed his cylinder shut and resumed slaughtering sport utility vehicles. The attackers were hampered by the fact there were women and children in the compound. Bolan raised his aim as riflemen appeared on the roof. The MGL thudded and two seconds later the men twisted and screamed as shrapnel tore their bodies. Bolan dropped the smoking grenade launcher. "Kante!"

The Malian handed Bolan the breeching charge and grabbed the MGL to reload from a bandolier he carried. The Executioner made a choking motion on his throat, and the Malian nodded. Bolan shouted across the link, "Covering fire!" Joseph and Heck advanced to the mullah's armored limousine and poured gunfire along the top of the wall. Bolan ran for the far western edge of the wall. Bullets whined overhead as he pulled the rip cord and lit the fuse. He tossed the charge against the wall and ran back, seconds counting in his head. At five he hurled himself to the ground as the charge detonated behind him. He felt the heat wash across his back and bits of wall rained down, then he rose and unslung his shotgun. "Joseph! Heck! Forward, move on—"

An RPG rocket hissed through the breach in the wall and streaked into the limousine. Joseph and Heck disappeared in a ball of smoke, fire and flying metal. Bolan's shotgun thud-thud-thudded against his shoulder as he poured buckshot into the breech. "Kante!"

The old man hurried forward, and Bolan dropped his shotgun on its sling as he took the reloaded grenade launcher. He lifted the muzzle to near vertical and pulled the trigger three times. "Masks!" Bolan yanked his gas mask out of his bag and pulled it down over his face and checked the seal. He moved the smoking breach in the wall as the three CS grenades dropped like a pair of rocks into the courtyard. Instantly, gray smoke began to ooze through the breech and into the sky. "Move! Move! Move!"

Bolan's team came at the run. Another RPG rocket flew out of the gas, but with no clear target it streaked into the trees and exploded against a palm. The big American leaped across rubble and into the compound. A two-man RPG team was furiously trying to reload their weapon. Bolan's shotgun boomed twice, and the patterns of buckshot slammed the two rocket grenadiers into their graves.

Lunk came through on the other side of the hole with a shotgun of his own leveled. Bolan moved through the gas toward the stairs. "Cover me!" He took the stairs two at a time. A door flew open down the balustrade and a man popped out firing a pistol. The shotgun slammed in Bolan's hands, and the buckshot took off everything above the man's eyebrows. "This is Striker Leader. I'm on the second floor."

Lunk came up the stairs on Bolan's six. They moved down the hallway to the next flight of steps. The Executioner reached Monahan's door and found it broken open. Saleh lay on the floor with the front of his robe bloodstained and riddled with bullet holes. He hadn't gone to his grave alone. A man lay near him with a snapped neck.

Monahan and the boy were gone.

"All units. Package Three is down, One and Two are unaccounted for."

All units responded. Grimaldi spoke through the link with

the sound of rotors beating in the background. "ETA three minutes!"

"Copy that! We have breached the west wall! Gas has been deployed. Red Leader, have your men mask up!"

"Roger that, Striker," Lord William responded.

Ticotin spoke from the bottom of the stairs. "Company coming!"

"Pope, get the SAW to the wall! Cover the courtyard!"

"In position!" A second later Bolan could hear bursts from the ex-Legionnaire's squad automatic weapon below and the *"Allah Akhbars!"* of the martyrs. Pope snarled over the link. "Jesus! They're coming out of the frickin' woodwork!"

Bolan took the stairs two at a time. Unfortunately the courtyard had a large fountain, huge earthen pots containing flowering trees and stone benches, all of which provided ample cover against small-arms fire. But they didn't have any cover from above, and the tear gas was clearly affecting their fire. Bolan and Lunk burst out onto the balustrade and began blasting buckshot down into the attackers. Few of the enemy appeared to be soldiers. Most seemed to be men with hastily grabbed guns that they fired wildly on full-auto. The two men rained lead on them like hail. The slaughter only stopped when they both had to step back and shuck fresh shells into the magazines of their shotguns. Both had fired seven rounds, and fourteen of the enemy had little left but applesauce above their shoulders.

One man rose and turned toward the balustrade. A single "pop" from Tymosh's submachine gun dropped the man without a left eye or much behind it. The door across the courtyard to the inner compound slammed shut.

Pope came across the link. "Courtyard clear!"

Bolan and Lunk kicked the doors along the second floor, but they all had been hastily abandoned. "Second and third floor, clear!"

The gas had abated, so Bolan shoved up his mask and shouted. "Kante!" The old man looked up from where he crouched behind wall rubble. He wasn't wearing a link because he didn't speak English, but he and Bolan had an understanding. The soldier pantomimed shouldering a heavy weapon and it recoiling and then pointed at Pun. "Pun!"

Kante nodded and ran to give the former Gurkha the MGL.

"Pun! Put three armor-piercing rounds through the door and then two gas! Got it?"

"Yes, Striker!" Pun slung his marksman's rifle, cracked open the MGL's cylinder and began strategizing shells. "Ready!"

Bolan and Lunk came down the stairs. "Do it!"

The MGL began spouting fire in Pun's hands. The antiarmor rounds hit the wooden door. Against metal armor, they would pierce it with their jet of molten metal and gas; but when the dry wood was exposed to the blasting jets, it burst into flame like paper with the first, and the second two burst it apart like kindling. The two tear gas rounds sailed through the sagging portal to spew gas within.

"Go!"

Lunk took point. His huge shoulders knocked aside the remaining fragments of burning door hanging from the hinges. Hallway clear— "Back! Back!" Lunk's huge paw shoved Bolan back through the door. At the same instant the Executioner heard the sound of a Claymore mine going off. The narrow hall was a perfect funnel. The range was point-blank. Lunk filled the door frame. The giant Welshman shuddered as the Claymore's seven hundred steel ball-bearing projectiles bee-swarmed through his body at supersonic speed.

Bolan grabbed him by his web gear as he toppled and hauled him back. "Pun!"

Pun fired a grenade into the hall to forestall any counter

charges. Bolan heaved Lunk back, but he knew what he would find. His body armor had protected his torso, but his arms and legs were pulverized meat barely hanging on his bones. The gas mask covering his face looked like a bloody sieve.

Lunk was gone.

Bolan glanced back around the doorframe. The narrow hall formed an L, and at the far end he saw the twisted remnants of the Claymore. Bolan scanned for further traps and moved down the hall. Banf and Ticotin were instantly behind him. Like Lord William, Lunk had been a legendary figure among the men of Aegis. The two mercs were looking for some payback. Bolan pulled a frag and tossed it around the corner. The grenade detonated with a whip-crack and was instantly met by the roar of the second Claymore. The man had been too quick on the trigger. Plaster ricocheted and flew as the bend in the hall was instantly cratered like the surface of the moon.

Bolan rounded the corner, flinging a second frag as he went. The grenade sailed through the door to the interior courtyard and shrapnel flew, accompanied by screams. "Pun! Gas!" Bolan, Banf and Ticotin crouched while the MGL thudded overhead behind them. Rifles crackled from the courtyard in response, and Bolan felt a bullet smash against his armor as he moved forward.

The men in the interior were of a different caliber. Bolan counted ten as he dived through the door and rolled up. All were similarly armed with short Russian assault rifles and fired in short, controlled bursts. These were the mullah's men and trained bodyguards. But they weren't equipped for tear gas, nor were they equipped for the Executioner. The semi-automatic shotgun sledgehammered in Bolan's hands, and it was instantly backed up by the rattle of Ticotin's and Banf's carbines. Two more CS grenades sailed into the courtyard. The multiple skip-chaser munitions broke apart and spun like gas-spewing hockey pucks. In the confines of the court-yard, the gas concentration turned the air into a dense white fog of death. The Executioner moved through it, reaping human lives like wheat. Bolan felt another hit on his armor, and a tug on the left side of his mask told him death searched the smoke for him, as well. Three men rose from behind a hastily constructed barricade of benches and tried for a fir-ing retreat toward the far door, but the men could barely breathe, much less see to shoot. Bolan blasted two of them off their feet, and the third collapsed in Ticotin and Banf's cross fire.

"Courtyard, clear! Banf!"

Banf looked over at Bolan through the gas.

"Banf!"

Banf suddenly sat down. Bolan shook his head as a large wet stain spread across the merc's right thigh. "Yuliya! Grab Kante! Drag Banf back into the hallway out of the gas and put pressure on that leg!"

"Yes, Striker!"

Bolan stared up through the CS toward the blue sky above. "Jack! I got three KIA and wounded. I need Second Team! ASAP!"

"ETA twenty seconds, Striker! Have you in sight!" The air began to shake with the sound of the Black Hawk helicopter's rotors.

"Jack, we're in the second courtyard! Give me a recon on the third! Let me know if you see the girl! If not, engage any hostiles!"

"Copy that, Striker!" The Black Hawk thundered over-head, turning the gas cloud in the courtyard into a whirling vortex. Rifles crackled and popped from the main courtyard beyond and bullets struck the Black Hawk's armored belly. "No sign of the packages! Definite sign of hostiles! Approximately a dozen! Engaging!" Two of the Aegis men from the second team leaned over their door-mounted M-60 machine guns and rained fire into the courtyard below. The return fire ended abruptly, and Lord William's voice came across the link. "Striker! Six hostiles down! The rest have taken cover under the balconies!"

"Copy that! Deploy gas! Heavy concentration!"

"Roger that, Striker!" Lord William replied. "Deploying gas!"

Gas grenades began raining out of the sky over the courtyard like party favors. "Second team, be advised we are entering the courtyard, deploying beneath the eaves!"

"Roger that!"

Bolan moved to the heavy door and shot off its hinges. He kicked the door and stepped back as an automatic rifle buzz-sawed at him and ripped wood chips out of the doorframe. Bolan gave the gas a few more seconds and dived through. The gunner fired at the motion, but the tear gas had destroyed his aim. The big American rolled up and destroyed him with a pattern of double-aught buckshot through his chest.

"Bastards!" Lord William's voice was a snarl of outrage. "Striker! Be advised! Civilians entering courtyard!"

Bolan's blood went cold. It was the same tactic he had used with the camels at the mine. Except these were dozens of screaming women and children being herded into the courtyard from behind to be used as human shields. The enemy was counting on the fact that Bolan and his team wouldn't kill them. It seemed the sheikh and the mullah were prepared to martyr the entire household.

Bolan wasn't.

"Jack! Get Zayid on the bullhorn! He needs to order

everyone to lie down! Bill, I need four of your men on the ground now!"

"Roger!"

"Copy that!"

The helicopter slid back over the second courtyard, and fast ropes deployed on both sides. Four men Bolan only knew as Rassmussen, Kidder, Wayne and Hyde slid down. The second their boots hit the tiles, the Black Hawk slid back over the courtyard beyond. Hakmoun's voice thundered in Arabic from the public-address system like an angry god of the desert.

Bolan drew the eight-inch blackened blade of his Marine Corps bayonet and held it up. "We're expecting zero civilian casualties." Seven gas-masked men nodded and drew their blades.

"Jack! When we're through, make a hole in the northern wall behind us!"

"Copy that, Striker."

Bolan nodded to his men. "Let's go."

The Executioner and the men of Aegis strode into the gas. Women and children were milling and choking, and the enemy was among them. Bolan moved straight in. A gunman saw him and hugged a woman tight to him and shoved out his pistol. The gun barked twice as Bolan closed and he felt the punch of a bullet against his shoulder. Fingers flew as Bolan slashed the gun out of the man's hand.

The entire compound shook as Grimaldi's first Hellfire laser-guided antitank missile struck the north wall of the compound and was quickly followed by a second and a third. Bolan caught sight of a man crouching in the milling, screaming throng and pushed his way through. The man wiped his eyes as he shouldered his rifle, waiting for the shot. He never saw the Executioner until it was too late and probably felt almost nothing as the eight-inch blade ice-picked down behind his left collarbone and impaled his heart. Bolan ripped the blade free. Another assassin was shooting as he tried to draw a bead on Pope. Bolan pushed aside a pair of screaming women, walked up behind him and slit his throat.

Hakmoun's voice continued to boom out orders in Arabic, and civilians began throwing themselves down. One of the gunmen was suddenly revealed as two women dropped. Pun's khukri flashed, and the gunman dropped down on top of them without a head.

Grimaldi shouted across the link. "Striker! Wall is down! Gas is venting out!"

"Jack, I need you to hover as low as possible over my position! Yuliya! What's the status on Banf?"

"Banf is stable! Bleeding controlled!"

"Grab Kante! I need you to start herding civilians out the hole in the north wall!"

"I understand!"

The Black Hawk dropped out of the sky, and the CS gas filling the courtyard blasted against the walls and billowed upward into the rotor wash. Kante and Tymosh ran onto the battle scene. The last of the civilians flopped down as Hakmoun's voice repeated the order. Eight shooters lay among them. It was a miracle that none of the civilians appeared to have been shot, but the miracle had been costly. Even with the gas and surprise on their side, Bolan's team had brought knives to a gunfight. Ticotin lay facedown with red hole in the back of his head between his mask straps. Kidder had taken a burst to the side of his head, and his mask was the only thing holding his head together. Hyde sat heavily on a bench while Rassmussen held a field dressing against a bloody neck wound that didn't appear to be fatal.

"Yuliya, you and Kante dunk each civilian's head in the

fountain. Zayid, I need you to order the civilians to evacuate back the way we came in and out the hole in the wall. Hyde, can you walk?"

Hyde nodded painfully. "Yeah."

"Get back with Banf. Make sure the civilians leave the way they've been told." Bolan sheathed his bloody bayonet and unslung his shotgun. "Bill, I'm running out of warm bodies. I need you and Cortez on the ground. Keep Zayid on the loudspeaker."

"Roger that, Striker." Lord William and Cortez stepped into the Black Hawk's door, fixed their masks and fast-roped down into the compound. Tymosh and Kante began dunking and shoving civilians toward the exit while Hakmoun thundered directions from above. Bolan scanned the shooters. They were randomly armed and appeared to be members of the sheikh's household. That left ten of the mullah's bodyguards loose on the premises. Bolan, Pope and Pun kept their weapons trained on the door the civilians had come out of.

Lord William looked around the courtyard. "Where's Lunk?"

There was no way to sugarcoat it and they were both soldiers. "Lunk didn't make it."

Lord William simply nodded. "Right, then. What's the plan?"

"Saleh's dead, and I haven't seen Bronwyn or the boy anywhere. I think we're about to have a hostage situation." Bolan pulled up his mask as the last of the gas sailed away up into the sky beneath the rotor blades. "How's our supply of gas grenades?"

"I think we're fresh out."

"We'll have to make due with stuns." Bolan glanced over to Tymosh. "Yuliya! How's your Arabic?"

The Russian looked back as she ushered the last of the coughing and weeping civilians out. "My Farsi is better."

"Stick close. I may need you. Everyone form up! Wayne, Cortez, have a couple of flash-stuns ready." The team formed into entry positions as Bolan approached the door. The door led to the "master cube" of the compound encompassing another box of rooms overlooking the inner courtyard. "Jack, what do you have on the courtyard beyond?"

"No movement, Striker. Everyone's either inside or hidden good."

"Copy that." Bolan's shotgun boomed twice and the door sagged on its twisted hinges. He kicked it and stepped back, but no gunfire answered the breach. "Yuliya, tell them to surrender and they won't be harmed."

Tymosh shouted into the courtyard. A voice shouted back almost instantly and just by the tone Bolan could tell it wasn't nice. "What's he saying?"

"I believe he is appalled to be addressed by woman soldier. He is calling me many unkind things."

"I'm sorry to hear that."

Tymosh smirked. "Most of them are actually true."

"Repeat the offer. Tell them to surrender now and they live. If they make us come in, then we kill them all." Bolan listened as the offer and response flew back and forth.

"He says they will kill woman and child if you attack," Tymosh reported.

Bolan checked his watch. There had been plenty of time to send out a distress call. "Control, this is Striker. How are we doing?"

"No undue traffic on the police and military bands. If they sent out for help, it was personal. No vehicles coming your way yet."

"Copy that." Bolan looked up at the slowly orbiting Black Hawk. "Jack, is there any access on that roof?"

"All three main buildings have a door up top. None are open."

"Copy that. On your next pass, see if you can slop a couple of the fast ropes on my position."

"Copy that, Striker."

"Bill, I want you to take command here. Wait on my signal. Pun and I are going up top."

"On your signal."

Fast ropes slithered across the roof above and fell to the courtyard. Bolan and Pun grabbed them and put their boots to the wall. As the helicopter continued its orbit, they were pulled aloft and walked up the vertical surface. The construction of the compound was clay and beam, and Bolan doubted anyone could hear them on the roof. It paid to be sure. "Bill, give me some covering fire."

"Roger that." Below, Pope's SAW snarled off bursts, and a flash-stun grenade detonated in the courtyard. Bolan and Pun moved to the horizontal door at the corner of the compound roof.

Stony Man Farm's mission controller came across the line. "Striker, this is Control. Satellite imaging shows helicopters coming your way."

"Civilian or military?"

"Undetermined. Still no traffic on military frequencies."

"Copy that, Control. I think the sheikh and the mullah are trying to extract. Bill, I think they're going to come up right through us. Begin your assault."

"Roger that. Assaulting now." Two more flash-stun grenades flew into the courtyard, and Lord William and the ground team came in firing. Across the horizon, Bolan could make out the shimmering black smears of the approaching helicopters. He pulled his Beretta and a flash-stun grenade. He and Pun stepped directly behind the door. Seconds later, it flung open and banged against its stop. Shouting came up out of the narrow stairwell, and Bronwyn Monahan appeared.

She was weeping and clutching her small blond child as rifles prodded her roughly from below.

Bolan pulled the pin. "Psst!"

Monahan stared around in shock, and Bolan jerked his head to come toward him. Monahan clapped a hand across her son's mouth and emerged onto the roof. A second later, a gunman followed her. He stepped onto the roof and only had a second to turn as Pun sank his khukri into his skull and yanked him back. A portly man in flowing Arabic robes wheezed his way up onto the roof followed by a thin man wearing a blue suit and the traditional turban of an Iranian mullah. The sheikh did Bolan a favor and pointed at the swiftly approaching helicopters. The mullah followed his finger, which gave Bolan the opportunity to drop the grenade down the doorway and kick the door shut.

The door rattled with the blast, and the sheikh and the mullah jumped and turned to find themselves staring down the barrels of Bolan's and Pun's pistols. The sheikh was appalled; the mullah sneered and waved a hand behind him. "I have two helicopters to your one and forty men with rifles and an RPG! You and your team surrender and you will be spared! Resist—" the mullah shrugged elegantly "—and my men will kill the woman and the boy regardless."

Bolan nodded. His pistol never wavered. He could see the choppers quite clearly. They were civilian Aérosptiale Super Pumas. Armed men hung out the doors. Neither chopper seemed to have any armament of its own. "Jack, be advised, helicopters have riflemen and RPGs."

"Copy that, Striker. They're just about in range." The Black Hawk was carrying a quad-rack of Hellfire missiles beneath one stub wing and a 2.5-inch rocket pod beneath the other. Rockets suddenly rippled out, trailing smoke and fire in a 12-round salvo and streaking toward the lead chopper in an expanding pattern. Two of the rockets struck the aircraft in the nose and detonated. The helicopter spun on its axis with the force of the one-two punch and boomeranged into the ground, spilling men out of both sides as it crashed into the sand.

The second helicopter lost one man over the side as it banked brutally and sped northward.

"Cowards!" The mullah lost his English as he screamed in indignation.

Bolan thumbed his mike. "Nice work, Jack. Bill, be advised. We have the package as well as the mullah and sheikh. There may be a few more armed men directly below my position."

"Roger that, Striker. So far we have met no resistance."

"Tell Yuliya to tell them if they don't surrender I will kill the mullah and then kill them."

"Roger that."

Tymosh shouted in a voice out of all proportion to her diminutive size. This time, no choice Iranian pejoratives were hurled back.

The sheikh stared at Bolan and began to sweat. The mullah drew himself up in a dignified fashion and folded his arms across his chest. "I shall tell you nothing."

Bolan stared into Roudbarian's eyes. He'd lost five men this day, and whatever the mullah saw in the Executioner's eyes made him take an involuntary step back.

Bolan nodded. "Oh, I think you will."

CHAPTER TWENTY-FIVE

The mullah talked. Sheikh Lawati, despite literally quivering with fear, had remained resolute. He was a true-blue fanatic, albeit a fearful one, but his fanaticism gave him a strength that had to be admired, however misplaced it was. Mullah Roudbarian, on the other hand, was like a lot of motivators and manipulators Bolan had met. He was full of fire and wrath for the true believers but somewhat less than willing to martyr himself. There was good money in terrorism and power. Roudbarian was a war profiteer in mullah's clothing. Unfortunately for him, greed for money and power at the expense of one's followers were not ideal pillars of testicular fortitude. It hadn't taken Bolan long to psychologically break him down.

Bolan had explained the facts of life to him.

They both knew Roudbarian had loudly and publicly called upon all Muslims to drive every last Israeli man, woman and child into the sea. They both knew that Roudbarian had recently been instrumental in the theft of Russian nuclear warheads. Israel was not aware of that yet, but Bolan had a cell phone and knew some people with very unusual

job descriptions in Israeli intelligence. The mullah had a
choice. He could talk to Bolan and then take a restful vaca-
tion in scenic Guantanamo Bay, Cuba, where he would be
given a copy of the Koran, a prayer rug and three square
meals a day, or he could take a one-way flight to Tel Aviv
where he could have a very long talk with the nice young men
at MOSSAD headquarters and then rest in peace at the bottom of the Mediterranean.

The mullah had decided Cuba was nice this time of year.

The plot was indeed to detonate the two Russian warheads
on Iranian soil to simulate an attack against the Iranian nuclear program, and the plot went right to the top. The first option was to inform the Iranians and let them handle it. The bad
news was there was no way to know how many top Iranian
officials would think the plot was a fine idea and let it happen.

Unfortunately, Roudbarian didn't have much more than
names, and those names were bad enough. The main man in
Iran was Mullah Hadi Mobali, and all reports indicated he
was made of far sterner stuff than Roudbarian. The mullah
held no office and outwardly eschewed secular life to devote
himself to religious study and a life of asceticism. CIA files
told a different story. Mobali was a "spiritual adviser" to
some of the most powerful men in Iran, and his son-in-law
was Major Ibrahim Nikbakht of Iranian Internal Security Police. Mullah Mobali was an *eminence grise,* a king-maker behind the thrones of power in Iranian politics and an impassioned
advocate of worldwide jihad.

At the sheikh's compound, Bolan and his team had interrupted a celebration instead of a weapons transfer. The two
warheads were either already in Mobali's and Nikbakht's
hands or on their way, and Roudbarian did not know their
route into Iran. Mobali and Nikbakht were extremely diffi-

cult targets. Getting to them would be nearly impossible. Even if Bolan could get his hands on them, the odds were slim. As a soldier in the Revolutionary Guard, Nikbakht had been captured during the Iran-Iraq war and survived torture without breaking before being exchanged. One of his main functions these days was passing on the experience of torture with members of Iranian opposition groups who became too outspoken. Mullah Mobali was a certified religious fanatic. Both men would rather die than divulge anything. Neither man would blink at martyring tens of thousands of their countrymen without their consent, and the clock was ticking.

Bolan looked up wearily from the files spread in front of him. "Bear, you have to insert me into Iran and put me in touch with their most hardcore resistance elements. We need people who will be ready to die to stop this."

Kurtzman sighed, and the face on the screen looked away for a moment. They both knew that was going to be a difficult feat. Relations between Iran and the U.S. had been strained of late. Bolan didn't speak Farsi, and possibly there were unpleasant people with long memories who could recall Bolan's face from previous missions. They both knew this one had gone from mission impossible to suicide run. "All right. I'll have Hal inform the President."

"I need the CIA to pull everything they have on the Iranian powers that be. I need at least one name that they think might be trusted to act on this information."

"Wasn't it you who said telling the Iranians was a bad idea?"

"It is a bad idea, but it's Plan Z if I'm killed or captured."

"Damn it, Striker…"

"I know. Just do it. I need clandestine insertion within the next twenty-four hours and a contact in place when I get here. Don't try to tell the contact what's going on. Just tell them they need to meet an American agent. I'll do the explanation, planning and legwork once I get there."

"I'll have a plan within the hour."

"Good enough." Bolan clicked off and turned. The scent of Lord William's personal tobacco and Tymosh's perfume had told him the baron and the Russian spy had been standing behind him for the past five minutes.

"You heard all that. You two have any ideas?"

Tymosh nodded. "Iran is major trading partner of Russia. We have fairly extensive intelligence operating within country. I told you I speak Farsi, and can insert into Iran with ease. I will give you secure link to GRU communications center in consulate and coordinate all deniable assets available. However, Iran is indeed major trading partner. In case of failure, Russia will deny all, and finger will be pointed at United States."

Bolan had been hoping she would say that. At least the first part. "Done."

Lord William lit himself a cigarette and stared meditatively at the ceiling. "I thought I might lend a hand, as well."

"Bill, you know I respect you…"

"Indeed." A shadow of the devil-may-care grin Bolan had first seen on a sodden heath in Guernsey passed across the baron's face. "And I've put that right next to my Victoria Cross. Serving with you has been one of the greatest honors of my life."

Bolan felt his heart lighten. He had fought his War Everlasting on every continent on Earth and seen selfless sacrifice from some of the greatest fighting men the modern world had known. From almost any other human being, the baron's statement would have been fluff and melodramatics. But Lord William was a dinosaur, the last of the English adventurers. The baron had lost everything. The business he had

built, his fortune, his family, his home and his last friend in
Lunk. Despite all that, duty to queen and crown was still his
shining pillar of strength, and Lord William Glen-Patrick
had not yet begun to fight.

"What do you have in mind?"

"Well, I'm Lord William bloody Glen-Patrick, aren't I?"

"Yes, you are, Bill."

"These sodding Iranians have been in this from the start.
With Jennings's and Parkhurst's help, they suborned my company, and I think by now they're bloody well aware that I'm
on to them. They know the chase is on, and it's a matter of a
day or so if not hours before they know about our little ex-
cursion into Oman. However, I am who I am. I'm a voting
member of the English House of Lords. If I take a trip to Iran,
I can make some outrageous inquiries, shoot my mouth off
and make myself a pain in the bum. This mad mullah and his
bloody black-hooded torturer of a son-in-law will be all eyes
on me. I'll have whatever slim definition of diplomatic immunity those Iranian ponces have, and if I don't? Well, hell,
I'll bet they think I've been leading this mission. They don't
know about you. If I go down due to natural causes or otherwise, they'll think they're aces. You and Miss Tymosh need
a diversion, old man, and believe me, I know something about
raising an embarrassing fuss."

"Bill?"

"Yes?"

"You're in."

"Jolly good! Do you know Hyde is a Devonshire lad?
Went to the MI-6 language school. Knows a bit of Farsi. I'll
declare him as my bodyguard and sneak in Pun as my valet.
God knows someone may need their head chopped off before
this is all over."

It wasn't a bad plan. Bolan knew he'd need every edge he

could beg, borrow or steal on this one, and it was the best deal he was going to get today. "I'll see you two in Iran."

20,000 feet

BOLAN FLEW over the night-darkened Elburz Mountains. Technically, he was gliding rather than flying, but he was as close to soaring like Superman as current technology would allow. Bolan literally had wings—an eight-foot carbon-fiber wing strapped to his back, to be exact. The firm of Elektroniksystem und Logistik und Draeger had designed the modular wing system for the German army, and it had been in use since 2003.

Rather than floating down in a parachute, the modular wing allowed a man to jump out of an airplane and engage in a shallow controlled dive of up to forty-eight kilometers, and the two vertical tail surfaces on the wing-tips allowed the operator to steer the wing just like a plane. The only thing the wing could not do was go up. Bolan was strapped into the latest model that allowed for a controlled glide of up to two hundred kilometers. A CIA-controlled commercial transport had filed a flight plan from Turkey to Turkmenistan, and Bolan had gone out the door at thirty thousand feet over the Caspian Sea. He was on a course due south for Tehran.

Clandestinely inserting into Iranian airspace was not the safest activity in the world. Iran had one of the most extensive and heavily armed air-defense nets in the Middle East. They used the very latest Russian radars and missiles, and they were constantly upgrading. In Bolan's favor, these systems were designed to locate and destroy planes, helicopters and, with luck, perhaps a low-flying cruise missile. Bolan was gliding and for all intents and purposes, he had no heat-signature. The modular wing was made out of carbon fiber and just about invisible to any current Russian air-defense radar. Bolan's body was seventy-two percent water, and the only metal he was carrying was his oxygen bottle and its radar cross-section was slightly less than three inches. The only electrical devices he was operating were his night-vision goggles and the global positioning satellite unit in his helmet. For a few seconds at certain angles of incidence when he was maneuvering, a highly sophisticated radar might perceive Bolan as a very tiny, indeterminate, fleeting, anomalous…something. Any radar operator not operating during time of war would very likely chalk Bolan up to a flight of birds or a freak atmospheric condition. Still, Murphy was always out there and his law, like gravity, was almost always in effect. It was highly unlikely that any Russian-made missile could lock on to Bolan, but MIG-29s carried 30 mm cannons, and it was very likely an investigating fighter pilot would take a dim view of Bolan soaring across Iranian airspace.

Luckily Bolan's course was a straight shot that involved almost no maneuvering, and the atmospheric conditions were favorable for gliding. The darkness of the mountains fell away beneath Bolan, and the glow of the capital became steadily brighter. Bolan banked just slightly eastward for the suburb city of Rey. He raised his flaps to slow his flight and began a wide circle over the city. His drop zone was a soccer field on the edge of town.

At a thousand feet, Bolan pulled his rip cord, and the modular wing deployed its parachute. He felt the tug on his straps as the canopy filled like an air brake. Bolan slowed, and when he lost enough momentum, the wing suddenly swung like a pendulum beneath the parachute, and he went from soaring like a bird to flying like a kite. Bolan took the toggles beneath the wings and began a tight spiral to the field below. The ground loomed upward and Bolan suddenly felt the weight of the wing as his boots hit the ground. He took a few running steps and hit his release buckles. When the modular wing hit the grass with a soft thud, Bolan stepped out of his flight suit and removed his helmet. Two men came out from where they had been crouching beneath the wooden bleachers.

Bolan palmed his Jungle Dart.

The knife was a product of the Cold Steel company. The handle and the leaf-shaped 3-3/4" blade were molded from a single piece of black Grivory. The fiberglass-reinforced plastic wasn't shaving sharp, but the needle point was strong enough to punch through a car door. His contacts were supposed to be friendlies, but in the world of espionage friend and foe could change in the blink of an eye.

The man in the lead was small, bald and bespectacled, and wore an ancient-looking tobacco-colored cardigan sweater, corduroy pants and penny loafers. He looked like an prototypical college professor. A young man in a cheaply made and rumpled suit followed him dutifully and might as well have had "grad student" tattooed to his forehead. Bolan held out his hand. "Dr. Khatibi."

The little man shook Bolan's hand. The big American noticed his left hand never left his pocket. "And you must be Striker. Allow me to introduce my protégé, Pejman."

Pejman shook Bolan's hand eagerly. Dr. Khatibi gazed upon the modular wing. "You flew here? With that?"

Bolan nodded. "From the Caspian Sea."

Khatibi shook a cigarette from a pack and lit it with a lighter in his right hand. He shook his head wonderingly. "Yankee ingenuity."

"We try," Bolan said.

"Let us be away from here. I have a pickup truck parked behind the bleachers. You and Pejman may load your...wing into the back. The city landfill is on the way to my home. We will dispose of it there."

"Good enough, and thank you."

"Do not thank me. I am assisting you for very personal reasons."

"Personal" was generally a bad thing when involved in operations behind enemy lines. Bolan kept his concern off his face. "Oh?"

"Yes, long ago I told my CIA contact I could no longer assist him. Twenty-four hours ago he called and lured me out of retirement. Something I swore I would never do."

Bolan had wanted to keep the nature of the mission on a need-to-know basis with people on the ground. The CIA had to have leaked something. "You were briefed on the mission?"

"Yes, I was told I would be saving tens of thousands of Iranian lives."

Bolan could read the man before him. "That wasn't why you agreed to help."

"No." The man's voice went clinically cold. "I decided to help the United States because there might be an opportunity to kill Major Ibrahim Nikbakht."

Rey

THEY SAT IN THE professor's kitchen while Pejman made coffee. Dr. Khatibi's hand still hadn't left his pocket. The professor brought it up without it being mentioned. "I no longer have the use of my left arm."

"You were in the war with Iraq?"

"Yes, I was, but happily I emerged from my military duty unscathed. I lost the use of my arm fifteen years later when I was a prisoner of the secret police. My bones were broken with iron rods. I recovered for the most part, but unfortunately my left arm was unsalvageable."

"The major?"

"No, I did not make the major's acquaintance at that time. Indeed, the men who tortured me were brutal and stupid men by comparison, armed with fanaticism and zeal rather any great skill at interrogation or police work. At the time I was a professor at the University of Tehran and a minor voice among Iranian moderates. The fact was, I had no knowledge of dissident movements and did not know any supporters of the former shah, nor did I wish to. However, these men operated under the belief that if they simply broke enough of my bones, I might produce some information. Wiser heads finally prevailed, and the secret police decided I had no useful information. Unfortunately by that time I had been reduced to a bag of broken sticks. The interesting and unintended consequence of their actions was that when I was dragged into that cell I was not a member of the opposition but by the time they dragged me back out I was."

Khatibi took a cup of strong Turkish coffee from Pejman. "It was then that I began supporting the dissidents. I recruited them from among the student body and teaching staff. We had secret meetings and met others of like mind or who had suffered under the government's hands. I used some of the young geniuses from the computer department to hack into Iranian government and military computer networks and gave vital security information to the CIA. I started opposition Web sites and published things that would embarrass the government on the Web. All of this I did under the guise of a crippled and cowed professor of literature. I thought I was very clever and became increasingly bold. It was at the apex of my cleverness that I, of course, came under the scrutiny of Major Nikbakht."

Bolan could guess at the horror to come, but it was clear to him the professor wanted to talk. He took a cup of coffee from Pejman and listened.

"The major was a man of some subtlety. My first incarceration was a decade before his rise to power. Perhaps he thought I would say nothing. I was a respected professor, a decorated veteran and had been tortured before and revealed nothing. Perhaps he thought I had iron within me that I did not. Torturing someone changes them fundamentally, I assure you, and having had it done once perhaps he thought it would not be worth a second try. Regardless of his reasoning, he did not lay his hands upon me." Khatibi stared back into a terrible place. "It was my wife and daughter he used against me."

That hung in the air between them.

"Did you know that it is against Islamic law to kill a virgin? So the secret police in Muslim states summarily rape any woman they kidnap so that sin may be avoided."

"I think I understand what you are telling me, Dr. Khatibi."

"I believe you do. It is not a happy story. Let us simply say that they broke me. I gave up everyone I knew and countless others, and their families undoubtedly suffered that which was visited upon myself and mine. My wife died of what was done to her. My daughter recovered, for the most part. I told her to take her dowry and get out of Iran. She is married now, with a daughter of her own, and a dental assistant living in your state of Iowa."

Khatibi leaned back in this chair.

"I will tell you something. People think I am a kindly professor, but I am a vengeful man. I was too old for army service, but I volunteered, long before they were drafting old men and boys, because I wanted revenge for what the Iraqis had done to my country. I joined the dissidents because I wanted revenge for my shattered body, and for years I have nursed a vengeance in my heart for what Major Nikbakht has done to my family. For a decade it has been cold and impotent, but now I feel that fire within my belly once more, and Allah forgive me, I will have it quenched once and for all."

"Then I give you my word. Unless I'm killed or captured first, I will kill Ibrahim Nikbakht."

A weary smile passed across the old professor's face. "Then I believe I am in a position to help you. I believe I know where at least one of the warheads will be, and I believe Major Nikbakht will be nearby."

CHAPTER TWENTY-SIX

There was a reason Rasoul Khatibi was a professor emeritus. His field was classical Persian literature rather than geopolitics, strategy and tactics, but he had an intellect that would have given Aaron Kurtzman a run for his money. Khatibi had no active way to get at his old nemesis, so his need for vengeance had turned into a patient and watchful vigil. More than anything, he was a keen observer. It was estimated the Iranians had around eighty nuclear technology sites. Some were large, open facilities that were clearly engaged in work to make nuclear electrical power plants. Others were buried deep beneath ground in hardened shelters that the government hoped might withstand the latest generation of U.S. Air Force GBU Deep Penetrator bunker-busting weapons; what was going on in these facilities was somewhat suspect. Other facilities were small, highly secretive and deliberately placed within suburbs outside of Tehran where Western military planners would have to face unacceptable levels of civilian casualties if they attacked them.

There was a facility of the latter type located right in the middle of downtown Rey.

Khatibi had driven past it many times. He had photographed it, and the people coming in and out of it, for the CIA. The second time he had been abducted by the Iranian secret police and shoved in the trunk of a car he'd had the wherewithal to mark the time of his journey in his head as well as the right and left turns. He had come to the startling conclusion that the Alternative Energy Resource lab he had photographed was the same place where his life had been destroyed. It was also a place that many of Iran's top nuclear scientists spent time at, a place that Major Nikbakht had been known to frequent. Given the situation, it was just about the perfect place to light off a tactical nuke. A mosque, a hospital and an orphanage were all within the blast radius of a twenty-kiloton nuclear fireball.

It might as well be worldwide Jihad Ground Zero.

Bolan scanned the city map of Rey. "I know Mullah Mobali would light up a nuke in Rey, but what about Nikbakht? According to my files he was born here."

The professor regarded Bolan dryly. "If this is not the good major's idea, then I suspect he dearly wishes he was the one who had thought of it."

"Fair enough." Bolan considered the Alternative Energy Resource Laboratory of Rey. "You got any hard-chargers?"

Khatibi considered the words. "Hard…chargers."

"People who are willing to die to make this happen."

Pejman surged up out of his chair. "I will!"

The professor's wry look returned. "You will take care of your pregnant young wife. I will shoot you myself if you seek to involve yourself any further in this matter than you already have." The professor sighed. "I have not spoken to them for some years, but if I explain the situation to them, I know a few men."

Bolan nodded. "The good news is we have the Russians

on our side. No matter what happens, they don't want anything with one of their nuclear signatures lighting up in Iran. They're not willing to deploy Special Forces, but they do have some expendable agents and they have expressed the willingness to procure money, weapons and whatever equipment of local manufacture we require."

"Interesting. I will need a gun for when we go in."

Bolan shook his head. "You're not going anywhere."

Khatibi put on his poker face. "My friend, I am afraid it is the price of my cooperation."

"Professor, I respect you, but 'personal' is an ugly word in clandestine operations, and unless you're willing to betray me and let Rey burn, I already have what I need."

"Indeed, I have told you everything you know." The professor's poker face was worthy of Vegas-level play. "But are you sure I have told you everything I know?"

Bolan gauged the man before him. Like Lord William Glen-Patrick, Professor Rasoul Khatibi was an old man with nothing to lose. "I'm asking you not to do this."

"I am begging you to do it," Khatibi countered.

"Professor, what is it you think you can do?"

"For one, I believe I will be your key to infiltrating the facility. Two, should all else fail, as an educated man, during my service in the Iranian army I was sent to the officer candidate school. Upon graduation I entered the Signal Corps as a lieutenant. I was quite good at my specialization, but as a soldier, marching in step, erecting a tent or carrying a heavy pack I was feeble in the extreme. The war had been going on for three years when I entered it, and I was a soft-handed scholar among hardened warriors. However, I was issued a handgun. To the surprise of my superior officers and messmates, I rated 'Expert' with it. The shah of Iran bought most of his weapons from the United States, and during the war with Iraq we still had large stockpiles of them." The professor shrugged. "I will require a Colt 1911A1 .45 automatic."

Bolan saw the steel in the man. "You tell me how you can get me into the facility, and I'll get you a .45 and carry you in on my back if necessary."

"Very well. When I was released after my second incarceration, I was told to inform the secret police if I was ever approached by the CIA or the dissident movement again. I will go to the facility and say I have been contacted by the CIA and wish to speak directly to Major Nikbakht. I trust the CIA or the Russians have someone following the major. I will go the facility when we know he is there. You will follow and use the opportunity to infiltrate it."

It wasn't a bad plan, but a few loose ends needed nailing down. "Why would Nikbakht believe you would come and willingly give him information? They know you have vengeance in your heart."

"Indeed, they must suspect I do, but I will not be giving them anything. I will be trading. More, I will be begging, and I believe they will open the door and let me in."

"Forgive me, Professor." Bolan looked deep into the man's eyes and tried to read what he saw behind them. "But trading and begging for what?"

"I will tell them I am willing to betray the CIA contact and a planned U.S. operation on Iranian soil." The professor's eyes took on the cold, clinical hatred Bolan had seen before. "I will tell Major Nikbakht I am willing to do anything he wants in exchange for telling me where my wife is buried."

THE RUSSIANS HAD COME through. Major Nikbakht was an Iranian player of some stature. Unless he deliberately went dark, he was not that hard to find. According to the GRU, the major had gone into the Alternative Energy Resource lab twenty-four hours ago and not emerged. The Russians had come through in other ways, as well. Yuliya Tymosh opened the back of a battered Renault 4 station wagon and pulled aside a blanket. Underneath lay a pile of Iranian army-issue weapons. Bolan picked up a Beretta Model 12 and checked the action. Tymosh opened a canvas satchel. "How many magazines will you require?"

"I'll take six." Bolan picked up a ZOAF 9 mm pistol. "Two for this."

Khatibi picked up his .45. "Will you please load this for me?"

Bolan took the pistol, slid in a magazine, racked the action and then ejected and replaced the loaded round. He shoved the magazine back in, and Khatibi had seven, plus one in the chamber. Bolan flicked on the safety and gave it back. The professor tucked the weapon away. He had produced two hard-chargers. Jalap Sedeghiani was an Atlas of a young man whose degree in Sufi ecstatic poetry was paradoxically being financed by an Olympic boxing scholarship in the heavyweight division. Hadi Ansarian, on the other hand, was a balding, bookish, homunculus of Professor Khatibi. However, the professor had assured Bolan that the young astrophysicist believed that the mullahs' iron-fisted rule over the spiritual and moral lives of the Iranian people was something worth dying to oppose.

Bolan measured the men in front of him. They had sand, he had to give them that, but as they picked up their submachine guns he had to push the muzzle of Hadi's weapon to one side so that he didn't point it at his teammates and Jalap held his like a poisonous snake. "Either of you two ever fired a weapon before?"

Jalap smiled helplessly. "Alas, no. It may sound ridiculous coming from a man who put himself through college hitting other men in the head, but I am rather confirmed in my pacifistic beliefs—that is until the professor told me what the mullah and the major intended."

"I, too, am unfamiliar with firearms." Hadi sighed. "But I am aware of my role and accept it."

Bolan eyed the young scientist. "And what's that?"

Hadi grinned. "I believe the American computer-gaming slang is meat shield."

The two men had sand, and on a suicide mission that was probably the most important thing.

Everyone looked up and trained weapons on the door as a car's headlights came through the dirty windows of the garage. The car halted and car doors opened and closed. A moment later a quick three raps came on the door. Weapons lowered as Lord William, Kidder and Pun came in swiftly and closed the door behind them. Lord William gazed into the car. "Did you bring enough for the rest of the class, then?"

Tymosh handed the baron a Beretta. "Good evening, your lordship."

Khatibi stared quizzically at the baron. "Lordship?"

"Lord William Glen-Patrick, but that's all pomp." Lord William racked his action on a loaded round and stuck out his hand. "Call me Bill."

"Bismillah!" Hadi lunged and grabbed the baron's hand eagerly. "I have read all about you!"

The professor shook his head. "Forgive him. For a man who has never handled a gun, Hadi is something of an aficionado of modern military history."

"I have read your biography twice!" Hadi gushed.

The baron retrieved his hand. "Just remember, old man, that was an *unauthorized* biography. I did not have a Playboy Bunny with me on safari when I was attacked by SWAPO terrorists." Lord William raised a cautionary finger. "She was a Penthouse Pet, and there is a difference, I assure you."

Hadi gazed at the baron in awe. Bolan rolled his eyes. Hero-worship wasn't a bad prerequisite for a suicide mission, either. "How'd you get away, Bill?"

"Oh, it wasn't hard. I just pulled the old Red-Hot Willy routine. I had dinner with the deputy of the Iranian Diplomatic Service, fine fellow, by the way. He feasted me brilliantly. I expressed Her Majesty's concern over the relations between our countries, appeared to have far too many drinks and then inquired where the finest prostitutes in the capital might be found. The deputy thought that was a smashing idea until I gave him and his aide the slip. I suspect several platoons of Iranian diplomatic corps clerks are feverishly combing Tehran's red-light district for me as we speak."

Hadi looked like he might burst into flames.

"So!" Lord William picked out a pistol and tucked it away. "What's on the agenda for the evening?"

"It's a pretty simple plan. The professor and Major Nikbakht have history. So he's going to walk up and knock on the door. If the major is stupid enough to open it, we go in."

"And if this Major Nikbakht is a clever dick?"

Tymosh held up one of several satchel charges. "Ten kilos Amatol high explosive."

"Brilliant."

Bolan tapped his finger on a Russian satellite reconnaissance photo. "The good news is that this is a small research facility rather than a manufacturing or testing site, and it's set in a suburban area. Their security will be geared more toward preventing interior espionage rather than fending off an exterior assault. However, the major is in there, and if the nukes are in there with him, we'll have to assume manpower has been beefed up. We secure the nukes. If possible, we extract the warheads and Yuliya takes them to the Russian embassy where they already have scientists in place ready to dismantle and dispose of them. If we get in but can't get back out, we disable the warheads' firing mechanisms and then blow them up."

Jalap's scarred brows rose. "We shall blow up nuclear weapons? Here, in Rey?"

"Nuclear weapons aren't like TNT. They don't explode if you hit them with a hammer. You only get a nuclear explosion if you blow the two fissionable masses together. We're going to blow them apart."

"If you say so." Jalap still seemed dubious. Hadi threw an elbow into his ribs and had a few choice words for him in Farsi.

Bolan checked his watch. "We don't know how much longer the major is going to stay. Once he leaves the facility, we have to assume the countdown has begun. Unless anyone else has any questions, we go in now."

No one had any questions.

"Let's do it."

CHAPTER TWENTY-SEVEN

Rey Alternative Energy Resource Lab

The Renault idled at the gate. Bolan and Pun lay under a blanket in the back with their submachine guns held against their chests. Hadi rode shotgun next to the professor. The hatchback was unlocked, and Bolan listened as Khatibi spoke with the gate guard. Bolan's Farsi red-lined at "drop your weapons," but he could read the tones of voices. The guard had told the professor to be on his way, and the professor had done some name-dropping, most notably Nikbakht and the CIA. Bolan could also determine that the guard was no longer talking to the professor but someone on the phone.

Bolan heard the gate raise and the Renault ground into gear. "Pun! Go!"

Pun threw off the blanket as Bolan kicked up the hatchback. The former Gurkha lunged out of the back of the wagon and hit the gate in a heartbeat. The guard had just enough time to recoil in horror inside his booth before two pounds of Nepalese steel cleft his skull to the bridge of his nose. Bolan rolled out of the back as the little man ripped his knife free.

Pun dragged the dead man out of the booth and into the dark.
Then he and Bolan trotted a few yards behind the car to stay
out of view of the security camera over the main door. The
professor pulled to a stop in the little parking lot, and he and
Hadi got out. Bolan and Pun moved into position behind it
to put the front door in a cross fire. Bolan spoke into his Russian radio. "Team Two, make your approach."

"Roger that." Out on the street, the van containing Lord
William and the rest of the group began pulling up toward the
gate.

The lab looked like any other small suite of offices, except
that the windows were facades and the front door was white-
painted steel with a camera peering down from overhead.
Professor Khatibi pressed a buzzer on the white-painted steel
security door. Long moments passed while Bolan and Pun
stared over their sights. The door buzzed, and a man in an Iranian military uniform and sand-colored beret filled the opening like a human gate. He wasn't the major, but he stood with
one hand resting on the grip of his holstered pistol while he
sneered down at the two men before him in open derision.
That was one advantage they had. The professor and his even
more diminutive sidekick looked more like the Iranian dele-
gation to a Sci-Fi Convention than men on a suicide mission.

Bolan could barely hear their words in Farsi, but he knew
the script. The man at the door would want to know what
made the professor think the major was here. Khatibi would
relate his tale of counting the time and turns in the trunk of
the car. He would say the CIA had contacted him. They had
operatives here in Rey. They were grim-faced men. They
seemed more like soldiers than spies, and they seemed desperate. They had finally threatened him to cooperate, but he
had refused. They had given him a twenty-four-hour window
of contact if he could learn anything of use. The professor

would give up the CIA contact and several people he knew who were cooperating with them, as would Hadi.

The sneer on the doorman's face as he loomed over the little professor told Bolan the man was telling Khatibi that it was his patriotic duty to tell him this information now. Khatibi stood his ground. He knew the major and would deal with him alone. He also pointed out that whatever was going on he doubted whether they had time to torture him, and the major knew there was something he would do anything to have.

Another soldier in a beret showed up on cue and leaned into the doorman's ear. They spoke for a moment or two, and the door guy nodded and stepped aside to let Khatibi and Hadi in.

Khatibi drew his .45 from beneath his sweater with admirable alacrity and shot the first man once in the chest and then once in the face.

"All units move in!" Bolan boomed. He vaulted over the hood of the Renault 4 and charged forward with Pun hot on his heels.

The second soldier clawed at his flap holster, but the .45 in the professor's hand told him goodbye twice in the same fashion, and he fell dead on top of his friend. Bolan and Pun bolted past the two academics and hurdled the two bodies and went into the facility. Lord William's van broke through the gate and screeched to a halt as armed team members poured out of every door.

Bolan charged down the short hallway. A man sat behind a counter with a telephone half raised in his hand. He froze as the cold, black eye of the Beretta Model 12 stared him down with its unblinking gaze. The man clearly had a pistol shoulder-holstered beneath his cheap blazer, but he wasn't wearing a beret and was clearly front-desk security rather secret police or a soldier. "Professor, what's his name?"

The professor asked.

"His name is Lach."

"Ask Lach where Major Nikbakht is."

Khatibi frowned at the answer. "The major is somewhere in the top-secret area."

"Where is that?"

"Below us. Underground."

"Where were they supposed to take you?"

Khatibi's eyes became hostile slits. "To the detention area."

"Where is that?"

"There was an elevator involved last time. I believe the top-secret area and the place of disappeared, like hell, are both below the ground."

The rest of the team was in. Kidder started handing out satchel charges, and Bolan strapped one across his shoulder. He turned back to the security man. "Tell Lach I want him to buzz the major and say there's an emergency. He needs to come up top immediately."

"I am not sure he will take that kind of bait. He will inquire as to the nature of the emergency, and I know from personal experience he has a very keen sense of smell about truth and lies."

Bolan glanced back at the pile of dead men by the door. "Who was that man?"

"That man is Sergeant Parviz. Corporal Parviz when I first met him, and he takes an unhealthy pleasure in wielding iron bars below. The private I have never met."

Bolan nodded. "Tell Lach he's going to say you and Parviz argued. Parviz demanded to know what you knew before he let you in. You refused, said you would only deal with the major. The sergeant struck. You fell and seem to have had a heart attack. If the major asks for Parviz, he and his friend are attempting CPR."

The professor scratched his chin. "It may be enough. Nik-bakht is clever, but he has a very bad temper and does not suffer fools gladly. There is a chance he will fly into a rage and come immediately."

Lach recoiled as Bolan suddenly loomed across the counter. "Tell him he'd better make this good. His life depends on it."

"He says he understands."

"Tell him to make the call."

Lach made the call. Bolan raised his weapon and pointed it at the security guard's face. Lach began babbling into the phone at a million miles an hour. Even on the other side of the counter, the big American could hear a deep voice immediately start to yell.

Bolan spoke low. "Jalap, Hadi, go a few steps down the hall and start panicking in Farsi." The two grad students went down the hall and started to shout in consternation. Bolan kept his eyes locked on Lach. "Professor, translate for me."

"I am ready."

"He has summoned an ambulance."

Lach's voice went up an octave as he gave the information.

"Khatibi does not seem to be breathing." Bolan pressed the muzzle of the gun between Lach's eyebrows. "Tell him to panic a little more."

Lach was clearly beginning to panic a lot. There was something to be said for Method Acting.

"He does not believe Sergeant Parviz and the private are resuscitating the professor correctly."

Lach got halfway through the sentence and suddenly flinched and lowered the phone with a shaking hand. A steely smile slid across Khatibi's face. "I believe the good major is on his way."

"Professor?" Bolan locked eyes with the little scholar. "I need that son of a bitch alive, at least for the moment."

Khatibi took a long breath and let it out, steeling himself. "I understand. Would you put a fresh magazine into my pistol for me?"

Bolan put in fresh 7-round magazine and shot the slide home on a loaded chamber. "Pun, take Kidder and Jalap and go watch the front. You've got our six. If police, medical or fire show up, you lock the door and fall back. Anyone wearing a brown beret? Burn him down and anyone with him."

"Yes, Striker. Kidder! Jalap!" Pun ran down the hall with the other two men in tow.

"Tell Lach to buzz us in."

The professor gave the order, and Lach went sickly pale as he buzzed open the inner door. It opened onto a T-shaped hallway with a pair of elevators directly ahead. One car was coming up. "I want a cross fire. Yuliya, with me. Bill, on the other side. Professor, you and Hadi down behind the counter with Lach. No one fires until I do."

Bolan's team moved into position without a word. The professor and Hadi knelt out of sight with their weapons pressed into Lach's kidneys while Bolan, Tymosh and Lord William dropped to one knee five yards to either side. The elevator pinged open and a tall, powerful-looking Iranian strode out angrily. Distinguished gray made a pair of wings from his sideburns and his face was flushed with the blood of rage. He took one look at Lach and roared. Like most soldiers, Bolan's grasp of foreign language, which was extensive, started with the swearwords. After "Parviz!" a stream of Farsi invectives spewed from the major's mouth. Two more men in sand-colored berets strode out and flanked the major in formation.

Bolan's Beretta tore off two 3-round bursts that ripped the major's legs out from under him. Tymosh and Lord William's submachine guns shattered the two men on either side. Professor Khatibi came around the counter and almost casually pointed his .45 at the major's head.

"Professor…"

"I am in complete control of myself." The professor gazed down at his nemesis. "Major, we will speak English for the benefit of my friends."

The major clutched his bloody thighs and spit something back in Farsi.

The professor put a foot on his chest and lowered his aim. "You will speak English or I will shoot you in the leg again."

The major glared bloody murder as the Executioner stood over him. "Where are the weapons?"

"I do not—"

Bolan shook his head. "Shoot him."

The professor took careful aim at the major's knee.

"No!"

"Allah blesses the merciful," the professor pronounced. "Cooperate, and I give you my word you will live this night."

"Last chance." The Executioner gazed down upon the major implacably. "Where are the weapons?"

"Below."

"Who's on the way?"

"I do not under—"

"If you have more men coming and don't tell me, I'll kill you."

The major's black eyes burned up into the Executioner's, but there wasn't an ounce of doubt in them. "Yes. I summoned a security detail, along with a doctor. They will be here within minutes."

"Where's Mobali?"

"He is below. With the weapons and twenty men."

Bolan read the major as he lay in a spreading pool of his own blood and didn't like what he saw. It was the same look he'd seen on Captain Goma's face in the last few seconds of his life. He was scared, but that wasn't why he was complying. "You're stalling."

Major Nikbakht grinned and glanced at the cell phone clipped to the breast pocket of his uniform. "And Mullah Mobali is listening to our conversation on speaker. Venerable one, initiate the detonation sequence—"

Bolan ripped the cell phone away and jerked his head at Professor Khatibi as he strode toward the elevator. "He's all yours."

The professor sighed. "Goodbye, Major. We shall not meet again. I fear you and I shall be going to very different places this night."

"I shall be having your wife in Paradise, little professor, as I had her and your daughter in this very—"

The .45 thudded once into the torturer's face and Major Nikbakht's reign of horror against his own people ended.

"You all right?" Bolan asked.

"I am all right."

Tymosh put a hand on Professor Khatibi's shoulder. "You wished him to suffer more."

"No." The professor's voice was strangely conversational. "My CIA contact was from Texas. He had many prosaic sayings. One of which always struck me was *If it foams at the mouth, shoot it.* I am a man of God. The Holy Koran allows me the killing of such a man as the major, but not to become him. He thinks he is a Holy Martyr." A snarl crossed the little academic's lips. "But he seeks to kill thousands of the innocent faithful, and he goes to his Maker with the rape of virgins proud upon his lips. His soul is consigned to flames, and his flesh shall rot in the earth."

Bolan brought the phone to his lips. "I hope you heard that Mobali. There's only one good man of faith in this facility, and it isn't you."

A few moments passed before a voice spoke back with the British accent of a second language. "Your deaths are assured."

Bolan motioned Lord William to the elevators. It was his turn to do a little stalling. "You won't have your tens of thousands of martyrs if you detonate below ground level. You need to rethink this."

Lord William punched the button several times and shook his head. The elevators had been disconnected.

"I will have enough," Mobali replied.

Bolan mouthed the words "flexible charge" to the baron and then replied. His one supreme advantage was that fanatics loved to talk. "Admit it. You have nothing. Give it up."

"Oh, but you are wrong. The orphanage behind this facility will be severely damaged. Al-Jazeera television will need but the face of a single dead child and pictures of the radioactive crater at the center of Rey, and the true jihad shall begin."

"I'm begging you not to do this."

"On your knees begging forgiveness is where you and your crusader governments belong."

Lord William and Tymosh pressed lengths of Russian flexible charge into the frame of the elevator. The baron gave Bolan a "keep him talking" motion as he set the detonator.

"You don't have to detonate the bombs." Bolan put an

edge into his voice. "Our attack on the facility will be enough. Innocents don't have to die."

"You are soft and weak, like all men of the West. Cringing at casualties. This is war."

"Against your own people?"

"You think I am a monster? I assure you, I am a moral person. You have no idea of the strength it takes to do this."

Bolan had been here before and knew the situation all too well. All it took was a sociopath with charisma and a few fanatic followers. He turned off the sound for a moment and nodded at the baron. The flexible charge hissed and the elevator door sheared and fell to the floor. Bolan turned the sound back up. "Listen, we can still negotiate this."

"I await you." The line went dead.

"Striker!" Pun shouted down the hall. "A vehicle comes!"

Time was running out. "Hold them off as long as you can!" The elevator car would be a killing box if Bolan and his team tried to climb down through the roof hatch one by one. Bolan pulled the rip cord on his satchel charge and dropped it down the shaft. "Fire in the hole!"

Heat and smoke roared up the shaft like a chimney, and the entire building shook as the twenty pounds of TNT and ammonium nitrate detonated. Bolan slitted his eyes against the acrid stink and the stinging smoke as he reached in and grabbed an elevator cable. He slid down two floors. The elevator car had been crushed like a tin can and the doors blown out. Bolan's boots hit wreckage, and he fired a burst out into the smoke-filled hallway. He pressed himself against the side of the shaft as automatic rifles returned fire. Gunfire was breaking out upstairs, as well. Tymosh shimmied down the cable followed by Lord William. Hadi was having heavy going helping the one-armed old professor down the scorched cables.

Hadi shouted breathlessly, "They found the dead guard, and they are through the front door! Your man Kidder is fallen! Pun and Jalap will hold them at bay from the security station!"

Bolan's radio crackled and Pun's voice spoke gravely. "Jalap is dead. I am wounded. Forgive me, Striker. I cannot hold them back."

"Pun! Get down the shaft!"

The radio clicked off. But the man from Nepal's battle shout rang down from above. *"Gurkhali!"* It was met by a crescendo of gunfire. When the British army had first begun employing Gurkha mercenaries, the English had been appalled to find that the Gurkhas had no war cry. The warriors of Nepal had the unnerving habit of charging their enemies in total silence. The British had insisted they come up with a battle shout. The Gurkhas had come up with *Gurkhali!* that literally meant *The Gurkhas are coming!* They considered it the most terrifying thing they could tell their enemies, and they only said it when they drew their knives and charged.

Subedar Thapa Pun had just died going forward.

The narrow hallway before them was a series of steel doors leading to the cells where the hell of torture was endured. Armed men lurked in the doorways, putting the smashed-open elevator into a cross fire. The enemy above would be shooting down the shaft within seconds. This was the end game. There was nothing left to do but to act on the former Gurkha's example and cowboy up.

"Hadi, you're with me. Yuliya, you and Bill next. After that, well, Professor, you just hit whatever you can."

Bolan stepped into the cross fire. He held his trigger down on full-auto, and the man in the nearest doorway screamed and yanked back into cover from the onslaught. The man in the opposite doorway made the mistake of shooting at Hadi rather than Bolan. The young scholar twisted and fell forward as an AKM rifle ripped the life from his body. Bolan swung his Beretta around and tore away the top of the shooter's skull. Bullets hit the big American's body, but the Russian soft armor he wore was rated to stop pistol ammunition, and the Iranian gunner behind the MP-5 screamed as Bolan refused to fall. The terrorist wasn't wearing any armor between his eyebrows, and Bolan's burst stove in his face. The Executioner strode up to the first door. Lead scored his hip as a man lurking in the cell screamed and fired. Bolan's burst hammered the man out of his crouch and splayed him dead upon the concrete floor.

"Allah akhbar!"

The Executioner turned at the scream of rage. He emptied his Beretta into the shooter in the next doorway down the hall, and his bolt slammed back on a smoking empty chamber. Drawing a second gun was always faster than reloading. The Model 12 dropped from his hands as he slapped leather for the ZOAF automatic under his belt. It still wasn't quite fast enough. Tymosh and the second shooter in the room exchanged fire. The shooter's head came apart like sporting clay beneath the Russian's burst. Her eyes went wide as her throat opened like a flower beneath the automatic rifle's assault. She put a hand to her neck and blood flew from between her fingers.

The Russian assassin went limp like a puppet with its strings cut and fell to the bloodstained floor.

Bolan kept moving forward. The two cells before him had only dead men in their doorways. Ten yards ahead the corridor took a sharp right turn. Professor Khatibi spoke softly. "These about us are holding cells. Around the corner lies the chamber of horror."

"The countdown has begun!" Mullah Mobali's voice

roared from around the bend in triumph. "But come! I implore you! Come, anyway!"

Lord William put a hand against the wall to support himself and a wet, rattling cough jagged through his body. He brought a hand to his lips and it came back bloody. "Professor, go get Yuliya's satchel charge."

"Yes, I shall."

Lord William pulled his own charge around on its strap. "Nice knowing you, Striker."

"You won't get close enough."

"Of course not. But if the mullah is yelling, then the door is open. The first blast will knock them down. The second will finish the job. Get in the closest cell."

"Bill…"

The baron pulled the cord on his charge and the fuse beneath the canvas hissed. "You have five seconds, friend."

Khatibi came back clutching Tymosh's charge. "What is—"

Bolan tackled the professor through the doorway of a cell. As they hit concrete, the Executioner heard the last words of Lord William Glen-Patrick.

"What the hell." The baron's boots thudded as he charged around the corner. "*Gurkhali,* you bastards, and God save the queen, you sodding sons of—"

The roar of automatic rifles drowned out the rest of Lord William's words.

Ten kilos of Russian Amatol high explosive drowned out everything else. Blast and smoke tsunami'ed around the bend and filled every cell with heat and stench. Bolan was up instantly as concrete dust rained down from the ceiling. He charged out of the cell and around the corner.

There was nothing left of Red-Hot Willy. There was something left of the men who had gunned him down, but which part belonged to whom was anyone's guess. Bolan strode through the gore-painted corridor and into the main interrogation room. Two men lay moaning across their rifles. The mullah appeared to have been blasted back against the far wall. His beard was scorched, and his mouth worked. Blood leaked from his ears and tear ducts.

His voice was a bare whisper. "You have failed."

Bolan walked up to the two nuclear warheads lying upon the floor. One had been turned on its side, and he righted it.

"The cleansing fire of jihad, it shall…"

Bolan ignored the mullah and examined the weapons. The warheads had been removed from their casings and the barbells of the "guns" were exposed. The timers were at twenty-nine seconds and counting down. Bolan's charge was in a three-sectioned loaf. He would have liked to have had the time to set three separate small charges, as Kurtzman had told him, to cut the gun tube, separate the nuclear detonator from its uranium bullet and send the target mass flinging itself out of the way into a concrete wall.

He was just going to have the blow the whole thing up and hope for the best.

The professor peaked into the room. "What is happening?"

"I'm going to blow the nuke. You need to be in a cell and close the door."

"I shall not require tackling." Professor Khatibi disappeared back around the bend.

Mobali smiled. "I shall ascend to heaven upon nuclear wings…"

TNT and ammonium nitrate were most likely going to shove the mullah's narrow ass straight to hell, but Bolan didn't have the attention to waste. He set down his charge and heaved to lean the two warheads on top of it.

"You shall serve me in Paradise. I am promised the souls of my enemies as slaves when I—"

Bolan checked the detonator. He tasted copper in his mouth. His ears were ringing, and he knew he'd taken damage from the concussions of multiple explosions. "You really want to see the countdown? You want to feel the fire and dissolve in the white light?"

"Oh, we shall experience them together, infidel."

"Get used to disappointment." Bolan drew his ZOAF and shot the mullah through the forehead. He yanked the rip cord and strode around the corner. He slammed a cell door shut and pulled two dead bodies on top of him.

There was no incinerating white light. The facility shook. Dust cascaded from the ceiling, and after a second Bolan pushed the bodies off him and went back out.

"Professor!"

The opposite door opened and Professor Khatibi coughed and came out. "We live."

"Yeah, so get back in."

"What?"

"Take off your clothes and get back in the cell."

"What do you mean?"

"I'll lock it behind you. You have no idea what has happened here, but tonight? Major Nikbakht came to your house and took you. He asked about the CIA trying to stop the unwilling martyrdom of twenty thousand Iranian men, women and children. That's your story. You stick to it no matter what."

The professor nodded. "I see."

"I give it a fifty-fifty chance. Your government will admit to nothing that has happened here tonight. You'll probably be interrogated, but if you stick to the story there's a chance they will let you go. If you're alive six months from now, one million dollars U.S. will reach you. Don't ask how, but it will. The CIA will provide you with papers and a false identity to let you cross into Turkey. After that, it's up to you. My advice is to go to America and be part of your daughter's life."

"And what of you?"

"Yuliya's dead and right now my cache with Russian intelligence is spent. The CIA will deny me until whatever happens here blows over, and I won't compromise the U.S. Embassy by making a run for the gate."

The professor shed his clothes and backed into a cell. "So what shall you do?"

Bolan closed the steel door and shot open the observation slot. "I'm going to climb up that elevator cable and kill any secret police son of a bitch who gets in my way."

"Then go with God, my friend."

"And you."

Bolan slammed the slot shut and scooped up three rifles and a second pistol from the bodies of the fallen. There were still a couple of soldiers upstairs. Iranian police and fire would be inbound.

The U.S.-held border with Iraq was still four hundred miles away.

James Axler
Outlanders®

GHOSTWALK

Area 51 remains a mysterious enclave of eerie synergy and unleashed power—a nightmare poised to take the world to hell. A madman has marshaled an army of incorporeal, alien evil, a virus with intelligence now scything through human hosts like locusts. Cerberus warriors must stop the unstoppable, before humanity becomes discarded vessels of feeding energy for ravenous disembodied monsters.

Available May wherever you buy books.

LOOK FOR

ACT OF WAR
by Don Pendleton

Technology capable of exploding cached nuclear
arsenals around the globe have fallen into the hands
of a group of unidentified terrorists. Facing an untenable
decision on whether to disarm or stand and fight, the
Oval Office can only watch and wait as Stony Man
tracks the enemy, where fifteen families of organized
crime will be masters of the universe—or blow it
out of existence.

STONY®
MAN®

*Available April
wherever you buy books.*

ROOM 59

A research facility in China has built
the ultimate biological weapon. Alex's job:
infiltrate and destroy. His wife works at the
biotech company's stateside lab, and Alex
fears danger is poised to hit home. But when
Alex is captured, his personal and professional
worlds collide in a last, desperate gamble to
stop ruthless masterminds from unleashing
virulent, unstoppable death.

Look for

out of time
by
cliff RYDER

GOLD
EAGLE®

*Available April
wherever you buy books.*

GRM592